To The
Health
and music !!

DISTANT
VENGEANCE

Nick Planas signature

Nick Planas

1

George Chappell leaned over the side of his engine's cab as his train shuddered to a halt alongside the down platform. It was a dark evening, and the rain was coming down in a light drizzle. As he looked back, he saw a young man walking briskly along the damp platform, armed with a couple of flags and an oil lamp. George recognised him as the young porter who'd directed shunting operations at the station in the past.

"Sorry driver," called the young man, "we've got to hold you here. There are some cows on the line up past the points. Mr Kemp's sent a couple of men up to see what's happening with them."

Just at that moment, the door of the telegraph office opened and Isaac Kemp, the stationmaster, emerged.

"The express'll be here soon, Isaac, won't it?" George called out, as if the stationmaster needed reminding. Isaac nodded and called out "Aye George. James, get this shunted as soon as you can, lad."

"I will, Mr Kemp, but the line's still blocked."

"Very well. As soon as you hear it's clear, we must move fast. The Squire is on the express tonight, and he'll be wanting to know the reason for the delay if we hold them up."

"We'll make sure he knows which farm the cows are from then, and he can sort them out." James

Palmer already knew which farm the cows would be from. Being in his early twenties and without the burden of responsibility that came with his superior's position, James had no patience whatsoever with the residents and workers of Rosfell Farm and would find any reason to complain loudly about them to anyone who listened.

Rosfell Farm was one of the goods yard's biggest customers, as farmer George Dove liked to remind them frequently, while also being the biggest thorn in the side of the railway's operations by way of its proximity to the lineside west of the station. When they weren't complaining that their milk cows were being affected by train whistles, steam, smoke, and other operational disturbances, they would frequently find reasons to legitimately - in their eyes - trespass on the main line. Isaac Kemp had got many years of experience of dealing with Farmer Dove and his workers, and had learnt to tread a fine line in his business dealings with them.

However, the local Squire, formerly Francis Webster Templeton Morphy, now Lord Morphy of Hallowfield, had recently been appointed a Director of the London and Western Railway. Perhaps, thought Isaac, he might be able to exert a little more pressure from above on his roguish tenant farmer.

The stationmaster grimaced at his porter's comment. Walking past them towards the front of the engine, he called out "Never you mind that, lad. You sort this shunting out sharpish, and let's hear no more lip." before disappearing down the end of the platform and across the lines to the opposite side of the station.

George Chappell grinned. "No use grumbling, lad. You'll not win whatever you do. Harry!"

George's mate on the footplate, Harry Lusby, was busy raking coal from the back of the tender to the front. He stood up and wiped his brow. "Aye?"

"Go and tell Wiggins we're held up by some cows on the line, and we'll whistle when we'll be starting the shunt. Better send him to the signalbox too; remind Bobby that we're here in case he forgets he stopped us."

Harry climbed down from the footplate, glad to have a small break, and sauntered along the shadowy rain-glistened platform towards the guard's van at the back of the train. The goods train, which had been slowly wending its way along the line since leaving Salisbury in the early afternoon, was too long to fit neatly within the station confines, and Harry had to walk down the slope and along the lineside for a few yards before reaching his destination. He clambered up onto the verandah of the van, and opened the door to the warm interior, where he found Harrison Wiggins, the guard, busy sorting out some sacks he'd taken on at the last stop. "We're stuck here a few minutes, Wiggie. Cows on the line. George said you're to go to the box and remind 'em."

Harrison moved a sack from near the bottom of the pile and placed it by the door. It was labelled 'Hallowfield', the next station on the line, where they were booked to stop.

"Right ho, Harry. They'll need to clear 'em fast. The express is due soon." They emerged from the warmth and climbed down from the verandah onto the ballast, the fireman heading back to his engine, the guard to the signalbox. One of the responsibilities of the train crew was to go to remind the signalman of their presence, and to check that he had protected the line behind them by putting all his signals to danger. The London and Western Railway was one of the first lines in Britain to fully adopt the Absolute Block method of working, which divided the lines into sections, or blocks, in which only one train was allowed under normal circumstances. By using telegraph instruments coupled with bell codes between each signalbox, each train would be offered to the next signalbox and either accepted or refused. If it was accepted, a train could be passed along the line safe in the knowledge that there was nothing in the section ahead of it.

On reaching the signalbox, Harrison Wiggins would check that the signals were at danger, and would sign the register to confirm that he had done this. At the same time his presence would serve to remind the signalman that there was a train there in the event he forgot about it, which was not unknown in busy signalboxes and during long working shifts. Salmsham was not usually a busy box, but like most of his fellow workers, the signalman worked long hours and tiredness was a constant companion towards the end of a long and miserable day.

As Harry Lusby arrived back at the engine, he saw two figures emerge from the gloom ahead. They stopped to talk to the stationmaster who was crossing back in front of the engine, and all three walked up the slope onto the platform by the engine. "Right" said Isaac Kemp. "The line is cleared, so we need to get this lot shunted. Where's young Palmer?"

Some three miles to the east of Salmsham Station, an express train thundered past the signalbox at Belcote Crossing. Percy Wingate watched the train pass, making sure he saw the red tail light on the last carriage. He tapped the key twice rapidly on his block machine, which sent the bell-code "Train entering section" to his counterpart at Salmsham, before walking over to his desk and logging the time, 7.41, in his register.

On the footplate of the express, Harold Pickford squinted uneasily through the inadequate round cab-glass of the locomotive, one hand on the regulator as he leant slightly to his left side, resting his arm on the cab side. Tom Jobson, his fireman, was busy feeding coal continuously into the voracious fire, trying to keep the boiler pressure high for the long climb to come. Both enginemen hoped that the signals would not be against them otherwise they would have to check their speed, and then work the engine even harder to get to the summit at Hallow Hill. On a good day, they could thunder through Salmsham Station at full chat and get a good run up the gradient. The long curve on the approach to the station was significantly canted so there were no restrictions on the speed of the expresses, although passengers would occasionally complain about being pushed roughly towards one side of their carriages.

It was a cold and windy evening and now there was rain which blasted against the cab as they travelled at over a mile a minute. The only good thing about the wind was that the steam and smoke from the front of the engine was being blown straight over them, so Harold had a fairly clear view ahead through the rain spattered glass. After passing Belcote Crossing there was a long gentle left hand curve before the line straightened out for just over a mile. Harold waited until they reached the straight, and then looked hard for the expected signal.

"It's off!" he called to his mate as he caught sight of the white light of the distant signal, three-quarters of a mile to the east of Salmsham. He relaxed his grip on the regulator slightly, but kept his hand there anyway as a matter of habit, ready to shut off steam at a moment's notice if anything up ahead gave him cause for alarm.

Despite leaving London seven minutes late, they had made up some time and were bowling along nicely now and gradually picking up more speed on the descending gradient; the steady clicks of the wheels on the rail joints told Harold they were doing about sixty-five miles an hour. Tom stopped shovelling coal for a minute, replacing his shovel with a long iron rod called a pricker, which he used to rake lumps of unburnt coal into the gaps which kept appearing in the firebed. Closing the firedoors, he stood up, threw the pricker back onto the tender, and wiped his brow with his sleeve. He checked the water level and pressure gauge, puffed his cheeks out and nodded to Harold. They were both satisfied with the run so far, and now Tom had a few moments of respite from firing before the hard climb ahead. He turned his attention to looking out for the Salmsham signals.

They had half expected to pick up extra carriages at Salisbury, but on arrival there they were told these weren't needed, which prevented any further delays. The front guard, James Garlinge, had come along to the cab to confirm the original load of ten carriages, and soon afterwards the train pulled away, now just five minutes behind schedule.

As usual, there had been a fair exchange of passengers at what was an important stop on the journey. The train was fairly full but not overcrowded; most of the compartments had spare seats. On board was a broad cross section of the British social classes; as well as the Squire of Hallowfield, with his valet, returning from his regular business trip to London as a recently appointed Director of the London and Western Railway, there were several professional men travelling away on business, or returning home from the capital, or the other stops on the way. There was also a popular theatre troupe on their way to perform at Weston, and many other middle class folk travelling to the West Country for leisure or familial purposes, all of whom were settled in their comfortable first and second class compartments in the modern six wheeled carriages. Further back in the third-class carriages, workers travelling home from the larger towns were enjoying, if that was the right expression, the relative comfort of high speed travel in the very latest carriages, despite the lack of properly padded seats, oil lamps and heating, which graced the other classes of carriage. Compared to travelling by stage coach, of course, this was still a luxury, and much faster too.

"Can you see it yet?" called out Harold, as Tom went to the right-hand side of the cab and looked ahead. "We must be close to Salmsham now!"

Tom leaned out of the right side of the cab and looked back towards the rear of the train. The countryside was so dark, he could barely see the outline of the trees that were growing on the slope of the cutting. Even worse, an intermittent fog of mist and rain prevented him being able to pinpoint any recognisable lineside features. As far as he could tell, though, they were still on the straight section of line. "We've still got another quarter mile yet, Harold!" he shouted above the roar of the wind screaming through the open cab.

Tom turned back and looked ahead through his cab glass. As the train was now approaching a right-hand curve he should be able to see the home signal before his mate could, but although there was little or no smoke ahead, he could barely see anything at all, not even an outline of the trees, or the first of two overbridges which should be right ahead.

"I can't see the home!" Tom strained his eyes. The curvature of the cutting told him they must be nearing Salmsham, and he was expecting to see a white light from the home signal, which would give them the all clear to hammer through the station and up the steep incline beyond. "Ah yes, got it!" he called.

Harold's hand remained on the regulator. They were now steaming hard at just over seventy miles an hour. The carriages swayed along behind them, shaking their inhabitants somewhat as they hammered towards the second overbridge, which took the road over the line before Salmsham Station. Once through the station they would be able to use their momentum to power up the steeper section of Hallow Hill, and then shut off steam and use the remaining gradient to help slow them down for the scheduled stop at Hallowfield.

—

8

Suddenly something caught Tom's eye – a glimpse of a red light and the outline of a goods van, and he called out "Watch out! Pull up!" In an instant, Harold pulled the regulator down to shut off steam. He pulled the whistle chain, calling for the guards to put their brakes on, as Tom moved across and began to screw the tender brake on hard.

Harold pulled the reversing lever back as far as he could, and then re-opened the regulator.

"The signals were off!" shouted Tom desperately.

"I saw 'em!" cried his mate.

Suddenly, as Harold opened up the regulator again, the reversing lever rammed itself forward from full reverse to full ahead. In an instant, the train lurched as full forward power was applied again. Harold slammed the regulator closed again, and tried to pull the reversing lever back again with both hands, and then his eyes widened… "Oh NO, NO!" he cried out. Those were his last words.

Still running at about sixty miles per hour, one hundred and eighty-five tons of locomotive and train ploughed into the stationary train of coal and paraffin wagons which was standing on the down main line at Salmsham Station. The brakes on the goods engine and tender were on, providing an almost immovable obstruction. The powerful express locomotive and its heavy train burrowed its way through the guard's van and two trucks, shattering them all into firewood and twisting their iron frames, and then struck a van full of paraffin barrels. As the engine's buffers smashed through the rear panel of the flimsy wooden van, the barrels split open and disgorged their volatile contents upwards in a huge cloudy spray of liquid, which splashed down on the engine and front carriages of the express train. In an instant, the hot coals which had spilled from the firebox ignited the paraffin, and the engine and first four carriages disappeared under a vast flashing cloud of smoke and flame. The remaining carriages continued to plough into the crushed wreckage. Unable to go forwards, instead they began to concertina upwards. The fifth carriage was lifted at the rear and toppled to one side onto the platform of the station, where it splintered into matchwood and spewed its human cargo out into the station surroundings, crushing two railway workers who were standing alongside the goods train. The sixth carriage went beneath the floor of the fifth, then the remaining carriages climbed up and over the burning wreckage in front...

2

February 2018 - Milnefield

"Dad, what is all this stuff in this old folder?"

Mark Phipps looked up from the bedroom floor, where he was kneeling somewhat uncomfortably, trying to work out which removals box to open from the twenty or so in front of him.

"Which old folder?"

"This one. It says 'Railway Disaster / Photos" It's quite bulky."

"Oh that. Gosh, haven't seen that for years! Where was it?"

"At the bottom of this box of books." Mark's son Alex pointed to another box, one of several which had been stacked neatly against the wall of the room. Mark intended this room to be his library and study, although it was built to be a fifth bedroom.

Mark hauled himself upright, briefly stretched his six-foot-two frame, and then and rubbed his right leg, which had gone to sleep while he was kneeling on it, and replied "There was a terrible accident way back. I did some research on it when I was younger. Some of our old family were there. They were railway workers. I think one of them went to prison for manslaughter. I can't actually remember much about it now."

"But why did you keep all this stuff?"

"Well, you know, I used to be into railways when I was your age. I used to have a big model railway layout in the loft. I spent all my pocket money and more on it, but then when I was older I just lost interest and sold it. But, you know, I've often thought about building another one. I suppose we could do it here, as this is probably going to be our home for quite a few years now." He knelt back down and opened another box, this one full of books on gardening. He quickly scanned the contents, closed it again, and then used a black marker pen to write "Gardening - Garage" on it. Freya could open it later in the year, once she'd sorted out all her other domestic priorities.

Mark was pleased with their new home. It was the first properly new house they'd ever lived in since being together for over nineteen years; he and Freya had bought it while it was still a building plot, and so were able to choose their own décor, carpets, and kitchen and bathroom designs from a fairly wide variety of options. It was also the biggest house they'd ever owned; a five-bedroom detached house, with a surprisingly large floor area, an 'almost triple' garage, and most importantly for the family, a large garden, which pleased everyone, especially Freya who had grand plans for it, gardening being her passion. Mark moved the box over to a space near the door.

He had originally been against buying a new-build home, as they were invariably built on what he thought were cramped estates, where no-one had much more than a small patch of grass for a garden, backing onto five or six other properties. But this place had been different. Milnefield was a small market town, which was expanding but at what the locals called a "gentle pace". The layout of the new Stratton Park estate was much more spacious;

naturally they paid a premium for living there rather than on the other new build estate to the south, but the house prices in Milnefield were comparatively cheaper than in their old home town of Attwell Crosby, just ten miles away to the north east. Mark reckoned the prices in Milnefield would rocket soon, and so he was glad to have snapped up this plot as soon as it came on the market.

Freya had taken responsibility for most of the interior planning – after all, as she had pointed out, she would be spending more time in the house than her husband, and not only that, she didn't think he would have much idea about matching colours or things like carpets and walls. Both of their children had been happy with their bedrooms; their rooms were of a similar size, and both had an en suite. Olivia had been allowed to choose her own colours, which she had done with much enthusiasm and a fair bit of restraint – her parents were expecting a somewhat Bohemian colour scheme and were pleasantly surprised at her choice of pale yellow walls and discreetly patterned curtains. Alex didn't share his older sister's enthusiasm for choosing his own décor, but he was pleased to have a room twice as big as his old one. Even with his new bed ("why would I want a double bed Mum?") he still had plenty of space. His parents had bought proper office furniture for both children so they had decent sized desks to work at. They were also mindful of the future potential for renting out the rooms fully furnished once their children had flown the nest, hence the choice of bed which had so puzzled their son. Olivia had already organised her room in an out-of-character burst of domestic enthusiasm, and was busy finishing off an essay for college, due for submission on the following Monday.

Alex was sifting through the folder. "So where is Sal... Salmsham, Dad?"

"It's pronounced *'Solmsham'*. Mark peered over his son's shoulder at the various papers. "It's one of those places where the name has been shortened over the years by the local dialect. It used to be spelt 'Saltmarsham' but the locals called it 'Solmsham' and eventually they shortened the name on the maps. It's not far from here, actually. I think it's only about fifteen miles south west. It used to be on the main railway line from London to Weston, but they closed the line in the nineteen-sixties. It's between Belcote, which is where I was brought up, and Hallowfield, which is also where some of my family came from. Remember Great Granny Phipps? She lived there most of her life. Hallowfield, I mean."

"Wow, look at this..." Alex pulled out an old photocopied document, consisting of quite a number of pages stapled together at the top left corner...

LONDON & WESTERN RAILWAY

REPORT of Lieutenant-Colonel Sir Francis Whey, on the Accident which happened on the 12th March 1874

> *Board of Trade,*
> *(Railway Department),*
> SIR,   *Whitehall, 27th April 1874*
> *I HAVE the honour to report, for the information of the Board of Trade, in compliance with the instructions contained in the order of the 13th ult., the result of my enquiry into the circumstances connected with the terrible accident that happened at Salmsham Station on the London*

& Western Railway on the 12th ult., by which an express train ran into the rear of a stationery goods train which had been held at the station due to a report of stray cattle on the line…

"Stray cattle! Really? Would they actually stop a train for that?" Alex chuckled.

"Yes, of course. You don't want to hit any animals on the line, especially cattle. They can derail even a heavy locomotive if they get under the wheels."

"When was all this again?"

"It says on the top. Eighteen-seventy-four."

"Wow, Dad, that's a hundred and… forty-four years ago! That's insane. And look how they spelt waggons, with two 'g's!"

Mark chuckled. "That was how it was spelt until quite recently." Father and son continued to read the document:

In this case the 4.50pm express passenger train from London to Weston, which was running three minutes late, ran at full speed past the distant and home signals…

"What are the distant and home signals, Dad?"

"I'll tell you in a bit. Keep reading."

…and collided at high speed with the 2.10pm goods train from Salisbury, which included two vans loaded with paraffin as well as 14 coal waggons and six general goods vans. The force of the collision completely destroyed the guard's van, two coal trucks and seven other vans, including the two containing paraffin, which instantly ignited and covered the first few coaches of the express. I regret to say that 17 passengers on the express lost their lives, and over 54 were injured, although only 22 of these are considered to be

serious. The driver of the express was killed, but his fireman had a miraculous escape from death, although he was seriously injured and is still off work. Sadly, two other railway servants who were standing on the station beside the goods train also lost their lives. The stationmaster and the fireman of the goods train were also injured by flying debris while they were standing on the platform, but the fireman was still able to protect the up line to the next block. There is a considerable amount of conflicting evidence about the status of the distant and home signals...

"Dad, what does that all mean? When they talk about the status of the signals?"

"Ah, well I think you'll need to help me put up this new model railway, and then I can teach you about signals, and all those sorts of things. I was actually thinking of modelling Salmsham Station as it used to be. I used to cycle there when I was a kid, when they still had the platform and station buildings. We used to play in the old signalbox. Now we're back in the area I can go over and look at the place and work out what era I'm going to model."

"Wow, that'll be cool Dad. Can we go and have a look at the place together then? I want to see where this accident happened."

"Yes, soon. But let's get ourselves settled in here first. Which means us, or rather, you not stopping and reading every interesting book or folder you find, and actually helping unpack all this stuff!"

"You were reading it too". Alex put the papers back in the folder, but left the folder out on top of the desk. He planned to have a good read later on. His curiosity about the accident had definitely been aroused now. He flicked his long light brown hair back from his face, and turned to his father, who was back on the floor sorting another box.

"So Dad, what about those signals? What does it mean – 'distant' and 'home'?"

"Well, bear in mind that trains can't stop quickly, even now. And believe it or not, in those days they only had proper brakes on the tender and a couple of coaches, so they needed a distant signal to warn them if they had to stop further up the line."

"What's a tender? Is it like the guard's van?"

Mark sighed. He'd forgotten just how much the last thirty years of modern railways had all but eliminated memories of steam, and his was the last generation to be really aware of the old steam culture; in his childhood he'd been surrounded by adults who seemed to regret the recent passing of steam as if it was a golden age of railway travel. Of course, when he asked deeper questions of his older relatives, they would be forced to admit that working on the railways in the 1940s and '50s was a dirty environment, but most people preferred a bit of coal dust and smoke mixed with steam to the choking black filth of diesel exhausts on the new locomotives. Mark had bought into the "steam is good, diesels are bad" culture of his childhood, although now he really enjoyed the clean and rapid high speed rail travel which modern electric lines such as the West Coast Main Line offered, as he frequently travelled to the north of England, and Scotland, on business.

"Remember those pictures of steam engines? Some engines had a tender behind, which was a truck attached to the engine, which had coal and water in it, so they would pump the water into the engine boiler, and the fireman would shovel the coal from the tender into the fire, boil the water and there was your raw power."

As they continued to open boxes and sort the various books into different subjects, Mark explained how the Victorian railway engineers were fixated with producing ever faster and more powerful locomotives, but seemed almost blind to the problem of brake power, so the stopping of trains was an art not only involving the driver shutting off steam, but also using the engine whistle to call for the guards on the train to put their hand brakes on, while the fireman did the same thing with the tender brakes.

"So the driver wasn't the only person in control of the train?" asked Alex.

"No. And the crazy thing is, he also wasn't technically in charge of the train, as far as the railway regulations were concerned. On many railways that was the head guard, who could order the driver to stop or move the train as required. It seems bizarre now, but that's because you're used to seeing me drive the car and make all the decisions…"

"Yeah, and not have to whistle to us lot to put the brakes on!"

Mark smiled and chuckled at the thought of that. "Yeah, one for each wheel. Can you imagine it?"

At that moment Olivia poked her head around the door. "Mum says tea's ready if anyone can be bothered. I'm bothering so I suppose you guys should too, otherwise I'll have yours – I'm actually starving."

Mark stood up and stretched his aching legs again, then made his way downstairs.

"I'll be with you in a minute" said Alex. He took the folder he'd left on the desk and went into his bedroom, and slipped it under his bed. He couldn't wait to go to bed tonight and have a really good read. For once, his laptop would remain unopened on his desk.

3

My Dear Sarah

Please forgive me writing you this it has been on my mind for too long and you are my closest relation you will understand I hope and forgive me what I am telling you.

Well my dear you know when I worked on the railway it was all my life since I was about 14 but even before that because my father was the signalman at Salmsham when they had the accident. They blamed him and my oldest brother and he died, suicide they said, and Pa went to prison an innocent man and when he came out he was broken and so what I did with some of us my brother ~~James~~ Hubert and my brother in law we knew who did the accident and it was not an accident and so we made sure the person never did harm again. Forgive me it was wrong and I should feel bad but I never felt that way because we did justice which my father never got. When we did it my brother in law would boast and we had to shut him up several times, well he died quite young and I even think my younger sister might have had a hand in that but that's just me thinking like that, she wasn't involved in the earlier things she was too young and know nothing.

20

I will tell you more soon I have to get this off my chest but not write it down too much in case people see it and theres more trouble for us. I will see you at Christmas my dear I hope if you will have me again and if I stay on this earth that long God willing - and I will tell you more then if you want, you might not want to hear it.

Love your Auntie Ath

PS I looking forward to seeing your family at Christmas your boys are the closest I have they are like children to me.

4

Christmas Eve 1946 – Belcote

"Here's your tea, Auntie" Adam Phipps put the china cup and saucer on the little side table by the sofa, where his Great Aunt sat, delight in her eyes at seeing him for the first time since the war ended. She held out a gnarled old hand and patted him on his.

"Thank you, Dear. It's lovely to see you again. You've grown into a fine young man! I bet all those young lasses are chasing you, aren't they?"

Adam blushed. "No Auntie! They're not, and anyway I've been away for a long time, remember? The army?"

"Yes, Dear. I expect you're glad to be home now though, and working on the farm again."

"Yes. I mean, my job isn't great but it's nice to just live normally again."

"Apart from the rationing, you mean?" Sarah Phipps commented as she walked in from the kitchen, duster in hand, to finish the chores she had been hoping to get done before her aunt arrived.

"Yes Mum. Apart from the rationing. But at least we have food. Where I was stationed, I've seen whole villages full of starving people."

"You'd think we lost the war, wouldn't you Auntie Ath?" said Sarah, running the duster around the frames of two small pictures above the fireplace.

Auntie Ath nodded, and stirred her tea.

22

"Mum, I tell you, we are much better off than most of the places I've been to. I've seen folk really suffering…"

"Listen, we didn't ask to fight the war. We didn't start it, and I don't see why we should still be suffering now." Sarah was now busy straightening out the few ornaments on the mantelpiece, so she could put up a couple of little Christmas decorations.

"You didn't fight it, Mum. I did, and it was pretty ghastly I can tell you."

"We had our own fights at home… for food, clothes. At least now you're working on the farm we can have a few extras, but it hasn't been like that until now. None of it's been easy, not for anyone." The inflection in Sarah's last comment told Adam the conversation was meant to be closed. He ignored that; how could she say such a stupid thing? She had no idea!

"Mum, it's not the same as being in the front line, people shooting at you, having to shoot back at them…"

"How many people did you kill, Dear?" Something about Auntie Ath's unexpected and almost impertinent question, asked very matter-of-factly, caused mother and son to stop in their tracks. It sliced through the conversation like a silent blade thrust between the ribs. Sarah and Adam exchanged shocked glances, and Sarah frowned at her aunt.

"Now then, Auntie, I'm not sure Adam wants to…"

"None, Auntie, as far as I know." said Adam. "Well, not directly. I spent most of my time patrolling behind the front line, and helping keep the supplies going, and… Well, the few times I fired my gun in anger, I have no idea whether I hit the enemy. I hardly ever saw them."

During the silence that followed, his great aunt looked at her cup of tea as she stirred it, her face expressionless. She had the appearance of a gentle, harmless old lady, but the tone of her question as well as its content made them both think that there was a lot more to Auntie Ath than met the eye. In the time-honoured manner of all adherents to the 'don't ask too much' culture of her generation and gender, Sarah continued rearranging the mantelpiece.

Adam stared at his aunt's frail hands as she endlessly stirred the tea. He recalled the one time he'd felt really trapped, when he'd truly feared for his life. Up until that moment he'd thought he was invincible – that this war was just an adventure, and that he'd be home soon as it was known that Hitler was losing the war on all fronts. Most of his work was routine patrolling of captured territory. On this occasion, he had been patrolling in a small village in Northern France with three other men, when they suddenly came under fire from what seemed like everywhere around them. They quickly hid in the shelter of a large, burnt out church, keeping their heads down while they tried to work out which direction the enemy was firing from, and how they were going to get back to safety. He remembered Spotty Coombs sticking his head up above a crumbling window ledge and straight away hearing a volley of shots. Coombs ducked down, and several stones on the wall behind them seemed to explode as the bullets ricocheted off them. A few minutes later, Coombs and Harris went back to the window and fired off a volley. They ducked as another hail of bullets passed overhead. Meantime Adam and his best mate Walter Manktelow moved to another window on the same side of the church, and fired off several volleys of their own, but then no-one replied.

After what seemed like an age, but was probably only about ten minutes of total silence, they crept back out of the ruins, and retraced their steps until they arrived back at the camp. They reported what had happened and were told there were a few rogue German snipers around but they'd either retreated or been shot. Later, another patrol found the bodies of two German soldiers less than a hundred yards from the ruined church. Adam wondered which member or members of his patrol had been responsible for taking out the enemy. He didn't dwell on the fact that he may have fired the bullets that killed the snipers, or that they were, like him, just young men obeying orders. They were the enemy, they were faceless, and if he hadn't fired at them they probably would have killed him.

A few days later, his friend Manktelow was caught in some crossfire and was gravely wounded. Adam saw him fall, and stayed with him until the medics arrived. They took him off on a stretcher. Later his CO told him Manktelow had died of his wounds soon after arriving at the makeshift field hospital. He suddenly felt a deep anger and frustration at the whole stupid, senseless war, and the puny part he played in it. When victory was declared he didn't feel any elation, he was just empty. He still was.

He wanted *not* to think about it any more.

"It gets easier, after the first one" said Auntie Ath, staring at the opposite wall, holding her saucer with her left hand, and sipping from the cup using her right.

Sarah looked at her uneasily. "What does?"

"You have to do these things. It's evil, but if it stops more evil, it has to be done."

There was an uneasy silence. Adam wondered what on earth his great aunt was rambling on about, when Sarah spoke.

"Is this anything to do with that letter you sent me in the summer, Auntie?"

"Yes Dear, it is. I wanted to get it off me chest. If you've got the time, that is? I hope you'll understand."

Sarah indicated to Adam, who got up to leave.

"No, he can stay, Dear. He's a grown man. He's seen death. He'll understand I'm sure. I just hope you'll both forgive me; it was all for the best."

Auntie Ath took a few sips of tea, placed the cup back on the saucer on her lap, and began to talk…

5

To the three helpless onlookers in the signalbox, the accident seemed to go on forever. James Palmer looked again at the signal levers, and the miniature repeater distant signal on the shelf above them. "How can this be, Pa?" he called out. "Everything's at danger".

Joseph Palmer was so shocked at what he saw he could barely think clearly, and yet when he looked back at the accident, he must have acted quite swiftly as he was already sending five beats - "Obstruction Danger" - on the bell to the boxes on either side of him while the last carriages of the train tumbled slowly but devastatingly across the running lines, having been piled up against the wreckage ahead. As they came to rest there was a brief and eerie silence, with just a distant hissing sound from the wrecked engine, before the fire began to roar loudly.

The third man in the signalbox, Harrison Wiggins, had stood with his mouth wide open as the guard's van at the back of 'his' goods train was pulverised and vanished beneath a torrent of splintering coaches and sheets of flame. He had been in the 'box for a few minutes, more than enough time to sign the register to say he had reminded Joseph of his train's presence, and to find out what the apparent delay was. He had waited while Joseph replied to a bell from one of the next signalboxes along the line – he didn't know which one – and then made an entry in his register, underneath Harrison's own signature.

Wiggins thought he could hear screams outside, and for a moment he wondered where they would be coming from, then he saw people spilling out of the last carriages, stepping, jumping, or in some case simply tumbling to the ground.

"Quick" said Palmer senior, "you'd better go back and protect the down line". Wiggins snapped out of his trance-like state, as Palmer went to the stores cupboard at the back of the 'box, took out a supply of detonators and a lamp, and handed them over. "Hurry man" said the signalman, as Wiggins grabbed the items, opened the door to the outside world, went down the steps and ran off to the left, under the bridge and away from the carnage.

"Son, you'd better do the same on the up line."

As James Palmer went to the stores cupboard, he heard someone coming up the steps, and a figure appeared in the doorway.

"What was that then, Bobby?" George Chappell used the nickname all train crews used for signalmen, a left over from the old days when they were properly sworn police constables, responsible for keeping the public away from the lines while standing for hours in one spot holding the flags and lights to signal to the trains.

Joseph ignored the question, and asked his own. "Are you the driver of the goods?"

"Aye. I've sent me fireman to protect the up line. What's just happened. Were your signals off?"

James turned around from the store cupboard. "The signals are all on. Look at the levers. The train just came on full steam."

"Did my guard come up here, Bobby?"

Joseph pointed to the figure stumbling alongside the line, heading towards the overbridge, his outline dimly lit by the glow from the inferno in the station. "He did, thank the Lord. He wouldn't have survived that. Oh my!" The signalman slumped down, exhausted, into a small wicker armchair and stared straight ahead.

"They must've missed all them signals then, Bobby."

Joseph didn't reply. He was certain that his signals were "on" against the express. He'd accepted the train from Belcote Crossing, the next box up the line, but kept his signals at danger. There was more than enough time and yardage between his Distant signal and Home signal to pull up a fully laden high speed express train.

The goods driver left the box, and disappeared down the steps.

"Shall I go and find Mr Kemp, Pa?" James was starting to worry about his father's state of mind. More people were milling about on the line outside the box; some were helping others out of the remains of the rearmost carriages.

"Yes, you'd better. I'll just do the register entries." Joseph stood up and went to the small desk where the register was kept. He looked again at his entries – they were all correct, and his levers corresponded to the narrative on the page. Noting 'Down Express overran signals, collision, sent Ob Danger 7.44pm' he looked again out of the window. Quite a crowd of people had already gathered and were starting to form an orderly line to assist people.

He thought he saw Police Sergeant Michaels – of course, he would have heard the crash from his house just at the end of the road. His two constables would surely be joining him too. He also recognised Jack Dove and couple of his mates, and assumed they'd been going to the inn as usual, and heard the crash as they were passing. Jack was right up at the front of a line of men, helping some passengers down from the wreckage high up above the crushed front carriages.

Joseph stared numbly at the scene. He could not leave his post unless he was relieved by someone, and yet he felt unable to function in any useful way. He had a nagging feeling that he must be responsible for the frightful destruction in front of him. He was snapped out of his numbness by the sound of voices at the foot of the steps. As he turned and looked towards the door, Isaac Kemp, the Stationmaster, walked in accompanied by a bedraggled looking man in engineman's overalls, blood oozing from a cut over his eye, one arm hanging limply by his side. Isaac also had a cut, on his forehead, and his face had a look of grim horror on it, as if he too felt the full responsibility for the tragedy which was being played out on his station.

"Isaac, I don't know…" Joseph stopped as Isaac held up his hand. The injured man spoke with some difficulty.

"We had white lights, Bobby, all the way in. White lights… those signals were off for us." said Tom.

"No, they can't have been – look at my levers" Joseph gestured to Stationmaster Kemp, who looked at the lever frame. All bar one lever was fully forward in the frame, and that one lever was for a set of points in the goods siding, which had nothing to do with the main line signals or points.

"I swear to it, Bobby. They were white, my mate saw 'em, I saw 'em." He sat down in the chair. Joseph poured him some tea from the pot, and passed it to him. "Are you the driver?"

The man shook his head. "Fireman. Tom Jobson, Salisbury shed. I don't know how I'm still here, still alive." His hands shook as he lifted the mug to his mouth and took a small sip. "We saw the white at the distant, then I saw the white by the bridge soon after. My mate saw it too when we went past it."

"You must have seen the tail lights on the guard's van?" said Isaac.

"Them's the first red lights I saw, them and the outline of the van in the moonlight."

"Oh come come, fireman. My signals were on."

"There weren't no red lights till the guard's van." He looked from the signalman to the stationmaster. "Nothing, Sir! I swear to it. Last thing I see was the light on the van, then I heard my mate cry out … he shouted "Oh NO NO!" and then we hit it. I don't know how but I got thrown up and out across the platform. I don't know about my mate. I think he's… he's still in the cab."

The three men fell silent for a moment. They all knew that anyone in the front of the express train would have been caught in the fire. Isaac Kemp walked across and began to read the register.

Joseph reflected on what the fireman had said. He'd put his signals to 'on' before the goods train even arrived at Salmsham, and only took the home off briefly once the goods had slowed down enough that it could crawl into the station. Then he replaced the lever to 'on' again. But there was no point in arguing; even if he knew he was right, this poor man was in no fit state and Joseph felt genuine sympathy for him. He'd just seen his driver and goodness knows how many people perish. A rush of blood went to his head.

"Where's James?" asked Joseph.

"I'm not sure. I assume he's helping out in the station. I hope so, we need all hands on deck. We're missing a couple of folk... I haven't seen Caleb or Arthur; they were on the platform." Isaac's voice began to crack. "My God, what have we wrought."

"I'll stay until Albert arrives." Albert was Joseph's fellow signalman, due to take over from him at ten o'clock. "I don't think I'll be much use out there. Shall I telegraph for more assistance?"

"It's done already. You stay put though."

"Isaac... I haven't touched my levers you know. They're exactly as they were. You ask the goods guard, he was in here, he saw everything. He signed the register and I showed him the levers."

Isaac nodded and walked silently out and down the steps. Tom sat staring into his mug of tea. It struck Joseph how calm it was in the box, while just yards away people were fighting the huge fire. Someone emerged from under the bridge, running along the line from Belcote. A young-looking man, Joseph thought he one of the farm workers from Hill Farm. He ran straight towards the wreckage and joined others who were helping with the rescue, beside the burning coaches. It felt so unreal, it was as if he were observing his worst nightmare without actually being a part of it.

"I know what I saw" said Tom Jobson, quietly.

Joseph nodded slowly. He had already guessed this would be the start of a long and painful journey, where he would be forced to question his own sanity at times.

6

Saturday 7th April 2018 – Salmsham

Mark got out of his car and wandered over to the corner of the yard. Alex was still in the front seat, busily replying to a text from his friend Hazel on his iPhone. He pressed send, slipped the phone into his top pocket, grabbed his fleece and hopped out of the car, calling to his father as he slammed the door shut. "Is this the old station then?"

Mark waited until his son was alongside him. "This is the old station goods yard; the actual station is over there behind that hedge. I'm just trying to work out a way in." He turned to his right, and wandered alongside the hedge for a few yards. At the corner of the yard, which still had a gravel surface, he noticed a little pathway which looked as if it was used regularly by dog walkers. He was about to follow the path when a man's voice called out angrily "Hey. You can't leave your car there, this is private land!" He turned, and saw a man about his age, walking briskly over towards him.

Mark held up his hands as an apology. "I'm so sorry, I didn't realise. I used to live near here many years ago and used to come here all the time when it was still a goods yard. I had no idea it was private now…"

"Yeah, well, it is. So you'd better move it. There's a spot across the bridge, up beside the churchyard." The man spoke less aggressively now, as if Mark wasn't who he expected to see.

"Fine. I'll park up there now. Sorry about that. It's just there weren't any signs…"

"There will be soon. We're developing those old cottages back there, and this is going to be the car parking area for them. There's some garages going up soon, right along here. Look, do you say you used to live around here?"

Mark nodded, and explained that he was just exploring his old childhood haunts with his son. Alex was standing by the car, the iPhone again commanding his absolute attention to the point where he barely noticed the stranger talking to his Dad.

"Whereabouts did you live, then?"

"Up at Belcote. I used to cycle down here a lot. I remember when it was still a complete railway station, with all the buildings, signalbox, and a few bits of track where the sidings were. I was planning to measure it up and maybe make a model of it – I used to do model railways when I was younger."

The man stuck out his hand "Roger Cooper – I'm from this very village. I'm not the most popular local though, as it's me who's bought up this land for… I'll call it development, rather than re-development."

They shook hands "Mark Phipps. Nice to meet you Roger. I'll just go and move the car…"

Roger interrupted him. "Oh, look, you can leave it there, it's fine. I thought you were some nosey bastard come to cause more trouble, that's all. I'm sure you're not doing any harm. You weren't to know. I really should put up a sign, I suppose."

"Well, I'm only nosey about the old railway really. Do you own that as well?"

35

"Not yet" said Roger. "I'd like to but..." He went on to explain that as a local man he was treading carefully, as his family had been the target of some fairly nasty treatment at the hands of some of the other locals. "I don't care for myself, but it's not fair on my family. My daughter's been getting some pretty ghastly hate messages on social media. Threats, name calling... people saying really horrible things. There's some really nasty people out there."

Mark agreed. "Give some people a keyboard and screen and they type stuff they'd never dare to say to your face, because they think they're anonymous."

Roger nodded. "Well some of them are just rude, but some are really vicious and they've been making it pretty grim for us. They all complain about the lack of facilities around here; you know, no railway, almost no bus service, poor road links, not much in the way of small businesses and so on, but when someone like me tries to inject more life into the place, they don't want to know. But anyway, I'll let you get on doing your exploring. How long d'you reckon you'll be?"

"About an hour, maybe two? Depends how quickly sonny boy here gets bored!" By now Alex had joined them. "This is Alex, by the way."

"Hi Alex. Look, seriously mate, leave the car here, it'll be fine for the rest of the afternoon. I'll keep an eye on it. I live in the end cottages along there." He gestured to the row of old railway houses which lined the small lane at the other end of the old goods yard.

Mark thanked him and made his way back to the pathway, with Alex following eagerly on. As they turned a corner, they came upon a slightly raised piece of smooth ground. "This used to be the westbound platform. There was a ticket office just…here." Mark walked along a piece of rougher ground. There was no sign of any building, not even foundations. Just what appeared to be a grassy mound.

Ahead of them lay some bushes, but it was possible to make out the line of the old railway between two rows of trees. The old track heading towards Hallowfield was very overgrown. They stepped off the remains of the platform, down into the space where the tracks ran. Here the ground was smoother, and much more level, but with large muddy puddles. Another small pathway seemed to snake along near the middle of the old tracks. They crossed to the other side of the pathway, where there was what appeared to be a low wall running beside the line.

"I do believe" said Mark "that this is the front of the other platform." He turned to the right, and started walking towards Belcote. The line of the old track was much less overgrown at the other end of the station.

Alex climbed over the wall and walked along the other side, a couple of feet above the level of the track way but not as high up as the old platform would have been. "This is weird, Dad. Where's the rest of the platform gone?"

"Who knows" said Mark. "I know some of the heritage railway companies like to take bricks and stuff from old disused stations, and reuse them on their own lines. Maybe there's a complete platform somewhere which came from here? Or maybe the locals took the materials away for their own walls and things."

By now they had reached the end of the station area. They walked on a bit further. A short distance away on the left was a large square of concrete. In front of it was a piece of metal, sticking up out of the ground, and a smaller concrete base with two very rusty bolts on top. Alex ran onto the large concrete square and turned around. I wonder what this was, Dad?"

Mark stopped. "This is the site of the old signalbox, son. That's where our family man worked. And this…" he turned around and faced the remains of the station. "…is where the accident happened. Right here, almost in front of the 'box."

They both stood in silence. Mark carefully took in the view. It all seemed very close. Over the years his memory had distorted things somewhat, and more recently he had imagined the signalman looking on from a great distance as it all happened, but it was here, almost right in front of him, where the edge of the flat grassy area began, just about a hundred yards from the 'box. In his mind's eye, he could see other things; shadowy figures, a mass of shattered wood and twisted iron, smoke and flames shooting high into the sky, a vision of long-past horrors, conjured up in his imagination from the hours of painstaking research he had done into the accident in his youth.

Mark shook his head sadly, took a big breath and then started to explore the site. He had been interested in railways since he was a small boy, and had read many books about them over the years. After his family moved to Frome, he was the spotty adolescent who would often be seen walking as near to the railway lines as was legally allowed, exploring the route of the line near his home, and then the branch lines, some of which were no longer in operation. Not for Mark the stereotypical train-spotting habits. He'd had no interest whatsoever in collecting train numbers, or ticking off different types of locomotive or freight wagons. He just liked to explore, and loved the feeling of walking alone (usually) down a disused track as it meandered through various countryside settings; bridging a stream here, or a lane there; across roads, through overgrown cuttings and along crumbling embankments.

Sometimes he would just sit down and listen to the sweet noises of the countryside; the birds twittering, the wind gently hissing through the unkempt shrubbery which often grew beside the old lineside, the occasional far-off sound of a farmer's tractor.

Once or twice he had visited the site of a well-known accident, either by chance or because his interest had been piqued by reading the stories about the human drama which always played out before the actual moment of disaster. He found these tales far more interesting than the often gruesome descriptions of the outcome. Usually these events happened because one or more people failed in some small detail to carry out their duties properly, and as mistakes piled onto mistakes, very often a tragedy would occur which would cause outrage and indignation for the immediate time, followed by inquests, inquiries and ultimately reports which would lead to improvements in safety designed to prevent such a thing ever happening again.

But this place… this was different because of the family connection. Today, he had driven the fourteen miles to Salmsham with Alex, to see once again the place where this particular drama had played out.

He had known since he was a small boy about "the accident" – his family made sure of that, because one of his ancestors was the signalman that day. This meant that this was more than just the visit of a curious railway enthusiast. He also knew that there was good deal of mystery and intrigue at the time surrounding the accident, but most of it was brushed over and forgotten within months. The poor signalman had become a scapegoat for the mistakes or sins of others, and he was imprisoned for manslaughter. But now Mark started to remember that there was supposed to be a letter in his family which told a different story, and his younger self had meant to get to the bottom of it. Then exams and girls took over and his teenage quest for the truth was dropped; the past losing out to the future. He'd put everything into a folder and filed it away, meaning to come back to it after his 'O' levels…

Alex stepped from the base of the old 'box, and stood on the path of the tracks, turning to face Mark. "Wow. We're on the very spot where it happened. Doesn't seem possible, Dad. It's such a peaceful place."

Mark nodded. "Yeah… it's all a bit strange, isn't it? I'm going to wander up the line a bit, see what's left of it. We used to ride our bikes up this way."

Alex bent down. "I wonder if there's any bits left of the trains."

Mark smiled. "I doubt that very much. The line was worked for another ninety years. It would have been searched and cleared thoroughly straight after the accident as well. They had to relay the line and get it open again quickly"

"All the same, Dad, I'll have a delve and see what I can come up with. You never know, maybe there's even traces of the people – you know, some old bones or something."

Mark frowned. "You've been watching too many films, son. This was a railway accident, not a plane crash. All the dead were accounted for, taken away and given a decent burial." All, he thought, apart from the two bodies who were so badly burnt they were unidentifiable, and were buried in the local churchyard. "Come on – I'm going to see if I can get to my old village. It's about two miles along the tracks, then a bit of a distance from the bridge. It's more like three miles if we went by road. Shouldn't take us too long."

Father and son began to traipse along the track of the disused line, away from the station, into the cutting to the left of the signalbox.

7

In complete contrast to the other end of the station, the tracks heading to the east were very clear and not at all overgrown at first. Following the wide path of the old double trackway, they passed under a stone road bridge, and the cutting curved gently to the left.

They walked on, and Mark's eyes carefully scanned the little details, the curve ahead, the old stone wall about fifteen feet up on the left, at the bottom of the sloping field, the wider patch of clear flat earth ahead, with a crumbling brick mound on the left, and a much smaller hump in the grass on the right. They were only about three or four hundred yards from the signalbox, but it was barely visible from this point, because of the curvature of the cutting, and the road bridge. Mark looked at the two mounds at each side of the tracks. "This used to be the old bridge to Hill Farm. It was already in a pretty poor state when I last came here. I'm not surprised it's collapsed. Shame though. The home signal for Salmsham Station was on the other side".

Sure enough, just past the bridge, Alex found a piece of metal sticking up out of the ground. It looked just like the one he'd seen by the old signalbox base. He knelt down and had a closer look.

Mark stopped and looked across at his son. "That's part of the old signalling system, probably where the signal wires went up to the post. Look, there's the hole there where the signal stood. If it was clear the train could steam on through the station."

Alex looked genuinely surprised. "I didn't realise they used electricity in those days."

"They didn't. The lights were lit with paraffin oil; they had slow burning wicks so they would not need re-lighting for a week."

"OK, so why did they have wires then?"

"Those weren't electric wires. They were wire cables connected to the lever in the signalbox. When the signalman pulled his levers, he had to pull all that cabling as well, and then the signal would move. So, if the distant signal was a mile away, he had to move a mile of cable AND the weight of the signal arm to pull the signal off."

Alex stood up again and brushed some dirt from his jeans. "That's insane, Dad. Those signalmen must have been really strong then!"

"They were quite strong, yes. Don't forget they also had to move the points manually as well, and they were just as heavy if not more so. Not everyone could just pull all the levers over, it really was a man's job."

"Don't let Livvy hear you say that." Alex imagined his sister getting irate about the 'man's job' comment. "She'll start on about female equality and all that glass ceiling stuff again."

Mark smiled. Alex was right about Livvy. He was very proud of his daughter's approach to gender equality – she had to make a speech to her year group about women's rights, and she was by far the most eloquent speaker in her year, he thought.

"Well, that's all very well but she would have found it incredibly hard to shift the levers. There were quite a few younger lads who just didn't have the strength, so some of them never even got the chance to be signalmen."

"If they weren't stopping, how did they know it was okay to keep going then? Isn't that what the distant signal is for?"

"No, the distant signal would give them a warning as to whether they would have to stop, but the home signal was the one they mustn't pass if it was on."

"You mean, if it was red?"

"Yes, or during the day, if the arm was straight out. But it was okay to pass a distant signal that was on, it just meant caution. Sometimes, the signalman would use it to slow a train, and then as it approached the home signal, if it was going slowly enough, he would pull the home signal off so the train wouldn't have to stop completely."

The two walked on further. The track of the line continued to curve around to the left, and when they looked back they could not see Salmsham at all, not even the houses or the church. As they were still in a slight cutting, they could probably not see more than about three hundred yards behind them. After a while, the trackway straightened out, and then the field on their right came down to the same level. Large wheel ruts began to appear in front of them, either from a Landrover, or a small tractor. The line of trees and bushes on the right of the trackway ended, and a wide gate appeared in front of them, with a smaller pedestrian gate to the right of it.

Passing through the smaller gate, they saw that the trackway had become a part of the farmer's field. Some cows were grazing fairly close by, and a few began to amble towards them. Alex looked slightly worried but Mark reminded him that they were just being curious. The cows stopped and stared as they walked on. At the end of the field there was another gate, but here the trackway became fairly overgrown, with just a narrow pathway through the middle. It was clear that this was still in use, presumably by dog walkers, or perhaps other railway maniacs, Mark thought.

"I used to cycle along this bit" said Mark. "It wasn't overgrown then. Before they took up the lines, there used to be another path alongside the line but the other side of the fence, which you could also cycle down." He pointed to what looked like an old pathway, on a slightly lower level. It disappeared under a large bramble bush in the distance.

"I think we're quite close to another bridge, and then beyond that is Belcote Crossing, which is near to the village where I used to live."

Just then the path widened slightly and they saw a girl coming the other way, followed closely by a youth with a baseball cap on back to front. The girl, who Alex thought was probably about Livvy's age, looked bored and grumpy. Alex looked away when she went past him. "Afternoon" said Mark, politely to the two youngsters. "Hi" grunted the youth. The girl didn't react at all. They walked on. As the undergrowth began to thin out, they saw that the line of the railway was now dead straight for about a mile or so. The cutting had now all but disappeared, and the fields on the left were now visible.

"You see that church tower on the left over there, in the distance?" said Mark. "That is Belcote. We used to live in a little cottage there, until I was about your age, then we moved to Frome, to the house where Nan & Grandpa live now."

Alex looked across at the village and then kept on walking. "Are we going to go there now, to your old place, or do we just turn around and go back?"

"I think we'll just go up to Belcote Crossing and turn around, otherwise we might outstay our welcome in the car park. But we can always drive back to the village before we head home, and I can show you the old cottage where I used to live."

They walked on. The old trackway became an embankment, and the fields on their left began to drop away. On the right were trees, which appeared to be growing out of the slope of the embankment for they seemed to be a similar height even as the embankment got higher above the fields. After another few minutes of walking they came to a bridge parapet. There was a plaque on the bridge that simply said '143'. They walked on over the bridge, which spanned a minor road. To Alex, it seemed weird walking on a trackway that had bushes growing on it, yet was actually quite high up over the road below.

"This is Belcote Crossing" said Mark. "There was a small signalbox here, but it had gone long before they closed the railway. It was in the middle of nowhere really. There was a set of really steep wooden steps up from the roadway. There was no other way in apart from walking along the track."

"So why did they have a signalbox but no station?" asked Alex.

Mark explained that the line was divided up into sections, or blocks, and that only one train was allowed in a section at any one time. When there was not much traffic they could use quite long sections, just between the stations, but later on when they needed to run more trains, the railway companies added extra boxes between stations so each block was only two or three miles long.

"So how come the train crash happened then, Dad? They must have run two trains in the same section."

"That is the question, isn't it? They blamed the signalman – our ancestor – for not putting his signals to red, but he insisted they were on all the time and that the train had run past them. There were witnesses who said they were off, and others who said they were on. One of the railway folk took his own life, so then they questioned his evidence. Eventually the inquiry decided our man had made a terrible mistake and he was sent to prison for manslaughter, but a lot of people thought he'd been made a scapegoat by the railway company."

They began to retrace their steps. "This is the start of the Salmsham block, right here" said Mark. "That old post there was the Belcote home signal, which let the train into the next block. Later on, we should find the Salmsham distant signal. In fact it could be seen easily on a clear night as the line is straight for a good mile or so." Mark imagined being the driver of the express that night, steaming along at high speed, clattering over the bridge past the Belcote 'box, taking the long gentle left curve and then eyes straining for the white light of the distant signal.

"Wouldn't they have trouble seeing it if it was foggy or raining?"

"Yes, but they knew where it should be, and also you must realise, there was barely any light at all in the countryside back then. There was no electricity, and gas-lighting was only in use in the larger towns. It would have been pitch black apart from moonlight, and the signal lights, so any artificial light would have been easy to see. The fireman said they saw only white lights, no red ones."

"White lights?"

"Yes," said Mark "they used red for stop, green or blue for caution and white for go. But I think the distant signals they used on this line also used white for all clear. They only stopped doing this when towns began to really be well lit, then they changed it to green instead of white, for all clear. Also, they reasoned that if the red glass fell out of the signal, it would show a white light, which would be a false clear. But if 'clear' was changed to green, the driver would know if the light was white that it was broken."

"Sounds a bit complicated, Dad."

"Mmmm, well it was simple really. But anyway, all of that was much later on. Our man says he saw a white light which meant the line was clear, and that's why the crashed happened."

They walked on, and gradually the embankment disappeared and they were once again level with the fields. They saw no sign of the distant signal at all. Mark made a mental note to look it up when he got home. Then he remembered something…

"Oh yes, Alex. Where is that folder I had about the accident? You left it out when we were unpacking stuff in my office, and I haven't seen it since."

"Ah. Sorry Dad, it's under my bed. I meant to read it and then got distracted and then just totally forgot. When you said we were coming over here I thought I'd actually put it back and you'd got it. Sorry."

"Okay that's fine. You didn't need to smuggle it out, there's nothing in there you shouldn't see. I was happy to let you read it all, just not while we were unpacking."

They walked the rest of the way mainly in silence, until they got back to the curve in the cutting before the station. Mark stopped and stared straight ahead.

"What's up Dad?"

"I'm just trying to work out what they would have seen from the cab of the loco. They've just gone into the curve, and they're approaching the first bridge, the Hill Farm one, so they would have been able to see the signal which they claim was white. Then they would have been steaming ahead blindly, because you can't see the station from here. If it was dark they wouldn't have even been able to see the gas lamps on the platform. So, they wouldn't have seen the goods train until they got much closer." He walked on again until he could just see the remnants of the old platform. "They should have seen the lights on the back of the guard's van about now…"

"How fast were they going?"

"Well the report said about sixty-five miles an hour. That's about ninety-five feet a second. About thirty metres a second to you. That means they had about seven seconds to react when they first saw the train. That's barely any time to do anything. Maybe whistle for the brakes, and start putting the hand brake on. But that's not going to make much difference in that time, probably none at all. Poor chaps, they must have known it was going to be a big one."

They stumbled along the rough bits of trackway until they were once again back by the station, and walking along in by the remains of the old down platform.

"Look Dad. Could this be a part of the wreckage?" Alex was scraping away at the edge of the platform area. "It's in about the right place," thought Mark before dismissing the idea.

"I very much doubt it, son. What is it anyway?"

"An old lump of metal, like a bolt or something." Alex pulled at something protruding from under an old stone. "Here it is..." They looked at the muddy object which Alex was holding, turning it over in his hands and brushing some of the dirt away. "Could be a bolt."

"It is indeed a bolt, son" said Mark brightly, "but I doubt very much it's from 1874."

"Still, I'll keep hold of it anyway, Dad, 'cos it's like, a bit of history or a memento. I'll clean it up when we get home."

They climbed back onto the low flat platform area. Mark turned and looked back down the line. In his mind's eye, he saw the dark outline of a train approaching at speed; he could hear the pounding beat of the pistons at work as the engine worked hard with her heavy train, her driver and fireman desperate to keep momentum for the long climb ahead. Mark looked to his right and pictured the goods train standing right there, just yards away, just out of view of the express crew, its driver standing beside the engine, calling to his fireman. "That's a train a-coming, Harry! Let's move!"

He imagined the bewildered look on the face of the signalman as he tried to make sense of the situation. Surely his levers were all on; surely the signal should be showing the red light. Surely this couldn't be happening to him…

"Dad!"

"Uh…" Mark snapped out of the daydream.

"Come on, Dad. Let's go home. I want to read that folder, and clean up this bolt."

8

Mark and Alex made their way back into the yard and looked towards their car, parked a few yards away. As they approached it they saw a note on the windscreen, badly scrawled on a scrap of lined paper. Mark pulled it from under the wiper blade. It read "No parking. Next time were going to clamp it. Thank you." Mark noted the missing apostrophe and chuckled. He screwed the note up, resisting the urge to drop it on the ground and instead, throwing it onto the back seat of his car. Then he noticed the girl they'd passed before on the old railway path. She was sitting not ten feet away, glaring at him.

"This is private land, you know" she said gloomily. "My Dad is on his way and he'll clamp it if you don't move it."

"If your Dad is Roger, we've already met and he told me we could leave it here as long as we liked this afternoon, but anyway, we won't trouble you again."

The girl seemed unmoved by this. "Oh, right" she said. "Well anyway, it's still ours and it's not the public's so… yeah anyway, if it gets damaged don't blame me."

"I'm Mark, by the way, and this is Alex, my son. I'm sorry to hear you've been picked on a bit about the re-development around here."

"Oh. He told you then. Yeah, well, people are just sh** aren't they? I mean, they write all sorts of nasty stuff online but none of them would dare to say it to me in public 'cos I'd beat the crap out of them."

Mark winced at her language. She looked about Olivia's age but if his daughter had spoken like that in front of him...

"Sorry" she said "it's not your fault. Anyway, I'll be glad to move out of this sh***y little place once he's finished all the building work."

"Vicky! Vicky!" A man's voice called from the end of the row of cottages. The girl looked up. "Over here Dad! I'm talking to some people..." Roger appeared and beckoned her. "Mum's got a pizza on the go, love, better get in there and clean up. Remember we're off to the cinema in a bit."

Vicky got up and shambled away wordlessly and without any sign of enthusiasm, towards the cottages. Roger came across to the car and smiled at Mark and Alex. "Good walk?"

"Yes thanks. I was just telling Alex all about the big accident back in the 1800s. Our ancestor was the local railway signalman."

"Really?" Roger looked surprised. "That's quite interesting. One of my great... great... something grandfathers was the porter on the station."

"Seriously. Gosh! Small world." Mark told him about the research he'd done as a boy. "We've got loads of family papers and letters and things over at my parents' place. I need to dig it all out and have another look. There was a lot of controversy about it at the time."

Roger nodded. "Yeah, my Dad told me his family reckoned there'd been some trouble with some of the locals, some sort of cover up and some no-good business. He reckons the railway company and some of the villagers covered it all up and blamed the station staff but it wasn't them who caused it."

"Well, I'm sure we'll be back in the next couple of months, so maybe if I find anything interesting out I'll let you know."

"Sure. Tell you what, here's my business card; it's got my email on it. Let me know when you're coming back and maybe we could have a jar or two in the local."

"It'll be a pleasure. I don't have my card on me but I'll email you when I get home."

They said their goodbyes, and Alex and Mark got back in the car. Mark pulled out of the car park and turned left, following the sign for Belcote. They drove up over the railway bridge, and past Salmsham Church high up on the left. The hill was fairly steep, and the churchyard wall, which had towered over the site of the railway, gradually got shallower as the road rose to meet it. There was a small layby, alongside which was the porched gateway to the churchyard. They carried on up the hill, curving to the right before reaching the summit. The road began to wind slightly but stayed mainly level, and soon they could see the steeple of Belcote Church in the distance.

Alex looked at the business card his father had asked him to hold.

"Roger Cooper. Property Developer slash Building Renovations. Oh, this makes him sound very posh. Email: rcooper@rmcproperty.co.uk telephone Oh seven seven four seven..."

"That's quite a coincidence – his ancestor being on the railway as well. I don't recognise his name from the old records, but we need to have another good look. Ah, here we are. 'Belcote welcomes careful drivers'. I wonder if it still welcomes old residents?"

"Probably depends how carefully they drive, Dad." Alex replied, glancing out at the large old houses lining the lane just past the village sign. "Did you live in one of these places then?"

"Ha! I wish! No, we were in that end cottage just there, Wheeler's Cottage." Mark pointed to a little row of houses in front of the church. "I could look over the churchyard from my bedroom window. It was quite spooky – Uncle Nige used to play horrible tricks on me and I used to think the people climbed out of their graves at night."

Alex laughed. He thought his Uncle Nige was the coolest guy in the family, the family joker. He could definitely imagine his uncle creeping about and scaring the wits out of his dad.

Mark stopped the car outside the church.

"What are we doing now?" asked Alex, as Mark undid his seatbelt.

"I just wanted to have a look around the old churchyard. Some of our family are buried here, and I haven't been here for ages. I was christened in this church too, not that I remember any of it."

The entrance to the churchyard was through a small wooden gate, with a small pathway made of paving stones, mixed with some very old headstones, leading to the church. Alex thought the church was very small, but as Mark pointed out, the village was very small too, and even now the population was not that large. The pathway split in front of them, the left fork heading straight to the church door, the right around the side of the church. They took the right fork, and started to wander towards the far corner of the churchyard, where there was a small memorial garden. Alex looked at the names on the old headstones as they walked slowly past them.

"That's where my grandparents' ashes are buried" said Mark, pointing ahead.

"Oh look!" called Alex suddenly, stopping in front of a large weathered headstone. "Henry Francis Phipps, died 6th January 1934 in his 49th year, and Sarah Ann Phipps his wife, died 8th October 1963 aged 79 years. Who are they, Dad?"

Mark thought for a moment. "I think they must be my great grandparents. Let's see, my grandfather was Adam Phipps, and he was born around 1920 or '21, so yeah, if Henry was 49 in 1934, he must have been born 1885 or thereabouts. So, he would have been mid-thirties when Grandad was born so, yeah, this is probably them."

Alex took a couple of pictures of the grave, and wondered what they were like, these ancestors of his, and whether there were any pictures of them anywhere.

"Do you have any photos of them, Dad?"

"I haven't no, but I'm sure my Dad has. He's got an old suitcase full of family stuff."

Alex glanced at the graves alongside the Phipps headstone, and began to read out their surnames. "Clode... that's a funny name. Weston... Oh look, Dad, there's a Thomas Cooper here. Wonder if he's related to that Roger guy?"

Alex took another picture, and read out the inscription; "Thomas Henry Cooper, died 9th March 1945 in his 80th year, and also his loving wife Julia who fell asleep... something-th of November 1916 in her 48th year. Together again".

Mark was already in the little memorial garden. "Here they are. My grandparents." He stood in front of the little plaques, one to Adam Seldon Phipps, the other Jeanette Eliza Ross Phipps. Alex took pictures of each.

"Oh, so is this Great Granny Phipps? Jeanette?"

Mark nodded. "Yep. My favourite Granny. Lovely lady. Don't think I could ever imagine a sweeter soul. She just made everyone feel so special, all of the time. She doted on you and Livvy, and Alistair and the twins. I don't think I can ever remember her uttering a cross word, to anybody."

"What if you did something wrong?" said Alex, who also remembered his Great Granny with affection.

"Well, the funny thing is, we must have been quite mischievous, but she never seemed to mind. She just had that twinkle in her eye, and would smile and wink at us, and suddenly we knew we were in the wrong but it didn't seem to matter. But we probably wouldn't do whatever-it-was again either. Just in case she ever stopped being like that to us."

"What was your Grandad like?"

"Adam, you mean? Oh, he was a lot more serious, you know. But then again, he'd fought in the Second World War, and seen some pretty horrendous things. Actually, I once wrote an essay on the war for a school project, and I... oh gosh, that's right! I interviewed him! Heaven only knows where the tape is now, but it was really interesting. He was once surrounded by German snipers and had to shoot his way out. He told me he really thought it was the end, but then he changed the subject and I couldn't get much more out of him. I think he preferred to forget it all, like many of his generation did. Actually, that's when he told me about the accident, and how... gosh, it's all a muddle now."

"We're doing World War Two in history at the moment, Dad. If you find that tape, let me know. I'd be really interested to hear it. I could take it into school."

"Maybe." Mark looked thoughtfully at the memorial plaques for a minute or so in silence, and then abruptly turned and said "Right, come on, let's get home. I told your mother we'd be home by now. She'll be wondering where we are."

Alex laughed "No she won't. I messaged her already. She knows exactly where we are and what we're doing; she's probably not expecting us home before midnight."

As they walked back to the car, Alex continued to look at the surnames on the gravestones. There were Pattersons, Clintons, Clodes, Marriotts, Fortunes, and Smiths, but no more Phipps or Coopers. He wondered out loud whether any of these families could be related to the Phipps', in which case they'd be cousins.

Mark pointed out that they would all be cousins anyway. "Anyone with English ancestry dating back several hundred years is likely to be around fifteenth cousins with anyone else."

As they drove home Alex thought about that last statement. "How is that possible, Dad? That we're all cousins with everyone else?"

"Well, think about it. We must be. I mean, there are some facts which have to be true; but we'll never be able to verify them."

"How do you mean?"

"Well, some things… I mean, for example, there must be a finite number of people drinking a cup of tea, right now, all over the world. There must be. It will be a true and finite figure. But the thing is, no-one will ever know what that exact figure is! You could take a sample and then use statistics to estimate the figure, but you'll never know the true figure. Likewise, we know that we are all related, and statistics show that the average is likely to be fifteenth cousins. But we'll never actually know, we'll just have to speculate."

Alex silently tried to get his head around the logic of his father's comments. He looked at the bolt which he'd found by the station platform. This bolt once did something important, that must be true. But would he ever know what?

As they left the village behind them, Mark began to wonder where he had last seen the tape of the interview, and where he'd left the old tape player. He remembered there was something quite revealing on it, to do with his aunt or something. It was about the railway accident. He decided to make it his priority to find the tape as soon as he got home.

9

The same day - Milnefield

Alex dropped the muddy bolt in the porch, kicked his shoes off on the doormat and rushed straight upstairs as soon as they got through the front door, colliding with his sister as the top of the stairs. "Thanks, Loser!" Olivia tried to slap him as he went past her. Alex ignored her and dived into his bedroom, and onto his front by the bed. He reached under but couldn't feel the folder. Putting his head to the floor, he looked underneath the bed. All he could see was his sister's feet on the other side of the bed, near the door.

"Alright Livvy, what have you done with it!" Alex shouted angrily.

"What!" his sister screamed back. "Done with what?"

"There was a folder, in here, under my bed…"

"I don't come in here, it stinks, and I certainly wouldn't look under your bed! I hate to think what I'd find…"

"Well who's taken it then? No-one else even knew about it!" The siblings' voices had risen to beyond normal shouting by now.

"Stop blaming me for all your little problems; if you can't keep your room tidy it's nothing to do with me, is it! I never come in here. You're just a little loser."

"Well you're in here NOW…"

"LOSER!"

"YOU'RE THE LOSER…!"

"WHAT IS GOING ON UP THERE!" Freya's voice called out from the stairs. "If you're going to kill each other, please do it quietly."

"It's him. He reckons I've been in his room and taken something. Why would I want to do that? God, Mum, do something; tell him I've got more important things to do like coursework." Olivia stormed into her room and slammed the door loudly.

"Right, what on earth is going on?"

Freya stood in the doorway of Alex's room. He was still kneeling on the floor, red with anger and trying not to cry. "Mum, she's taken a folder I left under my bed…"

"No she hasn't. If you mean that railway folder, I took it. I put it in Dad's office, as it's his folder."

"Why? I was going to read it!"

"Don't shout at me. I moved it because I was cleaning up your room and hoovering under the bed, that's why. This place doesn't clean itself, and I'm certainly not going to wait for either of you kids to do it. Besides, what's the big secret?"

Alex explained that he and Mark had had a quick look at it, and they'd started to read the reports about the railway accident at Salmsham, and he'd simply taken it away to look at that night, and then he'd just forgotten about it.

"Right, well, when you've calmed down, and when you've apologised to your sister, you can come downstairs and have some dinner, and ask your father if you can have it back again."

"I'm not apologising to her!"

"I said, when you've apologised to your sister…"

As Freya started back down the stairs, Alex stood up, huffed to himself and then stomped out of his room, banged once on Olivia's door, flung it open and shouted "Sorry!" and slammed it shut again, turned around and stomped down the stairs.

"I'm fed up with being treated like a child by everyone." he moaned as he walked into the dining room, where Freya had laid the table out for a full three course meal. Mark, who was opening a bottle of red wine on the sideboard, said "Well, you were perfectly capable of behaving like an adult today, but if you talk to your sister like a piece of dirt, she's not exactly going to treat you kindly is she?"

Alex ignored him. "Anyway, Mum says the railway folder is back in your office. Can we have a look later on, after tea."

"Yes, once we've helped your mother clear up." Mark poured himself a glass of wine, sipped it, and then poured some for Freya and Olivia.

"How come she gets wine and I don't?" Alex demanded.

"Because she's nearly eighteen, and anyway, you can have some if you like. A little. But you usually turn your nose up at it. Here you are…" he poured a small amount into a glass and put it by Alex's place.

Freya brought in a joint of beef and put it on the table. As she turned to go back out to the kitchen, Olivia appeared in the doorway. "Oh good, you can help bring the vegetables in." said her mother. With a sigh, her daughter turned back into the kitchen. She returned a moment later with a large pyrex dish and plonked it in the middle of the table, glaring at Alex. "Don't you EVER barge into my bedroom like that again. EVER! OK? Got it?"

Alex ignored her, and took a sip of the wine. He thought it was truly disgusting.

Dinner was a remarkably mild affair despite the siblings' mutual animosity. At one stage Mark asked if anyone had seen the old tape player, and Freya reminded him that they'd thrown it out when they were packing. "You said something about never needing it again, Dear" she commented.

"That's a pain," said Mark "because I think I know where that interview tape is that I did. It'll be interesting to hear the old man's voice again."

"Which old man, Dad?" asked Olivia. Although she had not wanted to go with him to Salmsham, she was still a little envious of her brother spending so much time with him and she felt the need to cosy up to him too.

"My grandfather. Adam Phipps. I interviewed him about what he did in the war, for my school essay. But he told me all sorts of other things too, about the family. Some of it was to do with that railway accident at Salmsham, or at any rate, the aftermath, I really can't remember. But we must have a listen to it, sooner rather than later."

After they had all polished off another one of Freya's amazing trifles, Alex eagerly helped to clear the plates from the table, while his sister took the glasses.

"Hey Loser, you never drank your wine!" she taunted as he stacked the plates up on the kitchen worktop.

"I don't know how you can drink that stuff. It's horrible. I'm sure you don't like it either, you only drink it to look all grown-up in front of the 'rents." sneered Alex.

"Oh please…" Olivia grabbed a cloth and took it in to wipe the table. Alex followed her in to collect the rest of the dishes and extras from the room.

"We met a girl today, about your age." Alex taunted. "She was really grumpy too. I thought maybe she was your long lost twin, although maybe not; she was much prettier than you…"

Olivia ignored her brother's comments, took the cloth back to the kitchen and then retired upstairs to her room. He heard the door slam, followed by Mark's voice, "There's no need to wreck the house already, Livvy!" Mark had gone upstairs to the office, and came back down with the folder.

"Right, let's sit down and have a good look at all this stuff." He sat back at the dinner table, poured himself and Freya another glass of wine and they pulled the folder open.

The first item was the copy of the Board of Trade Report into the accident. Then there were various old photographs of Salmsham Station and the surrounding area. There were a couple of colour pictures of the trackway when it was still clear, which Mark told them he'd taken with his own instamatic, when he was out riding his bike. There was also a copy of a model railway magazine from 1988, with a picture of an old locomotive on the front. The only other things were a fair number of handwritten notes, on lined paper, and some plans for a model railway layout.

"Dad, didn't that Roger guy say his grandfather or someone was at the station during the accident. How would we find that out?"

"Well, I suppose the best thing to do is to read the accident report. Why don't we read it thoroughly and we'll make some notes. Look out for anyone called Palmer, that was their name. They were on my side of the family."

They poured over the report, noting any names that were mentioned, rather than the details of their evidence. Alex jotted down a list of names, with added notes scribbled alongside:

Isaac Kemp, Stationmaster. Cut over eye
Marriott, porter. First name Arthur
Ganger Strong. Killed, standing on platform near back of goods train
Stopps, Porter. Caleb. Killed on platform crushed under coach.
James Palmer, shunter – son of Joseph?
James Maltby, farm lad.
Joseph Palmer – signalman our ancestor?
Ganger Faulkner. Robert
Reynolds, District Inspector.
George Chappell – engine driver (goods train)
Harry Lusby – fireman on the goods train
Wiggins, Guard (goods) First name Harrison!

"So which one of these was our ancestor then, Joseph or James?" Alex asked.

"Joseph I believe. He was the signalman, wasn't he?"

"Ah yes, so James must be his son… yes it says so here. So, is James also our ancestor then?"

Mark frowned. "I can't actually remember. We'll have to do some research on one of those family history things on the net. I'm not sure how we can find all those links and things out."

Freya piped up. "I'll ask my mother. You know how she's done some of this tracing stuff. I think she uses Ancestry.com. I'll email her later. What are the dates again? Eighteen seventy…"

"Four." said Mark. "So if James was an adult, he would have to be at least 20, so born around 1854. My Dad was born in 1950, his dad around 1920, so let's say thirty years for each one, he'd have been something like my great great grandfather. Gosh, that seems so remote."

"What I don't understand though, Dad, is why the signalman went to prison."

Mark scanned the report. "Me neither. There seems to be a lot of contradictory evidence in here. The last pages of this report are missing. I'm not sure if I got them all copied. I wonder if I got any other notes on it."

He pulled out the rest of the file. There were sketches, photographs of the station, pictures of a young Mark on his bike underneath the railway bridge (which was now collapsed), and some handwritten notes by Mark himself. One note said simply 'Action' and then listed three things; transcribe tape; newspaper reports; family papers (Granddad). Mark thought that was pretty much the current state of play too, and made a mental note to pick up where he'd left off all those years ago.

"Freya, isn't Livvy registered online with the British Newspaper Library for her 'A' level research? Maybe we could use her membership and do some searching."

"Good idea. I'm sure she won't mind if we ask her." Freya got up and took her empty wineglass to the kitchen, then disappeared upstairs.

"Dad, where are all your family papers then?" asked Alex. "They weren't in those boxes, were they?"

"No, I'm pretty sure they're with Grandpa in Frome, but I need to check. I think the priority has to be to find that tape. I know it's around somewhere."

They heard two lots of footsteps on the stairs. Freya came back into the dining room. "Livvy's just coming, she's just getting a drink."

Olivia came in with an empty glass, and went to pour herself some more wine. Ignoring her brother, she sat down and said "So what is it you need, Dad?"

"We're looking for any newspaper reports to do with this railway accident in 1874. Anything at all; inquests, general reports, you name it. The date it happened was 12ᵗʰ March 1874 and the inquests and things might have gone on for several months. Also, anything about a Joseph Palmer going to prison. He was our ancestor."

Olivia asked for a pen and wrote the details down on a sheet of notepaper, from the pad Mark had been using. "Where was this accident?"

"Oh. Sorry, Salmsham. Spelt S-A-L-M-S-H-A-M. I would think it'll be the only thing of interest flagged up for that village anyway."

"Well, it depends whether the archive has any local papers of the time. There are a lot of gaps and it's not the biggest archive yet, but it's growing all the time. But it is the most satisfying when you get a result. You can print off the whole page, or just the article, and it highlights every single reference to any keyword you use. I'll go and have a look later when I've finished this essay." She got up to leave, taking her wine with her.

"Thanks Livvy. We went to see the site of the accident this afternoon and it was quite eerie, standing there knowing what had happened and how many people were injured and died there, even if it was 144 years ago."

"Cool" said Livvy." I'll let you know if I can find anything…" The last sentence was shouted from afar as she dashed back upstairs.

"Right," said Mark, scooping up the various documents and loose sheets of paper and replacing them in the folder, "we can't do any more now. I'll email Roger Cooper tonight and thank him for letting us park there today, and then I'll have a good rummage for that tape I made. I suspect it's in my trunk of childhood memories."

"And I'll email Mum tomorrow about tracing the family and see what she says." added Freya. "And you had better think about bed, young man."

"Yes Mum." said Alex, with surprisingly no hint of an objection as he got up quickly from the table. Freya raised an eyebrow as he left the room.

"Did you see that? I've never know him go upstairs without moaning before."

Mark chuckled. "You may have sent him upstairs, but don't believe for one moment he's going to go to bed. He'll be on that laptop researching everything he can about this accident, I'll bet. It will probably do him some good, at least he's focusing on something other than games."

"You know, we could always switch the Wi-Fi off early" grinned Freya.

"Oh wouldn't that just go down well, you wicked mother you! You'll have both kids banging on our door demanding their online rights. Besides…"

"You're going to do some research too?"

"Well, apart from emailing this Roger guy, I was going to see what there is, if anything, on the net that is new, about this accident. There's probably not, but if I can find any more official stuff from the time that would be handy."

"Well, I'm off to bed, and I don't need any Wi-Fi for what I've got planned."

"Oh yes?" Mark raised his eyebrows.

"Sorry Dear…sleep! Lots of sleep. I'll email Mum tomorrow, but meantime I'm exhausted."

As they made their way upstairs, Olivia burst out of her room. "Dad, there's loads of stuff in the newspaper library. I mean, tons of pages and things. What shall I do with it all?"

As Freya went to the master bedroom, Mark went into his daughter's room and sat on the wicker chair next to her, trying to make sense of the various items on the screen. There were lots of tabs open.

"Look at this, Dad: 'Inferno at Salmsham. At least fifteen passengers and three railwaymen were killed when an express train charged at breakneck speed into a paraffin-laden goods train at the little station of Salmsham last Thursday. Many more people are thought to be injured. No-one yet knows what caused the accident but there are conflicting reports that the signals gave a wrong indication to the doomed enginemen. The signalman, Joseph Palmer, has been relieved of his post until the Board of Trade have completed their enquiry which is due to start this Monday in the Dukes Head, Salmsham. The line was blocked and station buildings destroyed in the fire. The London and Western Railway Company say they expect to be running through trains by Monday morning on one line only, and full repairs to both lines and equipment should be completed by Wednesday. Eyewitnesses have paid tribute to the gallant rescuers, who helped to pull passengers from the blazing train. Several local people have been named as heroes for undoubtedly saving the lives of many people. Many people from the village brought food and drink and looked after the injured, in many cases putting up travellers who could not reach their destination. The more seriously injured were removed by train to the municipal hospitals at Hallowfield and Weston. The fireman of the express train had a miraculous escape from almost certain death as he...': oh dammit, that's the end of the page. Where's the next column..."

After a few minutes of futile searching, with Olivia flicking between various open tabs, they both realised that the best thing would be for her to simply download every page she could find as a PDF, and then they could have a better look in the next few days.

"If we try to make sense of this stuff on the screen we'll be here forever" said Mark. "Download as many as you can, and maybe if you could name the file by the original date and page number the pages will be in the right order then."

"Okay Dad, I will. Do you mind if I stop now, this is doing my head in. I've got to finish this essay tomorrow, then I'll have another go later in the evening. Oh, and Jake's coming round."

Mark grinned. "I'm sure Jake won't mind helping you with this research, Dear."

"Actually Dad, he'll probably love it. He seems to prefer the company of computers than me, so you needn't worry about us being all alone up here, if that's what you were implying."

"I wasn't implying anything, but if he really is interested, two heads are better than one when it comes to absorbing all this data."

Mark left his daughter shutting down her laptop, and sat down in his office, He dashed off a quick email to Roger, thanking him for his hospitality with parking, and almost immediately got a reply.

From: rcooper@rmcproperty.co.uk
Sent: Saturday, April 7, 2018 10:11 PM
To: mark@phippstribe.net
Subject: RE: Thank you

Hi Mark, great to meet you too. We had a great time tonight thank you. You got me thinking about the train crash, and I spoke to my dad tonight and he says he's got some papers or letters somewhere, he's going to have a look. It's to do with our family. One of them was the porter but another one on another side of the family was a railway clerk much later on. He said there was a lot of goings on at the time and someone got stitched up and there was a bit of a family feud. Anyway when I find out more I'll let you know.
Don't forget to tell me when you're coming back and we'll have that pint or two in the local
Cheers
Roger

From: mark@phippstribe.net
Sent: Saturday, April 7, 2018 9:57 PM
To: rcooper@rmcproperty.co.uk
Subject: Thank you

Hi Roger

Just a quick note to thank you for letting us park at the old station today and also to tell you that we've found out quite a lot already about the train crash there. My son is quite eager to find out the facts, unusually for a 14 year old boy who normally prefers computer games.
I hope you and your daughter had a nice time at the cinema too.
Best wishes
Mark Phipps

Mark shut down his computer, and went across to the shelves on the other side of the room. On the top of the deeper shelving unit was a fibreglass trunk with wooden straps. He gingerly pulled it towards him and then took the weight and lowered it to the floor. Flicking open the latches, he opened the lid. What had been neat piles of carefully stacked old school books and papers was now a jumbled mess. He spent several fruitless minutes rummaging through the 'archive' of his school life, before realising that the best way would be to empty the trunk bit by bit. After several more minutes, he noticed two exercise books which seemed to have something stuck between them. On closer inspection he found an old cassette tape with and partly torn label which said "Adam Phipps inte.." on it.

As he pulled it out he realised that some of the tape itself had come out from the cassette and was jammed inside yet another book. He carefully extracted the tape, which had become somewhat creased, and then, using a hexagonal pencil, he carefully wound it back into the cassette. "Now all I need" he thought to himself "is a tape player."

10

Tuesday 18th November 1879
St. Mary's Church, Salmsham

It was a freezing cold morning, and the onlookers were well wrapped up, with the thickest coats and scarves to keep the bitter wind at bay as best they could. It had been cold in the church too, adding to the gloom and misery of the occasion. Many of the villagers had turned out for the funeral of the late landlord of the Dukes Head, George Whitmore. He was a popular figure in Salmsham; as well as running the Inn, he also sat on the parish council, and was a churchwarden and great personal friend of the Reverend Michael Ferber, who was conducting the funeral service.

Six men dressed in long black coats and top hats bore the coffin from the church, led by the Reverend Michael, along the path and then across the grass past several fairly recent graves, to the side of the freshly dug grave. George's immediate family stood closest to the graveside, including Jennifer, his youngest child at just ten years old.

His oldest surviving son, George Junior, stood with his head bowed; his wife Jane stood stoically just behind him, cradling their eleven-month-old baby son in her arms. Their other son, just four years old, stood holding hands with his aunt, George Jnr's sister Susanna, who had taken over the responsibility of looking after her younger siblings after the death of their mother ten years before. Another son,

William, stood arm in arm with his wife Martha. They had left their three children back at the Dukes Head, in the care of Martha's sixteen-year-old sister Katharine; Martha had said she wanted to mourn properly and not be distracted by the children, who were in any case too young to know what was happening.

George Snr's remaining children, Horatio, Lucy and young Jennifer sobbed quietly as the coffin was lowered slowly into the frozen ground. Watching from behind the immediate family, Sarah Palmer could hear snatches of the vicar's words; "Forasmuch as it hath pleased Almighty God of his great mercy to take unto himself the soul of our dear George here departed…"

Sarah caught sight of her brother Hubert and a fellow railway worker Arthur Marriott. Arthur looked up at her and winked. Sarah quickly broke her gaze.

"…ashes to ashes, dust to dust; in sure and certain hope of the resurrection to eternal life through our Lord Jesus Christ;…"

She looked up again and this time caught the eye of Hubert. He nodded briefly, then looked across the grave at Martha Whitmore. Martha stared straight back at him, her face slightly puckered in the cold wind, and cold tears rolling down her cheeks. He tried to work out whether Martha harboured any suspicions. She had been in on their plan to begin with, but had expressed reservations and so in the last few weeks they had acted without her knowledge. But Hubert knew his older sister felt just as strongly as he did; she wanted revenge, but not the way he had planned it.

"...that it may be like unto his glorious body, according to the mighty working, whereby he is able to subdue all things to himself." As the vicar finished his intonation, the assembled crowd muttered "Amen". Several people began to throw clumps of earth into the grave, until the coffin was almost completely covered.

Joseph Palmer stood alongside his wife Charlotte, just behind Sarah, staring straight ahead. How many times had he done this in the last few years; how many more gravesides would he have to stand beside in mourning, before his own demise. George Whitmore had been a good friend to him; one of the few villagers who had stood by him in his darkest hours. Now, he was tolerated by others, but not really liked. People avoided him as if somehow being close to him would turn them into bad people. If he talked with folk, they would be polite, and surely if they'd been asked to look deeply into their hearts, most of them would accept that Joseph Palmer had been seriously wronged and made a scapegoat. But no-one would take the time to think like that. The fact is, he had been to prison for a crime for which he had been found guilty by a jury, and in their eyes he was forever tainted.

Curiously, despite the time of the year, the sun began to break through the cloud, a brief respite from the bitterly cold wind. A few people looked up and squinted, feeling a hint of warmth on their faces. Joseph basked in the slight glow he felt on his cheeks.

"Come on, Joe." Charlotte took his arm and led him along the path, in the middle of the line of mourners who were slowly making their way out of the churchyard to the Dukes Head, where food and drink would be put on for them. They were followed by their daughter Sarah, then William and Martha, also arm in arm in silent grief.

"He was a good friend to me; to us."

"I know, Joe. He was. And there are others too. Not everyone thinks badly of you. We'll probably meet some more at the wake."

Just then Arthur Marriott appeared beside Sarah. "Glad that's over, aren't you?" he said in a low voice. Sarah shushed him and flicked her hand at him. "Go back in line, Arthur, and be quiet."

"Sorry, I can't help it. It's just…"

Just then, Hubert Palmer caught up with him, grabbed him roughly by the arm and pulled him back into line, behind William and Martha. "Just stay quiet, Marriott. Just… don't speak. This is a funeral, and Mr Whitmore deserves your respect, our respect."

"I know, but…"

"Stay quiet. I mean it, or I'll deck you."

The wake passed off as many did and still do - for some people it was a time for shared grief; for some, happy reminiscences; for some, a chance to look forward. For most of the guests, though, it was a mixture of all of these things. After about half an hour, once he was certain everyone who was going to attend was there, George Whitmore Junior proposed a toast to his father's memory, and then to his late mother's memory, and then a further toast to his younger brother William who had recently taken over the tenancy of the Dukes Head from his ailing father. After a few more smaller toasts, food was announced and served, the whole Whitmore family pulling together to serve their guests.

Martha Whitmore came over to the table where Joseph Palmer sat quietly, his wife having gone to talk with some friends. "Hallo Pa. How are you bearing up?"

Joseph looked up and kissed his eldest daughter on the cheek. "I'll be all right, love." he said. "How's William coping?"

"He's doing very well, Pa. I think being busy in here all the time is helping."

"And how the plans for the new place going?"

"Oh, William reckons they'll start building very soon. It's out of his hands really, it's all down to Squish. He's as keen as anyone to reclaim the land here so I expect he'll have it done in no time. William says the new place will have five more rooms and a much bigger bar, and of course we'll be closer to the station so that'll be good for business."

'Squish Morpho' was the nickname of the local squire, Richard Stephen Templeton Morphy. Quite how he got the childhood nickname was a mystery to many folk, including Squish himself, but he revelled in it. He was a popular figure in the area, with no airs or graces that the villagers were aware of. He had inherited the manor of Hallowfield and Salmsham on the death of his father in the 1874 train crash. Following a suitable grieving period, Squish had announced plans to expand the farms on his land, and redevelop Salmsham village and the hamlet at Hallow Hill, in a way which would benefit almost everyone in the local population. Expanding the farms meant more workers were needed, and almost everyone in the village would be employed. His popularity in and around the area was thus reinforced, not least because he cancelled his late father's plans to build a branch of the railway, which would have wiped out Rosfell Farm and severely cut back the land around Hill Farm. Under those old plans, some of the locals would have been forced out of their homes, and two families would have had to seek new tenancies. Now, however, both farms had been reprieved, and would both have more land south of the railway line, once two old decrepit cottages had been demolished, and the Dukes Head relocated.

"Do you have an idea of he wants to do with this place?" asked Joseph.

"Apparently, it will become part of the new farm expansion. Who will live here I have no idea. But it's looking good for the village, Pa. I'll see you later." She moved away to greet some late arrivals at the wake.

"Aye, Squish is a good man. A good man." Joseph said quietly. He remembered how Squish had been one of the few people directly affected by the accident who thought that he, Joseph Palmer, had not been treated fairly. When he was imprisoned, and his family evicted from the railway cottages, Squish had provided a decent sized new home for them at a very low rent "until you're straight again". His wife Charlotte was taken on at the Manor as a housemaid, and Joseph had never forgotten Squish's words on his release: "Don't worry, Joseph, I know you were not in any way responsible for my father's death, and the least I can do is to help you get back into village life again."

He'd welcomed him back and given him employment helping out around the grounds. Joseph knew he wasn't really doing very much proper work, but he was ever grateful for the chance to earn some money and have an occupation again, even if it was not as responsible or as exciting as working on the railway.

He had almost got his life back on track again, with some semblance of pride, before the tragic loss of his daughter Agnes, back in July. She was 22, and had been living and working as a housemaid for Farmer Dove at Rosfell Farm. Something had happened between her and Jack Dove – nobody knew what, although most folk knew that Jack had been wooing her since his wife had died in childbirth. Agnes had told Jack, and everyone else, that she was not interested in being his wife or anything else, but he was very persistent. Then one morning she was found in bed, having died of an apparent fit during the night. There was an inquest, and several people said she had been very unhappy and was also 'prone to fits'. This was the first Joseph had known of his daughter's apparently fragile health, and he was sure his family were keeping some other things from him too. The thought of his beloved Agnes dying alone ate into him, and it was all he could do to stave off the blackest thoughts.

"Grandpa!! Grandpa!! Look what Aunt Katharine made for us!!" Joseph's gloom was swept away in an instant by his four-year-old grandson, Joseph Whitmore, waving a pair of blue knitted mittens around his head. He was joined by his little sister, three-year-old Alice, who sported a green pair. Both children were jumping up and down in excitement.

"When it snows we can go out and play and our hands will stay warm!"

Joseph Palmer smiled. "And when's that then?"

"Auntie Katharine says it will snow … tomorrow!" shrieked Alice.

"Does she now!" said Joseph. "Well, if it does, I'll come and find you and we'll build a snowman. How's that then?"

The children grew even more excited, and ran off telling everyone they were going to build a snowman. Joseph reflected that when his own children were that age, he would have stopped them making such a noise, especially at their grandfather's wake, but he thought the whole world could do with some innocent excitement. After all, the children were the future of both families. Most people smiled as they ran in and out between guests and tables; if anyone objected they did not let it be known.

Hubert Palmer came and offered his father a drink, which he gratefully accepted. After a quick trip to the bar, Hubert returned with two pints of ale.

"What was all that about at the churchyard, with young Marriott?" Joseph asked.

"Oh… nothing Pa. Nothing at all. He's a strange one, that one. Lives in his own world half the time."

"Well, he'd better not be too strange, seeing as he's started courting our Katharine."

"I… er, thought you didn't know about that." Hubert looked down at the carpet.

"I wasn't born yesterday, son. I've seen them together, when they haven't realised. She's always been sweet on him, hasn't she? Remember? And… I also know something's brewing over other matters. Are you going to tell me what's been going on?"

"No, Pa. I'm not." Hubert asserted, surprising himself at his tone of voice – probably the first time he'd ever spoken in that way to his father. "What you don't know won't harm you, but let's just say things are sorted and there's nothing going on now. Let's leave it at that."

"Look, I don't want anyone coming to any harm, if that's what you're cooking."

"No-one" said Hubert slowly, "is coming to any harm, Pa. I can honestly tell you that."

"Well, you keep an eye on that young Marriott. He can be a law unto himself. I hope Mr Kemp's keeping him under tight control."

Hubert laughed. "He's fine Pa. I often see him when I'm passing through the station and I can tell you, he does everything by the rule book now. I don't think he'd dare step out of line again. Oh, here's Mother."

Charlotte Palmer came and sat with them. "Hubert, could you go and check on Sarah and Katharine please. I think they've got their hands full with the little ones."

"Of course, Mother".

As Hubert disappeared into the crowd around the bar, William Whitmore and his wife Martha came over and stood in front of the older couple.

"Joseph, Mother." said William "We have a little bit of good news to lighten the gloom of the day. Martha is expecting another baby. We thought you should be the first to know."

"Congratulations, you two." Joseph got up and shook his son-in-law's hand, while Charlotte hugged her daughter. "Right, this time "said Joseph, "I'll get the drinks in, you three stay right here. And you sit down, young Martha!"

As the others laughed as his sudden concern for his daughter, Joseph went to the bar and caught the eye of George Jnr. "George, my good man. Please fetch me two pints of ale, two gins and whatever you're having. This is on me!"

While he waited for the drinks to be poured, he reflected with sadness that his good friend George Whitmore would not be there to celebrate the birth of their next grandchild. He hoped personally to be around to see many more, but was not sure his wish would be granted; he was already beginning to feel older than his 54 years.

"On the other hand" thought Joseph, glancing towards the table where his wife and daughter sat laughing and discussing baby matters, "this good news is just what my family needs right now."

11

MISSING PERSON

Any information as to the whereabouts of Jack Dove of Rosfell Farm Lodge, Salmsham would be gratefully received by his family. Mr Dove, a widower aged 32 and father of two young daughters and a son, was last seen Monday 17th walking south along the footpath across the railway line from Field Mount to Lower Bank. He does not appear to have travelled from the village by other means. Mr Dove was not in debt and had no known reason for disappearing from his home. He is the only surviving son of Mr George Dove, the tenant farmer at Rosfell Farm and resident at the farmhouse. Please contact the abovementioned George Dove with any intelligence as to his disappearance which is entirely out of character.

12

Olivia opened the door of the living room. Her parents were huddled together on the sofa watching a TV re-run of Schindler's List. "Hi Dad, Jake's done a really good job on those newspaper files. He's logged them all page by page, so they're sort of ready whenever you want to see them."

Mark looked up. "Okay thanks, I'll come up when this has finished."

"Yeah well… are you going to be long? I mean… well, I've been doing my essay all evening on my laptop, and Jake's been on my PC and… well, we've hardly spoken to each other. And now we've got Alex wanting to come and have a look as well. I mean, I'd like a little bit of privacy in the holidays…"

With a sigh, Mark eased his way up from the sofa, stretched and stroked his wife briefly on the head as he slid his feet into his slippers and then shuffled off, following Olivia upstairs into her room. A tall gangly youth with curly fair hair and piercing blue eyes sat at the desk, staring intently at the screen, tapping away with his fingers on the keyboard. Alex sat beside him, both boys concentrating hard.

"Hi, Jake." Mark said, standing behind the two youngsters.

"Hi, Mr Phipps." said Jake, without looking away from the screen.

"Dad, look at this! It's a description of the court case when they find out who was killed in the crash!"

Alex was pointing excitedly at the screen, and Jake was trying to zoom the image in.

"You mean the coroner's inquest, son. Whenever there's a death on the railway, the coroner is informed so the death can be investigated."

"Yeah, it's all… oh that's horrible." Alex read out a short extract: "'The inquest will be adjourned until next Monday as there is more work needed to identify the remaining bodies. Mr Fieldhouse will carry out further post mortems on the remaining bodies to try to establish how many men and how many women and children there are.' Oh gosh, why couldn't they just tell?"

Mark said quietly. "There was a fire, remember? People were burnt, often so there were no extremities left. Sometimes you might end up with just a torso, a trunk, or maybe just a head."

"Oh Dad, that's gross!" said Olivia. "Why would you want to know all this stuff anyway?"

"Well, because one of our ancestors was accused of causing all this, and I've always been led to believe it wasn't his fault at all, and he was made a scapegoat. I think the least we can do is try to find out the truth."

"Yeah but… why do we have to read all that stuff about bodies?"

"Livvy, there are two unknown graves in the churchyard at Salmsham. They were people who couldn't be identified after the crash. Now, it was a hundred and forty-four years ago so does it really matter? Well, to me it does, especially knowing our family connection. I'm curious to know who they were. I mean, they were someone's children, parents, husbands, wives? Anyway, we have to sift through all this stuff to get to the key bits of information about how the crash happened."

Alex and Jake were opening still more files on the screen.

"Look at this one" said Jake. "Oh, it's the same old stuff as in the other one. They've copied the reports."

"Yes, that says Glasgow Herald," said Alex. "What would the Glasgow Herald be doing printing news from the south of England?"

"How else would news spread, Alex?" replied Mark. "Remember, no internet… no television or radio. The only news you could get you got through the newspapers, which is why there are so many pages and they're so large. Remember, we could win or lose a battle in Europe and it might take several days for anyone to know we'd even fought it, let alone won it or lost it."

"I thought they had the electric telegraph though, Dad." Alex pointed out. "Surely some news could travel that way."

"Good point; of course, the newspapers would be getting some news that way. Anyway Alex, I think Livvy would like a bit of space again now, so maybe we could stop for now."

"Oh Dad! There's so much to read here!"

Mark suggested that Jake could email all the files to him and Alex. "I'm working this week, but maybe Alex, you'd like to have a trawl through and see what you can find out. Oh… Jake, do you have a tape player by any chance? We threw ours out before we moved."

"If you mean one of those ghetto blaster things, I think so, Mr Phipps. I'll have a look and bring it over next time if I find it." Jake was busy at the PC sending the email and attaching all the newspaper files to it. "I'm sending this in three batches – the files are too big otherwise."

"That's great, thank you. Right, come on Alex, let's leave these two in peace."

They left and went into Mark's study, and decided that the best course of action would be to try to read all the accounts of the accident, and then make any notes about anything unusual. As Mark was going to be away in the week, Alex said he'd read all the papers, in between doing his homework and writing a English essay. "Actually Dad, did you say that tape from your granddad had stuff about World War Two on it? I could do with some extra stuff."

"Yes, but to be honest most of it was of no interest historically. It was mainly about him, what it was like for him, and one time when he was shot at. He really didn't want to talk much about the war. But I remember he did go on a lot about this crash. I just wish I could remember what he said."

At that moment they heard shouting from Olivia's bedroom. "I thought you came over to see me, not to read all this stuff. Oh for goodness sake, come on, I've finished my essay… Oh JAKE!"

Mark and Alex smiled at each other. They couldn't hear what Jake's reply was, but a few seconds later Olivia came bursting out of her room and stomped downstairs. Jake came out too, but came into the study to talk to them.

"Mr Phipps, I've found something which might be of interest. There was a girl who they would not allow to give evidence at the inquest because she was only twelve, and the guy in charge said her story was too fantastic to be believed and so they didn't take it into account. It doesn't say who she was but anyway I thought it sounded interesting."

"Thanks for that Jake. Now, I think you'd better go and talk to Livvy…"

"Oh, I'm off home now. It's all right, I'm used to her strops." He padded along the landing and down the stairs. Mark and Alex heard them talking downstairs. They could hear Freya too, then the front door closed, and they heard Jake drive off. Livvy came back up and walked straight into the office.

"Thanks for taking my boyfriend away from me everyone. I was hoping to spend some quality time with him tonight."

"Quality time. Urgh, sickening" said Alex, getting up. "I'm off to have a read of that page again, Okay Dad. See you tomorrow."

"Mind you don't have nightmares!" called out Mark as his son shut his door. "Right, Livvy. Sorry about all that; maybe you two could go out this week to the cinema or something…"

"Dad, I don't want to. I just want…"

"On me?" Mark interrupted "I'm grateful to you both for getting all this newspaper stuff together. It's really interesting."

"It is pretty cool what you can find on the 'net these days, Dad. It's really helpful with research and stuff. As long as you can get original documents and things. I never trust these online encyclopaedias too much as they're too easy to edit."

"Yeah, the best thing is to look at the links to other documents at the bottom. Never take just one source when you're on a fact-finding mission, always cross check every fact."

"Ah, that's what our teachers tell us too. So, I'm confused, are those two unidentified bodies... people... really our ancestors? Is that what you were saying?"

"Hardly. They were unidentified! No, they were people who were on the train, we assume, when it crashed, and because the fire was so intense they couldn't get them out until the fire was out, which was about seven hours after it started."

"Oh, that's awful. But surely someone must have missed them? Family, friends?"

"You'd think so. But what if they had no family or close friends? Anyway, we'll have to do some more research. Sorry about nearly wrecking your relationship." Mark grinned, knowing that Jake was not the slightest bit put out by helping them out.

"Oh, it's OK. I'm not in a very good mood anyway, I just took it out on him. He doesn't seem to care that much; he always comes back for more moody me."

"Must be love" Mark grinned.

"Oh don't you start!" Olivia smiled and kissed her father on the cheek. "Night, Dad"

"Goodnight love."

"Oh, were you serious about the cinema?"

"Yes. My treat. I'll buy you dinner too."

"What, you're coming with us?" Olivia looked horrified.

"No, love. I'm away this week, remember. No, you pay for it and I'll pay you back."

"Thanks Dad! You're the best!" Olivia disappeared into her room.

Mark turned back to his computer. Some of the emails had come through already, despite the large attachments. He spent the next few minutes downloading the files into a new folder marked 'Salmsham 1874' and then opened the first file, which was the first real account of the accident from the following days' papers.

It was quite a sensationalistic piece of prose, and was obviously written before the reporter had actually spoken to any real witnesses. It didn't tell him anything he didn't already know, but it did give an idea of how quickly the 'true cause' of the accident was established in the minds of the reporters, and hence the readers and the general public. What he found odd was the immediate assumption that the signalman was at fault, just because the express fireman insisted that they had seen white signals. Surely at this stage, if the reporter had been given two opposing views, he (for it was, of course, a man) should not have arbitrarily decided that it was one or the other. There had been an inquest opened and adjourned while they identified the bodies, and so although some people had been called as witnesses, there had been no particular pattern to the investigation. The Board of Trade Inspector had been invited to sit in on the inquest, and was already conducting his own enquiries. There was also some mention of the evidence of a young girl not being admitted due to her age and unreliability. The name of James Palmer came up, and one witness said he thought he saw James Palmer climbing up the ladder on the home signal after the accident had already occurred, although he 'couldn't swear to it definitely being him, just looked like him'. What he really needed was a detailed description of the inquest, and he wasn't sure he'd be able to find that.

He typed 'British inquests 1870s' into the search engine and was told that the documents for these were in the National Records Office. What's more, many were destroyed but if any were reported on, then of course there would be newspapers containing the relevant information. But of course, as Mark well knew, the papers would often only print what they had space for, and what they thought would sell papers, and not necessarily every little detail and verbal exchange from the courtroom.

There was a sudden 'ping' sound and Mark found he had a new email; this one from Sheila Bagley. He clicked it open and noticed the subject line 'Your family tree'. His mother-in-law was nothing if not prompt, and sent him several attachments with various charts attached. Opening the one marked "Pedigree" he found himself staring at a list of his known ancestors, right back to his great great great grandfather Joseph Palmer, Railway Signalman. A little shiver of excitement ran through him; here it was, evidence that it was indeed his ancestor who had been one of the key players at Salmsham on the day of the accident. The essence of Sheila's brief message was that some time ago, when his children were younger, she'd decided to trace Mark's ancestors back as far as she could without any real trouble, and she'd found it easier than expected.

Mark sent a quick reply to thank her, and then realised that he was meant to be leaving home in less than eight hours, so he shut down his computer, turned off the office light and went to bed. It was very late, and there was no light showing from under either of his children's doors. As he pulled the covers over himself he started to think about Joseph Palmer and what he must have gone through that day. Shutting his eyes, all he could see was a train steaming around the curve towards the station but never quite arriving…

13

Extract: The Hallowfield Courier, page 3, columns 4 - 5
Saturday 14ᵗʰ March 1879

THE HORRIFYING RAILWAY INFERNO AT SALMSHAM
DISCOVERY OF TWENTY-ONE BODIES, SOME UNIDENTIFIABLE INQUEST OPENED AND ADJOURNED

Readers will no doubt be fully conversant with the knowledge of the dreadful railway collision and inferno at Salmsham Station on Thursday, in which 17 passengers and four railway servants are known to have died, with many more injured. An inquest into the deaths was opened and adjourned yesterday, as there is some difficulty in identifying many of the deceased due to the terrible inferno, which was caused when the 4.50pm London to Weston express collided with a goods train carrying barrels of paraffin oil. There is confusion about whether the express ran past clear signals, as there is much conflicting evidence due to be heard at the inquest.

Below is a list of persons known either to have travelled in the express train, and who are missing, or whose remains have been identified in some way or another amongst the dead:- Francis Webster Templeton Morphy (Squire of Hallowfield);

Christopher Hinton, valet; William E Jackson, Merchant of Weston; Mr John Parry-Elms, Hallowfield; Mrs Parry-Elms; Miss Amelia Adcroft, Horsham, Surrey; Jane Taylor, maid; Mr Jason Abercromby solicitor, Chelsea; David Andrews, 23, Actor; Michael Sparrowhawk, 41, Impresario; Harold Slater, 37, Actor; Mrs Harriett Slater, 35, Actress; Arthur Slater, 10, son; Mrs and Miss Pettigrew, 43 Old Town, Hallowfield; Anne Chase, maidservant; Mr Alexander Stainesby, Wisbech, Cambridgeshire.

Railway staff known to have died were Harold Pickford, 53, driver of the express engine; James Garlinge, front guard; Beresford Strong, 41, ganger; Caleb Stopps, 17, Station Porter.

THE SALVAGE.

From the moment the inferno was finally extinguished at about 1 o'clock in the morning, railway workers from the rescue trains were busy removing wreckage by the light of many additional oil and gas lamps, and by daylight most of the less damaged railway waggons and carriages had been removed from the immediate vicinity of the accident. By mid-morning almost all the human remains had been found and carefully removed, notes having been taken as to their position in relation to personal items which can be an aid to identification.

In the front two carriages, scarcely anything is whole and nothing in perfect condition, nevertheless the salvage is of great value. It includes a great number of keys, single and in bunches; there were five silver watches, one with a chain of the same material attached to it, and two gold watches. Several brooches, a meerschaum pipe, three travelling bags, one of which was almost completely burnt away,

94

several jewellery boxes, quite a few loose jewels which are thought to have belonged to a necklace, and many other personal items of little value were handed into the custody of Inspector Wilding of the Weston Constabulary. Several of the items were known to have belonged to Squire Templeton Morphy and were identified formally by his son and heir Richard Stephen Templeton Morphy, the new Squire. Sadly two hounds that were travelling on the train were also killed when the cage in their van was crushed by the carriage ahead of them as it telescoped through the van. A list of everything found was made by the direction of the local Magistrate, and the articles will remain in the custody of the police until claimed by the representatives of the deceased.

NOTES AND INCIDENTS

Mr Gregory Swift, a coachman, was waiting in the station yard to collect visitors from Weston on the later train when he heard the express train whistling and then saw the collision. He recalled hearing a series of loud reports, and then seeing a cloud of liquid spray high in the air, and dust and splintered wood flying. He tried to calm his horses, when there was a flash and then a silent explosion and a sheet of flame engulfed the wreckage. Once the horses were secure, he went into the station to help and saw several passengers who had been thrown out of the train onto the platform. One man was still alive, and Swift gave him a drink from his flask but the man said "I'm done for" and then expired in front of him. Soon he helped the injured passengers and took those who were not badly hurt in his coach to the Dukes Head, where he handed them over to the care of George Whitmore, landlord, and his oldest son and daughter. Swift made two or three journeys, also at one time delivering Dr. Balderstone from the village to the scene of the accident.

One passenger who was unhurt said he had joined the train at Salisbury and had tried to find a seat in the front of the train but was unsuccessful, and eventually sat in the second-class carriage in the rear, just ahead of the guards van. His carriage came to rest perched half on top of the carriage ahead, and half on the platform. He was able to escape through the door which had flown open, and step out unharmed. He saw that his carriage had hit a man on the station and he was clearly deceased. The carriage ahead of his had been shattered and people had been thrown out onto the platform, many suffering fatal injuries. Passenger then helped to rescue several people from high up on top of the wreckage before the flames would reach them. He praised several of his fellow passengers and especially some men from the village who had heard the crash and run straight to the scene, immediately helping to pull people from the remains of their carriages.

Another passenger, a lady, was travelling in the third carriage from the rear and was stuck in her compartment high up above the ground when she was rescued by Mr Jack Dove, a local farmhand who helped to lift her and her two children from the wreck. She saw Dove and two of his fellow rescuers then go into the carriage and break through into the next compartments to try and rescue other people. They brought out a group who were very badly injured, one of whom she thinks was already deceased, and she then was able to help one of the others in the group by bandaging them until they could be attended by the doctors. At one time the fire was licking around the bottom of another carriage but she said that Mr Dove was not deterred and bravely plunged into a small space to try and rescue other passengers, but he was forced to retire because of the heat.

Mrs Geraldine Samways, of High Lane, was standing in the front garden of her dwelling when she heard the engine whistling followed by a terrible sound. She knew instinctively that a disaster must have occurred and she called for her husband, and her maid, to prepare to help. The three went to the station and while her husband helped directly with the rescue, Mrs Samways and her maid provided comfort for the walking wounded.

The front guard who died was James Garlinge, about 45 years old, a Basingstoke man. He was highly regarded by his managers on the railway, and had no marks whatever against his name in nearly 30 years of railway service. He was a very popular member of his town's local community, and a prominent member of the church, where he had been churchwarden for some twelve years. Garlinge was due to walk his eldest daughter down the aisle in July, she having been betrothed to another railwayman since Christmas day last. He leaves a grieving widow and two other children to mourn a loving family man.

Great sadness has been also expressed at the deaths of the well-known acting family, the Slaters, who had recently completed a short run in Woking and were travelling to Weston where they were due to appear this Sunday in their popular show. Their colleagues the impresario Mr Sparrowhawk, and actor David Andrews also died in the accident. Five remaining members of their troupe, who were travelling further back in the train, were slightly injured but four have since have travelled back to London to recover and try to make arrangements for the troupe's future.

Mrs Kemp, wife of the Stationmaster, threw open the station house and provided sheets, blankets and bandages for all who required them. Once the immediate rescue was completed and all passengers who could be removed safely had been, Mrs Kemp turned her attention to providing refreshment, water, food and hot drinks as and when needed for the many rescuers.

The paraffin oil in the two vans which were the source of combustion, was contained in thirty barrels, in transit to Weston, and was for use in the many lamps which light the stations, public buildings and of course, railway carriages and signals on the line. The company which supplied the oil stated that it was "contained in excellent casks, and the igniting point was far above the parliamentary standard for carriage in a normal goods train." They made the point that no container known to man could survive the impact of a heavy high speed express train weighing over 150 tons travelling at over 50 miles an hour.

PERSONAL NARRATIVES
THE FIREMAN'S STORY

The correspondent of the *Weston Observer* says:- the express fireman, Thomas Jobson, is recovering from his injuries at a small cottage in the village of

Salmsham, tended by staff from the Manor. The account he gave me is best given in his own words. He said, "The train had left London a few minutes late, but by the time we reached Salisbury we had made up some time, and we did not have to add any carriages at Salisbury as sometimes happens. We left Salisbury about five minutes late. Our train was made up of the engine and tender, a front guards van also filled with luggage, two first class carriages, a composite first and second class carriage, two second class carriages, three more composites, and the rear guards van which was also filled with luggage. We had been able to gain quite a bit of time and were only about three minutes late as we approached Salmsham. My driver was standing on the left of the cab and saw the distant signal was 'all right'. He told me "It's off!" I usually stop firing for a minute to look out for the signals, because the track curves on the right as we come into Salmsham. I told him I couldn't see anything at first as it was very dark, but there was no sign of the signal, but then I saw it, and he put on more steam. We like to get a clear run through to get up Hallow Hill after the station, because we could make up probably two minutes at that speed. Anyway, then I saw a red light and the outline of the goods train ahead and called out. My mate put the engine into reverse and I went for the brakes. He whistled for the train brakes as well, then just before we crashed the engine shot into forward gear. My mate said "No, No, No!" and then there was a terrible bang. When we hit I just thought I was finished but the floor pitched up and I flew out of the side of the cab and somehow missed being crushed. The engine went under the trucks but I went over them and found myself lying on the down platform under a piece of wood from a goods truck. The stationmaster got me up as I was very confused. We went up to the signalbox and then I felt a lot of pain. The signalman told me his levers were 'on' but I know that my mate saw a white light at the distant, and I saw a white light at the home signal by the bridge just before we came to the station. I stayed until the doctor came and then I am here until I get better. I am still shocked that my driver died, he was a good man and easy to work for. I have broken my arm badly and have some cuts on the head but I want to go back to work soon."

MR STANLEY CRAWSHAW'S ACCOUNT

Mr Stanley Crawshaw, a passenger who was travelling near the rear of the train gave the following account to the *Salisbury Gazette*:- "I was on my way to visit a friend at Hallowfield, and was reading a book when I heard the engine whistle and felt the brakes go on. Almost immediately my carriage was jolted severely and seemed to bump up and down, then there was a sudden shock. I had my back to the direction of travel, but a man who had been sitting across from me was thrown violently against the seat beside me. There was a tearing sound and then we were thrown sideways, and stopped quite suddenly. I helped the man gather himself up, fortunately he was not hurt. We could not open the door onto the platform side as it was jammed, so we climbed out of the other side, and found that our carriage was on top of part of another, and we were quite up in the air. We had to clamber down, and then we helped several other people to climb out. I looked towards the engine and saw lots of smoke and flames and heard lots of roaring and hissing. I thought then that maybe the engine boiler had exploded. It was only after we walked behind our train, which was much reduced in length, that we realised how much destruction there was, and also that the fire was still raging and extended to the first two or three carriages. We heard no cries for help from this part of the train. Some local men were helping with the rescue until the rescue trains arrived. I helped to carry a few people down from the upper part of the wreckage; there was a lady and her two children, and another man who I think was in a very bad way. The guard from the back of the train had been quite badly injured about the head, and had been knocked senseless by the collision. Apparently, he was hidden from view under a large pile of luggage. He eventually emerged from his doorway and then collapsed onto the platform, where we tended to him. I saw many people who had died, they had been quite disfigured by being thrown out of the carriages and onto the platform. I stayed for several hours and helped to cater for the injured passengers. Eventually the rescue staff came and sent us on to our destinations by road or by train. I was taken on to Hallowfield by another train. There were quite a few people from the express who were taken on. We did not speak much – I think most people were in a state of shock and yet relief at having survived such a disaster."

A VILLAGER'S HARROWING TALE

Miss Frances Lowther, a nurse, lives in a cottage across from the railway yard. As soon as she heard the accident she hurried to the scene and helped tend for the injured. She described to this reporter in graphic detail some of the injuries she encountered, including a young child who had lost the sight on one eye from a large piece of wood, and a man whose fingers had been crushed terribly when he was thrown out of his seat and onto the tracks underneath another carriage. Later on, she helped to gather up the belongings of the victims, both living and dead, and helped with the doctors to assess the seriousness or not of some injuries. Many people were transported in the guards van of a rescue train which took them to the infirmary at Hallowfield. Some of the less seriously injured were sent by coach to the Dukes Head and Manor Farm, where the generosity of their hosts has enabled them to begin the long road to recovery by the most comfortable means possible. Miss Lowther also helped begin the process of identifying the dead, whose bodies were moved into the goods shed as soon as possible so as to assist with the rescue operation, and where she took charge of laying them out in such a way as to be as presentable as possible to relatives who would be called to identify them. Miss Lowther has previous served in military hospitals and stated the injuries, human destruction and misery she saw at Salmsham were as awful as anything she had seen beside the battlefield.

14

Extract: The Hallowfield Courier, page 3, columns 6 - 7
Saturday 14th March 1879

THE INQUEST

The inquest was fixed for three o'clock Friday. Those summoned on the jury (18 in number) met at the Dukes Head, and after a short wait the coroner (Mr. William Hammond of Weston) came in and asked Inspector Wilding how many bodies there were. The Inspector said he made them into 21 but at this stage he could not say with certainty how many men or women there were from the remains as he could not tell one from the other in several cases.

The Coroner, before swearing the jury, said: "This is a very serious case. Eight of the bodies are not yet identified. We should view the bodies first and see how the identification is moving on. If we cannot identify people we should not carry on with an inquest. If we hold an inquest on people without proper identification, and then afterwards some of the people are found alive we would have failed in our duty."

A gentleman said that several bodies had been identified. The coroner agreed that the jury should be sworn, and then should immediately view the bodies. The eighteen jurymen were sworn. They were all respectable and intelligent looking men. Mr Dyer, of Kelby Farm, Meresham, was foreman. Each juryman was individually asked whether they were shareholders in the London and Western Railway, and whether they had any known personal connections to anyone employed by said railway, and they said they were not. The Coroner invited the representatives of the friends and relatives of the deceased to see that the jurymen kissed the book. The jury having been sworn, the Coroner said they had a very painful duty to discharge, and they would begin by viewing the scene of the accident, and then the bodies. They then proceeded to the station and were shown the accident site by senior railway staff. They were then taken to the place where the remains were lying. Eighteen bodies, or portions of bodies, had been placed in coffins, and the jury were informed that another three were currently the subject of a post mortem examination by the various doctors whose services had been called upon. Some of the bodies were easily identifiable and had already been identified by relatives, however some were to be subject to further medical examination. On returning to the Dukes Head, the Jury all answered their names, and the Coroner said that he would allow any evidence of formal identity so that some bodies could be released to their relatives for internment.

Humphrey Albert Tracy said: I reside at 9 Woodchurch Road, West Hampstead, and am a theatre owner. I have today viewed the bodies and am able to identify four people.

The Coroner: Are these relatives or friends?

Witness: They are colleagues in the theatre. I have identified Mr David Andrews.

Coroner: What was his age?

Witness: He was 23 last November.

Coroner: Was he in an occupation?

Witness: He was an actor. He was travelling with a troupe who I work closely with and help to fund. He was a single man with no known family. He came from the orphanage.

Coroner: Who else did you identify?

Witness: Mr Harold Slater, Mrs Harriett Slater and Master Arthur Slater. They are all actors.

Coroner: And their ages?

Witness: Mr Slater, 37 years. Mrs Slater, 35 years. Arthur Slater 10 years.

Coroner: Are you aware of any relatives surviving?

Witness: Mr Slater has a brother living in Manchester. He has telegraphed to say he will be arriving on Sunday and I have agreed to stay until such time as he can take charge of the arrangements. Witness had great difficulty in maintaining his composure during this exchange.

The Coroner then asked the jury if they had any objection to make to the removal of the bodies at a time convenient to Mr Tracy. The jury acquiescing, Mr Tracy expressed his thanks in a broken voice. The Coroner said to the Witness: You are the first witness we have examined, and I hope you will leave with the satisfaction that every investigation will be made into this melancholy affair.

Mr Tracy: I am quite satisfied of that, and I am willing to leave it in your hands. My only regret is at the death of my dear friends.

Ezekiel Stopps was the next witness called. He said: I reside at Elm Cottage, Hallow Hill, and I am a railway ganger. I have seen the bodies and I identify that of my son Caleb Stopps, who was a railway porter at Salmsham. He was seventeen years of age, and was on duty at Salmsham Station when the accident happened.

The order for removal of the body by the family was at once made out.

Thomas George Low was then sworn. He said: I have seen the bodies and identify that of Miss Amelia Adcock of Horsham, Surrey. Miss Adcock was 26 years of age and was travelling to visit her aunt in Weston. She had been known to me for many years and we were due to marry in the summer of 1875. Her mother is in deep shock and is not ready to travel. I have received a request by telegram to arrange for the removal of the body into the care of the family.

James Pettigrew, ironmonger, 43 Old Town, Hallowfield. I have seen the bodies and I identify my wife Elizabeth who was 37 years of age, and my daughter Anthea who was 9 years of age. I was myself injured in the accident. We were returning home from a visit to my mother and father in Andover. My son who is seven years of age was unhurt. I cannot identify my maidservant, Anne Chase, who was also with us.

Mr Hugh Sparrowhawk: - I am a retired civil engineer, residing at 3 Piercebridge Terraces, Grimsby. I have viewed all of the bodies and identify my nephew Michael Sparrowhawk, who was 41 years old and an impresario and actor residing in London. He has no wife or children, and both of his parents are deceased. He was brought up by my wife and myself as our own. We have two other children who were like siblings to him.

Sarah Strong, Railway Cottages, Salmsham: I have viewed all the bodies and identify Beresford Strong, my husband and the father of my three children. He was in his 42nd year and a ganger on the railway for the last twenty-five years.

Mr Martin Geohagen: I am a solicitor residing at 17 Kings Road, Chelsea. I have seen all the bodies and I identify Mr Jason Abercromby, solicitor of 35 Abbey Mews, Chelsea. He is my business partner and I have known him for more than thirty years. He was widowed three years ago and has four children between the ages of 12 and 18, who are currently at school in Norfolk.

Benjamin Jackson: I am a stonemason living at Cobbs Yard Buildings, Weston. I have seen all the bodies and I identify my father William Edwin Jackson of same address. My father was a Merchant and was travelling home from a business meeting in London. I identified him from the buttons on the coat he was wearing and from the gold ring on his right hand.

Susanna Pickford: I reside at 32 Railway Lane, Weston. I have seen all the bodies and I identify my husband Harold Pickford, the engine driver of the express train. I recognised him from the wedding ring on his left hand and from his shoes and other clothing with which I am familiar. He was 52 years of age and he has left three grown up children.

The order for removal of the bodies of all of the above named was made out.

The Coroner then adjourned the Inquest until Monday when he hoped that identification of the remaining bodies could be completed following their post mortems. He would also begin to take evidence from those directly involved in the accident with the assistance of the Inspecting Officer of the Board of

Trade. The Inspector of Police would be compiling a list of all witnesses required to attend, and said witnesses would be summonsed to appear in due course.

Before the adjournment, Mr Fullager, the General Manager of the London and Western Railway, with the permission of the Coroner, wished to say one or two words on behalf of the company, of the directors, and of all the persons connected with the company. In the first place, he had to express their great grief and regret at that terrible and melancholy accident. They were only too desirous that every possible information which the Coroner and jury wished should be forthcoming, and that every investigation they directed should be made. He added that the directors themselves had been personally affected by the death of Squire Templeton Morphy, one of their colleagues on the Board. He wished also to state, on behalf of the directors, that they were anxious and desirous to make every arrangement in their power to consult the convenience of the of the relatives of the deceased and injured, so that everything could be done for them which was possible. Of course they were also desirous of removing the unfortunate debris from the side of the line, and they would be glad to have the jury's permission to do so tomorrow (Saturday), if they had no objection to make.

The Coroner: Everything connected with the cause of the accident will be seen, I hope?

Mr. Fullager said that everything would be inspected as it was removed, by both the company's senior engineering staff and the Board of Trade Inspector. He also promised an accurate plan of the line and station from the previous signalbox to the sidings at the foot of Hallow Hill incline.

The Coroner and the Jury agreed that all this was in order, and that they would sit again at the Dukes Head on Monday at 10 o'clock for identification of the bodies not yet claimed, and then for evidence from the key railway staff involved directly in the accident.

CORRESPONDENCE

A letter has been received from 'A concerned villager' who wishes to call attention to evidence proffered by a young girl who is prepared to swear that she saw a man atop the home signal by the bridge several minutes before the accident. This appears to be in direct conflict with the evidence of one of the rescue workers who stated that he clearly saw a man whom he thought he could possibly identify at the inquest, at the same place but a short time after the accident. The young girl swears that the occurrence was before the accident and not afterwards. As this fact could turn out to be crucial in the investigation, we advise the correspondent to bring forth all the evidence at the coroner's inquest on Monday where it will no doubt be fully investigated.

From the *Salisbury Times*:- "Sir. I was a traveller in the express train which collided last night with the goods train at Salmsham and wish to express my great thanks to those people who helped to rescue me and my fellow travellers from our carriage which was crushed beneath the following carriage to the extent that our roof was about three feet at most from the floor. I was for a brief time trapped by my legs but a man called Jack and a porter named Marriott helped to free me from opposite sides of the carriage, and I was gratefully ejected from the wreckage after about ten minutes. A lady who was sitting beside me was unhurt but also trapped and the two men then were able to help her too. Only when we were both free did we see how close the flames were to our carriage. Our compartment was subsequently consumed by the fire. Fortunately, another two people travelling in the same compartment were able to scramble free once the lady and I were freed. Had it not been for the prompt rescue I would not have been writing this letter today and for that I will forever be in the debt of our rescuers. I would also like to offer my sincerest condolences to those who have lost loved ones in the crash, and to those who have suffered injury.

15

"Jack Dove! I want to talk to you!" The voice called up from the pathway alongside the railway cutting.

Jack Dove put down the sledge hammer he was using to drive in the new fence post, wiped his brow and turned towards the voice. At first he did not recognise either the caller, or the young man's short figure as it came into view, climbing up the path towards him.

"What have you been telling them about me, eh?" the man, slightly out of breath, called out again, and Jack recognised the pale face of James Palmer, the signalman's son and station clerk.

"Oh, it's Mister James Palmer. Haven't seen you for a while, thought you might have run away." He sneered at the approaching figure. "I told 'em nothing as such, Palmer. Nothing they can really pin on you anyway. Just told of my suspicions. And I've certainly got those, after everything that's happened."

"What suspicions, *Mister* Dove?" By now James was standing right in front of him. Dove picked up the sledge hammer again, and James flinched before he realised that Dove was about to resume his hammering of the fence post. Jack Dove was a stockily built man twenty-seven years old, who was used to the physical challenge of outdoor work, as senior farmhand on his father's farm. The sledge hammer looked as light as a feather as he swung it back behind his shoulder, and then brought it swiftly down. There was a thud as the ten-pound steel head connected with the top of the post, driving it further into the ground.

"Well, having seen what happened yesterday…" *Thud!* "…and seen all those poor folk dead and injured…" *Thud!* "…and helped to get some of those people out of the train…" *Thud!* "…and helped to remove those poor dead folk who were so badly burnt…" *Thud!* "…well, I wondered to myself 'where was the station clerk all that time, eh?'"

He put the sledge hammer down, and tested the firmness of the post. "And then I wondered maybe if he couldn't bear to be near the fire, see. Because maybe he knew how it had all happened, see? And maybe he felt a bit guilty…"

"I have nothing to feel guilty about, Jack Dove." James growled, his face was red with anger. "I know my job. I did everything by the book. I didn't make that train run past those signals!"

"And I suppose you think I did, eh?". Dove picked up the sledge hammer again.

"No, I…"

"And how would I have done that, Palmer, when I was enjoying a drink in the pub, and you and your father was in the signalbox, eh? How do you think I made the signals go to white, eh?"

"I never said you did anything, Jack Dove. And I know you rescued a lot of folk too."

"Ah, you know that, do you? I suppose that's because people must have told of what I did. But I bet they never told you what that was like, did they?

Crawling on top of burning carriages, getting splinters in my hands… look!"

He dropped the sledgehammer on its side, opened his right palm and pointed to an angry red swelling under the skin. "Bet they never mentioned that I had to crawl underneath the frame of a carriage so I could get some people out of the one which was being crushed underneath it."

"I never…"

"Bet they never told you what it was like to pull out the dead bodies, did they? When I say bodies, I mean, pieces of burnt flesh…"

"Shut up, Dove! I never said you didn't do all those things. I never said what you done yesterday wasn't brave. But you've been telling stories about me to the Sergeant and I want to know why. What's your game, Jack Dove? What's your little plan about, eh? Is it to do with my sister…"

"Agnes?! Don't you bring her into it. This is nothing to do with her and me."

"No? Why can't I believe that, Dove? Is it because you're a known liar?"

Dove suddenly grabbed James by the collar and drew his face up close. James could smell the stench of ale on his breath, and was annoyed to find himself shaking with fear. Dove lowered his voice to a husky whisper. "Now you listen here, *Master* James Palmer. I happen to know that a man was up that signal post last night after the accident, because I see him myself. Now, I just happen to mention this to the Sergeant, and he said did I recognise him…."

"You bastard…" As James said it, the grip on his collar was tightened.

"…and do you know what I said? I said 'I'm not sure, but it looked a little bit like the signalman's boy, James Palmer' and he said 'What would he be wanting to be doing up the signal after the accident' and I said 'I don't know, why don't you ask him' and he said 'I will' and that was all. A little bit like, that's what I said. Now, if you think that was telling tales…"

"You bastard, Dove! You know full well I was nowhere near that signal!" James glared in Dove's eyes.

The grip on his collar loosened, and then Dove let go altogether, surprising James so much that he stumbled and almost fell back.

"I don't know if you was near that signal or not, Palmer, but I know where you *wasn't*, because I was there. You wasn't pulling folk out of the wreck, you wasn't on the platform helping all them injured folk, you wasn't pumping the water from the tenders to help put the fire out. You wasn't anywhere really, was you?"

"I wasn't up that signal. Why on earth would I be up there anyway?"

"Well now, there's a question to be asked, isn't there? 'Dear Sergeant Michaels. Can you think of any reason why on earth the son of the signalman who claims all his signals were red, would be up the ladder of a signal just after a crash, when the fireman says the signals was definitely showing all clear? No? You can't? Well, that's all right then. Master Palmer had no reason to be up there then. It can't have been him then…"

"You bastard!"

"You keep calling me that, Palmer. But if you'd like to go on up to the farmhouse I think you'll find *my* father is in there right now, sorting out his accounts for the week. I don't suppose I should ask what your father is doing right now, eh? Maybe shaking in his boots in case his son gets found out for tampering with the signals?"

"I'll get you for this, Jack Dove, I swear it" James started to back away, pointing a shaking hand at Dove. "You'll pay for this."

"Pay for what, Palmer?" Dove moved towards James, grabbing his hand and throwing it down to his side. "I done nothing except state my opinion. Just an opinion. So if you've got nothing to hide it'll be alright then, won't it."

"Will it?"

Dove spoke in a smooth, mocking tone "It'll just be your word against my word."

"That means I'll be alright then. No-one will believe a word you say anyway. No-one does, do they?"

"Quite right, Palmer. Why would they believe a man who was seen by lots of folk, *railway* folk, helping out until early this morning, over the word of a man who was directly involved with a terrible accident, who might even have helped to cause it, and who went missing right afterwards."

"You're a case, you are, Jack Dove. You think just because you acted heroically last night…"

"Oh, did I?"

"You did, actually. I grant you that, and I will not let anyone say otherwise…"

"Well that's so noble of you, Palmer."

"But if you think that means somehow my sister will come running to you…"

"Like I just said, your sister and me is none of your business."

"Oh yes it is, Dove, because you know full well she don't want to see you ever, and she never did. There is no 'sister and you'. You stay away from her, alright?"

"I'll come and go as I please, Palmer. And remember Agnes is my father's housemaid, so she's there under my feet all the time. I can't 'stay away' when she's in my own family home now, can I."

"Stay away, I said. From all of us. The whole family. We don't none of us want nothing to do with you."

"Well, let's leave it there until the inquest then, shall we? Let's leave it as I won't come round to yours, and you get off my land, and then after everything's been cleared up, we'll see what happens."

"Fine by me, Dove. I'm warning you though. You stay away!" James stomped off angrily.

Jack Dove smiled to himself, sighed deeply and then turned back to his task of repairing the fence. They'd nearly lost five or six cows onto the railway last night, after the breach in the fence. He was determined that it would be a lot stronger alongside the line. If nothing else, it would mitigate against the inevitable fine which would be imposed on the farm for yesterday's escape.

His father had already heard from the Inspector of the Railway Police that they would be investigating how the cows managed to breach the fence without being noticed sooner. Jack couldn't help but chuckle at that one. He wondered just how patiently his father would point out that when it's dark outside, seeing everything that dark brown cows get up to from the far side of the field is not quite as simple as a country policeman might think.

After another hour, he had replaced three fence posts and fitted thick cross bars to them, in addition to the original wire, which he stretched and tied firmly to the existing fence posts either side of the breach area.

Jack was certain that there would be no more cows on the railway line from Rosfell Farm in the future, most definitely not from this field at any rate. With satisfaction at a job well done, he made his way up across the field to the farmhouse for some welcome refreshment.

16

James Palmer slammed the front door of the cottage and stood shaking angrily in the tiny front room. His mother sat in her usual place, with a girl's dress across her legs and a sewing needle in her right hand. "Where's Pa?" he demanded. "I've got to talk to him!"

"Your father has gone to the 'box with Mr Kemp and the Sergeant. I'm sure everything will be alright, Jimmy." Charlotte Palmer was anything but sure that it would, but she was not going to let her children know her deepest fears.

"No it won't. Mother, that bastard Dove has told the Sergeant that I was up the signal ladder after the crash. He's lying, Mother, he's making it all up. He's trying to make me and Pa look like we done this crash deliberately, and I won't have it. He's a snake, a liar, a… a…" James spluttered. "And he reckons it's got nothing to do with him and Agnes. I reckon is. It's *all* about him and Agnes. He wants her, he won't let go, he won't take no for an answer and he's out to get me and Pa and all of us if he can't have his way!"

"Jimmy, please just calm down. It'll be alright…" Charlotte found herself shaking too.

"No it won't, Ma! Sergeant Michaels has already questioned me about it. Says he believes I was up there, and comes out with 'why would Jack Dove be lying about such a thing?' I mean, Jack Dove lies about everything, Ma!"

"Sergeant Michaels said nothing of the sort. He said that Jack Dove thought he saw someone who looked a bit like you…"

"That's it though. Everyone will believe it now. They'll think I was trying to cover up for Pa."

"Your father didn't need anyone to cover up for him. He's got the register and witnesses to show he did everything correctly."

"That's all very well, until Dove puts doubt in people's minds."

"He can't. It'll all be dealt with on Monday at the inquest. Now hush, here's your sister from school. She doesn't need to know about this."

The front door opened and a slim young girl with slightly curled fair hair came anxiously into the cottage, carrying a small leather satchel which she dropped down beside the table.

"Hello Mother," she said solemnly, and bent down to kiss her mother's cheek.

"Katharine. How was school?"

"It was awful, Mother. Everyone's talking about the crash. Miss Parkinson says we should hush up about it all and try and get on with everything like it was. But I couldn't stop thinking about it. About poor Sarah, and Caleb…" she broke into a large sob and stood with her head bowed in front of her mother's chair.

James Palmer looked on for a moment as tears welled up in his mother's eyes. She looked at him and shook her head, then looked down at her daughter. She put the sewing down on the table, and opened her arms. "Come on, little Kate. Give your Mother a hug."

James gave a big sigh, and turned around to go back out. He grabbed a small bag from the wall hooks and slung it over his shoulder.

"Where are you going, James?" said Charlotte, still fighting back tears.

"I don't know. Out. Maybe to the Dukes Head."

"They've started the inquest there."

"Well then. Perhaps I'll walk into Belcote."

"Would you try and look in on Sarah for me, please. She's staying with Alice Hunter's folk up Hawkes Lane by the church there. She couldn't bear to be near this place while it's all going on."

"Of course. Yes, I'll do that for you, Mother."

"Don't do it for me, do it for her. She's just lost the young man she thought she wanted to marry, Jimmy. And she's only a child, she don't really understand…"

"I know. I know. I'll look in, don't worry Mother. You'd better look after this one then. I'll be back later on. If they want me, I'll be at the Black Horse or the Kings Arms, dunno which one."

He left, this time shutting the door gently behind him. Charlotte held Katharine closer, and rocked her gently from side to side.

"Where's Pa?" asked the girl.

"Oh don't you start, little Kate. He's over in the 'box with the Inspector. They're just going over…"

"They reckon it was Pa's fault, don't they?"

Charlotte was shocked at her daughter's words.

"No they do not reckon it was Pa's fault. They are just simply checking everything and going through the registers, and making sure…"

"I mean, everyone in the village. They reckon Pa forgot to put his signals to danger."

"Says who? Who told you that?"

"Some people. Thomas Bullard told me at school. He said 'your father's a murderer' and…" her voice shook, "anyway I told Miss Parkinson and she told him to stop it and he did, but then the others kept saying about it and…"

The front door opened, and a grim-faced Joseph Palmer walked in. Without saying anything, he took off his railway hat and coat and hung them on a hook on the back of the door, and then kicked off his shoes. Katharine looked at him through her tears.

"Oh Pa! Pa!" she broke away from Charlotte and ran to her father, who hugged her tightly.

"It's all right, my darling Kate. It's all right."

"They said you… you made the accident happen. You forgot the signals."

Joseph was alarmed by his daughter's words, and exchanged glances with his wife. His face looked even grimmer, but he spoke softly to his youngest child.

"Well I don't know who 'they' are who says that, but the Inspector of Railway Police, and the District Inspector, and Mr Kemp, have just looked at my register and seen that everything was in order. That train ran past danger signals, and that's why it crashed."

"But Pa, someone said…"

"It don't matter what 'someone' said, Kate, because what they don't know is that I got a witness who was in the box with me, who saw the signal levers at danger and signed the register to say that he'd seen them at danger. So unless your 'someone'

121

knows something I don't, you can tell them they have got it all wrong."

He gave his daughter an extra strong squeeze. Nothing he'd told her was a lie. He had indeed been with his two superiors and the Police Inspector, and they had all agreed that everything was in order. But there were several little things gnawing away at his mind; not only the statement from Jobson the fireman, who insisted that he saw the home signal showing 'all clear', but another witness who was walking by the line up near Belcote Crossing, and who said the distant signal was also showing a white light.

He loosened his hold on Katharine, and went to sit by his wife. She held out a hand to him and he took it in his, and squeezed it gently. Katharine took off her coat and put it on a hook at the bottom of the tiny staircase, and disappeared off upstairs.

Joseph looked down at the floor. "Isaac has suspended me until next week... until after the inquest. On full pay. They've got Dan Quittenden, the relief man in for the next few days."

"Suspended you? Why? What will you do?"

"Well they had to really. As he said, it's for my own good really. I'm in no fit state to think clearly at the moment. I'd be no good in a 'box, that's for sure. And I'll just prepare to defend myself against these stupid rumours. Make sure I know exactly what happened. Try not to think about what we could have done differently."

"Jimmy's in a bad way. Apparently, Jack Dove..."

"Jack Dove!? What about him. What's he been doing to Jimmy now?"

"He hasn't been doing anything. Apart from telling Sergeant Michaels that he thought he saw Jimmy up the signal pole after the accident."

Joseph frowned. "*After* the accident? Why would anyone go up the signal *after* the accident?"

"That's the point. Jimmy reckons Jack is trying to frame him, or you, or both."

"How the... and anyway, Jimmy was nowhere near the signal. He was in the box with me, then he left to go and get Isaac. And I still don't see what he would do up the signal that could possibly help me, or change what happened. Dove has got some nerve, hasn't he?"

"He's got a lot of people saying how brave he was last night."

"Aye, well, he did rescue a lot of people. Just goes to show that you don't need much of a brain to be a hero."

Charlotte smiled. "That's a bit cruel, Joe."

For the first time in the past twenty or so hours, Joseph Palmer allowed himself a brief smile. But then, he thought about what Dove had been saying, and wondered what on earth he was cooking up. He stood up, and went into the tiny kitchen.

"Cup of tea for you, my love?" he called. Charlotte smiled and picked up her sewing again.

"Yes please Joe. I can finish off this dress then. Poor Sarah, she ripped it yesterday."

Joseph didn't reply. He realised he had not even thought about his poor Sarah, and yet she had suffered the loss of the young man she loved. He wasn't sure if it was really true love; she was only fourteen after all, but Caleb Stopps doted on her, always treated her well, and had promised him,

Joseph, that he would not do anything he shouldn't with her, and that when she was old enough he would like to marry her if it was still what she wanted, and if he, Joseph, would allow it. He had no doubt that Caleb meant every word, although he wasn't sure the young lad wouldn't succumb to certain temptations before walking his daughter up the aisle. He was a nice lad nonetheless, and a diligent worker. Joseph had always got on well with his father too; they'd known each other many years and were on friendly terms. And now, thanks to this appalling situation, they would never be able to strengthen that friendship by the mutual bond of a shared grandparenthood. The kettle having boiled, he lifted it off from the hot stove and poured the boiling hot water into the teapot.

"Pa, can I tell you something?" Katharine had come into the kitchen almost silently. Joseph managed not to drop the hot kettle in surprise.

"Of course, little Kate. What is it?"

"Pa… what Jack Dove said about James."

"Don't you worry about that, Kate."

"No, I'm not. But I saw something too. Before the accident. I don't know…"

"What did you see then, Kate? You can tell me."

"Please! Pa! Please don't be cross with me. Please!"

Joseph frowned at his daughter. Her face was still tear-stained, but she was still so innocently pretty, and her eyes were so pleading, he couldn't think of bringing himself to be cross with her even if he didn't yet know what she had done which was so wrong, in her mind.

"Go on then. Tell me, Kate."

"I saw something. I was out yesterday, before the accident. And I saw someone... up the signal."

"Which signal, Kate?"

"That one by the bridge. There was a man up the top of the signal, I thought it might be Mr Faulkner trimming the light."

"No, the signal lights were trimmed in the morning. Caleb does them... did them, not Bob Faulkner. When was this, Kate? Before the accident?"

"Yes, Pa. Before. About ten minutes or so before."

"Now, are you telling the truth?" He spoke sternly, but he already knew from her expression that she was telling him what she believed she saw.

"Yes Pa, I really am."

"Because what you've told me, you need to tell other people. The Inspector, Mr Kemp, the Judge, everyone."

"Yes, Pa, I know. I will do that."

Charlotte came and stood in the doorway.

"What were you doing out there, Kate? They'll want to know all that. When did you see this man.? Where were you when you saw him?" Charlotte's voice was angrily inquisitive.

Katharine stood stock still, with a look of guilty fear in her eyes.

"Kate?" Charlotte looked stern. "Is there something you've not told me?"

Joseph held his hand up. "Please... Lottie... let her speak."

Kate looked down at the floor. "I... I was out... round the back of the station..."

"What?!" Martha cried sharply. "What were you doing out there, child? You know you're not allowed round there when its dark!"

"I was… I was seeing someone. A friend. I wanted to talk to them but… I know I shouldn't have been."

Charlotte took in a breath to speak, but Joseph once again put his hand up to silence his wife. He knelt down in front of his daughter. She was still looking down, shaking with the fear, tormented by the thought that whether she chose to say something, or say nothing, it was going to make life difficult for everyone.

"What friend was this, Kate?" he asked softly.

"I… I can't say, Pa. I mustn't say… and anyway it doesn't matter. It has nothing to do with what I saw. It has nothing to do with the accident, or anything."

"That may be so. That may well be so. Maybe it doesn't. But if you're going to stand up in front of the Judge, or the Inspector, and say you saw someone up the signal, they're going to ask you lots and lots of questions. If you don't tell them everything; if you don't tell them the truth, they'll think you're making it up."

She remained silent. Joseph saw a tear splash onto the stone floor.

"Kate? Kate, whoever you were seeing, it doesn't matter…"

"But it does matter, Pa. You'll be angry. Everyone will be angry. It's not fair on h… on my friend."

Joseph stood up, and took a deep breath. His voice grew harder. "Right, Kate. Listen to me. Your brother has been accused of being up that signal, tampering with it, after the accident. If people choose to believe him then he, and I, will be in a lot of trouble. Now, we both know it's not true but *they* don't know that. The people out there, who weren't there, but who have to work out why that train went steaming straight past those signals. *They* will listen to the stories and either believe them, or not. If they believe them, that will mean they'll think I caused the accident. Now, if you are telling me that you really saw someone messing with that signal before the accident happened, then that changes everything. But if you are going to say that, you must be telling the truth. All of it. I don't care who you were meeting, you must tell us. You must."

Charlotte joined in "Kate. This is really important. Please. We won't be cross with you, if you tell us who you were meeting."

Katharine lifted her face. Her eyes were closed, tears still leaking from under the lids, her mouth puckering, sobbing under her breath.

"Arthur." She said simply. "I was going to see... to talk to Arthur."

"Who's Arthur?" asked her mother.

"… porter." She looked back down at the floor.

Joseph's face changed. "You mean Arthur Marriott?" Katharine nodded. "That... that young idiot who can't push a handcart in a straight line or unload a sack of potatoes without dropping it. What on earth were you doing talking to him? What's he been doing to you, eh?"

"Doing to me? Nothing, Pa! He hasn't done anything to me. We just talk a bit."

"He's seventeen years old and you're not yet thirteen and you're out there talking to him, in secret. And you say he hasn't done anything? What is he playing at! I'll go and see him, and find out what's been going on! Seventeen years old. He should know better!"

"Pa! No! You said it didn't matter!"

"Has he messed with you?"

"Messed with me? I don't know what you mean!"

"Has he kissed you? Or anything like that?"

"NO! He wouldn't. I like him. I talk to him a lot, and he talks to me, but... Anyway, I never got to talk to him because... Pa, please don't go to him. Please. He hasn't done anything. I went to find him; he didn't know I was coming. I saw him but he was..." Katharine tugged at her father's coat sleeve. "Please, Pa! Don't go to him!"

Charlotte grabbed her daughter, and pulled her away from her father. "You are in so much trouble, young Kate!" she said, and slapped her hard around the face. Katharine shrieked, shook from her mother's grasp and ran off and went upstairs, still sobbing.

"That was uncalled for, Lottie." said Joseph angrily.

"No it wasn't. She's been out seeing a boy... a young man. What will people say? What has he been doing to her? What does that say about our family, Joe?"

"It says nothing. She's not doing anything she hasn't seen her sister doing with Caleb. Now look, I am going to go to Marriott and just check what's been going on. If what she says is true she just likes him, and he's a young lad, and she's young pretty, and what young lad wouldn't like the attention..."

"She's twelve!"

"... I know she's twelve, and it sounds like he's worked that out too! Now, let's get back to the *point* here, Martha! That snake Dove is accusing our son of tampering with the signals. Our Kate, who I would

128

trust a thousand times over Dove, says she saw someone up the signal before the crash. If we're going to have that heard in a court, we have to make sure anything that's said is true, and honest, and they can check it with anyone else. They'll question her and find out anyway, so let's find out the truth first, the facts of it all, otherwise there's no point."

Charlotte sat back down, and sighed.

"What will you say to Marriott then, Joe? Mind, if he's messed with her…"

"He hasn't, Lottie. He hasn't. I'm not sure he'd know how anyway. He might be an idiot, but he's a decent idiot. She's seen the way Sarah was with Caleb and…" He stopped in mid-sentence. "Sarah. Oh, my poor Sarah too. I hope she's going to be all right." He sat down and put his hands over his face. "What is happening to us, Lottie? What are we going to do?"

His wife leaned over and put an arm around his shoulder, and held his hand. "We'll get through this, Joe. We've got a good family, good children. Now, you go and see Arthur Marriott and find out what his side of the story is, and we'll take it from there. If what Kate says is true, she needs to be heard, and she needs us to be behind her when she speaks out."

17

40 minutes later

Tom Marriott had just unhitched his horse from the coal wagon, which was now parked neatly in one corner of the coal yard, with a wooden chock under a back wheel. As he led the horse into the stable, he heard his name being called. Bolting the door behind the horse, he turned and saw Joseph Palmer heading across the yard.

"Tom. Is your lad about, by chance?"

"Aye, Joe, that he is. And what would you want with him? He's had a fair old shaking the last few hours, what with seeing his mates killed, and seeing all them bodies in the train an' all that."

"I know, Tom. It's a rum thing, but I do need to talk to him. I don't mean him any harm. It's a favour actually. He could be of help."

"Oh?" Tom looked quizzical. "Help to who?"

"Me. Well, my lad really. Someone's been putting stories around about him and the signals. But they ain't true, Tom. Someone's got it in for him and I need Arthur's help…"

"What lad of yours? Hubert?"

"No, Jimmy. Hubert's been working the rescue trains all night. He's not even been home yet."

"Now listen here, Joe. We've known each other a long time, and I know you're a good man. But my lad's not in a good way right now. He's been shaking like a leaf most of the day, and I don't mind telling you he's been crying like a baby, and he's taken to his bed, and he's probably asleep right now…"

"I know, Tom. I understand and I don't blame him for it. We're all pretty shaken up. I wouldn't ask but… it's urgent. He's not in any trouble, I promise you that. Not with me, not with anyone as far as I know. He's a bit of a hero actually, for what he did."

Tom headed towards the door of his cottage, beside the yard. "Come with me, Joe, and we'll see what the wife says. But don't hold yer hopes up man."

They went in to the back entrance of the cottage, straight into the kitchen. Tom took off his cap and threw it on the table, revealing his balding head with just a few shocks of wispy grey hair at the sides. He looked vaguely comical; his thick grey beard made him look almost as if someone had turned his head upside down on his shoulders. On another occasion, Joseph would have allowed himself a smile at the thought, but he was in no mood to smile tonight.

"Lizzie? Lizzie? I got Joe here from the railway. Needs to see Arthur."

"He's not well, he's had a terrible shock. Let him alone, Tom. He's sleeping right now." Elizabeth Marriott emerged from the front room, her slightly bent figure eyeing Joseph keenly from the door. She looked much older than her fifty-nine years; a life of working outside on the farm, then bringing up a large family, and then helping her husband moving sacks of coal bags about the yard had taken its toll. "Hello Joe, how are you? The pot's brewing – you'll stay for a cup." This was said almost as a command rather than a question. Although the Marriott's were quite a bit older than Joseph, they looked up to him

131

as a pillar of the village community, and the man who had put in a good word with Isaac Kemp for their youngest boy Arthur, when he had applied for the job at the station.

"That's very kind, Lizzie. I will if I may. Only, I need this favour. You see, Jack Dove…"

"Jack Dove!" Tom interrupted. "Now why did I think he had something to do with all this then?"

"He's nothing but trouble, that man!" added Elizabeth. "See how he treats them poor kids of his, like they was dogs, or worse. I'd like to give him some of his own medicine if I had the strength. He still chasing around after your Agnes?" She poured three cups of tea, added milk from a jug, and then put the cups out in front of them all. The men joined her, sitting down at the small wooden table.

Joseph nodded. "Yes he is, but that's not the problem right now. He's only been and told the Sergeant that he saw my lad up the signal a few minutes after the accident. And my lad were nowhere near it. I know that for a fact. I don't know what Dove's game is, but it's put Jimmy and me in a very awkward place."

"He's a one, ain't he?" said Tom, sipping at his tea. "Arthur's been singing his praises today, though. Can't deny he put himself out there. Helped rescue a lot of folk from that those carriages. They'd have been burnt to a cinder like the Squire was if he hadn't been there."

"So did your lad, Tom. He helped a lot of people too. And so did lots of other folk. It's just Jack was the first one there, so he was seen to be leading them all from the front, if you like. But your Arthur… you should be proud of *him* too." Joseph took a long swig of tea, and suddenly realised he was feeling very thirsty, and hungry. He'd barely eaten since the accident. "I saw him from the 'box. He were crawling underneath the wreckage and I could see the flames licking round the carriage right above him, but I hear he helped get four people out who were trapped."

"Aye. He said summat about folks' legs trapped between the seats. Him and Dove got 'em out. But anyway, how is that going to help your lad over this signal business?" Tom put his empty cup down, and pointed to the pot. His wife dutifully refilled it for him.

"Well, it's a bit… difficult, but my lass Kate, she says she were seeing him just before the accident."

Tom stared at Joe. "Seeing him? What do you mean, seeing him?"

"She went to see him… Arthur. But she never got to see him. She came straight back. That's all she'll tell me. Won't say what she was seeing him about. I'm not saying there was anything else, and anyway she says it weren't anything like that, though mind, I think she's sweet on him. Thing is, she says she saw someone up the signal before the accident. If that's so, she'll have to give evidence in the court, and they'll want to know what she's doing out, being only twelve years old and all that, and why she was where she was." Joseph went to take another swig of tea, and then noticed Arthur Marriott standing at the kitchen door.

"Who's seeing me, Mr Palmer."

"Arthur. You need to rest." His mother stood up and moved towards him. "You need to get back up to bed."

"I can't sleep, Ma, and anyway I heard what Mr Palmer said. "

"You can call me Joe, lad."

"Well, alright then... Joe. If it's true, your Kate was trying to see me, well, if she did come round... I was meant to be cleaning the waiting room but... I was meeting someone else. I saw Kate in the distance, coming towards me and... and she saw us... she just turned round and ran away. I was out back of the station where Mr Kemp couldn't see us."

Tom Marriott glared at his son. "What have you been up to lad. She's twelve-year-old."

"Pa, I wasn't seeing Kate."

"Who's 'us' then?"

"It's... I'm... look, Kate, right, she's... she likes me. She's told me that before. And I like her but not like that. I mean it. I said we could be friends and everything, but I'm seventeen and she's twelve and that's all really. It's not her I'm seeing."

"Well who is it then?"

Arthur looked nervously at Joseph Palmer.

"Please don't be cross, Mr Palmer. Please."

"Go on, Arthur" said Joseph slowly.

"I'm seeing your Agnes."

"Agnes?"

"We've been seeing each other... sort of... for some time. And I've not done anything with her that I shouldn't have neither. But... well, Kate must have come to see me, and seen us together and then maybe got upset and run off."

"And what were you doing with Agnes, when you were meant to be cleaning the waiting room?"

"We were talking about playing a prank on Caleb and Sarah, jumping out on them when they were..."

"When they were what, lad?" Joseph Palmer fixed a benign stare on Arthur. He wasn't angry, he wasn't feeling anything except exhausted. He had passed the point where anything would surprise him. The shock of the accident was so great that a few small shocks such as finding out that three of his children were involved in some way with the lads at the station meant nothing to him right now. He knew Sarah and Caleb were in love, for they had told him, and he also knew they been seeing each other discreetly. Sarah had insisted that they did nothing more than hold hands and he believed her. She was already working as house servant to the Kemps, and the stationmaster's house was on the up platform, so they had plenty of opportunity to snatch a few moments together if they wanted to.

Arthur Marriott was shaking his head. "Caleb..." He sobbed as he thought of his workmates lying dead under the carriage frame on the platform. "One minute him and 'Mighty' Strong are chatting to me about how the cows got on the line, next minute they're... gone. I could've been there, on that platform. I should've been with them. And because I bunked off from my job, I'm still here. It's all wrong."

Joseph looked away in sympathy for the young lad. There was a brief silence.

"Look, Arthur. Just tell me what they were doing? Caleb and my girl. It doesn't matter now anyway, does it? It's not so important."

Arthur looked at his mother, then at the floor. "They been kissing sometimes. Not any more'n that. And cuddling, but always just on the seats. And we was just going to jump out on them, just for a tease.

135

That's all. It's childish really, but we wouldn't mean no harm…"

"That's fine, Arthur. I'm not worried about that. Now, listen, Kate says she saw a man up the signal about ten minutes before the accident. If we tell the Sergeant that, and you tell the Sergeant what you just told me, then if it were all true, there's nothing to worry about."

"Please, Mr Palmer! If it comes out, Mr Kemp will get rid of me for bunking off work, I should have been on the station but I wasn't. I was meant to be cleaning…"

"I'll talk to him. I'm sure he'll be fine. You're a hero in most people's eyes. You rescued quite a few folk yesterday, he'll not want to do anything to you. But just make sure if anyone asks you any questions about Agnes, or Kate, you just tell the truth, right, and don't hide anything. And don't worry what you think they might say about you, or her, or Agnes. None of that matters, it's nothing compared to what will happen if they believe what Jack Dove said about Jimmy."

"What's Jack said then?"

"He says that he saw Jimmy up the signal just after the accident happened. Or someone who he thought might be Jimmy."

"He can't have done! He was helping to get people out of the wreckage. You can't hardly see the signal from where we were."

"Maybe you can, maybe you can't. But that's what he said. So you see, what Kate says is really important, and they'll rip her story into little shreds if it don't match up with yours."

"Right. I promise you that, Mr Palmer. I'll tell them. And I really haven't laid a finger on your Kate. She's a lovely little lass, and we've had a few chats, and I wouldn't want to hurt her feelings, but... I'm worried about Agnes."

"Why?"

"Because Jack Dove won't leave her alone, and if he finds out she's been seeing me, he'll do for us both"

"No he won't lad. Because everyone knows that she's not interested in him, so if anything were to happen, he knows everyone will point the finger at him." Joseph wondered if this was all beginning to sound too fantastic for words. As he spoke it occurred to him that just one day ago, he was a happy working man, with a good wife and six children, all of whom made him proud. And now? It was as if half of his family seemed unknown to him, as if they'd been carrying on with different lives, right under his nose, and he was just an outsider, a token figure in a dysfunctional household.

He looked straight at Arthur. "Look, son. Don't worry. Agnes'll be fine, so will Kate, and so will you. We've got all this to worry about now. Now, you get some rest and I'll have a word with Mr Kemp. I won't tell him what's happened, I'll just tell him to go easy on everyone, and that you're not in a good way." Joseph got up to go. "Thanks for the tea, Lizzie... Tom... and sorry to trouble you."

"It's no trouble, Joe. We'll stand up for your lad, don't you worry. We'll see to it that everyone knows what they need to know, and no more." Tom stood up and saw Joseph to the door. "Now Joe, you take some rest too. You look just 'bout done in."

"I am, Tom. But yes, I will go and rest now, thank you."

Joseph ambled slowly home. The night was setting in, and he walked up the lane towards the station. His route took him past the Dukes Head, and he looked in as he walked past. The bar was quite empty, and then he remembered that it was closed for the inquest, which was being held in the larger room around the corner, out of sight of the road. As he passed the inn, he could just make out the lights of the station, about a quarter of a mile away. He shivered as he ran over the events of the last twenty-four hours. Everything seemed so confusing, and he was conscious of a nagging doubt creeping in to his thoughts. Yet he knew, deep down, that he had done absolutely nothing wrong, nothing against the rules, nothing he wouldn't ever do again if he ever got to work in the signalbox again. But something was wrong, and there were parts of the story in his own mind which just did not make sense. He wanted to understand why a perfectly capable and highly experienced engine crew had steamed past two adverse signals – his signals – to their doom. What was someone doing up the signal? Was the light out and they were trying to relight it? Didn't the express fireman say he saw a white light? Well, it was lit then… except of course it would have been a red light… His head was spinning with the conflicting stories he was hearing.

He heard a horse and cart approaching from behind, and he stood to one side to let it through. He saw the outline of three passengers as it passed him, but the moonlight was barely enough to see his own hands by, let alone recognise them. After a few minutes, he came to the station road and stopped. There was still a great deal of activity in the station, with the rescue gangs beginning the task of clearing the debris from the track and platforms, so that the tracklaying gangs could swoop in and repair the lines in time for the full scheduled service to be resumed, probably late Sunday but certainly by early Monday morning. Joseph stared as the steam crane lifted what looked like the frame of a truck up and onto the back of a flatbed wagon. He wondered why they were doing this now, and then remembered that for a while they had been told to leave the wreckage until it could be viewed by the coroner's jury, and the Board of Trade's inspector. He stood for about ten minutes, almost in a trance, before turning and ambling along to the short row of cottages built especially by the London and Western Railway for the exclusive use of their employees.

The first cottage he passed was that of Beresford and Sarah Strong and their three young children. The curtains were drawn, and there was no light showing. He had heard that Sarah's mother was coming down from Hallowfield to stay with her daughter to help with the children. Poor Sarah, she was devoted to 'Mighty' Strong as he was known. He was one of four men who patrolled the lines between Hallow Hill and Belcote Crossing, and he had been standing at the edge of the platform beside the goods train when the accident happened. Bob Faulkner had been standing right with him, and escaped without a scratch. Bob would be working on the lines right now, no doubt, while his mate's body lay in the good's shed in a simple coffin. He made a note to look in on Sarah at first light tomorrow. He walked on past the Faulkners' house, then John Anderton's. Anderton was the signalman at Hallow Hill, and had been his neighbour and friend for many years. He would be on duty now, busy sorting out the many movements as trains ferried the wreckage away, or brought materials for the new track and station buildings. There was a light from the front window, and he could see the figure of Jean Anderton sitting bent forward in an armchair, probably sewing, thought Joseph.

He turned into his garden, and went to the front door. He could hear raises voices from within. Turning the handle, he stepped in to find James and Katharine talking animatedly with Charlotte, who was clearly becoming short with them.

"What's this then?" he said sternly.

"Pa, I brought Sarah home, and Mother says I should have left her at her friend's. But she wanted to come home with me."

Charlotte took a deep breath. "She's upstairs in her bed. She's in a terrible state still, Joe. We've got enough to worry about without her whining and pining about that poor Stopps boy."

Joseph ignored his wife's insensitive comment. "Kate. I've had a word with Arthur Marriott."

"No, Pa! What's he said?" She shook her head and tears began to well up again.

"It's all fine, Kate. He's told me the truth and it sounds like it's what you told me. Well, most of it. So, tomorrow we'll send a note to the Sergeant…"

"What this about, Pa?" said James. "I've already seen the Sergeant and told him I was nowhere near the signal. He don't need to come again."

"Kate saw a man up the signal…"

"I told you, I wasn't there!"

"I know son, now will you just listen to me a moment… please! Calm down. Right, Kate saw a man up the signal about… ten minutes before the accident happened, all right? Now, we had to clear up how it was she was out there when she was meant to be in here doing her reading, but anyway, now I know the truth, I can't see any reasons why she can't stand up and tell the judge…"

"It's the Coroner, Joe" Charlotte interrupted him. "The Coroner is the person running the inquest. And they've called you and all the others for Monday morning at 11 o'clock."

"Right, well, we need Sergeant Michaels to know that we have some important evidence, and we'll get Kate along there too. Are you alright to talk to the judge… the Coroner, Kate?"

"I'll talk to him, Pa. Is it alright to tell him about seeing Arthur?"

"It's… it should be fine, love. Now, there's going to be some men there too… there's a jury of men who will be asking you some questions. Don't be scared, they're just trying to work out how this all happened. Just mind you answer them truthfully. Truthfully, you understand. Don't try to hide anything and it'll all work out fine. Don't make anything up, if you're not sure about something, say you're not sure."

"Yes, Pa. I promise I'll try and do that."

He gave his youngest daughter a quick hug, and sent her upstairs. Then he turned to James.

"Jimmy. I suggest you get to bed, son, and sleep. And try to sleep easy. We know you wasn't up that signal, and we'll make sure you get someone to stand up for you. Mr Kemp said that the company would be sending some lawyers to act on our behalf, so they'll make sure to ask the right questions and check anything that don't add up."

"Thanks, Pa. What's this about Arthur and Kate?"

"It's nothing, son. Kate's a bit sweet on Arthur and went to see him and… well he's seeing Agnes, as I expect you knew about even if I didn't."

"I thought they might be."

"Well they happened to be talking, that's all, just before the accident, and Kate went to see Arthur, saw them together and was just coming home when she saw the man up the signal. That's all. There's nothing else. Nothing at all."

"If Marriott's been messing with Kate as well, I'll deck him, Pa."

"No you won't, Jimmy, you'll leave it. Forget it. Nothing has happened, I've spoken with Arthur. You need to just save your strength for the inquest."

James followed his sister up the stairs.

"You alright, Joe?" asked his wife soothingly. "You look as if you need to sleep more than the rest of us."

"I can't yet, Lottie. I need to think this all through. There's still something nagging me."

He crashed down into their only armchair, and stared straight ahead. Charlotte folded up the clothes she had been repairing, tidied a few things away, picked up the clothes and went to carry them upstairs. At the bottom of the stairs, she turned to wish her husband goodnight, but he was already fast asleep.

18

Mr William Hammond, the Coroner for the District of Weston, seated himself at the head of the large wooden table, and consulted his notes briefly. "Is everybody present, Mr Dyer?"

The Foreman of the jury had already counted his fellow jurors in. There were no gaps in the ranks of seats in the room, all eighteen men were there.

"All present and accounted for, Sir."

"Very good. Well, now that we have concluded identification of all but two of the bodies, I am ready to take evidence from anybody who can help to explain how this terrible accident occurred. But before we do that, I would like to formally introduce you to Lieutenant-Colonel Francis... er, Sir Francis Whey, who is the gentleman from the Board of Trade..."

The man sitting at the top right side of the table, who looked younger than his sixty-two years, with a slim but healthy visage, and a neatly trimmed moustache, nodded to the assembled jurors and others in the room, and said "Good afternoon, gentlemen."

There was a slight murmuring in the room as mumbled greetings were returned in low voices.

"... also Mr. Gray, who is representing the London and Western Railway Company, and Mr. Seale, who is representing the family of Squire

Templeton-Morphy and has agreed to ask questions on behalf of the other bereaved families. Finally, Mr. Moss who has also been appointed by the Railway Company to represent its employees who were directly involved in the accident."

The three legal gentlemen, who were seated side by side at a smaller table, near the entrance of the room and across from the rows of jurors, nodded their heads in response to more mumbled greetings.

"Perhaps Sir Francis would like to take this opportunity to explain why he is present at the inquest, and what his role is in the proceedings."

"With the greatest of pleasure, Mr. Hammond. Gentlemen of the jury, my role as Inspector of Railways for the Board of Trade requires me to conduct an inquiry into the circumstances of any accident on the railway. As many aspects of my inquiry will involve questioning witnesses – the same witnesses as this inquest, it is useful and expedient for me to be present as an expert in railway operations, to enable relevant questions to be asked of any witnesses without in any way compromising the role of the Coroner, to whom I am most grateful for allowing me to attend. I would just add that the purpose of my inquiry will be simply to establish what happened, why it happened, and how such an accident may be prevented in the future. The results of my inquiry will be sent immediately to the directors of the company for their attention and action, if such action be required."

One of the jurymen raised his hand, and asked "Will you be apportioning blame for the accident, Sir?"

"Once I have heard all the evidence, and have heard additional evidence which may not be completely relevant to this inquest, I will indeed draw a conclusion as to the likeliest cause of the accident, yes, but I do not seek to specifically blame individuals unless they have been truly negligent in their duties. Most accidents are caused by many factors, and not just one. If I do reach a conclusion, however, it will probably not be before you have delivered your verdicts."

Sir Francis finished speaking, and nodded to the Coroner.

"Thank you, Sir Francis. I would remind you once again, members of the jury, that we are here to establish a cause of death for these unfortunate people, and not necessarily to apportion blame as such. We are only concerned with these unfortunate victims, and not with the injured people, nor with the operation of the railway other than where it impacts upon the cause or causes of the deaths. And now, may I suggest we hear our first witness today, Mr David Woodbridge."

David Woodbridge, the Engineer for the London and Western Railway, was sworn in, and then described the railway line and surrounding area with the aid of a large map which showed the layout of Salmsham Station, its various buildings, lines, points and signals, and their critical distances from each other, and the next signalboxes along the line. He also described the gradients either side of the line:

"Travelling from Belcote Crossing, which is on Bridge Number 143, the line is on a slight downhill gradient of about 1 in 300 for about three quarters of a mile, then is level from Bridge Number 144 until just after the station. Almost as soon as the down platform ends, there is an initial gradient to Hallow Hill of 1 in 90 for about 700 yards then a short section which is almost level followed by a severe gradient of 1 in 57 for 1100 yards before it eases to around 1 in 110 up until Hallowfield Station."

Woodbridge then went on to describe how he had arrived at the Salmsham at about 10.30pm the night of the accident, and initially went to the signalbox to inspect the levers, check the register and check that everything was working as it should have been. He had found no faults with either the signals or the mechanism for changing them. He had also checked the signal interlocking frame and found it in proper working order. He then went and helped to co-ordinate the breakdown gangs so as to try to lift the coaches to get to anyone trapped underneath. "The fire was burning very intensely and I could see there was little or no chance for anyone trapped in the front four carriages, but people had been rescued from the seventh carriage which was balanced on the top of the wreckage. The fifth carriage appeared to have been shattered and threw many people out onto the platform, and the sixth had gone under the carriages in front, and was also starting to burn. The last three carriages were more or less upright but were derailed sideways across both running lines. The crews had managed to pull some of the wrecked carriages back away from the flames, but all of them had been derailed, and only the last carriage could be rerailed onto its own wheels."

"I'd like to ask you, if I may, about the home and distant signals. I understand that you inspected them in more detail on the Friday morning, in the daylight." Sir Francis Whey asked. He already knew the answer, of course, as he'd been there with Woodbridge when they'd carried out a thorough examination of all of the equipment, all the way up the line towards Belcote.

"Indeed so, Sir Francis. I first inspected the home signal, and found all of the mechanism to be in perfect working order. I checked the lamp glass, and the spectacle frame. The only unusual thing I found was a screw missing from the spectacle frame. There are normally three screws securing the spectacle glass in the frame, and one was missing."

"Please explain how the spectacle glass is affixed, Mr Woodbridge."

"The glass is cut to size, and then affixed with putty. Then, three small screws are used to secure the glass and prevent it from moving within the frame and thereby cracking the putty and falling out."

"How might you account for the missing screw?"

"The only thing I can surmise is that the screw was somehow loosened over time through the constant movement of the signal. Either that or someone may have attempted to remove the spectacle, but I find that hard to believe. However, it must have happened recently as the hole was fresh and not clogged with dirt or putty."

"But there was no sign of the screw on the ground?"

"I could not find it. But it is small, and may have fallen between the ballast stones."

"And what was the state of the putty around the lens?"

"The putty around the lens was cracked and not sealing against the spectacle frame any more, as one might expect to find with a spectacle which has been outdoors for several years in all weathers."

"Quite so. And how about the distant signal?"

"The distant signal was also in perfect working order. I checked the tension of the wires, and found them to be perfectly in adjustment. The lamp glass and spectacle lens were in perfect condition."

After a few more questions, Mr Woodbridge had finished and been dismissed. The inquest then heard from James Agnew, the Superintendent of the line. He explained how he had written the rules for the signalboxes, when the new telegraph system had been installed about seven years ago. He described in some detail how the signalmen could communicate by their bell telegraph, using bell codes to request and confirm particular trains through each section, and how they could also use the speaking telegraph to communicate the more complex messages, such as details of special trains, and last minute changes to timetables. He confirmed that he and Woodbridge had checked all of the signalling equipment and could find no fault with it.

Responding to a question from Sir Francis, Agnew said "As far as I can tell, this accident was caused by one of two things – either the driver and fireman mistook the signals which were actually against them, or the signalman at Salmsham failed to return his signals to 'on' when the goods had pulled up at the station."

"And which of those do you consider most likely, Mr Agnew?"

"I shouldn't like to say, Sir Francis. There is conflicting evidence and I would need to ask more questions of the people involved."

"Indeed so."

"Er…There is one other possibility, of course, but it is a quite absurd one."

"What is that, Mr Agnew?"

"Well, it is just possible that someone tampered with the signals, to make them show a false clear."

There was a sharp intake of breath from the jury, and the three legal gentlemen began to look uncomfortable. The Coroner looked genuinely surprised, but Sir Francis did not as he'd already discussed this theory with James Agnew in private when they were both inspecting the accident site.

"How could someone do that, Mr Agnew, and hide it from us?"

"Well, this is the point. I don't think they could. It would need more than just one person mucking about with a signal. You'd have to tamper with both the distant and the home signals, and then return them to their normal state straight after the accident so that the problem is not found. It would take quite some planning, and would amount to a conspiracy. Whoever did it would need to have quite some technical knowledge to make sure their crime was successful and remained hidden. It would also need a motive. I don't think it is very likely at all."

"Quite so. But, in the absence of firm evidence of a clear cause for this accident, it is something we must keep an open mind about." Sir Francis finished speaking, and then indicated to the Coroner that he had finished.

"Thank you, Mr Agnew" said the Coroner. "You may go now. You are, of course, welcome to stay in the public area and hear other witnesses should you wish to do so."

"Thank you, Sir" replied Agnew. "I will do just that." and he stood up from the witnesses' chair and walked over to the line of public seats along the wall behind the jurors, nodding at the jurors as he went.

19

Isaac Kemp

"I should like to call the Stationmaster, Mr Isaac Kemp please." The Coroner out his pen down and sat staring at the door as Isaac's name was called to the outside world.

There was a murmur from the back of the room, and a shuffling of papers, then Mr. Gray coughed and said "Mr Kemp is still at the station, Sir. He was due to be here about now but his relief has only just arrived at Salmsham. I will check but I think he will be no more than a few minutes."

The Coroner looked displeased. "Very well, no more than ten minutes or we will call other witnesses ahead of him." He made a few scribbled notes and shuffled some paper, then took a sip from his drink.

Meanwhile, Sir Francis Whey took out a sheet of lined foolscap paper which already had some notes written on it, and added some additional thoughts, whilst the assembled jurors began to speak quietly amongst themselves.

The inquest had had another fairly harrowing morning, with the additional identification of various bodies. Once again the jury had been taken to view the remains, and had stayed in the temporary morgue at the goods shed during the identification process. The newly entitled Squire of Hallowfield, Richard Stephen Templeton Morphy, known as 'Squish Morpho' to all in the community, had been sworn in and somehow managed to maintain enough emotional restraint in front of the jury to identify the charred remains of his father Francis from the metal buckle on the front of his shoes, despite those shoes being almost completely burnt away and the metal badly distorted. A further inspection by one of the doctors appointed by the Coroner had established beyond doubt that the body was that of a man of a height know to match that of the former squire. By a process of elimination, the body which was found next to the squire was identified as Christopher Hinton, his valet, who possessed a small trunk which was found in the vicinity. A bunch of keys found beside his body matched the locks at Hallowfield Manor, and once again a post mortem had helped to confirm his identity.

Miss Florence Elms, from West Wittering in Sussex, had confirmed the identities of her cousin John Parry-Elms and his wife, from personal items found on their bodies.

Jasper Stainesby, from Wisbech, had formerly identified his father Alexander, who had died from being thrown out of his carriage onto the platform.

Two bodies remained unidentified, however. Zebedee Taylor, a market vendor from Uxbridge, had arrived looking for his daughter Jane, who was employed as a maid to Mr Barry Pinsent. Pinsent had escaped unhurt after freeing his legs from under some carriage seating, but Jane had been ejected into the gap between two wrecked carriages. Apparently unconscious, she had been burnt when the flames reached the wreckage, long before the fire was put out. The other body was thought to be that of Anne Chase, a maidservant to the Pettigrew family. Both the bodies found were known to be female, and the

Coroner had ordered further examination to try to identify them.

Just as the Coroner was about to ask for a new witness, the door was opened, and an attendant announced "Mr Isaac Kemp, Sir."

"Please, Mr Kemp. Sit down." Isaac walked in slowly, somewhat taken aback by the thick tobacco smoke. He was used to the men's waiting room at the station, but at least that admitted fresh air whenever someone stepped in or out. This room seemed to have no obvious ventilation of any sort, and there was a large cloud of smoke seeping its way over from the group of people he assumed to be the jurors. The attendant showed him to the witness's chair. He was in his full railway uniform, and held his hat in his hand. His thinning hair was neatly brushed back over his head, and a scar was visible over his left eye.

"Mr Kemp. Thank you for attending. Please try to answer any questions put to you by any of these gentlemen here" – the Coroner indicated the jury and the three lawyers – "or from this table. If you are unable to answer, please just say so."

"Yes, Your Honour." Isaac coughed a little. He had never had to attend an inquest before, and hoped never to again, especially if the atmosphere was as polluted as this. He was very uncomfortable and also had the feeling of being on trial. He had been advised briefly on Friday by Mr. Moss, who assured him that he had nothing to worry about as long as he just told everything that he knew. In his own mind, he thought he had done his job correctly, but had maybe been let down by one or two of his staff, which of course meant he was still ultimately responsible for what had happened.

"I believe you have already met Sir Francis Whey, the Inspector or Railways?"

"Yes, Your Honour."

"Very well. Please would you now take the oath."

The attendant who had shown him to his chair passed him a bible and a sheet of paper. Placing his hand on the bible, Isaac read out his name and took the oath.

The Coroner began his line of questioning. "You are Mr Isaac Kemp?"

"Yes, Your Honour, I am."

"Mr Kemp, you may address me as Sir. And please tell us, what is your job, Mr Kemp, and how long have you been with the company, and doing this job?"

"I am the Stationmaster for Salmsham. I have been with the London and Western Railway for twenty-seven years and Stationmaster here for the past sixteen years."

"Now, Mr Kemp. I understand that the 2.10 goods train from Salisbury had been stopped at your station. Why was that?"

"I was informed by a farm labourer that some cows had escaped onto the line near Hallow Hill."

"I see. And what did you do when you received this intelligence?"

"I sent the porter Marriott and ganger Strong to check the line, and Marriott came back and confirmed that there were several cows on the line, and some farm hands were rounding them up."

"And what did you do then?"

"I sent my other porter, Stopps, to the signalbox to get the goods stopped, and also the passenger train which was due shortly from Hallowfield. We decided to shunt the goods at Salmsham as otherwise it would take too long to get to Hallowfield."

"Who decided that, Mr Kemp?"

"I did, Sir."

"You just said 'We decided'"

"Yes, Sir. It's a joint decision which can be taken by either me or the signalman, based on the when the express is due. Whoever decides makes sure the other gets the message."

"I see. Is there any good reason normally to shunt the goods at Salmsham?"

"Because of the steep gradient up Hallow Hill, the goods will be very slow between Salmsham and Hallowfield. If the goods is running late, we shunt it at Salmsham so as not to delay the express. The rulebook expressly states that goods trains must be shunted clear no later than ten minutes before an express is due."

The Coroner made a note, and glanced at Sir Francis, who raised his eyebrows in request. The Coroner nodded, and Sir Francis asked. "Mr Kemp, good afternoon. Please could you tell the jury where you would normally shunt the goods, if it was not late."

"The goods is usually shunted at Hallowfield."

"I see. And have you had reason to shunt it at Salmsham in the recent past?"

"We have shunted it three or four times in the last few months. We planned to shunt it this time, and I sent my clerk James Palmer to take charge of the shunting, however he told me the line was still blocked beyond the siding points."

The Coroner asked "And why would this affect the shunting operation?"

"To shunt the train requires it to be drawn forward past the siding points. They are trailing points; that is, they don't face the direction of travel. The train has to go past them, stop, and then be backed into the siding."

"Was it a long train?"

"The train was not longer than usual. It was longer than our platforms, but not too long for the main siding."

"So, knowing that the line was blocked, what did you do with the goods train?"

"We held it in the station."

"For how long?"

"I would say we held it for about 13 minutes."

Again, notes were scribbled down by the various parties in the room.

"How did you know when the line was clear, if it ever was?"

Isaac Kemp coughed again. The atmosphere really did feel quite poisonous.

"James Maltby, one of the farm lads, came back with Strong to tell me the cows were all rounded up and the line was now clear."

"Did you go and check for yourself? Or did you send someone back to check it was clear?"

"I did not check the line myself. I did not send anyone else to check the line. I was keen to get the goods shunted as I knew the express would be due any time."

"According to my notes, you didn't actually proceed with the shunting. Why was this?"

"I could not find James Palmer when I heard the line was clear. I now know that he had gone to the signalbox to get the authority to move the train and to tell the guard to come back down to his train."

Sir Francis asked "Did you send Palmer to the signalbox then?"

"I did not send him to the signalbox."

"I see. And why was the guard in the signalbox?"

"The guard of the goods train went to the box to remind the signalman of his train's presence on the line."

"Mr Kemp, why did you ask Palmer, who is your station clerk, do carry out the shunting, and not one of the porters?"

"James Palmer used to be a porter, and he is also an experienced shunter, and more senior. The two younger lads have not carried out shunting operations before."

One of the jurors asked again why the train wasn't moved straight away. Isaac was starting to feel that maybe he could have played things a little differently on the day, with the benefit of hindsight. He coughed again nervously, then used the excuse of the thick smoke to exaggerate the cough. It seemed no-one particularly noticed though.

"We would have moved the train sooner had Palmer still been on the platform."

"Well, how long was it before the accident happened?" pressed the same juror.

"I estimate it was about four minutes between when I heard the line was clear and when the accident happened. We heard the express whistle and the goods driver called his fireman to get on fast."

"Four minutes? What were you doing in all that time then?"

The Coroner interrupted the questioning by pointing out that this was an inquest and not an inquisition, at which point the foreman of the jury asked another question, which meant that Isaac did not have to try and recall exactly what he was doing for that four minutes.

"May I ask you, Mr Kemp," said Dyer, the foreman "what you did when the accident happened?"

"When the accident happened I jumped behind the station building as I knew the goods train had paraffin vans in it."

The Coroner stepped in. "And were you injured in any way?"

"I was cut on the forehead by a small piece of flying debris." Isaac pointed to the fresh scar on his temple.

"What did you do then?"

"After the accident I went straight into the telegraph office and sent messages for help to control, and asked Weston to send their breakdown gang."

"And once you had sent those messages, what did you do?"

"After the accident I found the platform was almost completely blocked."

"And what did you do then?"

"I tried to work out what to do about rescuing people. I was a bit confused at first; I think the knock on the head might have dazed me more than I realised."

"Did you see any other railway staff on the platform?"

"I saw the fireman of the express who was sitting dazed on the platform, and I got him up."

"Were there other people helping with the rescue?"

"Some passengers from the last coaches of the express train were unhurt and able to help but the fire was too intense to help some people. There were lots of people helping who came from the village."

Sir Francis then asked Isaac what he had done to prevent further catastrophe. Isaac explained that the goods train driver had told him that he'd sent his fireman to protect the line. The Coroner then asked what Isaac had done after sending for help.

"I went to the signalbox with the express fireman, Jobson, who had ended up lying on the platform near me, and I spoke with Joseph Palmer, who assured me his signals were on. I sent ganger Faulkner to see the position of the signals and he came back later and confirmed to me that both the home and distant signals were on."

"And what else did you do?"

"I got the goods driver to use the water from his tender to try and put the fire out, then District Inspector Reynolds arrived with two light engines and we used the water from them as well."

Sir Francis Whey made a note to ask why Isaac had not sent the goods engine on to Hallowfield for help; it may have saved time. He felt now was not the time nor the place to ask this question.

Isaac carried on; "Another train arrived from Mereham and helped with the rescue, taking injured people back."

"How long was the fire burning for?"

"The fire went on for several hours, Sir."

The Coroner made a few notes during the brief silence that followed. Then he put his pen down and looked straight at Isaac. "I must ask you, Mr Kemp, what were the rest of your staff were doing at this time?"

Isaac's voice began to falter as he recalled the horror of discovering two of his workers dead on the platform. "I saw my porter, the lad Caleb Stopps who had been crushed by the frame of a coach on the platform…" he faltered for a moment "…he…he was clearly dead. Ganger Strong was also killed in the accident. Strong had been standing on the platform near the rear of the goods train. I was… I was quite shocked by it all."

"I'm sorry. This must be hard for you, Mr Kemp, and we are all sympathetic to your plight. When you can, please tell us about your other staff, and what they were doing. There is another porter, I believe?"

"I… I couldn't find my other porter… Marriott… but later on I found he was unhurt and had been helping with the rescue work, from the other side of the train."

"I see. And how long did you carry on with the rescue?"

"We worked on for quite a long time until we had rescued all the injured passengers. I saw Mr Agnew and Mr Woodbridge and we talked about how the accident might have happened. I did not go to bed that night, my wife brought drinks for the workmen and passengers and we had help from the villagers. We arranged for some people to stay in the village."

"Thank you, Mr Kemp. And how long was it, as far as you know, before the bodies were cleared from the wreckage?"

"We did not clear all the bodies from the express train until the next morning but I was quite exhausted and I was relieved from duty at 11.30 by Mr Pick."

"Thank you, Mr Kemp. We have now covered all the events relevant to the actual occurrence of the accident, to the best of my knowledge. Does any jury member wish to ask further questions?"

After a short consultation, Dyer confirmed that no-one wished to know any more from Isaac.

"Thank you. And other gentlemen in the room?"

The three lawyers gently shook their heads. "Sir Francis?"

"I do have a couple of questions which are technical and which do not immediately concern the accident. I don't think it's fair to Mr Kemp to ask him these in a formal environment. I will consult him as and when I begin to make my final report."

"Thank you, Mr Kemp. We appreciate that this is a difficult time for you, and we thank you for your time in assisting this inquest. Before I dismiss you, I would ask you to thank your wife on our behalf for her help in providing refreshments and assistance after the accident." Isaac nodded.

"You may go, Mr Kemp."

Isaac thanked the Coroner, and then the jury, nodding to the other people present. He stood up somewhat shakily, and made for the door but then the room seemed to swim before his eyes, his legs gave out and he collapsed in a faint onto the thickly carpeted floor.

When he woke up a few moments later, he found himself sitting outside on a bench, with Martha Whitmore, the Landlord's daughter-in-law, patting him on the arm. Martha, who had been married to William Whitmore less than two years, also happened to be Joseph Palmer's eldest daughter.

"Martha... my dear, I'm so sorry. I must have fainted. The air in that room."

Martha chuckled. "What air? You mean, that fog. I don't know why people have to smoke, Mr Kemp. It's filthy. I would rather sit in a busy engine shed all day, and that's saying something."

Isaac stood up. "Yes... well, I must be off, Martha. Thank you my love, and I'm truly sorry your family is having a tough time over this."

He brushed himself down, and walked back to the station, with a vague sense that he had missed something important in all the goings on at his station on that fateful evening.

Back at the Dukes Head, the Coroner had adjourned the inquest for a short lunch break. In the inquest room, the jury men had finally concluded that the atmosphere was too thick, so a window had at last been opened.

20

The train crew, and Robert Faulkner

After lunch the inquest heard from the engine crew of the goods train, driver George Chappell and then fireman Harry Lusby, who told their side of the events of the previous Thursday. They were followed by their guard, Harrison Wiggins who stated that he had been to the signalbox but did not recall seeing the signalman move any levers while he was there. The guard also told them that while he was there "the shunter who I now know as James Palmer came into the box and asked what he was to do about moving the train. I told him I would await his instructions... I thought he would leave the box but he stayed there and was talking to the signalman... I knew the signalman was his father... I think they were talking about someone in the village pestering his sister... I heard James Palmer say he would do for him if he laid a finger on her... I think I had been in the box about ten minutes when we heard the express train whistle... I thought it was my driver at first but then the express train came out under the bridge and hit my train... I thought it had steam on. It was hard to see if the brakes were on... I'm certain it was still steaming but the driver may have been in reverse." Wiggins then went on to describe the accident and the start of the fire, and how Joseph Palmer gave him some detonators and told him to protect the line back towards Belcote Crossing.

Sir Francis asked him "Where did you put the first detonators down?"

"I put two detonators by the home signal."

"Did you notice the signal? Was it on?"

"The signal arm was on. I did not notice the light."

"So you don't know if the light was on or not?"

"I cannot say that it was on or off."

"Wouldn't you have noticed if it was off?"

"I think I would notice if it was off but I can't be sure. I thought if the arm was on, the light would be too. I was in a hurry to get the detonators down, and I was looking up the line back towards Belcote."

"And where else did you place the detonators?"

"I put more detonators down between the home and distant signals, and when I got to the distant I placed the last two on the line. I kept running with the flags until I reached Belcote Crossing."

"What happened then?"

"I returned later on with the first rescue train and helped fight the fire."

"When you returned, did you see the signals?"

"Yes. I saw both the signals, distant and home, and both signal lights were 'on' when I returned."

"Were those signals well lit?"

"Yes, both lights were well lit and very clearly 'on'."

"Thank you. I have no further questions, Mr Hammond." Sir Francis made a few more notes, as the Coroner rounded off a couple of questions about Wiggins's further role in the rescue, and then called Robert Faulkner as the next witness.

After Wiggins had been dismissed, Sir Francis Whey leaned across to the Coroner and said quietly "I'm very interested in the condition of this home signal. We've had some very unusual reports about it, and none of them make any real sense."

"Well, Sir Francis, please, as you're the technical expert here may I suggest you ask any questions you like around this. It certainly seems to be an area of contention and I should be pleased to be able to explain to our jury exactly what was going on." The two men had just finished their exchange when Robert Faulkner appeared.

As he sat looking at the imposing group of gentleman staring at him from behind the large oaken table, Robert felt a curious mixture of anger and bitterness about the whole set up, and yet he knew this was something that had to be done, and that the gentlemen who questioned him were simply trying to establish the facts and were not accusing anyone of wrongdoing. Nevertheless, his answers were rather terse and matter of fact. Although he was not an educated man, he had already had a sense that he was being used by 'them' – who 'they' were he could not have said – to help to frame some poor hard-working railway employees so as to be able to sweep the real causes of the accident under the carpet.

At the Coroner's request, Robert described his role as the ganger responsible for patrolling the three miles of line between Salmsham and Belcote Crossing, and also the sidings at Salmsham. He told them that his work for the later part of the day had been to repack the ballast around the older siding rails near the points with ganger Strong, and confirmed Isaac Kemp's description of events up until the accident.

Sir Francis Whey had taken over the questioning from the Coroner, who considered that most of the details would be technical until the point of the accident at least. Sir Francis asked Robert "Where were you when the accident happened?"

"I was standing on the platform with Strong when we heard the whistle and saw the express train coming in."

"And when you saw the train, did it appear to be stopping?"

"It seemed to have full steam on."

"I see. And were you able to see either of the men on the footplate?"

"I did not see the footplate men because I quickly dived down onto the ground. I could see we were about to have a big accident."

"I see. That was very wise. You were lucky to escape."

"I believe I have had a miraculous escape, yes."

"And were you hurt at all in the accident?"

"The wreckage flew all around me but somehow I did not have a scratch. I… I saw Strong, he had been hit by part of a coach roof… and was quite dead."

Robert's voice faltered, and he looked down in embarrassment. Rather to his surprise, not one person in the room appeared to show any sort of sympathy for him. He supposed later that they had probably been battle hardened by having to identify the remains of the victims, but even so he was angered by the silence that followed his last words.

The Coroner took over the questioning from Sir Francis.

"What did you do then, when you got up and saw that your colleague was dead."

Faulkner began to shake and cough. It was only after a few seconds that the assembled men realised he'd started to laugh. He continued for quite a few seconds, shaking his head from side to side and laughing at the sheer insensitivity of the Coroner's question.

"What did I do? What did I do? I did nothing. I stood there. I looked at my friend lying there. I got angry. What did I do. What a daft…" but his sentence remained unfinished as his speech turned into a sob.

Again, there was no reaction from the assembly.

Sir Francis Whey stepped in. "Did you see Mr Kemp at this time?"

Robert regained his composure. He decided he would just answer every question straight in as unemotional way as he could, so that he could be out of there quickly.

"Yes. He came along the platform a few moments later. He sent me to check the signals. As I left I saw a man, a farm hand running along the line towards me, asking what had happened, I told him there had been a big accident and he carried on to the station."

"Who was this man?" asked the Coroner. "Was he known to you?"

"I recognised him from one of the farms, but did not know his name."

"And what did you do after seeing this person?"

"I ran to the home signal and found it was 'on'. I also climbed up the signal to check whether the lamp was burning clearly, and it was. I went on to see the distant and that was also 'on', and I also went up that signal to check the lamp."

"And were the lamps in the signals working?"

"The lamps were properly alight in both signals."

"What did you do then?"

"I went back to the station and told Mr Kemp about the signals, then helped with the rescue until the fire was put out."

"What did you do then?" asked the Coroner. To Robert, it seemed as if he was asking a child what they did when they went out to play… "and after playing in the sand pit, what did you do then?" Anger rose inside him, and he was aware that his neck and face were reddening with the anger he felt building inside him.

Gritting his teeth, he almost spat out "I went home after that. I was very shocked about Strong, he was my neighbour and a good man."

The Coroner nodded; for the first time Robert thought that maybe he understood. Sir Francis, who seemed to know what he was about even if he had a rather impersonal manner, then spoke.

"Mr Faulkner, I am truly very sorry about your friend Mr Strong. He was killed doing his duty, and it must be a very great shock to you and his other workmates. Please accept our personal sympathies."

There was a murmur of 'hear hear' from various people, including jury members and the other very learned gentlemen sitting around the table, who had not yet spoken. Robert nodded in thanks.

"Although we are here to deal in hard facts, I'm going to ask you for your opinion now, because we do value your experience as a railwayman, because you know the line in great detail, and because you were there and we were not. Can you think of any reason why the express train would have been driven at high speed through the signals?"

Surprised to be entrusted for his technical opinion, Robert thought carefully and in a calmer voice answered "I can only think that the express driver didn't actually see the signals, or maybe thought he saw white lights. It was a dark and rainy night. He may have been mistaken about what he was seeing. Then, knowing that there was a steep gradient at Hallow Hill, if he believed the line was clear he would have been steaming as hard as he could so's to make light work of it."

"Should he not have been able to see the goods train sooner perhaps?"

"You cannot properly see into the station from the home signal due to the curve. You cannot see the station lights until about a hundred yards away."

Sir Francis made a few notes and then looked at the Coroner before saying "I think that's all for now, Mr Faulkner. Once again, thank you for the assistance you gave after the accident and please accept our sincerest condolences on the loss of your friend Mr Strong."

"Thank you, Sir, and" he nodded to the Coroner "you also, Sir."

As he got up to go, he realised he may have been mistaken about the imposing gentlemen behind the big table. Perhaps they were, after all, really trying to find out why this terrible accident happened. He also felt he could talk to Sir Francis Whey if he needed to – they spoke the same language, the language of people who had the railway coursing through their veins. There was a respect there which he hadn't expected. As he left the room, he even managed a chuckle at how 'Mighty' would have felt about being referred to as 'Mr' Strong.

21

Arthur Marriott and Katharine Palmer

Arthur Marriott was already shaking with fear when he was shown to the witness chair. After a few gentle questions, he felt slightly less threatened as he confirmed that he was a porter, and had been so for three years, was seventeen years old and was also able to use the telegraph. He described being sent with ganger Strong, to check that there were cows on the line.

"We went as far as the siding points and I could see the cows quite close to."

"How many cows did you see?"

"There were five or six of them. I went straight back to confirm this."

"What about Mr Strong?"

"Strong went on to see whether he could help the farmhands move the cows. He liked cows. I don't, they scare me."

There was a suppressed giggle, and Arthur relaxed slightly.

"What did you do after returning and informing Mr Kemp about the cows?"

"After this I went across to the up platform and I was on the other side when the accident happened."

"Did you see the accident?"

"I did not see the accident."

Sir Francis frowned. "You say you went across to the up platform, and yet you did not see the accident? How is this possible?"

"I was cleaning the waiting room on the other platform, Sir."

"Mr Kemp, your stationmaster, said he didn't know where you were. How do you explain this?"

Arthur paused. A little tinge of guilt made him blush. He wasn't going to say exactly why he didn't see the accident, or why he couldn't be found straight away. He had not heard back from Joseph Palmer as to whether Mr Kemp knew about his bunking off just before the accident, and so he had resolved not to mention meeting Agnes if he could possibly help it. Aware that his face was reddening, he put on a thoughtful frown and did his best to look as if he was trying to recall some trivial details. He took a deep breath.

"I don't know why Mr Kemp could not find me as he had sent me there earlier to clean up, before the business with the cows."

"I see. And what happened after the accident. What did you do then?"

Arthur visibly relaxed as he realised that his answer had been sufficient, and now he would be able to describe his actions after the accident, which were very real, very heroic in his own eyes, which he wanted the world to know about. He described seeing the fire take instant hold, and how he ran towards the back of the goods train and saw the remains of the express carriages piled up. There was a carriage half on its side across the up line, and he had helped people escape from this. Some of them were trapped, and he had helped to free them, particularly one lady whose legs were caught between two seats, whom he subsequently helped onto a stretcher. Eventually, when he could do no

171

more on the line side of the accident, he went onto the platform and saw the stationmaster. "Mr Kemp told me to stay and help with the fire."

"What else did you do?"

"I spent the rest of the time helping to put the fire out. It took a long time."

"Did you assist with the removal of any bodies?"

"No. Once we got the main fire out I saw the carriages were very burnt and I saw that there were several bodies, but I did not move any."

"And did you then go off duty?"

"I stayed after the fire was out and helped with the movement of the rescue trains."

"Thank you Mr Marriott. I think that is all. You appear to have done sterling work in what must have been shocking circumstances. Please accept our sympathy for the loss of your colleagues."

Arthur stood up to go, and was about to open his mouth to thank the jury when he became overwhelmed by the events of the last few days, and he found himself sobbing like a little boy as he was led from the room.

For a few moments, the jury chattered amongst themselves, and there was a certain muttering between the occupants of the large oaken table before the Coroner coughed and asked for quiet.

"Gentlemen of the jury, our next witness is very young, and I would ask you to bear this fact in mind when weighing up the value of her evidence, and when asking any questions of her. However, please feel free to question any aspect of her evidence which you may find wanting."

After that somewhat patronising introduction, Katharine Palmer was led onto the room. For one so young, she appeared remarkably confident, however her innocent appearance, and the ever-so-sweet smile she gave to the assembled jurors masked a pulsing heartrate and a very dry mouth, a state which she became aware of as she was sworn in. As she had passed Arthur Marriott on her way in, he had shaken his head to her, which she took to mean he had not mentioned meeting Agnes, or seeing her in the distance. Mr Moss had briefed her earlier and told her simply to answer what was asked and not to volunteer any information.

After she had been sworn in, the Coroner began to question her. His patronising tones were not intended to put her at ease. If anything, his own opinion as to the value of asking any twelve-year-old, let alone a girl, give important evidence at such a hearing, meant that he would like her to be gone as soon as possible so he could move on examine more reliable witnesses. The gentle and sympathetic voice which he had used on Arthur Marriott was no longer to be heard.

"Your name?"

"Miss Katharine Mary Palmer, Sir." Katharine spoke with her 'reading' voice, very clearly and with a boldness that belied her dry mouth and thumping heart.

"And your age and… er… occupation."

"I am twelve years old, Sir, and I am a scholar."

Several jury members chuckled at this. The Coroner was slightly irritated by this and glared at them before sweeping his gaze back to her.

"Do you understand that this is a very serious matter, Miss Palmer, and that your evidence must be given honestly and clearly, as it may be used in court at a future date."

"I do understand that, Sir. It is because this is a serious matter that I am here. My brother…"

"Miss Palmer. I will ask the questions and you will answer them. Is that clear?"

"Yes, Sir."

"Now, you told Sergeant Michaels that you saw a man up a signal, the signal by Hill Farm Bridge, before the accident happened. Is this true?"

"Yes, Sir."

"May I ask you what you were doing when you saw this man?"

"I was walking home, Sir. From the Station Yard."

"The Station Yard?"

"Yes, Sir. On the passenger side. I had been around there."

"What route do you take home from there?"

"I have to cross Belcote Road Bridge, and then turn right into the goods yard."

"Why would you turn right into the goods yard?"

"Because I live in the Railway Cottages at the back of the yard."

"I see. And tell the jury what you saw when you were crossing the bridge?"

"Well, as I got onto the bridge I saw a movement across where the signal is. It was quite a dark night and it was raining a little, but I saw the outline of a man at the top of the signal."

"Would you be able to identify this man?"

"No, I wouldn't, I'm sorry."

"So you have no idea who this man was, who you think you saw?"

"I thought it was Mr Faulkner, the ganger. And I did see him. There was really a man up the signal. I wasn't making it up."

"No one has accused you of making this up, Miss Palmer."

"But you just said I thought I saw him." Katharine stared at the Coroner, inwardly more terrified than ever. Her piercing blue eyes bored into him and made him feel suddenly uncomfortable, and he looked down and pretended to make notes.

Sir Francis sat forward. "Miss Palmer. I am Sir Francis Whey, the Inspector of Railways. I believe you are the daughter of Joseph Palmer, signalman?"

"Yes, but that's got nothing to do…"

The Coroner interrupted her. "Just answer yes or no, Miss Palmer. Please do not try to add extra points to your answer."

"Yes, I am Joseph Palmer's daughter."

Sir Francis continued "I'm interested to know why you thought it was Mr Faulkner up the signal, Miss Palmer. He is, after all, the ganger, not a signal engineer or a porter."

"Yes, I know that, Sir Francis. But when I saw this man, I knew Mr Faulkner was on duty and so I thought it must be him. Who else could it be?"

"Who else indeed, Miss Palmer?" His question hung in the air. Katharine swallowed and looked down, suppressing the urge to cough. She was used to smoky rooms but this one was just awful. She could not understand how these men could breathe, let alone speak without coughing and spluttering.

"Miss Palmer. I asked you who else could it be?"

"I… I'm sorry, I don't understand you, Sir Francis."

"I asked you a simple question, Miss Palmer. You told me you thought it must be Mr Faulkner, because he was on duty. I ask you who else it could be, because he was not the only person on duty, was he? It could have been ganger Strong, for example, or one of the porters, or even your brother."

"It was none of those, Sir Francis, and I would have known my own brother."

"How do you know it was none of those? You did not see their face, did you."

"It can't have been Mr Strong because he was shooing the cows off the line…" (laughter from the jury) "…and the porters are young and wear hats." (more laughter)

"How did you know that Mr Strong was shooing the cows off the line?"

"Because people have told me since."

"Ah, so what you're saying is you now think it must have been Mr Faulkner, but at the time you weren't sure it was him."

"I didn't really give it too much thought at the time, but I know that I saw a man up the signal."

"Very well, Miss Palmer. I will note that you cannot say with certainty who it was, however, could you state what time this was?"

"I don't know the exact time, but it must have been about ten minutes before the accident happened"

"How do you know that?"

"Because it took me about five minutes to walk home, and then I went inside to make myself some tea. The kettle had just boiled when we… my mother and I, heard the crash."

"Thank you, Miss Palmer."

The Coroner then addressed Katharine somewhat sternly. "Miss Palmer, has your father put you up to telling this story?"

"What? NO! It's not a story. It's the truth! My father was annoyed with me when he found out I'd been out without telling my mother where I was going. The only thing he said was that I might not be believed, because I'm so young."

"Hmmm. Members of the jury, does anyone have a question for this witness."

Several of the jury shuffled, and some hands went up. The foreman turned and pointed to one of the jurymen, who coughed and then asked "Miss Palmer. You have stated that you are twelve years old. What were you doing out in the dark at that time of night?"

Katharine blanched slightly at the question, but she had been half expecting it and decided to go on the attack to deflect the implications of the question.

"It was not at night, Sir. It was half past seven in the evening, and I'm not a little child."

"So your mother knew you were out then? She had said you could go out?"

"My mother did not know where I was. I let myself out without telling her. I have done this before. It's not such a terrible thing."

"Right. So, what were you doing then?"

"I was walking back from the passenger yard…"

"You've already said that. What were you doing at the passenger yard then?"

"I was… hoping to meet someone."

"To meet someone? I see. And who is this someone you were hoping to meet?"

"It's a private matter, Sir, and it has nothing to do with the accident."

There was a sharp intake of breath.

"With respect, Miss Palmer," said the Coroner, "it has everything to do with this accident! You will tell us who you were meeting."

"I will not, Sir. I say again, it is nothing to do with the accident, and it is a private matter between me and the other person, and anyway they did not know I was going to meet them, and as I didn't meet them anyway they would not be able to confirm it."

"Miss Palmer, you are obliged to answer my question."

"No I am not, Sir."

At this moment, Katharine was rescued by an unlikely source. Horace Moss piped up "The witness has already stated that the meeting was private and not pre-planned and therefore does not have anything to do with the accident. Also, it did not take place anyway. She has a right not to disclose this information. I believe we should take her answer at face value and not pursue this line of questioning any further."

The Coroner looked straight at Katharine.

"I take your point, Mr Moss. Very well, Miss Palmer, the fact that you refuse to answer my question is your right, I am informed. However, it places your evidence in a rather poor light if you do not tell the whole truth."

Katharine felt tears welling up in her eyes, but was determined not to cry. Pa had warned her about this hard questioning, and she was ready for it, but when the Coroner had told her that her evidence might not be believed she saw red.

"Why is that so, Sir? I have told you honestly what is important in this matter. I know that I saw a man up the signal by the bridge! I will not tell you who I was planning to meet, and anyway I did not meet anyone. I have also not told you what I had for breakfast or luncheon that day, does this make any difference to my evidence, Sir?"

"Miss Palmer, we have heard quite enough from you. You are dismissed."

"Thank you, Sir!" she said in the most dignified voice she could muster. Several jurymen burst into laughter, and as she turned to leave she glared across at them. "I told you the truth!" she said, spitting the words out as she stormed to the door.

22

Deliberations over dinner

"This whole business of the man up the signal is most perplexing, Sir Francis." William Hammond sipped a glass of red wine which had just been poured for him by Martha Whitmore, who was waiting on the gentlemen at their table in the inquest room. The jurymen and Mr Seale (representing the Squire's family) had retired to the main bar for the early dinner, leaving the Coroner, Sir Francis, and the two remaining lawyers to eat a fairly hearty meal at their working tables, surrounded by various sheets of paper and a couple of maps.

Sir Francis finished a mouthful of gammon, one of his favourite light dishes, and nodded.

"I agree. I can't work out whether it's the key to the whole thing, or a distraction. I know that there is some conflicting evidence about a man seen tampering with the signal after the accident, and of course this person Miss Palmer claims to have seen before the accident."

"Do you think there is sabotage?"

"Well of course there could be, but it's highly unlikely. What have we got? A missing screw from a spectacle glass that was otherwise present and correct. These railwaymen spend their whole working days devoted to trying to run the railway as smoothly as possible. However competently they go about their daily work, you cannot deny that this is one of the most efficient railway companies in the country, and they wouldn't be able to maintain this reputation without some very hard working and effective men running every part of the show."

"Nonetheless, it is possible."

"Anything is possible, Mr Hammond."

At this point, Horace Moss held up his hand and joined in the conversation. "As the man representing these railwaymen; all of them, I would just like to say that I have seen and heard nothing which would make me question their honesty and integrity."

"Mr Moss…"

"I have heard that someone has said he thought he saw, or might have seen, someone who might have been one of the station staff, up the signal after the crash. Now, I ask you, what is the likelihood of that being sabotage. Surely, he simply saw Faulkner or someone checking the signal."

"My thoughts exactly, Mr Moss" said Sir Francis.

"But we cannot simply dismiss this evidence." said William. "We must hear it, and the jury must hear it, and they must decide."

"What about Miss Palmer's claim she saw someone up the light before the accident?" Horace Moss was determined to have Katharine's evidence taken seriously.

"Well I'm not so sure about that girl, Mr Moss." replied William. "There are three things working against the reliability of her evidence; her age, the fact that she is the daughter of the man central to the circumstances of the accident, and the fact that she has not given a good account of her reasons for being where she was."

Horace Moss bristled at this apparent dismissal. "She may be only twelve years old, but I have every confidence that her evidence is as reliable as any grown man or woman's. Let's face it, some of these young lads on the railway are but fifteen and sixteen. Her evidence should not be dismissed because of her age, Mr Hammond. I wish to make that very clear, and I would like the jury to understand that."

"Mr Moss. I can assure you, if anyone has had any reservations about her evidence, it will become apparent once the jury have concluded their deliberations."

The fourth man at the table, Percival Gray, had remained silent throughout the above conversation. Now he had finished his main course, he carefully placed his knife and fork on his plate, wiped his mouth with his napkin, and then spoke.

"I do hope that all of us here are not trying to prejudice this case before we have heard all the remaining evidence? As I see it, the matter rests on three possible causes. Either the driver misread, and ran past the signals at danger, or the signalman forgot to put his signals to danger, or some unknown person has tampered with the signals so that they showed clear when they were not. Whichever of those causes, the railway company will acknowledge its responsibility, and I for one will not attempt to influence the jury towards any of those potential outcomes."

"That's all very well, Mr Gray, but as the representative of the railway staff, it's important for me to be able to…"

Horace Moss's sentence was cut off by William, who banged his fist lightly onto the table, as if he were holding a gavel.

"Gentlemen! May I suggest we speak no more of this awful business until we resume the hearing. I for one would like to stretch my legs and get some fresh air into my lungs. This room is damnably stuffy."

With that, William Hammond, District Coroner, got up from the table, left the room and went through the bar to the large garden. Walking down to the far end, beside a low stone wall, he lit a cigar, and stood quietly gazing out over the rolling fields as dusk began to dull their patchwork colours. Out of the corner of his eye, to his left, he saw a rapidly moving column of white smoke approaching behind the darkening line of trees. The railway was already up and running again, and there was another express train about to thunder through the newly rebuilt Salmsham Station, as if the events of the five days ago were already a distant blur. Perhaps they were even unknown, at least to many of the passengers on the train, but to the men still working at the station everything was still very raw, and William was aware of the tensions beginning to rise between the various factions.

"I do wish..." said a voice next to him "that we could just go back in time and watch everything, and see who did what. It would make life so much easier."

Sir Francis Whey lit his own cigar.

"But if we could do that, we could stop it all going wrong, Sir Francis."

"Indeed. Which is what I have to try and do now. Stop it all going wrong in the future."

"I think that's what we're both here for, aren't we? Just coming at it from different directions."

"It is just so, Mr Hammond. Sadly, I think we'll always be needed. Whenever we find one problem, and find the means to overcome it, the human element means that something else rears its ugly head. I for one would be grateful never to have to attend another accident in my life. Although I find the technical puzzles rather fascinating, the human element always confuses the issues. Human beings are quite extraordinarily complex persons, don't you think, Mr Hammond?"

23

James Palmer

James Palmer sat quietly shaking in the witness chair. He had been called immediately after dinner – the next witness after his little sister – and tried not to show his nerves as he was sworn in, but his voice wavered enough that he knew that he had failed already. He had already had dealings with Sir Francis Whey, who he found very intimidating when being asked informally about his actions leading up to the accident. He was particularly unnerved by Sir Francis's lack of comment whenever he replied to one of the inspector's questions.

It was the Coroner, however, who spoke first, asking him his name, occupation, and length of service. James stated that he had been the station clerk at Salmsham for the past three years, and had worked for the railway for eight years. He was originally a porter and so he was often called upon to take care of the shunting due to his greater experience compared to the two young porters, Marriott and Stopps.

At this point Sir Francis jumped in. "Tell us what happened that day."

"On the day of the accident, it was decided to shunt the goods train at Salmsham. Mr Kemp told me to take care of the shunt, after he had been told the line was blocked by cows. I checked with Marriott who told me the line was still blocked."

"Did you send anyone else to check after this?"

"I did not send anyone else to check as he said Strong would tell us when the line was clear."

"I see. What did you do then?"

"I then went to the signalbox to ask what I should do and to confirm the signalman's permission to shunt as soon as the line was clear."

"The signalman being Joseph Palmer, your father."

"The signalman is my father."

"What did you do when you got to the box?"

"My father was busy at the time and the goods guard, who was also in the box, told me he was awaiting my instructions."

"So what did you do after that?"

"I thought I'd stayed in the box for no more than a minute or so, but looking back I realise it must have been longer."

"Is it true that you discussed some personal matters?"

"I may have talked briefly to my father about personal matters."

"What personal matters are these?"

"One of the villagers was pestering my sister."

"Do you mean your sister Katharine who we have recently met?"

"No, no. I have four sisters. Agnes, I meant."

"I see. And what did you tell your father you would do about this? Did you make any threats?"

"I may have made a threat if any harm came to her."

"So are we to gather from this that you were distracted from your duties, or perhaps your father was distracted, because of this conversation?"

"The conversation did not distract me from my duties, nor do I think it distracted my father."

"How can you be sure of this?"

"I heard him answer the bells, and saw him keeping his register."

"I see. Did you see the position of his signal levers?"

"All of his down signal levers were forward, that is, the distant and home signals were 'on' as was the station starter."

"What happened next?"

"I heard the express train whistle and I thought at first it was the goods, but only for a moment. Then I saw the express train come under the bridge at full steam and collide with the goods train. I think I said to the signalman 'How can this be?' and he replied that everything was at danger."

"What did the signalman do then?"

"He went immediately to his instruments and sent 5 bells in both directions."

"And what did you do?"

"I was not sure what to do, but he told the goods guard to protect the down line back to Belcote Crossing. He told me to do the same on the up line as far as Hallow Hill. I was collecting the detonators from the store when the goods driver came into the box shouting."

"Shouting? What was he shouting?"

"I think he said 'What's that then, Bobby?' and my father told him all his signals were on."

"And you then left to protect the line, did you?"

"The driver said he'd already sent his fireman to protect the line. Then he left the box and I asked my father if I should go and get Mr Kemp."

"And your father confirmed this. What happened when you left the box?"

"I left the signalbox and saw Marriott in the six-foot way, trying to help to free someone from the wreckage. I went around him and around the front of the train to find Mr Kemp."

"Did you go back past the signalbox at all, in the direction of Belcote?"

"At no time did I go in any direction other than to the station."

"You never went to the home signal?"

"I never went to the home signal. I never climbed the ladder to the signal."

"You didn't think it would be a good idea to go to the signal and check the light?"

"The thought did not occur to me to do that."

Sir Francis nodded to the Coroner, who took over the questions.

"So, Mr Palmer, when you left the signalbox, you went and found Mr Kemp?"

"I could not find Mr Kemp as he had already gone to the signalbox with the fireman."

"Surely you passed him on the way?"

"I did not pass him as I went the long way around the train... along the 'up' platform."

"I see. And after you had gone around the train, where you saw Marriott helping to free people, what did you do then?"

"I went on to the down platform and saw some people lying against the wall of the station building. I could tell some of them were dead."

"What did you do then?"

"I don't remember much after that as I was sick. I… I thought I was somehow something to do with the accident by not shunting the goods train, even though I now realise I could not have been as the train was protected by signals. I think I may have fainted."

"You think you may have fainted... I see. And when you... came round, what then?"

"Mrs Kemp came out of the stationmaster's house to help some other people. She gave me some tea."

"And did you stay and help with the rescue?"

"I couldn't... I felt funny, so I went to my home which is in Railway Cottages and I fell into a chair and I think fainted with the shock of it all."

"And you never left there for the rest of the night?"

"No."

The jury foreman raised his hand and asked "I'd like to ask you again whether you went to the home signal after the accident happened?"

"I can honestly say that I never went near the home signal, before or after the accident. I'm not a porter now, so I have no reason to go to the signals ever. That's their job."

"What do you say to the rumours that someone says he saw you?"

"I know someone has said he saw me on the ladder after the accident, but he is mistaken."

"You think he is mistaken?"

"Yes. I know he is. He must be. I don't know why he would accuse me of doing such a thing."

"Perhaps you were trying to remove the spectacle glass, so the signal showed white, so as to protect your father's reputation?"

"I do not need to protect my father's reputation as I know for a fact his signals were 'on'."

The Coroner stepped back in with the next question. "Have you been to work since the accident?"

"Mr Kemp has suspended me for not doing my duty properly after the accident."

"In what way did Mr Kemp say you did not do your duty?"

"Well, because I was very shocked, I went home, but I didn't tell him first. I just went off."

There were general murmurings in the room at this news. One or two jurors murmured to their colleagues.

"Mr Palmer, have you been given any advice about answering any questions put to you? Have any of these legal gentlemen spoken with you?"

"They have, but I should just like to say that I am willing to answer any proper questions put to me by anyone."

A juror called out "In that case, I'd like to ask you - did you help in any way at all with the rescue?"

"I… I did not help with the rescue in any way as I was too shocked."

Another juror asked "Mr Palmer, were you shocked because you knew you had not done your job properly?"

James was taken aback by the question. He had expected to be asked about the signal, but not to defend his integrity, or ability in carrying out his duties.

"I am certain I did my job correctly up to this point."

The same juror asked "Don't you think you spent too long in the signalbox, talking, when you should have gone back to check if the line was now clear?"

"I don't believe I waited too long in the signalbox. I was about to go back and check whether the line was clear when the accident happened."

After this, the Coroner called for an end to the questions, and dismissed James from the witness stand.

As he got up from the chair, one of the assistants showed him to the door, but unlike most of the previous witnesses, James chose to stay in the room, and sat alone on a bench seat at the back. He knew that Jack Dove was the next witness, and wanted to hear what he had to say.

24

Jack Dove

As Jack Dove entered the room, it was clear he had prepared himself well and was determined to make the best impression he could. He was not wearing his working clothes; his hair was brushed neatly, and he had dressed up well. He also had an air of self-confidence about him – he knew he had nothing to lose; he was, after all, not an employee of the railway company and so he had nothing to fear as far as the questions were concerned – not that Jack Dove feared anything anyway. Swearing on the bible using his christened name, John, only after the formal introductions did he comment that he had been known as Jack for as long as he could remember. He gave his age as twenty-seven years, and his occupation as farm hand at Rosfell Farm, which he stated was his father's farm.

Before the Coroner began his questions, he introduced Sir Francis as the man who would take over when it came to some of the more technical aspects of the accident. Jack then related how he and two of his fellow farm workers were about to have a drink in the Dukes Head, 'this very inn, Sir,' when they heard a long train whistle followed by a 'terrible sound, like an explosion'. They left the inn and ran straight up to the station and, seeing the wrecked carriages piled one on top of the other, they proceeded to run across the yard and up onto the platform. Hearing cries from the wreckage, which they identified as coming from the carriage which was sitting high on top of the others, Jack immediately climbed up and saw that people were trying to open the doors. He then helped quite a few people out, some of whom were unhurt, but others were quite badly hurt. He passed them down to his friends below.

When he thought he had rescued everyone from the upper carriage he became aware of a group trapped beneath it, in another carriage which had been compressed down and had telescoped endways too. He managed to rescue them quite easily, and then saw that someone was trapped beneath that carriage as well, which was half on its side and slightly across the other running lines. He described how, with the help of the porter Arthur Marriott, who was working from the opposite side of the carriage, he managed to free an elderly lady whose legs had become trapped between the seats of her compartment, which had been compressed. He also rescued several other people from the same compartment, and soon afterwards he saw that the fire had reached that particular carriage.

When he had finished telling his story, he was thanked by the Coroner, who then asked Sir Francis if he wished to answer any questions.

Sir Francis coughed, said "Mr Dove…" and then hesitated, looking straight at him. For a moment Jack was taken aback, but managed a weak smile and stared back at the inspector. "Sir?" he replied.

"Mr Dove, you have made a statement that you thought you saw a man up the signal by the bridge after the accident occurred."

"The home signal, that's right, Sir."

"The home signal, that's right. Can you tell me…
us, when exactly you saw this man?"

"Yes Sir, it was while I was on the very top of the
wreckage, Sir, and I turned round and could see the
signal very clearly as I was quite high up."

"I see. You used the term 'home signal', Mr Dove.
Is that what you usually call it?"

"Yes, Sir."

"Why do you call it that?"

"Because that's what it is, Sir."

"Well yes, it is indeed. But most people just say
'the signal' – they don't know what it's called."

"I know what it's called, Sir, because many years
ago I worked on the railway. I was the station clerk,
so I know what the signals are for."

"Ah, that explains it. Thank you. Now, did you
recognise this man that you saw up the signal?"

"I thought I did, Sir. I thought it looked like James
Palmer, Sir."

"You say you thought it looked like James Palmer.
But you are not certain?"

"No Sir, it was dark. I couldn't quite see his face."

"Quite so. But you could see the signal clearly."

"Yes, Sir."

"Very well, Mr Dove. What was the signal
showing when you saw it?"

"The signal was 'on' Sir. That is, the arm was
straight out."

"You could see that clearly, then?"

"Yes, Sir. The back of the signal arm is painted
white, and I could clearly see it reflected in the light
from the signalbox."

"And did you see the light from the signal?"

"I don't recall seeing it, Sir."

"But you saw the signal arm, and you do still think the man you saw was James Palmer." Sir Francis consulted his notes, and a murmur began amongst the jurors. James Palmer shuffled uneasily in his seat.

"Mr Dove, the home signal is precisely 268 yards from the end of the down platform, where you were assisting with the rescue, and you contend that you could see who this man was, who you claim to be up the home signal, at night. Is there any chance you could be mistaken?"

"I might have been, but of all the people I know from the station, it looked mostly like James Palmer."

"But you are not certain, which means it could have been someone else. If, for example, I were to put to you that Mr Faulkner, the ganger, went up to the signal to check it after the accident, could you possibly have seen him instead?"

"Oh no, Sir. I saw Faulkner go up there much later to check the signal was still on. This was before that. As I said, I was still pulling people out of the top carriage. It can't have been much after ten minutes that I'd been there."

"Thank you very much, Mr Dove." Then, to the Coroner "I have no more questions for Mr Dove."

"I have," said Horace Moss, "if you'll permit me, Mr Hammond. Mr Dove, you stated that you used to work for the railway as the station clerk."

"That is so, Sir. About ten years ago."

"Was this at Salmsham?"

"Yes, Sir."

"Why did you leave the railway, Mr Dove?"

"Because my father asked me to help him on the farm. He holds the lease in perpetuity, which means I should inherit the farm one day. I needed to work for him to learn all about farming."

"I see. Now, Mr Dove, do you realise that if what you say you saw is true, you are accusing Mr Palmer of tampering with the signal, which means tampering with the evidence of the possible cause of the accident."

"I'm not trying to accuse anyone of anything, Sir. I'm just pointing out what I saw."

"But you accept that if it was indeed Mr Palmer, this is quite damning for him."

"It must be, yes."

"Why do you think he would be going up the home signal after the accident, Mr Dove?"

"Maybe because he knew his father had forgotten to place the signals to danger, and so if he maybe tampered with the lamp glass after they'd put the signal back to danger, there would be an explanation why the train past the signals. They could say the driver would have seen a white light because the glass was missing."

"Isn't that a highly unlikely scenario, Mr Dove?"

"I don't know. I just said what I saw, Sir."

"Isn't it true that you have a dispute with the Palmer family, Mr Dove?"

The Coroner stepped in "Mr Moss. This is an inquest into the deaths of the victims of a railway accident. It is not a court for deciding family disputes"

"I understand that, Mr Hammond, but this man has accused a railway worker of tampering with a signal, which could have been the cause of the accident…"

"Mr Moss. The man has stated certain facts. I think we can leave it at that."

The foreman of the jury called out "Mr Dove. What was the nature of your dispute with the Palmer family?" and before the Coroner could stop him, Jack replied "I have no dispute at all with the family. None at all. It is true I am wooing Agnes Palmer, who is a housemaid at my father's farm. But I personally have no argument with her family."

"That statement is not relevant to this inquest, and should be struck from the record. Mr Dove, you are dismissed. Thank you for your time, and also for your rescue work which I'm sure is much appreciated by everyone in this room, not to mention those who were able to escape the fire."

As the jury muttered "Hear, hear!" James Palmer stood up and jumped onto the bench seat, stamping his feet down as he did so. "The man's a liar! He's lied about seeing me, he's lied about the family, he's lying about my sister...!" A police constable grabbed him by the arm, and pulled him down to the floor, still shouting "He's a liar!" Jack Dove was led to the door, and as he passed near, James wriggled and aimed a kick at Jack.

"Filthy liar, Jack Dove! I'll get you for this!"

The Coroner called for order. There was a fair amount of chatter from the jury as James was dragged from the room by the constable.

Outside the door he was still trying to break away. "Palmer, if you don't stop wriggling and calm down, I shall be obliged to report you for breach of the peace."

"I don't care. HE'S A FILTHY LIAR!"

"I'm warning you..."

"LIAR. LIAR!

"RIGHT! James Palmer, I'm arresting you for breach of the peace. You'd better come with me down to the station house."

As James was led away, handcuffed to the constable, Jack Dove leaned against the bar and calmly ordered a pint of ale. "Some people, eh George?" he grinned.

George Whitmore glared at him. "You... out. You're nothing but trouble, Jack Dove, and I'm onto your game. In fact, we all are. You can get out, you're not welcome in this inn, and neither are your mates."

"Fine. Fine, if that's how you want to play it, George. But you'll regret this. I'll see to it, you'll regret it."

"I'm not scared of you, Jack Dove, nor your threats. Looks like the constable's got the wrong man, doesn't it, eh? Well, if there's any trouble around here, we'll know who the cause is, that's for sure, won't we."

Jack spat on the counter, turned, swept a couple of ale glasses onto the stone floor, and stormed out.

25

With a surge of excitement, Mark Phipps slipped the old cassette into the old 'ghetto blaster' tape player that his daughter's boyfriend had brought over, and pressed the Play button.

Nothing happened.

He took the cassette out, turned it over, replaced it in the machine and tried again.

Still nothing.

"Try rewinding it, Darling" said Freya. "You know how those old cassettes used to get stuck, and so we used to wind them back and forth to free them up a bit."

The family were sitting at the dining table, having finished lunch, and Alex, who had been eagerly telling his father about the various accident and inquest reports he'd been reading up on, had suggested that now would be a good time to listen to the tape. As Mark had been away on business all week, this moment was keenly anticipated. Even Olivia was interested, though more with a fascination with hearing her great grandfather's voice than listening to war stories. Freya was mildly thrilled too – she had adored Mark's grandmother, Jeanette Phipps, and wanted to hear the voice of the man who had won her heart.

And now the tape was jamming.

Mark pressed Fast Forward and the little tape spools began to whirr. He stopped it and pressed play. The tape was moving, but there was silence. He flicked the lid open again, and turned the tape over.

As he pressed Play, they were startled by a voice blaring out from the speaker, which was on full volume.

"… *thought…well, I nearly didn't go back there, but anyway, that's what that business was all about."* Adam Phipps' voice was typical of the English blue collar worker of the 1940s and '50s. He had a rural accent, but his speech was clear and didn't drop his 't's.

"*Coming back to the war then, Granddad…*" the young Mark Phipps' voice made the whole family laugh. Mark pressed Stop and then Rewind. "I sound so young" he grinned. "Let's hope I don't give you kids any stupid 1980s cool teenage phrases to mock me with."

"There wouldn't have been any back then, Dad" said Olivia, witheringly. "Cool didn't start until about a week after we were born."

The tape reached the beginning, and Mark said "Everyone ready?" Alex switch on his iPhone to record this, a precaution in case the tape didn't work again, and the family listened keenly as he pressed Play.

Mark's young voice blurted forth from the machine. "*This is Mark Phipps, on Saturday 8th February 1992, talking with his grandfather Mr Adam Phipps about his life. Hallo Mr Phipps.*"

"*Hallo, Mark.*"

"*Mr Phipps, when and where were you born.*"

"*I was born on the sixteenth of June, 1921, right here in this cottage. Wheeler's Cottage, Belcote.*"

"*And what did you do for a living?*"

"Well, I was at school until I was twelve, and then my father died and so I had to go to work on the farm."

"Emmet's Farm, Grandad?" Young Mark had already forgotten his initial formality.

"That's right. Old Farmer Goldthorpe took me on. He was a good man, very fair and easy to work for, and he'd been at school with my Dad so he was sort of like an uncle to me. He didn't have any sons, just girls, so I think he saw me as a bit of a son, when I wasn't in trouble on the farm, hehe"

"In trouble?"

"Oh, the usual pranks and things us young 'uns used to get up to...."

The family listened intently as Adam Phipps went on to describe his early life, the countryside around Belcote, his frequent trips to Hallowfield to see a certain young lady ("Jeanette Davey her name was – I fell in love as soon as I saw her")

"Awww that's so sweet" said Olivia quietly, as the others shushed her. The interview went on, with a few questions from Mark, and a lot of rambling answers from Adam. Then the subject came up of the war.

"I was what was called a reserved occupation, on the farm, see. Because we needed more food than before the war, because they didn't want to rely on imports. So I didn't have to go to fight. But I wanted to, and Mr Goldthorpe said he needed to get someone to replace me. In the end I think he got a couple of girls in, and so I was able to join up then."

"Why did he need two girls to replace you, Grandad?"

"Well, he didn't, but he could afford it because first of all you didn't pay girls the same because they said girls couldn't do what a man could do, which was all rubbish but... anyway the farm was doing well because we were producing more food and it was guaranteed money from the government and if you were efficient you did well. So… these girls went to the farm and I went off to war."

"What did you do?"

"I joined the Somerset Light Infantry. I had to go off to Taunton for training. It was July 1943, I was just past my 22nd birthday and I'd never been away from home before."

"That must have been hard for you?"

"No son. It was the best time of my life… I mean, up to then. The first few days were a bit funny, because everything was so different but there was good camaraderie, because we were all fighting to stop Hitler, see? He was a real threat. He had to be stopped. Now I'm not really a fighting man myself, I don't like war, I didn't really like it then, and I don't agree with most war anyway. But that man was… well, if you want to define evil just say Hitler. So anyway, we did most of our training and then we ended up just in south of England, but we knew something was brewing. Well of course, they were planning for the invasion, weren't they…"

"What, you mean the Germans coming."

"No, no, son! Us. Invading them. France. We were going into France, and that took some planning I can tell you. We were moving supplies around here there and everywhere. Course I know now what we were doing, but back then we just followed orders. But we were dummying stuff so the Germans thought we were going to invade at Calais. We had inflatable tanks [he chuckles out loud] so when they took pictures up in the air it looked like real ones. Thousands of 'em. We moved some across to Kent, we were stationed there awhile, helped set 'em up. Anyways, then I was moved to a different Battalion, and our division was moved into France. We were patrolling along near the front line. Usually we were a mile or so back, so we would be looking for stray Germans, or more often just making sure no-one tried to steal our supplies."

"Why would they do that, Grandad?"

"Well, see, some of these villages in the front line. Well, some of them had very little rations, and some had been pretty much wiped out by the enemy, so there were people, lots of people, living in awful conditions. Very little water, or food, and so anything they could steal they would. Couldn't blame them. We were meant to challenge them and shoot anyone we caught but we never shot any locals. Just shooed them away."

"Did you ever fight in the front line, Grandad?"

"No... No... I mean, I was never right up the front, if that's what you mean. But we used to go on patrols, just four or six of us at a time. Making sure there weren't any Germans or spies creeping along behind our lines. We were never meant to be right up front, although we were ready for it if we had to do it. But our battalion were more supporting the frontline infantry and the supplies. But I... well, we had a few close calls, but there was only one time I thought I was a goner."

The tape when quiet for a few seconds.

"What happened, Grandad?"

"Well... see, there were four of us. Me, Spotty... Spotty Coombs, his name was. You can guess why. And Len Harris. And Walter Manktelow. He was my mate. He was from Hallowfield. I knew his folks and we were at school together though he was younger than me. Yes, so me and Spotty, Harris and Walter... we were meant to be patrolling through this old village. Can't remember where it was... somewhere... northern France anyway. And this place, well it was a ruin in places, but there were still a few people living there in what's left of their homes. So, we're on this patrol and suddenly BANG BANG BANG all around us, so we ducked down, and then there was more BANG BANG BANG BANG – lots of gunfire. And it sounded like it was coming from different places. Well, we saw this old church which was pretty ruined – had no roof and half the wall was gone high up, but it was solid so we ran in there and dropped right down. There was a bit more gunfire. Well I tell you, I was really scared. We all were. Whoever it was was still firing. I thought the Germans were back in the village, you know. Well, then it went quiet so old Spotty Coombs just peeped over this window ledge and BANG BANG BANG they were off again. So he ducked, and then the wall on the opposite side of the church seemed to sort of explode in little bits. Of course, that was the bullets hitting it, so we knew where they were coming from. Anyway, Spotty and Harris, they went back to the window and quickly fired off a volley and the Germans fired straight back. Me and Walter, we went to another window, same side, and we fired a volley too. Then another one… and then Coombs and Harris fired, and then me and Walter. Then… silence. That was worse, that, because, you know, had we hit them, or were they just creeping closer and ready to send a grenade in? Anyway, we waited ages and when there was no more, we crept back out of the church and went straight back to our base, which was about a kilometre out of the village. We made our report and our CO said there were some rogue German snipers around but they'd either retreated or been shot. Well, later on another patrol went where we did and found two dead German snipers, just about a hundred yards from the church. So I reckon me or Walter got them. Probably us, because when Coombs and Harris had fired, they fired back. When we fired… well, nothing back. Anyway, they were only young lads, like us, probably younger. I was relieved to have survived that, but didn't really feel good about those Germans."

"Even though they'd have killed you?"

"Even though they'd have killed me. Because, you see, they weren't Hitler. They were just young lads, like me and Manktelow, and we'd killed them. And I had no fight with them, not really. But at the time, we didn't say that, of course. Wouldn't have dared, anyway. We just got on with things. Anyway, then… then Walter got it. One week later, we were out again, and there was another patrol to our left, and they got engaged with some German patrol not far off, and we took cover, and were just sitting there, and then suddenly Manktelow just sort of said "Oh!" and fell down, and he had a bullet right through his back and chest. Well, I lay him down, and stayed with him, talking to him though he was hardly hearing me. Harris went and got help and they came with a stretcher and took him away."

"What… was he dead, Grandad?"

"I went back later, and saw the CO and he told me, he was still alive when they got him to the field hospital, but he died soon after… [silence] yeah. So much for war… I'd known him since we were both little lads, and now he gets a bullet that could have been for me. He was right next to me. So… I don't think anything else happened of interest really. I wasn't in any of the big battles, didn't do hand to hand combat, didn't do anything heroic. But it was still war, what I did, and still dangerous."

"When did you go home?"

"Well, I was due some leave, soon after that all happened, so it was September '44, I think. And I asked to go home on leave, and when I was there they said they needed us back in England for more home support, so that was my adventures in France in the war. Sorry it's not much for your project, son. But that's how it was. And soon after VE Day, I was discharged, because I was never full militia, see, because I'd been in agriculture, so we were the first to be demobbed back to work on the farm.

205

Goldthorpe took me straight back. And I was very glad to be home, I can tell you. The nice thing about being on the farm was we were growing food, so of course we got plenty, we never went without."

"I bet your Mum was pleased to have you home."

"She was, although she was always moaning about the rationing, and all the hardships she'd been through, but that didn't mean anything to me, because I thought she'd had it easy compared to those poor French villagers. We had some real rows about it. But I remember one time... now son, here's something you might be interested in."

"What's that?"

"Well, I hadn't been home long and my Auntie Ath came to stay. Christmas '46 I think it was. Have you heard of Auntie Ath?"

"Can't say I have, Grandad."

"Well now, she was one heck of a lady. I loved her to bits, and she loved me too – she never had kids of her own so I was like a grandson to her. Well, she used to work on the railways, and you've heard of the big crash at Salmsham, haven't you?"

"Yes, quite a lot about it."

"Well, it was Auntie Ath's father, my mother's grandfather – he was the signalman who they blamed for the crash. But she told me that it was not his fault at all, and that she and her brother and her brother-in-law, they found out wh..."

At that moment, the voice stopped and there was a sudden whirring sound from the tape player.

"Oh no!" said Mark. "I don't believe it. The tape has snapped!"

"No!" said Alex. "This was starting to get really good."

"Oh well, that's that." Mark sighed, and switched off the tape player. "We won't hear the rest of that ever, will we?"

"Can't we fix it, Dad?" said Olivia. "I mean, it's all there, on the tape, isn't it? You just need to fix the tape and then it'll work again."

"I'm not sure…"

"Here…" said Alex, who had searched online. "You just need to use some splicing tape."

"Oh, I'll go and get some from the drawer in my office" said Mark sarcastically. "I mean, couldn't it have waited until we'd got to the end?"

"Right" said his wife. "That can be my project for next week, when you're at work, I'll sort it out. Leave it with me, I'll order some splicing tape. In the meantime, at least we have some interesting stuff for Alex's history work."

"True. I wonder who this Auntie Ath was, though. I must get your Mum to do a bit more digging for me."

"They're coming over for lunch tomorrow, Dear. Maybe you can ask her then?"

"I'll email her now, then maybe she'll have the chance to look it up tonight."

26

"It's lovely to see you, Clive... Sheila, kettle's on."

"We would have been here earlier, Mark, but you know what Sheila's like, and today she was worse than ever..."

"It's his fault, Darling... sending me all those questions last night – I was up half the night dredging up family histories of all these strange new people."

Clive and Sheila Bagley shed their overcoats and shoes in the porch. "I'll take those" said Mark, grabbing the coats and hanging them up on the coat hooks in the hallway.

"Hi Mum, Hi Dad!" Freya emerged from the kitchen wearing a flowery apron, and with a glass of white wine in one hand, which she put down on the key ledge before giving her parents a quick hug. "Come on through. The kids are laying the table. We're running a bit late as per usual; I had to dash out for supplies at the last minute."

"Don't worry, Dear," said her mother "your husband's had me up half the night tracing his family, which is why we're late too. Hallo Olivia, hallo Alexander!" Both children rushed to hug and kiss their grandmother. "I've got a little something for you each, but it'll have to wait until after lunch."

The family settled down for Sunday roast and simultaneous conversational catch-ups, interspersed with fair portions of wine. Once again Alex had a glass of red, which remained virtually untouched through the meal. Olivia, however, had managed two glasses, and was busy sipping from a postprandial third when the doorbell rang. "Oh crikey!" she spluttered "Jake's here already. Do you mind if I…?"

"Is this her boyfriend, Freya?" asked Sheila with glee. "Ask him to come in and meet us… Olivia! Bring him in here, Darling!"

"He's such a lovely boy, Mum." Freya said "and he's been helping Mark and Alex as well, with this railway mystery."

"I dunno how he puts up with her, though." chimed Alex. "She's horrible to him."

"That's enough, Alex" said his mother, as Jake came shyly into the room, followed by a smirking Olivia.

"This is Jake, everyone."

"Lovely to meet you Jake. What a handsome young man, Olivia. You make sure you keep a hold of him, Dear."

"Yes, Nana" Olivia blushed.

"Sorry Jake, I'm Sheila, and this is Clive. We're Freya's parents, but I expect you knew that"

"Very pleased to meet you both" said Jake, on his very best behaviour, shaking hands with Clive who had stood to greet him. "I gather you're the family historian…erm, Sheila?"

"That's right, Dear, and your father… Mark has had me working half the night to find out more about his folk from the railway at Salmsham. I've dug up quite a lot of interesting people, so to speak."

"Well, I'd love to know more as well. I've got rather into this railway accident thing. It's becoming quite a mystery, you know."

"Oh, GREAT!" Olivia rolled her eyes, turned and stormed out of the room. "Nice to see you Jacob..." her voice disappeared up the stairs. Alex suppressed a grin as his sister's door slammed.

"Erm... I'd better go and see if she's OK" Jake stammered. As he went out to follow Olivia, Sheila said. "What a nice young man. Now, Mark... I suppose you want to know what I've discovered so far..."

While Freya and her father cleared the table, Sheila pulled a stack of papers from a large buff-coloured envelope. "I thought the best thing was to work back and then come forward again, so having got back to your great great great grandfather, Mark, who was Joseph Palmer, I looked at each of his children and worked forwards again."

Sheila laid a couple of rough charts on the table. "Now this one here, this is Joseph Palmer's family. You see, he married Charlotte Ann Lovell in March 1851, and they had six children; James born 1851, Martha in 1853, Hubert in 1855, Agnes in 1856, Sarah in 1859 and Katharine in 1861. Martha is your great great grandmother, Mark. Charlotte died in 1881 so she would have been forty-nine – quite young. Now, as for the children; James never married. In fact, he died in 1874, so he would have been 23..."

"Hang on Nana. Did you say he died in 1874?" Alex perked up.

"Yes, Dear. Why?"

"That's the year of the Salmsham train crash. When did he die?"

"Well, I don't know the exact date, but… his death was registered in the second quarter of the year, so April, May or June, which means he could have died in March if they'd been a long time registering the death."

"The accident was 12th March, Nana. Maybe he died in that after all."

"No, he can't have done Son" said Mark. "He gave evidence at the inquest, remember?"

"So, when exactly did he die then?" Alex asked his Nana.

"I don't know, love. But I can order his death certificate if you like."

"Yes please, Sheila," said Mark "and any others we might need. I'll pay you back of course."

"OK, well there's no hurry. I'm rather enjoying this, even if it's quite not my own family. It's a fascinating business. Anyway, carrying on; Martha Palmer married William Whitmore, who is your ancestor. Hubert Palmer never married as far as I can tell, and he died in… 1913 aged fifty-eight, in Salisbury. Then you've got Agnes… this is sad. She never married either, she died aged twenty-three in 1879."

"OK, do you think can you get all their death certificates too?" asked Mark

"I can get them all, I think. Now, Sarah Palmer… I couldn't find her marriage at first, but eventually I found her marrying in 1899, so she was forty. She married James Athey, and as far as I know they had no children. Now she died in December 1946, aged eighty-seven…"

"Hang on, Nana. What was her husband's name again?"

"James Athey."

"Athey. Athey. That might be Auntie Ath, Dad" said Alex excitedly.

"Of course! We were looking for an Athena or someone" said Mark "and all the while it was her surname. I wonder why they did that."

Sheila smiled "Well, probably because there was another Sarah in the family. Sarah Whitmore, your great grandmother. Martha's daughter. She married Henry Phipps. It was quite normal for families to use other names for the older folk. She was probably called Sarah Palmer or Sarah P until she married, and then Auntie Athey shortened to Ath."

By this time, Freya and Clive had finished clearing the dishes and loading the dishwasher, and brought in tea and coffee which they'd made over a catch-up chat in the kitchen. Clive brought in a tray and laid out the mugs on the table, carefully avoiding the various sheets of paper his wife had produced. "Freya's just gone to get the young lovers down." He chuckled as Alex turned his nose up.

"Jake's OK. You can leave Livvy up there for all the help she is."

"Alex!" Mark glared at him. "Come on, let's find out more about this family of ours. Whereabouts had you got up to, Sheila?"

"Well, the last child was Katharine Palmer, and she got married in 1882 to Arthur Andrew Marriott…."

"Marriott!" cried Alex. "Arthur Marriott! He was the porter. The one who was helping out with the rescue. You know, he was cleaning the other platform or something when the crash happened."

"That's right" said Mark, leaning forward. "So… he ended up marrying young Katharine eh? Did they have any children, Sheila?"

"Yes, let's see…   Right, Arthur & Katharine Marriott had three children. James Andrew Marriott who married Sophie Ann Cooke, and they had a daughter Josephine who married Thomas Cooper. I didn't go any further than that. They also had a Martha Marriott who married Leonard Cherrington. The third child, Mary Ann, died aged twelve."

"Hang on, go back a second, Sheila. Did you say someone married a Cooper?"

"Yes Dear. Josephine Marriott – that's Arthur's granddaughter, married Thomas Cooper."

"That was Roger's name. The chap Alex and I met when we went to Salmsham. He was Roger Cooper. He said his ancestor was a porter on the railway when the accident happened. Good heavens!"

"Well, if he is related to Arthur Marriott, then he's also a cousin of yours."

"Well I never!" exclaimed Mark. "He'll be surprised at that one. I'm due to meet him for a pint next time we go over there."

"You were right then, Dad" said Alex, "everyone is related in the end. Except that means we're related to that Vicky person. It's bad enough having a sulky girl as a sister, now I've got one as a cousin as well."

Mark started shuffling through a couple of the charts his mother-in-law had found. "So, Sheila, can you do me a massive favour, and get all the birth, marriage and death certificates for all of this lot, do you think?"

"Darling, they're £9.25 each, you know"

"I know. I'll pay you back. It's just… well this has blown me away. There are so many names here that I recognise from the inquest and accident reports. Also… how can we work out what relation I am to this Roger Cooper chap?"

"Well, I'll have to do more research on that line. It could take me a long time. I tell you something else I haven't looked at yet, and that's the census returns. They did a census every ten years. That's a whole new area of research, but I could find them on the census, and that also tell us what they do for a living, and what their relationships are in the house. Also, where they live."

"Sheila, this is amazing. Would you mind doing all that for us?"

"Of course I wouldn't mind, Dear. It's my hobby, and I love doing it. And I rather like this little project or yours. It'll keep me out of mischief for a couple of weeks at least."

By now, Jake and Olivia had joined them at the table. "Guess what, Jake" said Alex. "We are not only related to that signalman, but also Arthur Marriott, the porter. I'm not sure what relation he is to us, but he's married the signalman's daughter, one of them."

"I'm sure there's a joke in there somewhere… she was only the signalman's daughter but… well I'll think of something." Jake smirked.

Olivia grimaced. "That was so lame, Jake. You're getting as bad as my brother."

Sheila had done a quick bit of calculating and plotting on one of the charts.

"Right, Alex dear, Arthur Marriott was your four times great uncle by marriage."

"Four times great uncle? What does that mean exactly?"

"Well, in the case of his wife, your four times great grandfather was her father, so she's your four times great aunt. Your great aunt is your grandmother's sister; your great great aunt is your great grandmothers."

"Nana, stop it! My head hurts!" said Alex with a grin. "How do you work all this out."

"It's quite easy. But I tell you what I'll do. I'll put all these names into my family history programme at home, and then print out a chart or two so you can see all the relationships."

"I've just thought, Dad. Katharine Palmer… she was the little girl of twelve they wouldn't believe at the inquest. She said she was going to see someone. I wonder if it was Arthur Marriott, because…"

"… he was not where he should have been." Mark interrupted. "That's a very good point, son. But she was only twelve, surely that's too young to think about meeting a boy of – how old would he have been at the time of the accident? – well, anyway, we might be reading too much into this"

"Twelve years old!" exclaimed Olivia. "That's gross! No way would she have been seeing a boy older than her like that."

"Well, she gave evidence at the inquest that she was meeting someone, and she refused to say who. Maybe it was Arthur, and she didn't want him to get into trouble." Mark frowned. "There's a lot of odd things about this case that don't add up, you know. And we haven't even got beyond the inquest yet. I still haven't read about the trial – Joseph's trial, where they sent him to prison."

"And then there's the tape, Dad." said Olivia. "There was all that stuff about the accident not being his fault, with the Auntie What's-her-name…"

"Auntie Ath… who we've found out was born Sarah Palmer. One of the signalman's daughters." Mark looked at the sheets of paper in front of him. He explained to his in-laws about the taped interview with Adam Phipps, and how the tape had broken yesterday. He'd ordered splicing tape online from a specialist dealer but would have to wait a couple of weeks for delivery.

"I must email Roger Cooper, tonight I think. He said something about a rumour in the family about some odd goings on. This is turning into a really convoluted mystery, isn't it?"

"Well, said Sheila "if you want me to trace his link to you, ask him for a few names and dates. Parents, full names, maiden name of mother, dates of birth, marriage… anything he can give you, because it speeds up the search. Cooper is quite a common name and so it's possible there may have been two or three families in the area."

"Will do, Sheila" said Mark. "And now, I think I need that coffee."

Alex turned to his grandfather, who was looking a little bored, staring at the carriage clock on the mantelpiece. "Grandad, you're good at engineering and things. Could you help me clean up this bolt I found at the railway station?"

Clive smiled. "Glad to be of assistance, young Alex." he said with the patronising tone of a man who was about five years behind in his assessment of his grandson's mental maturity. "Let's go and see what you've discovered, eh?"

27

From: mark@phippstribe.net
Sent: Sunday, April 22, 2018 10.32 PM
To: rcooper@rmcproperty.co.uk
Subject: Your railway ancestor

Hi Roger

Hope this finds you and your family well

My mother-in-law has done a lot of research for on our family, and found a connection to Arthur Marriott, the porter at Salmsham Station when the accident happened. His granddaughter married someone called Thomas Cooper. Is he any relation of yours? Arthur is my 4x Great Uncle as his wife was the daughter of the signalman Joseph Palmer who they blamed for the accident.

If it's OK with you, she's asked if you could tell us any names and dates of your parents / grandparents and so on, to see whether we are related. If you don't want to though I would understand.

We've been looking at all the inquest stuff from the newspapers. There's a lot of info to go through, and some of it is fairly gruesome, but we're trying to work out how they decided to blame Joseph Palmer when he doesn't seem to have done anything wrong! But we haven't read it all yet, there's about 60 pages of newspaper to read.

Dare I ask how the building developments are coming along?

Best Wishes

Mark

Tuesday afternoon

From: rcooper@rmcproperty.co.uk
Sent: Tuesday, April 24, 2018 1.19 PM
To: mark@phippstribe.net
Subject: RE: Your railway ancestor

Hi Mark, that's quite a coincidence. Thomas Cooper was my granddad, but he was killed in the 2nd world war so I never knew him but I did know my great granddad Cooper, his name was Henry, not the boxer haha, and he died when he was 93 and used to go on about the crash. He said his grandfather was something to do with it, he was always up to no good and someone got him for it. I rang my Dad and he is really interested in all this. He says he has an old suitcase stashed away in his loft with some old family letters, I think he got them from his granddad Henry.

In answer to your mother in law, I was born 29th November 1969, my Dad is James Cooper, he was born 1941, he married Barbara Andrews she was born in 1942. The Thomas you said is my Granddad he was born in 1919 and so was Josephine my grandmother. I never knew her she died in another train crash in 1967. That's a bit of a coincidence we thought but it was up in York. I think I'll keep away from trains, they haven't done us much good eh?!

The building stuff is going well, hoping to have the cottages on the market properly soon. You really must come along soon.

Roger

From: mark@phippstribe.net
Sent: Friday, April 27, 2018 5.57 PM
To: rcooper@rmcproperty.co.uk
Subject: RE: Your railway ancestor

Hi Roger

OK my mother in law confirms we are 4th cousins as we share 3xgt grandparents Joseph and Charlotte Palmer! This makes your daughter and my son 5th cousins.

I'm fascinated by your great granddad Henry saying his grandfather had something to do with it. I can't find a record of anyone Cooper connected with the accident at all. I've sent a copy of your email to my mother in law. If she replies her name is Sheila Bagley.

I've got a lot of other work going on at the moment but I'll be back in touch when I have something more.

Mark

From: sheilabagley@phonetalkinternet.com
Sent: Sunday, April 29, 2018 1.56 AM
To: mark@phippstribe.net
Subject: Cooper family

Dear Mark

Your cousin Roger has really hit the jackpot with his family. Without going into too much detail yet, it goes:

Roger Martin Cooper born November 1969 married Jacqueline Draper born 1970

His father: James Henry Cooper born July 1941 married Barbara Andrews born 1942

Grandfather: Thomas William Cooper born January 1919 married Josephine Marriott born August 1919

Gt.Grandfather: Henry Arthur Cooper born December 1896 married Sarah Cantor in 1917

Gt.Gt. Grandfather Thomas Henry Cooper born 1865 married Julia Dove born 1869

I haven't gone any further back yet. I've ordered loads of certificates as you asked!

I'm also going to start on the census searches soon. I hope you've got a spare filing cabinet for all this stuff dear!

Oh gosh look at the time! Clive will have me certified.

Love to all

Sheila x

Sunday morning

From: mark@phippstribe.net
Sent: Sunday, April 29, 2018 9.20 AM
To: sheilabagley@phonetalkinternet.com
Subject: RE: Cooper family

Sheila

That's amazing, thank you so much. I'll send a copy to Roger.

Can you do some research on Julia Dove? We have a Jack Dove who was one of the witnesses at the inquest, and he also rescued some people from the burning carriages.

I do hope you've had a big lie in today? Hopefully Clive's brought you breakfast in bed!

Love

Mark

PS Freya says she'll ring you later tonight as per usual

Sunday evening

From: sheilabagley@phonetalkinternet.com
Sent: Sunday, April 29, 2018 6.45 PM
To: mark@phippstribe.net
Subject: Julia Dove

Dear Mark

You have me more fascinated by the minute!

Julia Dove was born July 1869. I don't know who her parents were yet, but I've ordered her birth certificate. There was a marriage between a Jack Dove and Anne Draper in Salmsham in September 1866. There were some other births
Harriett Dove born Salmsham January 1867 so they had to get married, if it's the same ones
John Dove born Salmsham March 1871.
Anne Dove died Salmsham March 1871, so maybe she died giving birth?

There are no further children, so I'm going to start on the census returns and see who was living where in Salmsham.

I'll let you know when the certificates arrive.

Love to all

Sheila x

From: rcooper@rmcproperty.co.uk
Sent: Sunday, April 29, 2018 7.09 PM
To: mark@phippstribe.net
Subject: RE: Your railway ancestor

Hi Mark

Glad you found the connection. You can park in the family yard any time you like haha!

Thanks for sending all this over. I've sent the details to my Dad and he says it was all spot on, and there was stuff there he didn't know about. He's still looking for that suitcase of papers but his loft is almost impassable these days! Next time I'm over there I'll help him have a look; he's a bit frail these days.

Dad also told me a bit more about my great granddad who was the one who reckoned there was no good in the family. Apparently, his grandfather was Jack Dove and he used to beat his wife and kids, and one of his kids ended up in an asylum because he was brain damaged or something. Jack Dove disappeared in the end; everyone reckoned he'd run off but my granddad said someone had done him in! Sounds very interesting I must say.

Our lives are quite boring compared to them I think.

Roger

From: mark@phippstribe.net
Sent: Monday, April 30, 2018 7.36 AM
To: rcooper@rmcproperty.co.uk
Subject: RE: Your railway ancestor

Roger

Just a quick note to say "Wow!" – your revelation about Jack Dove ties in with info my mother-in-law just sent me last night. I'm actually on a train on the way up north on business today, but next weekend I'm definitely going to do some more research and try and tie things together. Maybe we should meet up sooner rather than summer hols as I originally planned.

My daughter has access to some newspaper records online and they've been pretty revealing about the inquest.

You're right about our lives compared to theirs – I don't recall doing in any of my family yet!

Best Wishes

Mark

28

Mark pulled the car into his driveway, glad to be home after a long and taxing week. He had been up exceptionally early on Monday morning to catch the train to Manchester, where he stayed for two nights before hopping onto another train for an overnight stay in Sheffield. After an early morning meeting on Thursday, he had returned to his employer's Reading office, and had stayed overnight with a colleague in Winnersh. Today saw three meetings, including one with senior management which went on for over an hour longer than planned. Mark had only had time to grab a sandwich for lunch, and he had got the distinct impression that it was way past its official sell-by date. He couldn't wait to get home and have a decent hot supper.

As he opened the front door her heard Freya's voice, talking on the phone. "Ah, here he is now Mum, I'll just pass you over."

He put his cases down, gesticulated and mouthed "What – give me a chance!" to his wife, but she was holding the receiver out to him.

"You talk to Mum, she's quite excited. I'll take your stuff. Go on, you'll enjoy this." She pecked him on the cheek and slipped the phone into his hand. With a sigh, he put it up to his ear.

"Hi Sheila, it's Mark. Listen, I've just got in…"

"Mark, Darling, you HAVE to hear this. The certificates have just arrived and… oh, well this is so exciting. James Palmer committed suicide, by poisoning himself, on the 7th April! It doesn't say why, it just says the certificate was issued by the coroner. Isn't this exciting?"

"Yes, OK, let me write this…"

"Oh, and Julia Dove's father was Jack Dove, and her mother was Anne Draper. And Anne Dove…Draper…died in childbirth when the boy was born."

"OK, go on…"

"Well, also I've got some of the census returns and it gives all the family details and where they all lived. It's ever so exciting. Agnes Palmer, she was a dairymaid at Jack Dove's farm. Now, Agnes died in her sleep in 1879…"

"Look, Sheila. This all sounds amazing, but I've literally just got in through the door."

"But I thought you'd want to know…"

"Yes, but I haven't even taken my coat and shoes off yet."

"Oh." Sheila sounded briefly crestfallen. "Well, look, I don't want to have to put it in an email, it would take me so long. Perhaps you could all come to ours for Sunday lunch? It would be so nice to have you round here for a change."

"That sounds great, Sheila. Listen, I'll pass you back to Freya, OK?"

Handing the phone back to Sheila with a certain amount of relief, Mark slipped his coat and shoes off, popped a pair of slippers on and went to the kitchen for a drink. He heard brief snatches of conversation and then Freya saying her goodbyes.

"Well?" he said, when she appeared in the kitchen beside him. "I gather we're going over on Sunday."

"No we're jolly well not, Mark." She said angrily. "I do wish you'd check with me before committing us to these things."

"I didn't…"

"We've got the Parkins coming over for Sunday lunch, remember?"

"Oh yes, sorry. Look, I didn't commit us. You know what your mother is like. She told me that's what we were doing, and then I handed her back to you."

"She's very excited. She's done a lot of work for you on this railway thing, you know."

"Yes I know. Look can we start again. Hello Dear, have you had a good week?"

"Yes, I have, as a matter of fact. I've got the splicing tape and I've started to try and sort the cassette out. There's only one problem…"

"Which is?"

"I had to cut some of the old tape away, as it was jammed in the machine."

"What?! Freya…"

"Don't worry Darling. I have kept every tiny little shred of it. If you happen to know any forensic scientists I'm sure they could put it all back together again. Meanwhile, I'm waiting for a spare couple of hours to do the difficult bit and splice it back together again – I don't want to have to cut any more of it."

Mark gave his wife a cuddle, and they just rested their heads on each other's shoulders in silence for a minute or so.

"Is that wine you've poured?" Freya said quietly.

"Nope. Ribena. Seriously." He chuckled. "I actually couldn't face another glass of wine, or cup of tea, or coffee. I've had too many meetings this week and too much of those vices."

Freya grinned. "Mmmm. Right, I tell you what I'll do now. I'll ring Mum back and tell her we can't get over this Sunday because we've got the Parkins' coming over, but how about we invite her and Dad over on Sunday the next weekend?"

"Sounds like a plan. It sounds as if she's got loads of info for us. Oh, and something about James Palmer committing suicide. That's a point; there'll be an inquest report, I'm sure. Is Livvy about?"

"Upstairs, with Jake."

"Brilliant. I'll go and disturb them then."

He smiled, slipped from his wife's clutches and made his way upstairs. Knocking gently on the door as he opened it, he found his daughter and boyfriend sitting up side by side on her bed watching a film. Olivia leapt up and gave her father a massive hug.

"Hi Daddy! Missed you loads! How was Manchester, or wherever you were?"

"Very Manchester-like. How's college been?"

"Oh, the usual grim place."

Jake paused the film and looked up from the bed. "Hi, Mr Phipps!"

"Please, Jake…call me Mark. Now, Livvy, a quick favour. Could you look up something in the newspaper library. We're looking for an inquest or a report for the suicide of James Palmer in April 1874. I can't remember the date except that it was less than a month after the crash. Your Nana got his death certificate."

"We'll get straight on it Dad."

"Thanks. I'm going to have a shower."

Twenty minutes later, the three of them were sitting on Olivia's bed, staring at a single sheet of A4 paper, with the old newspaper report on it.

Extract: The Hallowfield Courier,
Saturday 18th April 1874

SUICIDE OF RAILWAY CLERK

An inquest was held on Monday last at the Dukes Head, Salmsham, before William Hammond, Esq., and a respectable jury, on the body of James Palmer, aged 22, who was found dead in the churchyard of St. Mary's Church. Following a post mortem it was found that deceased had died from strychnine poisoning, and from the evidence adduced it was clear that this had been self-inflicted. A letter written by the deceased to his parents confirmed his intention to take his own life, and made reference to the pressure he was feeling having been accused of tampering with the signals after the dreadful railway accident last month. His mother and father had arrived home from an afternoon walk the previous Tuesday and had found the note in their home, which they shared with deceased. They immediately sent for help to search for the unfortunate man, and he was discovered not forty minutes later

> by Patrick Connor, a farm labourer
> who had joined the search. He was
> lying serenely on his back, with his
> arms across his chest, upon the
> grave of the two unidentified
> victims of the accident. Sergeant
> Michaels was then notified, and
> medical assistance was sent for. Dr.
> Melrose attended and confirmed
> that death had occurred within the
> previous hour. After a very short
> deliberation, the jury returned a
> verdict "That the deceased poisoned
> himself whilst in an unsound state
> of mind."

"Wow." said Jake, quietly. "I wonder how they knew he was in an unsound state of mind then?"

"Oh, that was a typical verdict in those days." Mark replied. "It meant that he could still be buried in the churchyard. If he was of sound mind, then he couldn't be, because being a suicide meant the church could refuse him. Personally, I think he really was in an unsound state of mind. If he knew he wasn't guilty then logically he had nothing to worry about. Unless they were framing him, of course. Poor lad."

"Who was he again, Dad?"

"The signalman's son. The one who Jack Dove accused of being up the signal after the accident had happened. This Jack Dove was, by all accounts, a nasty piece of work. I've been talking to Roger Cooper. His Great Grandfather told him Jack Dove was his grandfather, and had something more to do with the accident, and that people found out and did him in."

"Wow, Dad. This sounds more weird by the minute. That must be what that tape is all about."

Mark nodded. "I'm off for supper now, guys. Are you joining us?"

The two youngsters said they would be down in a minute or so, and ten minutes later, they were all sat around the dining table, with a large dish of pasta bake to share. Alex was the only one absent, having gone away for the weekend on a Duke of Edinburgh practise hike 'somewhere in Wales'. The main discussion was, of course, the suicide and accident.

"What I can't understand, Dad, is… why would anyone want to accuse this James guy of doing what he did to the signal?"

"Good question. I can't fathom it out." Mark said. "I mean, if he genuinely did fiddle with the signal lamp, that would mean he was trying to cover up for his Dad. But by all accounts, from what I've seen so far, the signalman actually did his job by the book. So, unless Joseph Palmer was so incompetent that he changed his signals to 'off' behind the goods train, it seems he can't have caused the accident. So why would his son cover up for him. It's getting very curious, this."

"Maybe," piped in Jake "the driver and fireman of the express train were mistaken. I mean, go was a white light, wasn't it? So what if they saw a streetlight or something?"

"Good thought, Jake…except they didn't have street lights then. The countryside was very dark. They would have had no problem picking out a red or a white light as it would have been the only thing they could see."

"So what, then?" said Olivia. "Are you suggesting that someone sabotaged the signals to cause a crash?"

"Could be."

"But why would anyone want to do that. That's like psycho country that. I mean, all those people killed. He must have been a motive."

"Who is 'he'?"

"This psycho. I mean, this Dove guy?"

"Well there's no evidence that he had any hand in this. And anyway, I'm sure all these things would have been considered at the time. I tell you what though; I'd like to have a look at the conclusions from the Board of Trade enquiry. For some reason I've got the first couple of pages but the last page is missing. I'm not even sure I ever had it. I think I only ordered a copy of the evidence. Maybe we should have another search online after we've finished supper."

"I'll do that, Mr… Mark" said Jake. "I can go onto The Railways Archive – they have lots of old accident reports on there, and you can download the whole report, if it's on there."

"I thought we were watching that film?" Olivia crossed her arms sulkily.

"Yeah… OK, when the film's finished."

"And then you're going home."

"Yeah, OK. Well, it'll only take a minute or so."

The next few minutes passed in relative silence, until Freya asked the two youngsters how college had been going. Mark tuned out of the conversation, and was busy trying to work out what on earth had actually happened that dreadful Thursday in 1874. He wished he had more data to hand, to try and work out what all the undercurrents were. Why would Jack Dove accuse James Palmer of tampering with the signals? What was in it for Dove? Why wasn't he satisfied with the glory and commendations he received for his heroic rescue work? Had he got a grudge against the Palmer family? What was this about Dove and one of the Palmer girls? Mark stared at the wall behind his wife's head for a few minutes. Then suddenly he felt very tired.

"Would you mind terribly if I go off to bed, Darling? I feel absolutely wiped."

"Of course. We'll do the dishes and things." Freya replied, and then promptly carried on gossiping with the youngsters.

Mark's head hit the pillow, his last thought being "what was in it for Jack Dove", then he slept soundly for ten solid hours.

29

Saturday 5th May 2018 - Milnefield

Sheila Bagley rang her daughter's doorbell excitedly, having driven over from her home just outside Chippenham, via Bath, where she had dropped her husband Clive off at an old school friends' reunion. She had freely admitted she had no interest in attending with him – which was just as well, as Clive had acidly pointed out that wives were not invited anyway.

"Hallo, Darling! I thought I'd just pop round…"

"Mum! I thought… how lovely, come on in! I thought we'd agreed you'd be over next weekend!"

Sheila put down the large 'bag for life' she was carrying, hugged her daughter, and kicked her shoes off in the porch. "I realised this morning that we can't come next weekend, because we're away in London with Jess and the children, but anyway, I had to drop your Dad off in Bath, and I thought I'd just carry on to here."

"Well, you took a chance. We might have been out!"

"No you wouldn't. You told me last night… a quiet day in, then friends round on Sunday. Well, I'm here to make your day less quiet, but in return, I'll help you get ready for your guests."

"Oh, Mum, you're a nightmare. But a wonderful one. I'm afraid I'm the only one up… Mark's shattered, and Livvy… well, she's a typical teen."

"Well, I've got all these things to show you all." Sheila picked up the bag, which was crammed full of documents, and took it into the dining room. "We'll use the table for now, Darling, and then I'll cook you all some dinner."

An hour later, Mark sat sifting through the various birth, marriage and death certificates which his mother-in-law had produced. He picked out the death certificate for James Palmer, and stared at it for a while, wondering why he'd decided to take his own life having protested his innocence of any wrongdoing at the inquest. Was it a sign of guilt, or had something, or someone, pushed him over the edge?

"Now Mark, I haven't got the one for Julia Dove yet, but as soon as that comes through, I'll let you know."

"Thanks, Sheila. I have to say, you're my best mother-in-law, I don't care what the others say."

Sheila grinned – she was used to his gentle teasing. He had once introduced her to a couple of workmates as his 'first' mother-in-law, much to her momentary concern. On that occasion, Freya had leapt instantly to her mother's defence, pointing out that there was unlikely to be a second mother-in-law as no-one else would take him.

"Actually," Mark said, thinking out loud, "how common was it for men to remarry if their wives died in childbirth, or when they were still quite young?"

"Well, it was pretty common, certainly. Don't forget, in those days, the man was usually the breadwinner, and the woman brought up the children. If the woman died, the man had to either

234

employ someone to bring up the children, or marry someone who was happy to be a stepmother to them. Some men even married the maidservant. It may not have been for love, who knows, but for practical purposes, but I expect it was better than the alternative."

"Urgh, that's gross, Nana!" said Olivia, who had sauntered in, still in her pyjamas. "You wouldn't catch me marrying some old man just to look after his ghastly little brats."

"Perhaps not in 2018, Dear, but in 1870 you might have had no choice. And what's more, you might have welcomed the chance. You also wouldn't have known any different. You would have been expected to be getting married otherwise people would think there was something wrong with you. You would probably have felt you wanted to be married, otherwise you'd live a poor life."

"Yeah, but that's just so awful, Nana."

"Also, you would be living in a small village, probably never travelling further than the next village, if as far as that. Then, all the boys of your age you would have known since they were babies. You probably knew too much about them to want to marry one."

"True. I mean, look at Alex and that Ellie Parkin. He really fancies her, I know he does, but she isn't the slightest bit interested in him."

"You don't know that, Livvy," said Freya, "she probably just doesn't realise... and anyway, Alex doesn't fancy her. I thought he was supposed to be seeing someone called Hazel, not that we've ever met her."

"I don't think he's actually seeing Hazel. I think SHE thinks he is – she's a bit schizo. He really does fancy Ellie, Mum. I text her quite a lot, remember. She thinks he's being creepy. He's getting all deep and everything. It's disgusting, she's only a few weeks older than him."

"Then it's just as well he's not home until late tomorrow, isn't it, seeing as her family are coming to lunch." Freya got up and started clearing the scattered breakfast things from the edges of table, where they had been carefully placed to avoid disturbing the ever-expanding pile of genealogical documents.

"How much do I owe you for these, Sheila?" asked Mark. "I don't want you out of pocket."

"Well, there's nearly £300 pounds worth there, Mark, but it's all on my credit card so you don't have to pay me back yet."

"No, I'll do it later. Let me have your bank details, and I'll do it online. There's bound to be more, of course, but that's not a problem."

"Dad! £300! For that lot? You're completely mad!" Olivia shook her head.

"Ahhh, the joys of youth. Everything comes to you for nothing – your education, your healthcare, your dentistry, your food, your transport. Wait till you know how much everything really costs, and then complain to me about how I spend my well-earned money, my favourite first-born daughter."

"Yeah, until I go to uni, Dad. That's not free, is it?"

"No, true, but you're still at school, and I don't see any bills coming in for that."

"Should've sent me to some posh public school then, Dad. I reckon I'm worth it."

"Of course you are. But this way, I get to keep you at home under lock and key so you can do more research for me. Oh, and by the way, if I wanted to become a member of your newspaper library, it would cost me £79 a year. You're getting it for free via your school. Remember all this stuff, Livvy."

"Still, £300 for a few bits of paper Dad…"

"Well, have you any idea how much this household costs to run? With the bills, the mortgage, the council tax, the food, the heating, water… all of those things?"

"Oh, here we go. I don't know, a thousand a month?"

"More like two and a half thousand a month. And that's before you add in the cars, saving for holidays, and all of that stuff."

"That's crazy, Dad!"

"Yep. You're right, I should start charging you rent."

"How would I pay it though?"

"Ahhhhhh, now she realises the problem. How indeed? Tell you what, I'll let you live here free of charge until after you return from uni… and you can stop telling me how to spend my pocket money? Deal?"

Olivia grinned. "Maybe? But I reserve the right to be a stroppy teen and tell you how wrong you are about everything."

"Would you do anything else?" Mark smiled and hugged his daughter. "Now go and get showered and dressed up properly for your Nana."

The family banter continued through the afternoon, before Sheila decided it was time to get back home.

"But not before I help you get everything ready for tomorrow, Freya darling."

"It's fine Mum. I've got plenty of help here. Thanks for bringing all that stuff over. Mark's going to have lots of fun filing it all, and Alex will be delighted when he gets home tomorrow."

Later that evening, Mark sat at his desk, once again sifting through the certificates. He stopped at a green certificate, and scanned the details.

'1882. Married solemnized at the Parish Church in the Parish of Salmsham in the County of Somerset. 14th October, between

Arthur Andrew Marriott, aged 25, bachelor, Railway Porter, residence – Salmsham, father's name Thomas Marriott, deceased,

Katharine Mary Palmer, aged 21, spinster, Dairywoman, residence - Salmsham, father's name Joseph Palmer, Groundsman'

"Groundsman?" thought Mark. "Whereabouts, I wonder?"

He made a note to ask Sheila if she could find out any more about Joseph after he had been released from prison. He looked at the names of the witnesses: Joseph Palmer, Elizabeth Marriott. A nice touch. Joseph was still living locally then, and was still the patriarch of the family. He didn't know Elizabeth Marriott; perhaps a sister? The information on the Marriotts had not yet come through, but never mind.

He had a quick think, and then found Joseph Palmer's death certificate. His residence was given as Hallowfield Manor, and his occupation as Groundsman. Cause of Death, Morbus Cordis, certified. Informant, Sarah Palmer, present at the death. A quick online search for morbus cordis told him it was contemporary term for heart disease. He wondered how much of it had been brought on by the stress of the last nine years of Joseph's life, since the moment of the crash.

He looked for any other marriage certificates relating to the Palmer children, but found only two more. The eldest daughter, Martha, had married William Whitmore in 1872 – Joseph was noted at "Railway Signalman". By the time Sarah Palmer (spinster – Railway Station Clerk) had married James Athey (bachelor – Farm Labourer) both her parents were long dead. He wondered about Sarah – she was one of several people who were keys to the whole mystery, but what was she actually like? Why had she left it so late to marry?

This whole mystery was beginning to take over his every waking moment. He dashed off a quick email to Sheila, thanking her for coming over with all the certificates, and asking her if she could find more about Joseph Palmer, perhaps from a census.

He also resolved to start work on modelling the railway station, as it was in 1874. Then, he could perhaps try to work out exactly what happened, and who was where. Thinking about where he was going to make this model, he realised that he'd need to use a smaller gauge than 'OO' otherwise he wouldn't be able to fit the whole station and yard into the loft. He did some more searching online, and after about half an hour he had decided to use 'N' gauge track, as he could model a mile of track in about ten metres. By the time he had shut down the PC, he had ordered a bulk pack of thirty yards of 'N' gauge track, assorted rail joiners, and a catalogue.

As he drifted off to sleep that night, he wondered how he was going to broach the subject of the model with Freya. After all, they had a nice big garden...

30

Thursday 12ᵗʰ June 1913 - Salisbury

The motorman shut down the power, took out the key which he had used to shunt the empty train into the carriage sidings, and stepped out of the driver's cab. Then he saw her, and stopped in his tracks. He hadn't expected to see her quite so soon.

"Oh… you're here. I wasn't sure if you were serious or not… about coming down, I mean." He stood awkwardly on the narrow platform alongside the electric multiple unit, which he had just emerged from. He felt strangely unsettled. There was something remote about her - she looked straight at him, without a hint of her usual smile.

"I just wanted to say that, I know." She looked at him with not a hint of emotion about her.

"Know? Know what?"

"I know everything."

"You know everything? About what? This doesn't make sense."

"Oh, I'm sure it does. I mean, I *know*. I know what happened, all those years ago. I know what you did and how you did it."

"If… if you think you know what happened, why are you telling me? Why don't you report me?"

"Because they probably won't believe me."

"Oh, you're right there. I *know* they won't. I think you'll find I'd get off scot free."

"Yes. You will. I know you will, you already have. That's why there's no point in reporting you. I've come to tell you; you've got away with it."

"I know that."

"No need to be looking over your shoulder."

"I know that too. Not that I ever was."

"I'm the only one who knows what happened"

"I know."

"So, no more secrets. I don't have the will to report you, or to fight you in the courtroom. No-one will ever believe me. It's all too fantastic for words"

He smiled thinly at her. "I'm glad you see it that way, at last."

"I do."

His smile widened and he relaxed, and started walking towards the end of the platform.

"Can we be friends again, then?" he asked.

"Of course. We always were, weren't we?"

"I'll see you later on then. We could… celebrate this. Put it behind us."

"My thoughts too." They had reached the slope of the platform, and began to cross over the sidings, heading to the canteen and staff changing room.

"Mind the live rail." He smiled again.

She nodded. "Later, then?"

"Later."

Twenty minutes later, his body was found lying beside one of the tracks, apparently electrocuted. He had inexplicably crossed the sidings away from the wooden foot crossing provided for train crews. As the person who found his body and raised the alarm, she gave her evidence at the inquest on the following morning.

31

"Dad, I can't find a report anywhere of Joseph Palmer's evidence. I think we must have missed a file or something. I can't work out why they thought he was guilty or anything." Alex Phipps was pleased to have his father home again, having been away the previous weekend. Despite spending the previous weekend tramping around the Mendips as part of his Duke of Edinburgh training weekend, he had not stopped thinking and talking about the Salmsham disaster, to the point where his five team-mates had avoided conversing with him unless there was a critical need.

Mark was sitting opposite his wife at the breakfast table, a piping hot mug of tea beside his cereal bowl, rubbing his eyes when his son came downstairs. He was still feeling pretty tired from yet another long week away, this time in Norfolk.

"Oh, you mean, the signalman. Right. I tell you where it is, though. It'll be summarised in the accident report in my file."

"Oh yeah, of course. I'll just go and get it."

Alex returned with the folder, and sat down at the table, shuffling through various sheets of paper before pulling the old photocopied report out.

"Don't you want some breakfast, Alex?" asked Freya. "There's cereal, or I'll do you some eggs?"

"Ah, scrambled egg please, Mum." Alex continued to scan the report. "Here it is... *Joseph*

Palmer (sworn). I am the signalman at Salmsham. I share this duty with another man, Albert Jobbins. I have worked for the company for 26 years, and as a signalman for the last 21 years. I have been based at Salmsham for 14 years. I was on duty from 8 o'clock in the morning until 8 o'clock in the evening. The 4.50pm express train is due to pass through Salmsham at 7.41pm. The 2.10 goods from Salisbury is scheduled to pass at 7.03 but it is often late. It is usually shunted at Hallowfield to allow the express to pass, which is correct by the rulebook. If it is too late it is shunted at Salmsham. The decision is made after signalmen on either side confer by telegraph. At about 7.15 the lad Stopps came into my box and said that the line to the west of the station was blocked by some cows and I was to stop all traffic until further instructions. I was offered the goods at 7.17 from Belcote Crossing, and I accepted it immediately. I left my signals on as I intended to shunt the goods at Salmsham. When the goods was near my home signal the driver whistled for me to take the signal off. He was going very slowly, so I pulled it off and I showed my green flag. When he got level with the 'box I shouted to the driver that he was to be shunted. I kept my starter signal on. I returned the home signal to 'on' as soon as the goods had stopped. This was about 7.29. A minute or so later the guard of the goods train who I knew slightly came into the box to sign the register which he did at 7.36. I showed him the levers which were all on for the down line and told him he may as well wait until the shunter came to the box. After this I never touched any down line levers at all. My son James Palmer came into the box and said he was in charge of shunting the goods. He confirmed the line was still blocked and I advised him to wait in the box until we were given the all clear. I thought it would save time to have all the key people in the box so when the line clear was given we would all receive it at the same time. I did not realise that my son had not been told to come to the box. We did briefly discuss a family situation between my daughter and a man who was pursuing her. That's Jack Dove and… Agnes, isn't it Dad?"

"Yes, this Dove character is popping up everywhere, isn't he?"

Freya put the plate of scrambled eggs on toast down in front of her son, and another mug of tea. "Right, put that down and eat up otherwise it'll get cold. Come on."

Mark took the report from Alex, who pointed to where he'd got to. "OK, here we are… *family situation… pursuing her…*right. *I was not in any way distracted from my duties. I was offered the down express at 7.37 and accepted it at once, but kept my signals on. It is not against regulations to accept the train provided I keep my signals on. We try not to stop the express but in the circumstances I had no option. The train should have pulled up at the home signal which is by the Hill Farm Bridge, about 200 yards from my box. I can see the signal arm from my box and I can usually see the glow of the backlight from my box, but it was a rainy night and the light was not visible. I assumed it was still on, but as there was light rain and a slight breeze I was not alarmed at not being able to see the light all the time. I was about to suggest that James should go and find out what was happening with the line clearance as I was having to delay the express. At that moment we heard a long train whistle and I realised the express was not stopping. It appeared to be steaming ahead straight into the goods train. I did not have time to react. It is difficult to judge the speed of a train from my window due to the curvature of the line. I can only see the train from about 200 yards away. There was no time for me to grab a flag. After the collision there was a strange thumping sound and a flash and then the front of the express was covered in a sheet of flame. I immediately sent 5 bells to Belcote and I remember seeing the carriages still moving while I was doing this. I sent 5 bells to Belcote, and then to Hallow Hill. I remember telling the*

245

goods guard to protect the down line back to Belcote, and I gave him some detonators from the stores. I was about to send James to protect the up line when the driver of the goods came into the box and asked me what had happened. I showed him my levers and he told me he had already sent his fireman to protect the up line. I told my son to go and get Mr Kemp and he went off. As far as I knew at the time, he found Mr Kemp because a few moments later Mr Kemp came to the signalbox. He also had with him the fireman of the express who looked badly hurt in the arm and head. He told me he saw two white signals all the way in. I showed him my levers and said they had been on all the time but he swore that it was impossible. I stayed in the signalbox to help signal the rescue trains in until Jobbins relieved me. He was late because he had stopped to help an injured lady on the platform. I think it was about 8.14 when he officially relieved me. I stayed in the box for a bit longer and then went and saw Mr Kemp who told me I should talk to Police Sergeant Michaels. I gave Sgt. Michaels a brief statement and was then told I could go. I was very shocked and upset by what had happened but I am certain that at no time did I pull my signals off after the goods train had passed.* So that was it then. He seems to have done everything correctly."

"So why did they send him to prison, Dad?"

"That's what I can't understand. We need to see the court case records. Perhaps they're in the newspapers too? Oh, hang on. Here is the PDF of the full report. Jake founded it and printed it off for us. Here we are; this is the conclusion to the report:"

[Extracts from the Report into the collision at Salmsham Railway Station on 12th March 1874]

<u>Conclusion</u>
The circumstances connected with this collision appear at first to be the subject of much confusion, due to the

clearly conflicting evidence of the signalman, the shunter, and the guard of the goods train, all of whom were present at various times in the signalbox; and the evidence of the express train fireman, and two lineside witnesses, one, a farm worker, and the other, a man walking on the path alongside the line as it approaches Salmsham Station.

To understand the reason for the collision, it is first necessary to select the principal facts, and arrange them in their proper order. [... ...]

The undisputed facts are as follows: Just after 5 to 7 o'clock in the evening, Mr Jack Clode, a farm worker, came to Salmsham Station and informed the stationmaster, Mr Kemp, that some cows had escaped from the farm onto the line west of the station. Mr Kemp immediately sent his porter, Marriott, and ganger, Strong, back with Clode to check and see whether the line was blocked. Marriott returned soon afterwards to confirm this, and Mr Kemp sent his other porter, Stopps, to the signalbox to inform the signalman, Joseph Palmer. Palmer then telegraphed signalman Anderton at Hallow Hill to advise of the blockage. Both men's registers agree that this signal was sent at 7.16 p.m. One minute later, signalman Wingate at Belcote Crossing offered the 2.10 goods train to Salmsham, which was accepted by Palmer. At 7.21 p.m. the goods train passed Belcote Crossing and entered the Salmsham section; both signalbox registers agree to the times.

Because of the blockage on the line, Mr Kemp and signalman Palmer agree to shunt the goods train at Salmsham, and a message was sent to Hallowfield to this effect. The Salmsham distant signal was kept 'on' and the goods train slowed almost to a stop at the home signal. As they approached the home, driver Chappell of the goods train whistled, and Palmer put his home signal to 'off' to allow the goods to creep forward.

From this point onwards some of the evidence appears to be conflicting. Palmer states that he shouted to the goods driver that he was being shunted, and then he replaced the home signal to 'on'. The goods guard, Wiggins, says that when his van passed the home signal it was still showing white for all clear; this would have been at least a minute later. This means that Palmer did not immediately replace the home signal to 'on'. In view of the conflicting evidence there is a possibility that he mistakenly moved the distant signal lever to 'off' instead. The distant signal is interlocked with the home and starter signals, however, and so to do this the starter would also have needed to be 'off'. There is also a repeater in the signalbox which would have drawn Palmer's attention to the position of the distant, had he been attentive, however had he pulled the lever thinking it was the home signal, he would not have been checking the repeater. However, Driver Chappell and Fireman Lusby both state that the starter signal was at red when they approached it in the station. At this point, therefore, I don't believe it is possible for Palmer to have accidentally moved the distant lever to 'off' as the interlocking would have prevented this.

The goods train was now stopped at the station platform, and the time was around 7.21 p.m. The fireman went to the guard's van to send the guard to the signalbox as the line was blocked. Guard Wiggins then went to the signalbox and signed the register at 7.36 p.m., claiming that he saw the signal levers 'on'. He remained in the box to await further instructions, as he was expecting the signalman to be aware of when the line was free. At 7.37 p.m. signalman Wingate at Belcote Crossing offered the 4.50 express, which Palmer accepted. Comments were made by the inquest jurors that Palmer was wrong to have accepted the express train when there was another train standing at the station, however he was perfectly entitled to do this under the Absolute Block method of working the line. In fact, had he not done so the potential delays to following traffic would have been further increased. The proviso is that the express would be accepted but would be stopped at the home signal.

It is at this point that the evidence becomes more conflicting. James Palmer, the station clerk and designated shunter (and son of the signalman), came into the signalbox to ask for instructions. Both he, and Joseph Palmer, and the guard Wiggins, agree that there was a conversation of a personal nature between Joseph and his son which may have caused the signalman to neglect his signals at a critical time. Shortly after this time, ganger Strong and the farm hand Maltby came to the station and informed Mr Kemp that the line was now clear. It was now 7.40 p.m. and there should still have been time to shunt the goods out of the way with only a little delay to the express, had Mr Kemp been able to find James Palmer, who had gone to the signalbox of his own volition. I believe Mr Kemp should have taken control of the shunting at this point, however he appears to have been busy trying to trace both Palmer and his other porter Marriott, who was by now cleaning the waiting room on the up platform. Because of this, the shunting was never commenced. Despite this inefficient situation, which would cause inevitable delay to the express train, nonetheless the express should have been perfectly safe had the signals been shown correctly against it.

The fireman of the express train, Thomas Jobson, says his driver, Harold Pickford, quite clearly saw the distant signal and said it was clear. Jobson then looked out for the Salmsham home signal and, despite some visibility problems due to the rain, and some smoke from the engine, he was able to see it clearly showing 'clear' as they approached Salmsham. The rear guard, Bartholomew

Mewes, was concussed in the collision and only remembered seeing the distant signal, which he stated was white, however he was unable to recall seeing the home signal and remembers nothing of the accident itself. Had Fireman Jobson not survived the terrible collision, albeit with serious injuries, I would most likely have been drawn to conclude that the engine crew simply and inexplicably missed 'red' signals, causing the collision, however an independent witness, Jesse Smith, a farm worker who was on his way to the Dukes Head from Hill Farm, states he clearly saw the home signal showing a white light and the arm down at an angle, showing all clear. Moreover, Charles Archibald, a stonemason, was walking on the path alongside the line, about halfway between Belcote Crossing and Salmsham Station, moments before the collision, and he states very clearly that the distant signal was showing 'white' as the express train passed it, and it was never returned to 'red' until after he had passed it. Soon after this he heard the sound of the collision and ran to Salmsham to render assistance.

However, the question remains; how could the distant signal be pulled 'off' if the starter signal was 'on'? Here is where I believe the local regulations may have caused a certain unintended outcome, for the rule about shunting at Salmsham reads as follows: "Where it is necessary for a train to draw forward for shunting purposes, the shunter must first obtain clearance from the signalman. Once this clearance has been obtained, the starter signal may be pulled 'off' but the train must not move unless under the direct guidance of the shunter, using flag signals or lights." This instruction carries the flaw that the interlocking for the distant signal becomes ineffective should the home signal also be pulled 'off' – a circumstance which I believe happened in this instance, for I believe that during the course of their conversation, the signalman pulled the starter signal 'off' and thereby informally handed control of the shunting to the shunter. In his defence, Joseph Palmer states that he had no reason to pull 'off' the starter as he was not aware that the line was now clear, but I feel that he may have acted inadvertently due to being distracted, and that he was now left with all three signals showing 'all clear'.

The conflict in the evidence is very clear. The express train crew claim they saw 'white' signals, and the signalman, shunter and goods guard claim they saw the levers in the box pushed forward to 'on'. One or other of these views is at the very least mistaken, at the worst unreliable and patently untrue.

There is a third possibility, which is that the signals were tampered with deliberately as an act of sabotage. I have investigated this, but conclude that this is highly improbable for the following reasons: Firstly, this would have required two signals to have been changed at the same time, and then changed back so as to hide the sabotage. Secondly, this would have required more than one person, thirdly, the persons involved would need a technical knowledge of the workings of the signal, and finally, there appears to be no motive or evidence for such an act. I have been forced to conclude that there was no sabotage.

There was, however, evidence presented at the inquest which places James Palmer at the top of the home signal in the minutes following the collision. He denied this, and the evidence is uncorroborated, however it is my sad duty to report that not long after the inquest, James Palmer took his own life. I can only conclude that he may well have been attempting to change the physical evidence to protect his father, the signalman, although there was no evidence found on the signal itself. James Palmer's movements after the accident were difficult to verify. Having been sent by the signalman to find Mr Kemp, he failed to find him and stated that he went straight home claiming to be in deep shock. Following the outcome of the coroner's inquest, which I attended, and where the jury concluded that Joseph Palmer should be charged with manslaughter, I am reluctantly forced to conclude that Palmer unwittingly placed his signals to 'off' when he intended them to be 'on', probably because he was distracted at a critical time by the shunter and goods guard, neither of whom should have stayed in the signalbox longer than was necessary to carry out their duties.

I believe the regulation concerning the use of the starter signal during shunting operations is flawed, and should be amended so that the starter remains 'on' during the shunt. The Directors may wish to consider the provision of a small shunting signal on the post below the starter, which would not be interlocked with the distant signal.

I am, &c.,

The Secretary
(Railway Department)
Board of Trade

F.L.Whey,
K.C.B.Lieut.Col. R.E.

32

Mark finished reading the report. "Well, that was a heck of a lot of waffle, wasn't it? I can't square the evidence given in the report with his conclusion – I mean, how on earth can he just choose from one conflicting report to another? Seriously. Everything points to sabotage, but he just dismisses it out of hand, as if it's just not possible."

"Dad, I don't get the bit about the distant signal and the interlocking. I mean, either the starter was 'on' or 'off', but assuming it was 'on', how could the distant have been pulled off anyway?"

"Exactly. This smacks of a cover up. It's almost as if someone's got to this… Sir Francis Whey. He's done all this investigating and then… well, he may as well have tossed a coin." Mark slammed the report down on the table, and sighed deeply.

Freya looked at her husband. "This is getting to you isn't it, Dear? Remember, this all happened years and years ago. It's all in the past. You can't change it, so why are you getting so worked up?"

"Because my poor ancestor got stitched up, that's why. I'd like to get a time machine and go back and shake Sir Francis Whey by the collar and ask him what on earth he was playing at!"

There was an uneasy silence at the breakfast table. Alex was not sure how angry his father had become, and didn't want to make him any worse. He pushed his empty breakfast plate away, and took a swig of tea, taking his time over it so as to excuse himself from having to speak.

Mark suddenly sighed "Ah, I don't know. You're right – I'm letting this get to me. Now, I really want to know what happened. I'd love to find the truth, and publish it to the whole world. Joseph Palmer was innocent. Joseph Palmer was stitched up by… the Board of Trade, the London and Western Railway, the Coroner's Jury, the villagefolk. Everyone."

"Not to mention our friend Jack Dove." Freya added. "I'd like to know more about him, and where he came from, what he did. There's something odd about this whole thing, and I think he holds the key."

Alex picked up the report again.

"Dad, what if the starter was showing 'all clear' after all. Would it have been possible for Joseph to pull all his signals off thinking they were on?"

"Well, he'd have had to have been really out of it, wouldn't he? I mean, you pull the signals 'off', which requires effort. When the signal levers are back away from you, they're 'on'. I'm sure even a tired and possibly distracted signalman couldn't make that big an error. And the other two people in the box corroborated it."

After another short pause, Freya piped up. "So what you're saying is, this Sir Francis Whatsisname has got conflicting evidence, with some doubt on both sides, but he's chosen a side so he can conclude the enquiry?" She was starting to get her head around the details now, and was as perplexed as the other two.

"So it would seem, Darling. OK, we must find that court case. Alex, can you check whether any of those files has anything about it again?"

"Yep. When I'm back from swimming."

"Yep, OK. Meantime, I'll get onto my Dad and see if he's found any of his papers yet."

A half an hour later, Mark was on the phone to his father, having given him a quick summary of their discoveries so far.

"I'm not sure I'll be much help, Marcus" said John Phipps down a somewhat crackly phone line. "I know I've got an old briefcase somewhere with some old letters in it, but I haven't looked in them since '93 when your Grandad died. Not even sure I looked at them much then; I just filed them in a brief case in the loft."

"Can you find the case, Dad?" asked Mark. "I tell you, we've got ourselves a real mystery here, and I know we were always told that our ancestor was wrongly blamed for the crash, but I reckon I can actually prove that he was. I've got Alex and Livvy getting stuff of the internet from old newspapers and things… it just doesn't quite make sense yet."

"Okay well, I'll go and have a look now, and call you back as soon as I find anything."

Mark put the office phone back on its charger, and went downstairs to make himself a coffee. He found Freya sitting at the dining room table trying to repair the cassette tape. "How's it going, Darling?"

"Hmmmmm," she muttered "well, it's going… to drive me round the bend at this rate. Just trying to line it up is a real problem. I think I need specialist tools for this, or maybe… I know, I need to make up a dolly so I can line the tape up perfectly straight."

"OK. I think perhaps you also need some caffeine to help you?" Mark went to the kitchen and made a fresh pot of Colombian ground coffee, their favourite. Returning to the dining room and putting their mugs down on the table, Mark told Freya about the chat with his Dad. "If he finds this case of family papers, I'm almost certain it'll give us some more clues. It's so… frustrating. All the evidence is out there for what really happened… or here, right on this tape which we can't get to yet!"

"I know. I'm really going to have to go carefully here. I'm worried I'll make it worse. It really needs a specialist, you know? I wonder if we should try and find someone to do it for us."

"Oh, I'm sure there'll be someone out there, but it'll probably cost a small fortune."

"Well, the amount my Mum has been spending on those extra certificates, which you've said you're paying for, I'm sure this won't be too much of a burden. Oh, and a large package has arrived for you. It's in the garage. If I had a suspicious mind I'd say it resembled rather a lot of model railway track, but of course I know you wouldn't have ordered so much because you have nowhere to put it…"

"Oh that, yeah. I meant to talk to you about that. I have an idea or three. Anyway, I tell you what, see if you can find a specialist company to do that tape for you. Meantime, I'm going for a run. I need to get some fresh air and get some fitness back."

Two hours later, having run five kilometres, Mark was taking a well-earned shower while Freya prepared a light snack lunch. Alex had by now returned from swimming and was poring over his computer, painstakingly opening the various newspaper files for references to Joseph Palmer's court case. Olivia had just surfaced and was still wandering about the house in her pyjamas when the phone rang in Mark's office. The two siblings raced to be the first there – Olivia won, and mouthed "Loser!" to her brother as she picked up the handset. "Hallo. Mark Phipps' office."

"Ah, you must be his gorgeous secretary that he's always going on about." said a man's voice.

"What? No! What do you mean... oh it's YOU Grandpa! Yeah, I'm his most truly gorgeous secretary ever. He's in the shower at the moment, shall I get him to call you?"

"That'd be good. You might tell him I've found the old case full of family papers, and it's a real treasure trove of letters and pictures and things. I think he'll be very interested to see it all."

"Wow, Grandpa. He's not the only one. Are you coming over any time soon?"

"No, Dear. But there's nothing stopping you coming over to me. We're out tomorrow, but any other time…"

"How about now, Grandpa? It's only an hour or so in the car?"

By now, Alex was standing in the doorway, trying to catch the gist of the conversation. She mouthed to him and pointed to the phone, with a thumbs-up.

"OK, well look, as soon as Dad's out of the shower, I'll tell him and see if he'll drive us over after lunch. That'll be really cool. Thanks. Yes… love you Grandpa! Byeee!" She replaced the handset. "Oh wow! He's got the case full of family papers, and apparently it's got some really interesting stuff in it. We just need to convince Dad he wants to drive us over there."

"I'll get my gear together." said Alex, as Mark emerged from his bedroom.

"Dad!" both siblings cried out together.

"Guess what, lovely father of mine." Olivia purred. "You're taking us to Frome this afternoon, to see a treasure trove which your very own papa has discovered in his loft."

Mark's eyes lit up. "Really? Wow, that's amazing. We'd better clear it with Mum."

Much to their surprise, Freya was happy for them to disappear straight after lunch, as she had more than enough to get on with and was happy to let them go for a few hours.

"I doubt we'll be too late back, Darling" said Mark, giving her a peck on the cheek. He actually very much doubted they'd be anything other than very late, knowing what they had in store at his parents' house…

33

Later that afternoon – Frome

The two siblings and Mark sat at the large wooden kitchen table that had graced both of Mark's parents' houses for as long as he could remember. John Phipps sat across from Mark, and Fenella fussed about the kitchen, offering and supplying various refreshments to them all.

On the table in front of them was an old leather tan-coloured briefcase, of the type which came together at the top, like a clam, and then had a single thick flap with a buckle on the end, which fastened onto a lock halfway down the opposite side. They'd already spent half an hour or so looking at old photographs. There were quite a few of John's parents, and a group picture taken of his grandmother, with his father and an elderly lady sitting on a sofa. John had identified the elderly lady as Auntie Ath, or Sarah Palmer, as Mark referred to her.

"She looks so fragile and docile," he commented "and yet she seems to have done some pretty evil things by all accounts."

"Well, you don't know that for sure, do you Marcus?" John replied. "It's all conjecture and hearsay."

"Well, I've got that tape of Grandad talking about her, but it's broken so until Freya fixes it, I can't really say any more. But I think she knew a lot about what went on then."

"Maybe. Let's look at these papers then." John unclipped the lock and pulled the case open.

"There's so much junk in here, rather than tip it all out, why don't I just take things out one at a time and you see if it's any use, eh?" John pulled an envelope out postmarked 8th August 1946, and addressed in a somewhat shaky hand, to Mrs S. Phipps, Wheelers Cottage, Belcote, Nr Salmsham. Inside was the letter from Auntie Ath, talking about visiting them at Christmas time, and about her father having been the signalman who was wrongly accused of causing the accident, and having something to confess. Mark gasped as he read the letter out to the others…

"'so what I did with some of us my brother ~~James'~~ crossed out 'Hubert and my brother in law we knew who did the accident and it was not an accident and so we made sure the person never did harm again.' Oh gosh, so she's as good as saying they bumped him off, whoever it was. You've already been through these, Dad, haven't you, and put this one on top?"

"Well," grinned John "I thought I'd put a teaser out first. Actually, there's a lot of stuff in here which I haven't looked at, but that letter was near the top. Look, try this one."

He pulled out an old white envelope which had a ribbon tied around it as it was bulging with letters.

"One at a time, folks" said Mark, as he opened the first letter.

Dearest Martha

Thank you for your note. I hope William and the children are well. I am enjoying learning the work and hope I will soon be getting back to Salmsham.

Please tell Pa not to worry at all about things. I can promise you we will never see Jack Dove again, whatever has happened to him he deserved more than you'll ever know. Please say and write no more about this, not to me or to anyone else.
Your loving sister Sarah.

"Wow" said Mark. "That must be one of the most incriminating letters I've ever read. I assume this is the Sarah who became Auntie Ath?"

"I wouldn't know about that, Marcus" said his father. "You've got more information on the family than I have. I've never really been through any of this. But I think Martha is my great grandmother."

"Let's look at another one, Dad." Mark said, unfolding a similar looking note.

Martha
Hubert tells me you have been asking him about things as if we've been up to something. I have told him what I asked you before, don't open old wounds, don't mention this matter any more.
Sarah

"Hmmm, not so 'Loving Sister' now is she?" Mark commented. "I get the feeling Sarah and Hubert have done something to Jack Dove, and Martha is suspicious about it, and is turning the heat up. Remember on that tape, just before it broke, he says she said she and her brother and her brother-in-law. Which brother-in-law, I wonder?"

"I've got Nana's charts here, Dad." Alex spread out a couple of sheets onto the table. "Right, here's

Sarah Palmer… Auntie Ath… and so her brothers-in-law are… William Whitmore…"

"Martha's husband, so we can discount him surely. She'd have been badgering him, not her sister."

"OK… well Agnes died without marrying, so the only other one is Katharine's husband, who was…"

"Arthur Marriott!" Father and son spoke together.

"Except…" cautioned Alex "according to this they didn't get married until 1882. And Jack Dove disappeared in 1879, didn't he?"

"Yes, but when she mentions her brother-in-law, she is talking in 1946. He didn't have to be her brother-in-law when they did whatever it was they did."

John Phipps looked perplexed. "Would either of you like to tell me what on earth you're talking about?"

"Sorry, Dad. OK, Jack Dove was a local farm hand, the son of the farmer at Rosfell Farm at Salmsham. Jack Dove accused Joseph Palmer's son James of tampering with the signals after the accident. No-one else saw James anywhere near the signals, but anyway, James then goes and commits suicide, leaving a note saying he couldn't stand the pressure of being accused of something he didn't do, then his father Joseph, the signalman, ends up going to prison for manslaughter."

John Phipps nodded. "Right… so what's all this other stuff then?"

"Well, we think Sarah Palmer must have found out and did something to Jack Dove. In fact, we think she confessed to your Dad in 1946, and told him all about it. But she says her brother and brother-in-law helped her. The thing is, what did they do to Jack Dove? All we know is, he was born, and married, and his wife died in childbirth, but there is no death certificate for him at all."

"Maybe they killed him, and hid his body?" John Phipps was starting to sound intrigued by this.

"Who knows? Livvy, have you brought your laptop with you?"

"Yes, Dad. Why?"

"Can you go into your newspaper thingy and type in Jack Dove… any time after 1874, and see what it comes up with?"

As Olivia set up her laptop, Mark peeled the next letter out of the file. "Ah, this is different handwriting."

Dear Martha

I have received your note, and spoken with Arthur. I can't tell you what he said, but you have caused him much distress and I must ask you to stop making these accusations. Arthur would not do such a thing – I don't think he is capable of harming anyone. Haven't we been through enough as a family without you raking over the past? Don't tell me that Pa put you up to this, because I see him every other day and he has said nothing to me. As far as I am concerned, I care not one jot about Jack Dove, whether he is alive or dead, as long as he is not here causing us trouble. Remember Agnes, and please for her sake if no-one else's, do not write or speak of this ever again.

Kate

"Who's this Kate, Marcus?" asked John

"Katharine Palmer. Joseph's youngest sister. She was twelve when the accident happened, and she reckoned she saw someone up the signal before the crash but they wouldn't allow her evidence to be admitted at the inquest, because she wouldn't tell them what she was doing at the time she saw them."

"I wonder" Alex piped up "if she was out seeing Arthur Marriott then?"

"Ah, now I think you're speculating too much, Alex" said Mark. "Remember she was twelve, and he was..." he looked at the family history chart "seventeen years old. I hardly think she would have been seeing him, do you?"

"She might have been, Dad. She might have had a secret crush on him or something. You know what girls can be like."

Olivia, who was listening with one ear whilst staring at her laptop, couldn't resist the open goalmouth. "You'd know all about crushes wouldn't you, Alex. Ellie Parkin? She's a bit older than you."

Alex blushed a little. "Ellie's my age, actually. Oh, and no I don't have a crush on her, actually. We're just friends, and text a lot."

"Yeah, I know – she's tells me everything you know. You creep her out."

"No I don't! And anyway, I'm seeing Hazel from my class, so you're wrong, as usual."

"What, psycho Hazel. The one who punches netball coaches when they send her off!"

"She's not a psycho! She's really cool..."

"She must be a psycho if she fancies a loser like you. She's probably got a whole string of little boys lining up to..." Olivia punched a couple of keys on the keyboard, and suddenly stopped and frowned.

"Come on kids, leave your bickering for school time. Let's see what else we have here." Mark was about to pull out another letter when Olivia suddenly gasped and pointed to her screen.

"Oh, wow! Everyone! You've got to see this… look. This is the Hallowfield Courier, dated Saturday 22nd November 1879."

She read out the request for information about Jack Dove *"last seen on Monday 17th walking south along the footpath across the railway line from Field Mount to Lower Bank. He does not appear to have travelled from the village by other means. Mr Dove was not in debt and had no known reason for disappearing from his home. He is the only surviving son of Mr George Dove, the tenant farmer at Rosfell Farm and resident at the farmhouse. Please contact the abovementioned George Dove with any intelligence as to his disappearance which is entirely out of character."*

Alex leaned over to see the screen. "Hey, look just above it. There's a Whitmore mentioned. In that column there. What's all this about?"

Olivia scrolled up the page. "It's a funeral. *'The funeral took place on Tuesday at Salmsham of George Whitmore, the landlord of the Dukes Head and a highly respected member of the church and local community'*…"

"Yeah, but Livvy! Look. On the chart here. George Whitmore is our ancestor as well. He was Martha Palmer's father-in-law."

"I'm confused already."

"Don't you think it's odd? The week Jack Dove disappears, they happen to bury George Whitmore. Maybe they swapped the body!"

Olivia sighed and looked witheringly at her brother. "Do us a favour, Loser, they'd notice if they'd mixed up the bodies wouldn't they."

Mark peered over as well. "I tell you what though. Alex… you might have a point. Dove is last seen on the Monday… and the funeral is on the Tuesday. That's a big coincidence, isn't it?"

"I don't see how though, Dad." Olivia frowned at the screen. "How would they be connected."

By now, John Phipps was also looking over their shoulders. "It's possibly just a co-incidence. But it's too good a co-incidence to just dismiss out of hand, isn't it? So, now, here's a thought. If you wanted to dispose of a body, where would be a good place?"

"Erm… well in a coffin, obviously, Grandpa." Olivia could not see where this was heading.

"You could go one better than that. What happens at a funeral?"

"Well… they have a church service, and then a cremation or a burial."

"No cremations in those days, I would imagine. Everyone was buried. So, what do you need to bury a coffin then?"

Mark picked up the scent first. "A hole. A grave. So, you wait until there's going to be a funeral, and you put the body in the hole which has been dug, and then cover it over with earth, and then put the funeral coffin in the next day and no-one is any wiser."

"Exactly. What do you think to that then?"

There was a brief silence while they absorbed this theory. Olivia was the first to speak. "Surely… but, wouldn't people notice. I mean, the funeral people, they'd have to look in the grave while they were lowering the coffin into it, wouldn't they."

"True, true," replied her grandfather "but if you dug out another foot of earth the night before, put the body in, covered it over again so that the body was invisible, you might get away with it. Especially if no-one is expecting it. I wonder… do you really think they did that? It's a very bold thing to attempt."

"Livvy, can you check what the weather conditions were on those dates? I mean, there must be something in the paper about the weather?"

"No Dad, but do you know what? The Met Office has a website and they have archives right back to the early 1800s. I had to use it for another project. Give me a few minutes and I can tell you what the weather was doing on the day of the funeral."

The others were seriously impressed with this. Alex watched over his sister's shoulder while Mark unfolded another letter.

Dearest Martha   *16th April '92*

Thank you for your letter. I am still in shock about poor Arthur. I can't believe he has gone, it was not like him to be so careless on the lines. He was crossing behind a goods train to see me and just tripped in front of a light engine. It was a horrible thing to see. I don't want to go near the railway ever again, it has not been good to us has it?

Little James is bearing up; he understands he will not see his Daddy ever again and is very upset, but also sometimes he is happy again. I will try to stay strong for him.

I will write as soon as I have a date for the funeral; we have the inquest tomorrow. I'm not sure how I will get through it. Sarah has offered to sit with me but I told her not to come along. I would rather be on my own.
Please hug Susie and Sarah for me
Kate

"This is becoming more gruesome every minute. How many more railway deaths in our family, Dad?" Mark Phipps handed the letter over to his father.

"Hmmm. We do seem to be cursed, don't we." said John. "Then again, the railway was a dangerous place, and if you're working there every hour God sends, you're going to end up getting into all sorts of scrapes."

"Look at this, Dad" cried Alex. "Livvy, you're actually a star, for once. You're definitely my favourite sister now."

"Gee, thanks little bro." Olivia was actually feeling quite proud of herself. There, on the screen in front of her, was a book in PDF format. The cover read 'Meteorological Office. Daily Weather Reports. 1st July – 31st December 1879'. Olivia scrolled down to the 17th November, then she and Alex scanned down the list of weather stations, not all of which were in Britain.

"Dad, which of these places should we look at?"

Mark looked down the list. "Hmmm, the nearest is Portishead. There." He pointed to the line of data. "Right, you can assume from this that it was raining on the 17th, freezing overnight, and cold and overcast all of the 18th. That would have been one heck of a job for them then. Digging out even more of the grave at night, in the rain."

John Phipps chuckled. "Unless the gravedigger was in on the plot, so to speak?"

"Don't be daft, Dad. This is sounding more and more crazy by the second."

"I'm not joking. Seriously, if you say this bloke Dove was a nasty piece of work, and three of our family conspired to get rid of him, who's to say more folk weren't involved, eh? Might be worth finding out who the church wardens employed as a grave digger. Could have been the sexton, or it could have been a gardener or even a farm worker. It wouldn't have been his only job."

Mark made a note to find out who the gravedigger might have been – another job for Sheila Bagley perhaps. It was the sort of thing she loved to find out.

There were a few more interesting documents in the collection, including a few newspaper clippings of various family events. One in particular caught their eye – a short newspaper cutting from June 1913. "ELECTROCUTED AT WORK" was the headline; there was no newspaper marked on the cutting. Mark read the short report out loud. "*'Railway guard Hubert Palmer was electrocuted while crossing the lines in the coach sidings at Salisbury Station. He was found by a friend who had stopped off to meet him after work. Harriet Brooks, a widow and railway clerk, of Salmsham, Somerset, gave evidence at the inquest where the jury heard that she had just entered the sidings when she saw a body lying behind a train. She realised that it was Palmer, and raised the alarm. After switching off the electric current, colleagues tried to resuscitate Palmer but it was later found he had suffered almost instant death from electrocution.'* Gosh, Dad, I think you're right. Yet

269

another railway death, and another one who's fallen across the line. This is getting a bit too crazy now, not that I expect there's any foul play here."

"I wonder who the widow was? Harriet Brooks. That's not a name we're familiar with." Alex was speculating. "That's another one for Nana. Find out who Harriet Brooks was and what her maiden name is – it'll probably be another suspicious relative."

There were many more items in the package, and two other packages full of useful genealogical information, but nothing more that seemed relevant to the railway mystery, although Mark was careful not to dismiss any of it yet.

"Any chance we could take this lot away, Dad?"

"Well… I'd rather you didn't, Marcus. I'd actually like to have a proper read of it all too. But I tell you what, if you want copies of it all, feel free. I've got a scanner in the study." Before John Phipps could move, though, his grandson took out his phone and started taking pictures.

"This is much quicker, Grandpa. This way, I've got an instant record and I can send it to all our devices straight away."

"And there was I thinking I was streets ahead of you young 'uns." John chuckled.

34

Surprisingly, having said their goodbyes and spent half an hour or so catching up on family gossip, Mark and his two offspring were home before nine o'clock. The conversation in the car was full of lively speculation, and they all agreed that there was so much new information, they needed to do a lot of careful sifting to make sure they hadn't missed anything subtle. More than ever they were convinced that the Salmsham Railway Disaster of 1874 was anything but an accident, and they were all determined to get to the bottom of the mystery once and for all.

Freya had just about got the house ready for the next day, and was happily chatting on the phone when they got in. Mark heard her say "Bye then, Mum" and then she replaced the handset and beamed at him.

"You'll never guess what?"

"Try me."

"Mum's got most of the certificates from the GRO. She's trying to sort them all out now, and she says she'll scan them in and email them to you, but she wanted you to know that Julia Dove was definitely Jack Dove and Anne Draper's daughter. So, your friend Roger is not only your cousin, but he's descended from Dove as well, which confirms what he says in that email."

"Gosh, this is turning out to be a day for data, isn't it? We've found so much more out at Dad's. In fact, we have a theory about what actually happened. It's full of holes, but I think we've got a new slant on the accident."

After they had brought Freya up to speed, Mark remembered that he had some more questions for Sheila; especially that he wanted her to try and find out who Harriet Brooks was.

"She was the person who found Hubert Palmer's body after he tripped and electrocuted himself on the lines in the siding. I wouldn't normally be suspicious but there seem to be so many deaths on the railway which look like accidents, I don't trust any of them anymore!"

Mark finished off the glass of red wine which he'd been sipping since they got in, and went upstairs to the office. He was soon joined by Olivia. He managed a little smile to himself – he fully expected Alex to be intrigued by the whole railway mystery, but he had not expected quite so much enthusiasm from his daughter.

"Dad. I've been thinking. You know this Roger guy… the one you met in Salmsham?"

"Yes… the one I'm about to email."

"That's right. Well, he's there, isn't he? I mean, he's right on the spot. Where it all happened."

"Yes. What are you getting at?"

"Well, couldn't we get him to do some local research? Like, chatting to the villagers, finding out if anyone else has any information on the accident, or on the locals. I mean, was there a book written or anything."

"That's a great idea, Livvy. I'm not sure he's actually that popular at the moment in the local area, but maybe he could find someone who is. He might at least know someone, maybe a local historian or someone like that."

"That's what I meant."

Mark opened his emails to find several unread messages, including one from Roger Cooper.

"Here you go, Livvy. This is our man." He clicked on the message.

From: rcooper@rmcproperty.co.uk
Sent: Saturday, May 5, 2018 1.21 PM
To: mark@phippstribe.net
Subject: Family papers

Hi Mark

I've been to my Dad's and helped him find some letters and things. There isn't as much as he thought, but I've got a couple of things which I think will interest you. Can you come over today at all?

By the way, let me have your phone number so we can talk or text.

Roger

Mark checked his watch. "Blast. It's gone ten, otherwise I'd give him a ring. Never mind, I'll email him and tell him I can pop over tomorrow..."

"Can I come too, Dad? I want to see this place, as well as meeting this cousin of ours."

"Of course. Let's try and get over for a pub lunch with him and his family."

"I'll let you tell Mum. She's been preparing a roast."

"I wouldn't be at all surprised if Mum wants to come with us." Mark was typing as he spoke. "You go and tell her and I'll let Roger know."

He finished the reply to Roger, and left his phone number with a suggestion that they meet up tomorrow in Salmsham for lunch or tea. Then he sent another message to his mother-in-law.

From: mark@phippstribe.net
Sent: Saturday, May 12, 2018 10.33 PM
To: sheilabagley@phonetalkinternet.com
Subject: More searches!

Dear Sheila

Can you find out who Harriet Brooks is? She is a witness to the death of Hubert Palmer in Salisbury. It said she was a widow and railway clerk from Salmsham, so maybe she worked at the station.

Also, how would we find out who the gravedigger was for George Whitemore's funeral. Salmsham, November 1879. Is there any way of knowing this?

We're heading off to Salmsham tomorrow. We've got so much information now I think my head is going to explode, but we're going to meet the Coopers. Apparently Roger has some old letters too.

Love

Mark

He pressed send as Freya appeared at the door.

"Don't worry about lunch tomorrow. Despite what Livvy says, I haven't prepared it yet, so we'll have our roast through the week while you're away. And yes please, I'd like to come over to Salmsham with you."

Like her daughter, Freya wanted to see the village where all the action had taken place. She hadn't felt this excited since she was a young child, on her way to the seaside for the summer holidays. Now, she was starting to understand why her mother was so hooked on family history – it seemed to be far more interesting and convoluted than the traditional 'kings & queens of England' approach to history, which had bored her to tears at school.

Another email came through from Roger.

"He says he'll meet us at the Dukes Head, Salmsham, for lunch at 1.00 tomorrow. He's booking a table for seven of us, so I assume we'll be meeting his wife as well. This is going to be amazing."

35

Mark opened the door of the Dukes Head, and was greeted straight away by Roger and Vicky Cooper, who had watched the Phipps family drive in. "Mark. Great to see you again. You remember Vicky, of course? This is Jacqui, my wife".

Jacqui Cooper was a short, slim lady with short brown hair, and what Mark considered to be oversized earrings. She was so obviously Vicky's mother too; he would have recognised her anyway. She leaned up and gave Mark a peck on the cheek. Mark introduced Olivia and Freya to Roger's family, and Roger ordered a round of drinks at the bar.

"I've already got a table sorted for us, over there in the corner. It's quite secluded. It isn't usually very busy in here on a Sunday, but there's a match on later, so the other bar is quite packed."

As the two families settled around the table, Mark explained where they'd got to in their searches, and particularly, how he now knew that Jack Dove was definitely Roger's ancestor.

"Your great grandfather Henry, who I think you knew…"

"Yeah, yeah. I was 20 when he died…."

"Well, his mother, your great great grandmother, was Julia Dove, daughter of Jack Dove and Anne Draper."

"Did you say Draper?" Jacqui had been listening intently and studying Mark carefully as he spoke.

"'Cos that's my maiden name. Draper. My family have lived here for generations."

Mark smiled. "Looks as if you two are cousins then, as well as us."

Roger grinned. "Oh dear. Vicky… just check how many fingers you've got on each hand? You're probably an inbred."

"Thanks a lot, Dad. I feel so much better now." Vicky grinned back. Alex thought she was a different person from the stroppy girl they'd met in the old station yard a month ago. For a start, she was smiling, and he thought she was much prettier when she smiled. In fact, he was struck by just how jovial everyone was. Roger seemed to be a fun person, with a lively sense of humour; nothing like the man who had shouted at them across the car park. Both families already seemed very relaxed in each other's presence, as if they'd known each other for years.

Olivia dug her brother in the ribs. "Stop staring. She's your cousin." Alex blushed and elbowed his sister in retaliation.

Mark was still talking. "Anyway, we reckon Jack Dove had something to do with either the accident itself, or at least framing the signalman, who was Joseph Palmer, and we also reckon that Joseph's son and daughter and your porter ancestor, Arthur Marriott, found out and did him in."

"Seriously? Jack Dove? What, you think they murdered him?"

"Yes. That's what we think *may* have happened. Now, look, Jack disappeared the day before they buried the landlord of this place, who is also one of our ancestors. So, we have a theory that maybe they put his body in the landlord's grave the night before the funeral, and then he ended up being buried underneath the landlord's coffin. I mean, what a great way to get rid of a body, eh? No-one can search under a buried coffin."

Roger looked thoughtful. "That's pretty outrageous, Mark, I must admit. But it's plausible, isn't it. And I tell you what, I would have dismissed it normally, but what with the stuff my great granddad told me... oh, and wait till you see what I've got here, and maybe it'll help it all make sense."

Roger brought out a large tattered envelope, and slid out a very old photograph, and a smaller, plain letter-sized envelope. He held out the photograph first. It was on a large faded white card, although the actual picture itself was relatively small. It showed a horse and cart, in what looked like an old yard, with a road in the background and a row of cottages in the far distance. There was a youngish man with a flat cap, holding the bridle of the horse, and looking straight at the camera. Standing next to the cart, wearing a top hat, a rough looking jacket, and loose trousers, was an older man with a whiskery white beard and large sideburns. Sitting up on the driver's seat were three young children, a boy and two girls.

"Who's this then?" asked Mark.

Roger smiled. "Well, we didn't know all of them until what you just told me, but on the back it says 'John aged 7, Harriet age 11, Julia age 9 – that'll be my Dove ancestor - and their father and grandfather. Salmsham Station Yard.' But it's undated."

"Ah, well dating it shouldn't be too difficult. We know when Julia was born so we can work it out from that. But that means... that means that must be Jack Dove, the one standing by the horse. He went missing early in 1879, so it's earlier than that. Also, it looks quite sunny and dry, so maybe a summer photo?" Mark pointed to Jack, and then showed the rest of his family.

"He looks a bit miserable, Dad" said Alex. "And so does his dad."

"Well, don't forget, they had to hold their poses for quite a long time in those days, so the best way to do that was not to smile. Look, you can see the children are slightly blurry. This is an amazing photo, Roger. Where was it you found it?"

"It was in my Dad's loft. That's the only thing we could find really, and that letter. He says he's sure there's loads more stuff, but I couldn't see any of it."

"Oh, yes, I missed the letter. What's in it?"

"Well, it doesn't make much sense to us, but it might make some to you. It's a sort of threat letter. I have no idea why it's come down through the family though."

Roger took the letter out of the envelope, and read it out loud:

'We know what you did to Agnes. You will pay for it and everything else you did. You will not get away with any more. You will regret… all…' ah, it looks like all crossed out and then it says *'everything. Watch out.'* Sounds a bit like childish cloak and dagger stuff if you ask me."

"Is it signed?" asked Freya.

"No signature. The envelope is blank and it was obviously hand delivered, 'cos there's no stamp and no address either."

"Roger, would you mind if we copied these. We've got some family letters on file, and we'll compare the handwriting." Mark got his phone ready.

With Roger's approval, he took a couple of pictures of the letter, and one close-up shot of the writing. Then he stood up and took a copy of the old photo, which Roger laid out on the table in front of him.

"Dad, I've got the other letters on my phone." Alex reminded him. He brought up the copies of the various letters and showed them round. They agreed the handwriting could possibly have been the same as one of the Palmer daughters, but without an expert to compare them they wouldn't swear to it.

Roger picked up the photograph again and chuckled. "This photo is a real classic though, isn't it? I mean, there's been various old photos of Salmsham, from around this time, but none of this family group. It must have been done privately."

"Where exactly is it?" His wife leaned over, and traced her finger across the left side. "Oh, look. Isn't that the start of the bridge? The Belcote Road Bridge, just there in the background? And there's a bit of that cottage on the end."

"Oh yes. You're right. It's the yard, out there, where you parked your car the other time, Mark. Look... you can see the bridge, and the slope of the road in the background. I reckon the local history society will be interested in this. I should get a proper copy done. And old Ted Crozier'll be interested in this too..." Roger pointed towards the bar. "Hey Ted! Come and look at this, young man!"

The 'young' man turned, raised his eyebrows, grunted something to his drinking companion with a grin, grabbed his pint from the bar and shuffled over to the table.

"Ted's our local history buff. Ted, take a look at this picture and see if you can spot where it is."

Ted Crozier, who Mark estimated must have been at least in his late-70s, squinted a bit, held the picture at arm's length, moved under a light and then said "Well, it looks familiar. Maybe the goods yard at the station?"

"Got it in one, Sir! Well done."

"Who's the folk?"

"Right, the little girl there" Roger pointed to Julia "is my great great grandmother, and that there is her father Jack, and that there is his father, Farmer Dove, of Rosfell Farm, which is still up there, isn't it?"

"Well, I never. Yep, the farm's still there. So, that'll be the infamous Jack Dove by the 'orse? I feel sorry for that 'orse then. There's quite some old tales about him in the records, I can tell you. He used to beat his animals, beat his wife, beat his kids, beat-up half the village…" Ted Crozier's sentence remained unfinished, as he studied the picture in more detail, checking little details and pointing to various things of interest with his gnarled index finger.

"Ted, these people here are distant cousins of mine, and they're looking into the train crash."

Mark introduced himself and his family one by one, and explained what they'd found out so far.

"We think, and this is a little bit fanciful, but we think that when Jack Dove disappeared, he may have been done in by one or two of Joseph Palmer's children, and buried underneath a coffin just before a funeral."

"Whereabouts? Salmsham Church?" Ted raised his eyebrows in surprise.

"Yes," said Mark "we think it was when the landlord of this place died, in 1879. George Whitmore."

"George Whitmore... that's right, yes. His son took over this place after him. William, I think it was. Yeah, William and Martha. Popular couple them. He held onto this place many years, he did. He was a real pillar of the village community too. Took over as churchwarden after his dad died. So you think Jack Dove is buried in old George Whitmore's grave?"

"Not in it. Under it. But we'll never know of course. Not unless we go and dig them both up."

"Hang on a minute, gentlemen – and ladies, of course." Ted tipped his head politely to the assembled ladies, put down the photo he'd been studying, and wandered back past the bar, disappearing through the swing doors.

Roger grinned at Mark. "Bingo! You've got him totally hooked already. This, my friend, is a very good sign. What old Ted Crozier doesn't know about the history of Salmsham isn't worth knowing... and if there's something he doesn't know, he knows where to look and who to ask!"

36

DCI Chloë Smith

A couple of minutes later, during which time several new conversations struck up around the table, Ted burst back through the swing door, accompanied by a tall but not overly slender early-middle aged woman with medium length brown hair, dressed in a smart blue blouse, black trousers and dark low-heeled boots, and carrying an almost full pint of stout.

"Of course… Chloë!" Roger stood up and shook the woman's hand. "I should have thought of you. This one's right up your street, my luv. Folks, this is WPC Chloë Smith of Hallowfield CID, our local Sherlock Holmes. Chloë, meet the Phipps family, who are our distant cousins. They're investigating the old train crash. This is Mark, Freya, Alex, and Livvy."

"Hello, nice to meet you all." Chloë Smith said, sounding as if she really meant it. She flashed a brief smile at the large gathering in front of her. "Roger's almost right. In fact, I would actually arrest him for belittling my rank, but I can't be bothered and anyway it's not an offence, except to me. But I'm actually a Detective Chief Inspector, not a WPC. And I gather you've got a little mystery on your hands?"

"Pull up a chair, Chloë, and listen to this."

As Chloë settled on a chair purloined from the next table, Roger indicated to Mark, who briefly covered the story of the possible framing of the signalman, and how his children seemed to have taken their revenge on Jack Dove, and how the families had concluded that Dove may have been murdered and then buried underneath another grave the night before a funeral. Mark got Alex to bring up his picture of the newspaper cutting, showing how Dove had last been seen the day before the funeral.

Chloë looked at the copy document on Alex's phone. "So, Mark, do you think there's really a dead body in the graveyard? Is that what you're saying?" She managed to keep an earnestly deadpan expression on her face. "If so, I'd better call the team in. We can't have dead bodies in the graveyard now, can we!" She suddenly smiled, and the others chuckled.

"Very good!" grinned Mark "I hadn't thought of it that way. But seriously, we think that's what may have actually happened."

"Well, OK, I'm going to ask a copper's question now then. Have you any real evidence for this?"

"Actually, we think we may have. But we just need to put it all together, in a timeline, and we're still waiting on a few things like death certificates. Why, did you want to check it over and see if we've done a good job?"

"No. Not necessarily. I'm sure you'll be very thorough. But in all seriousness, if you came to me with chapter and verse… all the evidence, and I mean ALL the evidence, which pointed to an unsolved murder with the probable whereabouts of a body, we would have to investigate it, even if it was as old as… when was this?"

"Well, Jack Dove disappeared in 1879."

"Crikey, that's pushing it. That's 139 years ago. It would more likely be an archaeological investigation."

"What if…" began Roger, "we had just found a body, and it turned out to be from that era, and obviously a murder. Would you then investigate it?"

"Yes of course. Well, maybe. It depends on so many things, Roger. I mean… once we had a body, we'd do a post mortem, and DNA tests and stuff like that. You know, see if there were any bits of clothes left, although that's unlikely. So, I'd have to do some enquiring. I've never had anything quite like this before. I mean, we have cold cases which we look at every now and then. But anyway, long before we did that, you guys would need to come up with a complete set of reasons, like, documentary evidence, that a crime is likely to have taken place. If we were pushed for resources we'd probably try and bat it away or farm it out, but it might make an interesting challenge for my unit, stretched as we are. I mean, you're also saying that the train crash maybe wasn't an accident?"

Mark leaned forward. "Are you serious? You'd actually investigate it?"

"We would look at it, with all the evidence, yes."

"Because the more I've looked at this, the more I think the railway accident investigation by the Board of Trade was a big whitewash. They couldn't bring themselves to entertain the possibility of sabotage; they threw out strong evidence that it might well have been sabotage, just because they didn't want to believe the testimony of a twelve-year-old girl, and then they had two conflicting scenarios, namely the driver went past red signals, or the signalman forgot to put his signals to red. In the end, they seem to have decided to take the easy option and make a scapegoat out of the poor signalman, when all the evidence we've seen makes him just about the only railwayman on the day who did his job by the book."

Chloë looked at her drink and thought for a few moments. "How many people died in the crash?"

"Oh, I think it was twenty-one altogether". Mark checked the notes in the folder he'd brought along with him. "Yep. seventeen passengers, four railway workers."

Chloë nodded. "And your man Dove. So, so far we've got twenty-two potential murders. Or at least, that's what you're speculating."

Mark nodded. "I hadn't thought of it that way."

"Well, yeah. I mean, if you went out today and deliberately fixed the railway track so a train crashed and people died, we'd do you for murder."

Mark and Roger both raised their eyebrows and exchanged glances. Vicky blew her cheeks out. The others looked intently at Chloë.

"The other thing you might try," she continued, "because there's so much local history and folklore tied up with this accident, is maybe getting one of the Universities to look into it; you know, a bit like the Richard the Third exhumation back in 2012. Because what you really need is to find out whether there is a body under the other grave, and you can't just go around digging up random graves."

"Would you guys do it? I mean, exhume the graves?" Roger asked. "I'm serious. I mean, they're only just up the road. I'm sure *we* could find them very easily."

Chloë shook her head. "Don't even think about it, Roger. I know what you're like. That's taking your redevelopment of Salmsham a bit too far!"

"Ouch! That was below the belt."

"Sorry, Roger. I know you've been getting grief from the other natives. I'm not sure this investigation will win you many friends either."

"On the contrary, Chloë." Ted Crozier piped up, having been listening intently. "I think this'd make a fantastic story, rewriting a bit of local history, and righting a wrong which has been passed down in folklore. I mean, when I was growing up, there were folk in the village who remembered their parents saying how they'd almost pilloried poor Joe Palmer for causing the accident, even though most of them knew it wasn't down to him. Easier to go with the baying mob than stop and consider the alternatives."

Chloë nodded. "OK, well, listen. In all seriousness then, if you can bring me all the evidence; letters, dates, death certificates, burial certificates, newspaper cuttings. That official accident report you had there, and your comments about why you thought it was wrong. All of that, and put it into some sort of coherent timeline, I'll try and see if I can put a little bit of resource into it."

"Thank you, Chloë. We really didn't expect this." Mark made a few quick notes and stuffed them into his folder. "There's only one thing I'm not sure of, though. It's been bugging me for some time now."

"Which is?"

"Motive. I mean, we know Jack Dove was supposed to be after one of the Palmer girls, and Joseph was supposed to be unhappy about it, but why would a local farmhand, son of the farmer, cause a railway accident and kill all those innocent people? Surely there would have been easier ways to get at Joseph Palmer, if that's what he wanted to do. I mean, just go out and thump him for a start."

"Hmmm," said Chloë "Shall I nick you for inciting historical violence, Mr Phipps? Only kidding, Mark. Look, you're right. A strong motive should form part of your evidence, if you can find one. I stand by what I said though. Bring us all the evidence you've got, and I'll see if I can help in any way."

"Thanks so much, Chloë. I think that deserves another pint, don't you?" Roger got up to go to the bar.

"No way, Roger. My round, I think." Mark scanned the existing drinks on the table, and went to order the next round. "Here's some menus, everyone. Let's have a bit of grub and get to talk about anything but railways."

The rest of the afternoon was a chance for the two families to get to know each other properly over dinner, while Chloë and Ted said their goodbyes and went back to spend the rest of the time with their original companions. Olivia and Vicky found themselves with much more in common than they realised, comparing notes on college courses, films, clothes, boys and changing the world. Alex was surprised at how much he was allowed into their conversations, even when they discussed boyfriends and their perceived inadequacies. His sister, for once, didn't tease him about Hazel, much to his relief.

The two wives were very quickly talking about their respective children, new homes, and lives in general. Meanwhile, despite their best intentions, Roger and Mark ended up earnestly discussing the intricacies of railway signal interlocking from the 1860s. As Roger pointed out with a grin, the only thing that was missing now was their train-spotter's anoraks.

"Why don't we all go for a quick walk?" suggested Roger. "I'll show you up to the station and we can see where it all kicked off."

The Dukes Head was less than 50 yards from the entrance to the old station yard, where Mark had parked the first time he visited. "You can just imagine Jack Dove dashing up here the moment he heard the crash!" said Mark to the group. "He would have been there in no time at all. I suppose that's how he came to be first to climb up and rescue folks from the top of the wreckage."

"What, you mean my evil ancestor?" Roger looked somewhat confused.

"Yep. The very same. Whatever else he may have done in his life, he was a hero when it came to rescuing folk from the fire. He got a special mention in the report, and at the inquest. Apparently, he was about to have a drink in the bar when he heard the crash, and ran straight up here with a couple of his mates."

"Well, I never."

"Well it just goes to show, most people aren't all evil, are they?" Jacqui ventured her thoughts on the matter. "I mean, he was probably as shocked as everyone else, so good on him for getting in there."

37

As the two families stood in the middle of the trackway between the old platforms, Mark showed them exactly where the collision had taken place.

"The whole platform was covered in wreckage. Apparently, they had to rebuild all of the station buildings on this side of the line."

As his father carried on explaining to the grown-ups what had actually happened, Alex wandered off towards the Hallow Hill end of the station. He looked across to his left, and saw the end of the line of railway cottages, and realised he was standing on the site of the old starter signal. He narrowed his eyes and looked up at the imaginary signal, wondering what it was displaying just before the collision. If it was 'on', showing a red light, then the distant could not have been pulled 'off' as the interlocking would have prevented it. Perhaps it was, after all, showing white? It just didn't make sense, though, and he turned and looked back down the line towards the Belcote Road bridge. A thought occurred to him that they could check the visibility to the old signal from here.

He also remembered the old bolt he'd found, and the disappointment when he and Clive had cleaned it up, only to find it was from an old car; a Javelin, he thought Clive had said.

As he walked back to the others, he heard Olivia talking fairly earnestly, and his ears pricked up at the mention of his name.

"Right, so Jack Dove reckoned he could see the man up the signal from here? Why don't we send Alex down there to stand where the signal was."

"Good idea. Right Son, remember where we found those bits of signal pulley, by the old broken down bridge. Could you go and just stand there – wave when you get there – and just look towards us."

A couple of minutes later, Alex was in position. The others could see him through the arch of the Belcote Road Bridge.

"OK, so... we can see the signal post from here. But if it was gloomy, or dark, and raining, could we see his face well enough to recognise him?"

"Not really, Dad," Olivia said "but you can at least see him. So, if Jack was up high enough, he could see a figure up the signal."

"Of course he could. But then, the signal was in clear view of the signalbox, which is another 100 yards or so up there. Now, let's go to the road bridge."

He called out to Alex to stay put, as the group walked past the site of the old signalbox, and took the path out of the goods yard, then left and onto the bridge. The bridge was fairly narrow – there was a bare sliver of pavement on one side – the side nearest to the station.

"Now," said Mark, stopping in the middle of the bridge, "imagine that you're a twelve-year-old girl, walking across this bridge in the dusk. From here, how well can you see Alex?"

Everyone agreed, he was clearly visible.

"Right, so, although there is no bridge where he's now standing, the signal would have protruded above the line of the bridge anyway, so as to be seen from the signalbox. In fact, it would have been quite tall, because in his evidence, Joseph Palmer says he could see the backlight. Now, the signal lamp was lower down the post than the signal arm, for him to have been able to see it. So, we're getting a worse view of Alex at ground level, than Katharine Palmer would have got of someone at our level. Now, could you make out Alex's figure clearly from here?"

"Yes, I can, although I'd find it hard to see his face in the dark," Roger volunteered, "but you can clearly see his figure, can't you."

"Exactly. Now, we don't know which side of this bridge Katharine was walking, because it was unpaved in those days and probably had no separate footway, but even if she was on this side of the bridge she would have seen someone easily."

They all agreed with Mark's assertion. He waved and beckoned Alex back to them, and indicated he should join them on the bridge.

"Dad, is that the church up there?" said Olivia, pointing further up the road towards Belcote.

"Yes, it is. Do you want to go and have a look around? It's quite a steep climb."

"Well, I'd like to, even if no-one else does." Freya said, making her way across the bridge. "Coming, Livvy?"

The two Phipps women started out for the church, with Vicky following closely. Roger and Jacqui waited on the bridge with Mark.

"I'm just trying to imagine what it must have been like, that massive train doing, what, sixty miles an hour, no brakes on, steaming straight on into the goods train, right there." Roger leant on the bridge wall, facing the old crash site.

"Well, they had a bit of a brake on the tender, but yeah, they must have been doing sixty. And of course, the fireman said the reversing lever jumped forward so that wouldn't have helped matters."

"Sixty doesn't sound that fast though, does it, gents?" said Jacqui. "I mean, we do that on the lane to Belcote."

"Yes, but your car doesn't weigh a hundred and eighty tons, and has brakes that work." Mark pointed out. "Also, even when the trains collided, the carriages at the back were still pushing on, as they had no brakes either. So it would have been like a giant sledge hammer pounding away. It's amazing they only lost twenty-one people."

They stood for another minute or so, before Alex joined them. "I could see you all really clearly when you were on the bridge, but not so well in the station. It's a long way off." he added. "I reckon Jack Dove invented that story to get at the Palmers."

"Which he did very nicely too, didn't he?" Mark commented, as they began slowly moving off up the hill towards the churchyard. As they ambled up the steeply sloping pavement, Mark mentioned that he was making a model of the station at the time of the accident, so he could try and make sense of the events.

"Good plan. You should make the model, and then make a film of what you think happened, show it to DCI Sherlock Smith back there, and see if she'll investigate." Roger chuckled. "I reckon she will. She's a local lass; also brought up on the tales of the crash. Let's face it, it was the biggest thing ever to happen here in the last few hundred years, so I think if she has a chance she'll try and open the case."

They met the others halfway round the churchyard, standing in front of some fairly recent graves.

"Found anyone of interest yet?" asked Mark

"Nope!" replied Olivia. "We're looking for Palmers and Whitmores, aren't we?"

"Well, and anyone else really, like Marriotts, Doves, Coopers."

"I can show you my great grandfather's grave." Roger said, leading them further down the path towards the far wall. "I remember the funeral and everything. It was only twenty-eight years ago – seems like yesterday. I can still hear his voice; boy did he have some spark, that man."

He led them into a shaded area, where young saplings had sprung up creating a gloomy, overcast feel to this part of the churchyard.

"Here you go. Henry Arthur Cooper, and Sarah, his wife. But she died long before him. Lovely old chap. I hope I live as long as him – ninety-three years and seven months. Mind, I'd have to be as active. He was right on it until the day he died. Sharp as a pin. Just dropped down stone cold dead in the street on the way to the pub. Way to go… but big shock for us, of course."

"Dad, can we go now. This place is giving me the creeps." Vicky grabbed her father's arm.

"This, my dear, is your great great granddad…"

"Yes, I know all that, but it's freaking me out."

She pulled him away, and they started to walk back towards the church, but Mark led them to a different path, taking them round the far side of the church.

Meantime, Alex and Olivia were enthusiastically leaping across the various grave plots, trying to spot as many surnames as they could. It took the two families nearly ten minutes to amble their way back to the church gate, but just as Roger was about to open it, they heard Olivia's voice shouting from behind a clump of small trees away to their left.

"Here! Here, everyone. I've found a Whitmore! Martha and William Whitmore. Wow, he lived till he was eighty-nine years old, in 1941. She died in 1906. So, they're both buried here then."

"Looks like it, Livvy" said Mark. "Now, let's look out for George…" and as he spoke, he saw the gravestone just behind William's. "There!"

George Whitmore's headstone was directly behind his son's. "It mentions his wife Sarah but only in memory of… which means she probably wasn't buried in this grave then."

"She's over here, Dad" said Olivia. "Look, Sarah Whitmore, beloved wife of George, who died 10th July 1869, and also their beloved daughter Hannah who died aged 14 in… something 1868 and also their infant son Harry who died May 1866." So, she's already in a full grave plot…"

"…which is why George is buried on his own, rather than with his wife. Of course, that would explain it." Mark could sense that their deductions about the disappearance of Jack Dove were becoming more likely at every turn.

"Anyone got a spade?" quipped Roger. We'll soon whip him out of there…"

"DAD! Stop it! You're really freaking me out now!" Vicky turned and stomped her way towards the gate. The two Phipps children took a few close ups of the headstones, and then everyone made their way back through the gate back down towards the old station.

Roger pointed to a large mound on the left as they got to the steeper part of the hill. "That is known as Field Mount. At one time, it was thought it might have been an old motte and bailey castle, but it's not a very likely place to build one."

"Wait… did you say Field Mount? Is there a pathway past it?"

"Yeah, look. It's a bit overgrown, but it's a public footpath to nowhere! It used to go over the old Hill Farm Bridge, but that's crumbled so it just stops at the edge of the field."

"What's on the other side of the bridge?"

"Lower Bank Field. Why?"

"Because this is where Jack Dove was last seen alive. Walking down that path, just there."

The two men stopped for a moment. Roger looked back up the hill towards the entrance to the churchyard.

"That's, what, fifty yards from here to the graveyard. That's' doable, isn't it? Kill Jack Dove just down here, and you could get him to the graveside in a couple of minutes without anyone seeing you."

Mark nodded. "This is going to be one hell of a case if we can get it looked into, eh? Blimey, Roger, we could be rewriting history here, I think!"

"I think you're right. Maybe the locals will forgive me my sins if I throw a village heritage museum into the mix. I could easily rebuild the station, you know. And we could put your model into it."

Mark laughed. "Good idea, Roger."

"I'm not kidding, Mark. It's what I do. See an idea, make it happen, while other folk just talk about it. Have a think, mate."

"I need to build the model first. Mind you, I've just bought the track. Haven't quite got planning permission from Freya yet, but I'll build the station bit first from the plans that came with the accident report, and a bit of help from online maps too."

They chatted model railways for the rest of the walk back to the Dukes Head.

"Right, well, you must come over to us soon." said Mark. "As soon as I get started on this model, and we've got some more info, come over. We can go through all the files and stuff."

"It'll be a pleasure, Mark, Freya... lovely to meet you all." Roger gripped Mark's hand. "And I meant what I said... if we solve this. Heritage Museum, right here, right in Salmsham, with your station model having pride of place. I'll get old Ted Crozier to dig out some pictures. Somewhere, there's a drawing of the aftermath of the crash. I'll send Ted's details to you."

As they drove off, waving out of the car windows, Mark commented that he wanted to make a start on the model, and if anyone wanted to help they were very welcome. When his wife agreed enthusiastically he breathed a gentle sigh of relief and smiled to himself; there would be no need to justify the space he was planning to use.

38

From: sheilabagley@phonetalkinternet.com
Sent: Wednesday, May 16, 2018 11.10 AM
To: mark@phippstribe.net
Subject: RE: More searches!

Dear Mark

I think your mystery is going to get deeper!

Harriet Brooks was the married name of Harriet Dove. She
married a John Brooks in 1888. As far as I can see they had
two children, a son who died aged 3, then a daughter who
married someone called Mellow. John Brooks died in 1895,
and Harriet died in 1915 in Hallowfield – I assume it's her
anyway. I've ordered the usual certificates for them all.

I wonder what she was doing in Salisbury with Hubert
Palmer? Were they in love, perhaps? What would Hubert
want with the daughter of a man who is meant to have
accused his brother of sabotage? Are you as suspicious as I
am that maybe she pushed him onto the electric rail?

As for the gravedigger: I've managed to find some online
parish registers. You can't get Belcote or Hallowfield, but
Salmsham is there so I can find actual marriage records
with their real signatures on them, and also burial records.
I've attached the burial record for George Whitmore.
There's also a page where they do the accounts. The
gravedigger in a church like Salmsham was usually either
the sexton, or someone appointed by them. It seems
Salmsham's sexton often used a local gardener, Joseph
Sands. I only know this because he appears in the annual

accounts, either for 'tending to the vicarage gardens' or 'grave digging'. There's nothing linking him to this burial though, and I'm not sure you'll ever know.

I do hope you're having an easier week after the last few? Freya tells me you're in the office most of the week for a change, and home every night for a week or so.

Love to all

Sheila xx

From: mark@phippstribe.net
Sent: Wednesday, May 16, 2018 7.37 PM
To: sheilabagley@phonetalkinternet.com
Subject: RE: More searches!

Thanks Sheila

Yes, I'm home, it's a quiet week at work, and less stressful but mainly because my line manager / director is away for two weeks.

I have my suspicions about Hubert's death too – and being near to a Dove child is just too much of a co-incidence. I'm clutching at straws here, but without getting certificates or anything, is there any way of finding out more about Joseph Sands?

While we're at it – Roger Cooper's wife Jacqui is a Draper, as was Jack Dove's wife. I'll leave that one with you...

Love

Mark x

From: sheilabagley@phonetalkinternet.com
Sent: Wednesday, May 16, 2018 8 25 PM
To: mark@phippstribe.net
Subject: Joseph Sands

Mark

You'll love this. Joseph Sands married Janice Palmer! I've gone back a bit further and she is Joseph Palmer's sister. There's no certificates as this is all before 1837, but there are baptism records. Their parents were Edward and Mary Palmer.

What's the relevance of the gravedigger?

I'll get back to you with the Draper stuff another time.

Sheila x

From: mark@phippstribe.net
Sent: Wednesday, May 16, 2018 8 46 PM
To: sheilabagley@phonetalkinternet.com
Subject: RE: More searches!

That was quick!

We think that the gravedigger could have been tipped to dig an extra depth so they could hide Jack Dove's body in the grave before the funeral. I thought it was a bit of a fantasy but now I'm not so sure; if the gravedigger was the uncle of the Palmer children he would have known how much they suffered because of Dove…

I've set Alex to do a complete timeline of everything – accident, deaths, etc, when he's not doing his homework.

While he's doing that, I'm making a model of the station as it was in 1874. It's taking my mind off the stress of the job at the moment. Did you know your daughter is a good modelmaker? She's been building the landscape out of plaster of Paris!

Love

Mark x

39

Tuesday 21ˢᵗ April, 1874 – Hallowfield Crown Court

Joseph Palmer sat in the dock, his head in his hands, as the prosecuting barrister cross-examined the various witnesses. He had barely managed to eat any lunch, not that there was much to eat anyway, but he had very little appetite. He listened to the two barristers as they questioned and cross-examined witnesses for the prosecution.

He knew that this was how the law operated – the prosecution would present the facts in a way most designed to seal his guilt firmly, twisting the words of witnesses to favour the barrister's arguments, whilst lightly dismissing anything which did not bolster the case for the prosecution. He just hoped he could be strong until such time as the defence barrister could have his say. His mind wandered back to the day of the accident. He knew that he had put all his signals to 'on' – and the register confirmed it. He knew this as much as he knew his own name… but then someone would question him and he would start to doubt himself. Still, he had the goods guard as a witness, a man who had no axe to grind either way. He should have had James too, although he was sure they would have given him a hard time during cross-examination. He wept silently as he thought of his son buckling under the pressure and taking his life, because he thought that would save his father from the inevitable incarceration which would follow a guilty verdict. He wished he could have spoken with him first; told him not to worry; told him it would be alright. He would even have offered to go to prison rather than lose his eldest son. They had only buried him last week, since when Joseph had barely slept.

He raised his head and looked across to the witness box, where the goods driver, George Chappell, was giving evidence. He only knew George slightly, but knew he was a good man, a solid worker, and a reliable driver. George was also an honest man, and was confidently explaining to the jury what had happened from his own perspective.

The counsel for the prosecution, Sir Hamilton John Milsom Dilkes, QC, cut an imposing figure in the courtroom. He had a fearsome reputation as a hard-hitter, with many high-profile successes to his name. Like all skilled barristers, however, he had the ability to put a witness at great ease before he went in for the kill, so to speak. The fact that he appeared to be a railway enthusiast, fascinated by the job of an engineman, was as much to do with his acting skills as with the truth. He did indeed find railways fascinating, and had spent a couple of happy hours on the footplate being shown the workings of a locomotive whilst working on another case several years back, but he had absolutely no desire to do it again. He held up a copy of the inquest into the deaths at Salmsham.

"Mr Chappell, you said in your evidence at the inquest that you pulled up in the station at the starter signal, which was presumably showing red at the time."

"Yes, Sir, that is correct."

"You're sure it was red?"

"Yes Sir. I would not have pulled up otherwise."

"But you also said the signalman had told you that you were to be shunted at Salmsham, so presumably you would have stopped anyway?"

"Yes, I would."

"So the signal might have been white?"

"No, Sir. It was red."

"But you just said, if it was white you would have pulled up anyway."

"I did, but what I meant was…"

"No, that's good, Mr Chappell. Thank you. I'll take your word that the signal was red when you stopped."

"Yes, Sir."

"Now… it says here, in your statement to the inquest, that, and I quote from your statement *"The stationmaster told me he would shunt us as soon as the line was clear. I stayed with my engine. My fireman was on the platform when we heard the express train whistle. I called out to him "There's a train a-coming. Let's move!" then I felt my train hit and heard the noise."* Those are your words, you'll agree, Mr Chappell?"

"Yes, Sir."

"Now, am I right in thinking you heard the whistle, and you thought correctly that the express was coming?"

"That's right, Sir…"

"…and so your first thought is to move forward, to try to get out of its way?"

"Yes, Sir. At that time I had no idea how fast he was going. The thought occurred to me that he might be having trouble stopping and so if I drew forward he might have more space."

"Quite so. I think we would all try and get out of the way if we heard the express train coming."

"Yes, Sir."

"Now, you fully intended to move forward, didn't you?"

"Yes, Sir."

"So what was the status of the starter signal?"

"Red, I think, Sir."

"Red. You're sure about that?"

"Pretty sure, Sir."

"I would ask you to think again, Mr Chappell. Are you sure that the signal was red?"

"Yes, Sir."

"So you're telling me that you were happy to start your train even though you were faced with a red signal? Isn't that against the instinct of any good engine driver, Mr Chappell?"

"Normally, yes, but to be honest, I didn't much care about the signal at that moment. I just needed to get my train out of the way."

"Even if you had to go through a red signal to do it?"

"Yes, Sir. I think I could answer to any inspector who might question my actions on that occasion."

"Quite so. And, if I may say so, Mr Chappell, had I been your inspector, I would have backed you up completely for starting your train and passing a danger signal, bearing in mind there was another train approaching from behind you."

"Thank you, Sir."

"That's quite all right, Mr Chappell. So you see, you did nothing wrong, and even though you did not move your engine, your intentions were clear and you could not have been accused of planning an action which was in any way wrong, don't you agree?"

"Yes, Sir."

"Good. Now, you have just told the jury, Mr Chappell, that you 'didn't much care about the signal at that moment', your words, and I put to you that maybe the reason was, that the signal was in fact now showing a white 'all clear', so in your mind you did not need to worry about passing a danger signal as there was not one to pass? Is this a possibility, Mr Chappell?"

"Well… I suppose it is. But I'm pretty sure it was still showing danger."

"Pretty sure… but not certain. I come back to my previous point, Mr Chappell, that perhaps you didn't notice the signal because it was now cleared for you and it was no longer something to be considered when you went to start the train."

"No, I…"

"Thank you, Mr Chappell. No more questions."

As George Chappell left the witness box, Joseph's heart sank. Sir Hamilton Dilkes QC was living up to his reputation as a hard-hitter. He'd just managed to sow enough doubt in the minds of the jury as to the status of that starter signal. If he could do that, he could argue that it was possible for Joseph to have pulled off the distant without realising it, and without being prevented by the interlocking bars beneath his feet in the signalbox.

The next witness was the fireman, Harry Lusby. He was equally unclear as to the condition of the starter signal, and had in fact said he was even looking in the direction of it when the crash happened. After a few minutes, Lusby was gone too, to be replaced by none other than Jack Dove.

Dove stood confidently in the witness box, and Joseph cringed as he was almost revered as the man who had helped to save many lives after the accident.

"Mr Dove, I understand you heard the crash as you were having a drink in the Dukes Head?"

"That's not quite right, Your Honour. I was about to have a drink. As it happens, I never touched a drop of drink, as the crash happened before I had a chance."

There was a quiet chuckle from the jury and the public gallery. Even Dilkes managed a little grin.

"Quite so. So you were perfectly sober when you rushed to the scene of the disaster."

"Yes, Your Honour."

At counsel's request, Dove then went on to describe what he had done to rescue people from the wreckage, confirming the evidence given at the inquest. Then Dilkes asked about the man up the signal.

"Well, Sir, as I said before, I happened to glance along towards the signal, and I saw a man clearly from where I was standing, on the roof of a carriage."

"You could see this man clearly."

"Yes, Your Honour."

"Even though it was dusk, and raining slightly/"

"Yes, Your Honour. I could see very clearly. In fact, I think it may be easier to see the signal from there than from the signalbox."

"How is that so, Mr Dove?"

"Because I was high up above the level of the tracks, but right in the centre of them. I couldn't miss seeing the signal clearly."

"Thank you. Mr Dove, can you identify this man?"

"I thought it looked like the signalman's son, James Palmer."

"You thought it was James Palmer?"

"Yes, Your Honour."

"Could you be certain of this?"

"Not completely, no. But it looked like him, and he was around at that time so I naturally assumed it was him, and not anyone else."

"Why would he have been around at that time?"

"Why, James Palmer was the station clerk. So he was there when the crash happened."

"Quite so. Did you see him after this time?"

"Never, Your Honour. I think he told us later on that he had gone home in shock, but he never helped with the rescue or nothing."

Joseph began to seethe with anger. Not only was Dove implying that James had tampered with the signal, he made the added statement, entirely unrequested, that James had gone home in shock.

"I see. Mr Dove, I would like to thank you for your evidence today, and I have no further questions."

"Thank you, Your Honour."

To his relief, counsel for the defence, Horace Ampleton QC, got straight to his feet.

"Mr Dove, you say that you could see clearly a man up the home signal?"

"That's right, Your Honour."

"I put to you that that is a nonsense, Sir."

"I... erm... no, it is true, Your Honour."

"What was the weather at the time, Mr Dove?"

"It was raining lightly, Sir, although I didn't really notice as I was busy trying to rescue people."

"Quite so. And what time in the evening was the accident, Mr Dove?"

"About twenty to eight, as I remember it?"

"So you would like us to believe that you could clearly see a man more than two hundred and sixty yards distant, in the darkness of the evening, and with light rain, and identify that man as James Palmer."

"Well, I did not state positively that it was Palmer."

"But you did, Mr Dove."

"I swear I did not, Your Honour."

"Just call me Sir, Mr Dove."

"Yes... Sir."

"So it would be reasonable for us to say that you cannot positively identify Mr Palmer as the man on top of the signal."

"Well... I thought it was him, Sir."

"But you have just said that you couldn't be sure."

"No, I couldn't be sure."

"Indeed, I will go further and state that you did not see anyone on the top of that signal when you say you did, Mr Dove, because you were too busy rescuing people from the train."

"No, that's not true, Sir. I saw someone. Definitely."

"But on-one else saw anyone. And no-one come forward who went up the signal at that time. However, I put to you that you may have indeed seen someone there, but much later than you remembered, and that you most likely saw Mr Faulkner, the ganger, who says in his evidence that after the accident he went up the signal to check that the light was on and displaying correctly."

"No, it was not Faulkner, Sir. I know him well as I used to work for the railway. I know his appearance, and it was not him."

"You are certain of this, Mr Dove?"

"Yes, Sir."

"Mr Dove, I find it hard to accept that you are capable of seeing a man clearly, from over two hundred and sixty yards away, in the dark, with light rain, with two overbridges between you. You must have extremely good eyesight."

"I have been told that, Sir."

The jury laughed.

"I would like to ask you another question, Mr Dove. I understand you have a disagreement with the Palmer family over another matter, not relating to the railway?"

"Not really, Sir."

"Not really. Oh, come come, Mr Dove. You are in love with Agnes Palmer, the daughter of the signalman, and she has refused your approaches, and what's more her father, the man in the dock here, has told you repeatedly to leave her alone. Is that not true?"

"It is true that I have been seeing Agnes Palmer for some time, yes."

"Now, Mr Dove, come come. You have been seeing Miss Palmer only because she is a housemaid at your father's farm. You have not been seeing her in the sense of walking out with her, have you?"

"Not exactly, Sir."

"Not exactly."

"Well, it's true I've… asked her."

"Asked her?"

"To marry me. You see my own dear wife died three years ago, and I have three young children, and I would like a wife."

"I'm sorry to hear that, Mr Dove. So, you have asked Miss Palmer to marry you, and she has rejected you."

"Something like that, yes. I'm still hopeful that she'll come round."

"I'm sorry, Mr Dove, but that is nonsense. You know perfectly well that Miss Palmer is not interested in you, and never has been, and that you have been warned away from her by Joseph Palmer…"

"Objection, Your Honour!" Dilkes rose to his feet indignantly. "Mr Dove is not on trial here."

"Quite so," the judge said. "Mr Ampleton, this is not relevant to the enquiry into the railway accident."

"My Lord, I believe this is relevant because the witness has reason to besmirch the good name of the defendant. It is known in the village that the two families are in dispute."

"Nonetheless, the fact that the witness wishes to marry the defendant's daughter is not material to the cause of the railway accident."

"My Lord, when he accuses the defendant's son of tampering with the signals, it implies that the defendant required assistance to cover up a mistake which I want to show did not happen."

"I think you have already shown that, Mr Ampleton. I would ask you to keep to questions directly relating to the case."

"Very well, My Lord. No... further... questions." Ampleton emphasised his final sentence to make it clear that he was not happy with the decision, following which the judge noted the time, and adjourned the proceedings until the following morning.

40

Jesse Smith stood in the witness box. A short man in his late twenties, with a long black beard, weather worn visage and glowering eyes, he looked and felt completely out of place in the courtroom. He had made a rudimentary effort to smarten himself up for the court, and had failed miserably in the process. Joseph recognised him as the young man he'd seen running along the line towards the accident soon after it happened. "He should have dressed in his normal work clothes" thought Joseph. "Right now, he looks like the perfect caricature of a village idiot."

Smith told the court he was a farm hand at Hill Farm, and related how he had been walking from his cottage on the other side of the farmhouse to the Dukes Head, and his route had taken him towards the overbridge, in front of which the home signal stood.

"What time did you set out for the Dukes Head, Mr Smith?" asked Sir Hamilton Dilkes.

"'Bout ten minutes past seven, I'd say."

"Thank you. And please describe your route from the farm, for the benefit of the jury here."

"Well, see, I 'as to cross the Upper Field, and then goes down to where the path runs along the bottom of the field, overlooking the railway. I turns along there, towards the Hill Farm Bridge."

"Thank you, Mr Smith. I want to stop you there for a moment. So, let me see, you are now walking parallel to the railway…"

"Wassat? No, I's walking along the edge of the field, see…"

"Yes, that's what I mean. The path you are taking runs next to the line…"

"No, no, no. Not next to the line. Over it. Above it. Same way the line goes, but high up."

"Yes, Mr Smith. I think what you are saying is, the path runs parallel to the line, but much higher up, on the top of the embankment."

"I don't know about parallel. Don't know what you mean by that."

The whole court seemed to burst into laughter. Even the judge smiled. Jesse Smith laboured on, under the misguided impression that he had managed to make the learned gentleman look foolish.

"Quite so, Mr Smith. The main point is, you could see the railway clearly from where you were?"

"Oh yes. Very clearly."

"And you could see the signal from the field."

"Yes, the signal is right there, in front of the bridge."

"And did you notice the position of the signal, Mr Smith?"

"I just said, didn't I? It was in front of the bridge…"

"Mr Smith. I meant, the position of the signal arm. Was it showing all clear or stop."

"Oh, I dunno about that."

"I'm sorry? In your evidence at the inquest you stated that the signal was showing 'white' for all clear."

"That's right. It was."

"But you just said you couldn't see it."

"No, no, no. You asked me if I could see the arm, and I said I couldn't."

"Very well, but you could see the light?"

"Of course. I told 'em that at the inquest!"

More laughter.

"Very well. What colour was the light showing, Mr Smith."

"White. It was showing white."

"Thank you, Mr Smith. And what happened after that.?"

"Well, as I was walking along the field, getting up near the bridge, the express came flying past, and then I heard 'im whistle. I thought he was in trouble, because they never whistle for long, but this went on and on."

"And then what happened?"

"Well, then I heard the crash, didn't I?"

"Go on."

"Well, then I runs down to the bridge, and just before I got there I saw a flash like lightnin' it was, right ahead over the treetops. It started the cows a moo-ing in the field next to me. I thought 'there's a pretty fire started' and then I ran over the bridge, and then jumped down onto the bank and ran along the line."

"What did you do then?"

"Well, then I helps with the rescuing until early next morning. Then I goes home again. Never got me ale."

The court laughed again.

"No further questions, My Lord."

As Dilkes sat down, Ampleton got to his feet.

"Mr Smith. Who else did you see on the bridge that night?"

"What bridge?" More laughter.

"The Hill Farm Bridge. The one you had to cross to get to the other side of the line."

"There was no-one on the bridge apart from me. When I crossed the bridge I saw no-one."

"Thank you. No further questions."

Joseph rubbed his face in disbelief. However much Jesse Smith had been made to look like an idiot, his evidence was pretty damning, and the defence counsel's cross-examination was shallow to say the least.

If he thought Smith's evidence was damning, however, it was nothing to that of the next witness. Charles Archibald was a highly respected member of the Salmsham village community. He was a master stonemason, and worked almost exclusively for the late Squire, either restoring the stonework on the manor house itself, or doing simpler jobs around the estate, and for many of the Squire's tenants. He was also known to create monumental carvings, in particular for the Squire's family mausoleum at Hallowfield church. Despite his advancing years, Charles was a supremely healthy man, and had no intention of retiring from his occupation until he could no longer lift a chisel.

After the initial swearing in and introductions, Charles was asked where he was on the evening of the accident.

"I was walking along the pathway which runs beside the railway line from Belcote Crossing to Salmsham, Sir."

"I must ask you, Mr Archibald, what were you doing out walking at this time of the evening?"

"I had just finished installing a small fountain at the home of Miss Bellingham, a friend of my employer, Squire Morphy. I had been taken over by trap, as the fountain was heavy, but I like to walk, and so I chose to return on foot, via the railway footpath."

"Thank you. Now, am I right in saying that the path does not follow the line all the way from Belcote Crossing?"

"That's correct. It starts off further south of the line, and then gradually climbs up the side of the embankment, until it is alongside the line, just where it becomes very straight."

"Quite so. Once you are beside the line, how far can you see along it?"

"Oh, at least a mile, a mile and a half. Certainly. Almost all the way to Salmsham, until the line curves to the right just before the station."

"So, you can see the signals from the pathway."

"Yes, that's right. You can see both the distant signal, and the home signal, on a clear day or night."

"And could you see both signals?"

"I could."

"And what time was this?"

"Well, I don't carry a watch, but as I was nearly at the Hill Farm Bridge by the time of the accident, I would say probably about twenty-five past seven when I was alongside the line."

"Thank you. And what colour were the signals at that time?"

"They were white. They were both white, and they stayed that way all the time."

"You are certain of that?"

"I am."

"Now, Mr Archibald, did you see the express train passing you?"

"I did, yes."

"And where were you when it passed you?"

"I must have been just approaching the Hill Farm Bridge... yes, that's right. I remember thinking he was going pretty fast for that bend. I thought the passengers might know about it."

"And then you heard the accident?"

"Yes, that's right."

"And what did you do then?"

"Well, by now I was on the bridge and heading up towards my house, so I thought I'd better drop my tools off, because they're valuable and I didn't want to leave them out in the dark. So I went to my house, left my tools there and then I went back down the hill to the station."

"Thank you, Mr Archibald, for your very clear and concise evidence. No further questions, My Lord."

Ampleton got straight to his feet.

"Mr Archibald. You say the signals stayed the same even after the train went past you?"

"Yes, Sir. This is true."

"They were showing white?"

"Yes, Sir."

"And you were how far from the bridge when the express train went past you?"

"Oh, let's see, about a hundred yards I think."

"You think a hundred yards. Can you be more specific? I mean, at which part of the bank were you?"

"That's difficult to say, Sir. You see, one bit on earth bank is much like another…" There was a certain low level chuckling from the court.

"I ask you because, you see, the collision must have happened very soon after the express passed you, mustn't it?"

"Yes it did, very soon after."

"And yet in that time you had moved from a hundred yards before the bridge, to being on the bridge, and not noticing that the signal was red."

"No… the signal was white all the time."

"I find this hard to understand, Mr Archibald. You see, even if the defendant had mistakenly pulled all his signals off, instead of having them all on, they were most definitely 'on' straight after the accident because we have witnesses who saw the signalbox and saw the levers pushed over. How do you explain this?"

"I can't, Sir. I can only explain what I saw."

"Well, I put to you that your evidence may not be as clear as my learned friend says it is, because apparently you were able to move at a very high speed from a point a hundred yards ahead of a signal, to the bridge behind the signal, faster than the express train could travel two hundred yards. You see my difficulty?"

"I do, but…"

"So I put to you, Mr Archibald, that your estimate of distance and time may be somewhat wayward."

"Well…"

"Yes or no, Mr Archibald?"

"Well, maybe a little. But the signals were still showing white, wherever I was on the line."

"Which could, by all accounts, be anywhere…"

"Objection, My Lord!" Dilkes jumped to his feet.

"Mr Ampleton, please! The witness is not on trial here" said the judge.

"Thank you, My Lord. Mr Archibald, all I am saying is, your estimates of time and place seem to be a little inaccurate? Am I right?"

"Maybe a little, Sir. But I know those signals were clear when the express passed them."

"But you were way past the distant signal when the express passed you. It could have been showing red by then, surely?"

"Maybe, Sir. But the home signal was definitely showing white when the train passed me."

"Thank you, Mr Archibald. No further questions."

By Friday of the case, all the evidence had been heard, and the first part of the morning was spent with the prosecuting counsel's summing up. Sir Hamilton John Milsom Dilkes, QC, pulled no punches as he portrayed Joseph Palmer as a hardworking and honest man who nonetheless was unsuited to the task of running a busy signalbox, and who had made such a glaring error as to have caused a major disaster, and who then compounded this error by attempting to cover it up with the aid of his son, who had sadly taken his own life to cover up his shame. Joseph thought that was a most despicable comment, but he was not surprised at hearing such a thing in court. He had been warned by his own solicitor that he would be portrayed in a way no-one who knew him would recognise.

He was more disappointed at the apparent abandonment of support for him from his work colleagues. In particular, Isaac Kemp gave the impression that he just wanted to shift the blame for the accident onto Joseph; the Directors were likewise keen to divert attention away from the possibility of sabotage and firmly onto their supposedly errant employee. The only support he felt he had from colleagues was from Arthur Marriott, who admitted he had briefly seen James Palmer just after the accident, walking past him in a daze, and from Harrison Wiggins, the goods guard, who was adamant that the signals were at danger, and who had signed the register to that effect.

He was similarly disappointed at the performance of his defence counsel. Horace Ampleton QC was no Sir Hamilton Dilkes, that was certain. However, he tried hard to sow enough doubt in the minds of the jury that whatever people said, the signals could not have been white unless they had been tampered with. It was Joseph's and Harrison's word against a 'bumbling farmhand' and a stonemason with 'no sense of time or space'. Joseph had asked for his daughter Katharine's evidence to be heard, but it was decided by both sides that she would not be able to be taken seriously.

He wished he had the energy to stand up and ask some pointed questions to each of the witnesses, but he had been told to say nothing to anyone. He felt empty. The past few weeks had drained him emotionally, to the point where he cared little for himself. In his own mind, he had let his family down, and he would take whatever was coming to him with dignity.

The judge's summing up was much shorter than expected, and as Joseph had feared, he was very much on the side of the prosecution.

It took the jury just under two hours to find him guilty on all 21 counts of manslaughter, and the judge just another fifteen minutes to sentence him to four years in prison. He sank down in the dock, but was almost immediately handcuffed and taken away, down the steep steps to the holding cells beneath the courtroom.

He had not looked up at his family in the public gallery – he felt too ashamed of himself. Had he done so, he would have seen his wife with her head in her hands, sobbing quietly, being comforted by her eldest daughter, Martha Whitmore. Agnes Palmer was absent from the court, having been forbidden to attend for more than one day by Farmer Dove. Hubert Palmer sat alongside his other two sisters, his jaw set, glaring angrily at the judge. Sarah Palmer held his hand tightly, her expression even more blazing than Hubert's, while young Katharine sat quietly with tears streaming down her face. It was she who spoke first, long after the rest of the public had left the gallery.

"I know he didn't do it. I know it wasn't him. They never even thought about sabotage, but I think it was, wasn't it? Pa is not a liar, but nor is Mr Archibald. So, someone must have tampered with those signals."

"You're probably right, little Kate," said Hubert, squeezing her hand, "so when the dust has settled, let's do some quiet digging and find out what's happened. Let's do this for Pa. Who's in?"

"I'm in." said Sarah. "I reckon I know who's behind all of this, and I'm going to prove it, and I'm going to tell the world, and he'll hang for it."

"Don't be silly, all of you. How will you prove anything? We've just heard all the evidence. No-one will believe anything different." Martha cradled her mother's head on her chest.

"Martha, you have not heard all the evidence. You've only heard what they want you to hear. What about all those questions they didn't ask, eh?" Hubert spoke through gritted teeth, as the family were ushered out of the public gallery and onto the broad staircase.

"Like what?"

"Well, like… they wanted to know everything about why our Katharine was out at night without Mother knowing, as if that was an important piece of evidence, but no-one checked up on whether Jack Dove was where he said he was before the crash, or who he was drinking with, or who else saw Jesse Smith, or Charles Archibald. In other words, they took everyone at face value, unless it didn't fit their idea of what happened."

"Well, you can do what you like, but Mother needs our help and support now…"

As they reached the foyer of the courthouse, Hubert tried in vain to keep people away from his mother and sisters, but quite a few wanted to offer their support. While they were busy making polite thank yous to a couple of well-wishers, a sprightly middle-aged man pushed his way through the crowd, and approached Charlotte Palmer.

"Mrs Palmer. My name is Seale; I have been representing the estate of Squire Morphy, and I would like to discuss something with you. I know that you are in shock, and I sympathise with you very much, but the new Squire is extremely sympathetic to your situation and has told me he is keen to assist your family in any way he can. I know this is not the time nor the place to discuss matters in detail, but please take my card and come and see me at your earliest convenience."

With that, Mr Seale nodded to the Palmer children, and again to Charlotte, and backed away in the crowd.

"What was all that about, I wonder?" said Hubert.

"It's Squish. He's always liked Pa. They go back a long way, remember? Squish used to like the railway, and he would go into Pa's signalbox and talk for hours. He'll look after you, Mother. He'll make sure you can pay the rent... he can make things happen. I think you'd be wise to go and see Mr Seale as soon as you can."

"I think..." said Charlotte, standing with great dignity, "that before I do that, I have to see my poor husband. Take me to him in the cells, Hubert."

41

Mark Phipps bent over the large trestle table he'd erected in his garage, and threaded a small pair of wires through the tiny hole he had drilled in the back of the family's new model railway layout. It was a fiddly job, but he felt very satisfied, and was looking forward to running the first train along the two 'main' lines, which he planned to do before lunch.

It was half-term week for both the Phipps children, and Mark had booked the time off work so that they could all work on the layout and the Railway Case (as they called it) together. Freya had spent the morning tidying up the new flower beds in the back garden, but was taking a keen interest in the model's progress. She had put a lot of effort into creating the lineside scenery, using photographs and paintings from the period, supplied with great enthusiasm by Ted Crozier. Meantime, Mark had carefully laid the track bed, taking care to model the curve exactly to scale, with the aid of Google Earth images as well as the maps supplied at the time of the inquest. The main detail work now would be to the buildings and signals. After much research, he had realised that no-one made contemporary 1874 signals, so he'd have to model them from scratch. He'd enlisted the aid of his father, who had helped with his original railway layout all those years ago. While he waited for John to supply those, he used cocktail sticks to mark out the position of the signals.

He'd used four 3 metre lengths of MDF as baseboards, which gave him more than enough length to model the complete station, and the line leading back to the distant signal. He was determined that on a fine day, he could put the whole model together outside, and be able to run trains right into Salmsham Station. He had also decided not to model the area beyond the starter signal, so whilst he was modelling the goods yard as well, rails and all, there was no actual connection with the main running lines. At the far end of the fourth baseboard was a 2 metre 'fiddle yard', which would have a cover so that the model trains could be marshalled out of sight of the viewing public, whoever they might be. The only unrealistic aspect of this was a tunnel mouth where there should have been a curve round towards Belcote Crossing, but the family was only concerned with the stretch of line from the distant signal to the starter; that was where all the action had taken place.

By the time Alex had shuffled into the garden in a pair of tatty jeans and a T-shirt which said 'Am I bothered?', the main lines were connected to the power, and Mark was running a little tank engine up and down both lines.

"Wow, Dad. That's looking cool. Can I help with anything yet?"

"Yes, you could start measuring out the bridges, especially the Hill Farm Bridge because we've only got drawings of that from 1883 or something. They're over there, on the workbench. You could cut out some of that thin wood and we'll sort out how to fix it all together later on."

While his father tested the other sections of the line, which were still on separate baseboards, Alex worked away on the curvature of the arch.

"It occurred to me, Dad. You know in that court case, that guy the stonemason who said he got up on the bridge when the crash happened? Well, he couldn't have done it that quickly, because the path went under the bridge first, and then there were steps up to the level of the field. Unless they changed it after the accident, I don't see how he could have seen what he said he saw."

Mark sucked in air through his teeth as he struggled with a small connecting pin beneath the third baseboard. "Well, you might be right. He seemed a very respectable witness, but some of his evidence did seem somewhat suspect. But the main thing is, they believed him at the time, and you have to have some faith in the jury members – they could see and hear how he spoke, and judge whether to believe him or not. We just see words on a page."

"True…"

"Not only that, but we're reading newspaper reports. They write down the bare conversations… you don't get the 'errrs' and 'umms' and all the other little asides."

"Fair enough. But I don't like him, Dad. I think he's a fraud. Well, I like to think that. Otherwise our Joseph must have really screwed up."

Father and son worked on for another hour or so, before they were joined by Olivia, for once showered and dressed before midday, carrying a tray with of mugs and a plate of jaffa cakes.

"Morning everyone!" she grinned. "Coffee is served. Mum, yours is here as well!"

There was bang on the garden gate, and a parcel was held up over it. A voice called "Helloooo! Post for you" as Freya unlocked the gate and took the parcel and a few letters from the postman.

"Ah. This is from the lab I sent the tape to. Folks... we have the rest of Great Grandad Phipps' interview, assuming they fixed it."

"Great – why don't we sit down and have a listen indoors over coffee?" Mark said. "My back is killing me and I've had it up to here with these silly little pins and wires. I think I've gone cross-eyed."

A few minutes later, the family were once again sitting around the tape player, listening to Adam Phipps's tales from the war, while Alex recorded the playback just in case it broke again.

"We've heard this already..." Olivia chimed in.

"Shhh! I'm recording!" said her brother, while Freya put her finger to her lips. They listened for a few minutes, then Mark raised his eyebrows and pointed to the tape player as his Grandad started talking about Auntie Ath.

"Well, I hadn't been home long and my Auntie Ath came to stay. Christmas '46 I think it was. Have you heard of Auntie Ath?"

"Can't say I have, Grandad."

"Well now, she was one heck of a lady. I loved her to bits, and she loved me too – she never had kids of her own so I was like a grandson to her. Well, she used to work on the railways, and you've heard of the big crash at Salmsham, haven't you?"

"Yes, quite a lot about it."

"Well, it was Auntie Ath's father, my mother's grandfather – he was the signalman who they blamed for

the crash. But she told me that it was not his fault at all, and that she and her brother and her brother-in-law, they found out who was responsible for it, and did them in, and hid the bodies."

"What, you mean murder?"

"Yes, I mean murder. I haven't told anyone this before. I mean, my mother heard it and told me not to tell a soul. But I went and wrote it all down, in my old diary, which of course I've lost now."

"But… what did they do exactly."

"Well, I can't remember all the details… names, or anything, but I remember the gist of it. See, while she was telling me all this, I was sitting there thinking 'Nooo, she's a harmless old dear, wouldn't hurt a fly' but I tell you what, I wouldn't have wanted to cross her after that. Really shocked I was."

[Silence]

"So, Grandad… what happened then. What did she tell you?"

"Right, well, it can't hurt anyone now, can it. When the crash happened, her young man was killed. He was standing on the platform, doing his job, he was a porter, I think. So poor Auntie Ath, she was only a young lass but she wanted to marry him, and he was killed. She saw him afterwards as well. She said she wanted to die right there, but anyway… they had a court case where they accused her Pa of manslaughter. She said that right after the case, where they sent her Pa to prison, she and her brother Hubert, and her sister Martha, they decided to find out everything that had happened. Like, all the little details, checking all the evidence and so on. They decided to do it very stealthily and over a long period of time, so they could make sure of all the facts and then get their revenge when folk weren't expecting it. Well, the first thing they did was checked up on this chap Dove. Jack Dove. That's who she said she thought had a hand in it. So they checked up on him. He was the one who had told a story about her older brother, said he'd tampered with the signal to cover for their Pa or something. Anyway, this older brother topped himself rather than face the court."

"Hang on Grandad. Do you mean, she lost her brother as well as her boyfriend? And her father going to prison?"

"That's right, yes. So, they started to ask around and it turned out Jack Dove had said he was drinking at the Dukes Head when the crash happened, and he'd run up there straight away. Well, he must have run ruddy fast, she said, because he was already there almost as soon as the crash happened. So they asked the landlord, and he said Jack Dove hadn't been near the place for days. So, he was lying, see, but no-one had checked. Then her little sister had seen someone up the signal just before the crash, see. Well, they reckoned it was Jack Dove, and he messed with the signal lens, took a bolt out or something, so the signal showed a white light. White was all clear then see, not green."

"That's sabotage, Grandad!"

"It is. But he didn't do it all himself. 'Cos, he had to put it back as well afterwards, so no-one would notice. There was another farmhand, from a different farm. He was part of the plan as well. And then they got someone else to tamper with the other signal so when the lever was pulled in the 'box, the signal still showed all clear. As soon as the train past, this other person put the signal back to danger, and then had the front to stand up in court and say he saw the signal showing all clear..."

"Archibald – the stonemason!" cried Alex.

"Shhhh! Alex, we know, we can hear it too. Quick, wind it back a bit, Mark" said his wife impatiently.

42

A few seconds later, and they were back to the same place in the tape, as Adam Phipps's voice carried on.

"...stand up in court and say he saw the signal showing all clear, which was true, he did, so he wasn't lying. Clever people, this lot. So anyway, they did some more digging and gradually built up a picture of what had happened, but then Martha got cold feet and told them she didn't want to have any more to do with it. She also said if anything happened to anyone else, she'd tell on them. So they waited and waited, and anyway, their Pa came out of prison, she said he was a very bitter man, quite broken, but then the local Squire took pity on him and gave him a job and so on. But then Agnes died. Now, Agnes was another sister, and she worked up at the farm where Jack Dove lived, and he wanted to marry her, but she was betrothed to one of the porters and didn't want to marry Dove. Apparently, he was a cruel man, and beat his first wife, and his kids. She died in childbirth, they reckoned he'd beaten her beforehand, because the baby was born all damaged and ended up in an asylum. Anyway, Auntie Ath said Jack Dove raped her sister and told her if she ever told anyone he'd kill her. Well, she told her man, the porter. He was so angry he threatened Jack Dove. He denied it, of course, and threatened to have him dealt with... 'cos this man Dove had some pretty nasty mates. Well, soon after that Agnes died in her sleep, apparently in a fit, so they said, but no-one believed that. They reckon he poisoned her. So anyway, Hubert, and Auntie Ath, and this porter chappy, they vowed to get Jack Dove, so they lured him to the churchyard on some pretext, and Hubert

and the other man confronted him, and then... I'll never forget her telling me this... she had her mother's carving knife and she just stepped out from her hiding place and stabbed him, right through the ribs, several times. She told me she was so angry, and he went down pretty fast but she kept stabbing him. Well, they had to get rid of the body but... hang on, that's right. They waited until someone died in the village, and they got the gravedigger... he was their uncle I think... and he dug extra deep, so they threw this body into the grave and covered it over, so when they had the funeral, no-one knew."

"That's crazy, Grandad. You mean, he's still buried there?"

"Yep, that's right Mark. If you go and dig up the grave, you'll find him underneath, hehe."

"How did they get away with it? I mean, he must have been missed?"

"Well, he was miss-ING, not missed, as such. Well, they had some cleaning up to do, that's for sure. But they made up some story about seeing him walking across the fields earlier in the day, and most people thought he'd probably left home because, let's face it, he wasn't liked much. I think only his father missed him. Not his kids"

"That's one heck of a story, Grandad!"

"Oh, it's not finished yet, not by a long chalk. Next they decided to go after the other chap, who they reckon had sabotaged the other signal and said it was showing white. Well, apparently Hubert confronted him, and he denied everything, but then the next morning he heard the old boy had died in the night of a heart attack. Auntie Ath said they hadn't killed him, but they were planning something and he did them all a favour. Well, then anyway, later on this porter chappy marries the younger sister... remember, he was going to marry Agnes, but he married this Kate girl. Well, he just couldn't keep his mouth shut, and boasted that he'd done Jack Dove in. So they sort of fell out with him. Hubert put the frighteners on him, then anyway, some years later, he stepped in front of a train and died. They all reckon it was an accident, and his wife saw it all happen, and so did lots of other people, but still Auntie Ath reckons her sister did him in somehow. Anyway, after this, Jack Dove's daughter, who is now married… her husband was friends with this porter chap, and told his wife that the porter had killed her father. Well, years later, after her husband died, she tracked Hubert Palmer and seduced him, because he'd never married, you see. Anyway, she got him thinking they were going to get married, but she pushed him onto the electric rails and got him killed, then had the nerve to say she'd found him. Well, Auntie Ath knew straight away this was a lie, so she lured this woman… I don't know her name, but anyway, Auntie lured her into a trap and killed her, and threw her body into a quarry. Now, I don't know how true that one is, because she must have been very strong, but anyway, she was found years later and they thought she'd fallen into the quarry."

"Gosh, this sounds like revenge with a vengeance, Grandad. If I ever write it down, that's what I'd call it."

"Don't write it down, young Mark. There's lots of people still affected by it."

"How come?"

"Well now, what you haven't asked is… why would Jack Dove want to cause this train crash in the first place?"

"Well that's obvious. He couldn't marry Agnes so he got his revenge on her by accusing her father of causing a train crash."

"No. That wasn't 'it. Look… I've told you enough. I think we should talk about other things."

"But surely it wouldn't do any harm now, Grandad? It's 1992… when did Auntie Ath die?"

"Well, now there's a thing I'd forgotten. I told you she said she had to get of off her chest?"

"Yes. It was Christmas Eve, wasn't it?"

"It was. And we had a lovely Christmas Day, although I was still a bit shocked, of course, I'd almost forgotten it all by the end of the day. I had my gentle old Auntie back again. And then, Boxing Day, my mother went in to wake her and she was gone."

"Gone?"

"Died in the night, probably about 3 o'clock they reckoned. Heart failure, the doctor said. Apparently it's very common over Christmas. The old folk, they eat and drink more than they have for a month, have a great time and then peg out."

"She must have had an inkling she was dying."

"Oh, I'm sure she did. It was probably the need to confess to my Mum which kept her going."

"So… are you going to tell me why Jack Dove did what he did? Or have I got to do some research of my own in the area?"

"No, no, don't do that. Don't mention any of this. Look, think about it for a moment. Who was killed in the crash? Which famous person?"

"I don't know? Was there a famous person on the train, Grandad? You haven't told me?"

"Oh, right, well… it was just a week after they'd had a general election, and the Squire was on the train. He'd been up to London, because he was a Director of the railway, and he was also a Lord… Lord of the Manor… Squire, whatever it was. Well, he'd been meeting the new government because he wanted to expand the railway. The story went that he wanted to build a branch line off from Salmsham Station to the north, to connect with the quarries about 5 miles north of Hallowfield, which he owned. Now, this would have taken the line straight through Rosfell Farm… the Dove's farm."

"Ah, so that's why Jack Dove did it."

"No no, listen. It wasn't only the farm that would be affected. It was the whole village. Two farms, not one. Hill Farm as well. They'd have to move people; jobs would go to further away down the line. Lots of folk would have to leave their old homes. They didn't want to move. So, there were powerful forces at play here, Mark. All I will say is, once the old Squire was dead, his son reversed the decision. I remember they had a nickname for him. Squish, they called him. Squish Morpho. Funny name, but he'd had it since he was a young lad. Well, he was a popular chap, and they say he saved Salmsham, and helped the village grow. He'd persuaded the railway not to build the branch, but anyway they didn't want to, and soon after that they were sold to another railway."

"But you still haven't told me who was responsible for the crash. Who put Jack Dove up to it?"

"It wasn't only Jack Dove. He thought he was the only one, but he wasn't. But… listen I can't tell you, Mark. I won't tell you. It's the one thing Auntie Ath swore me to secrecy. I said I'd never tell, and I won't but… It's best left alone. But anyway, you'll probably work it out one day."

"Thank you, Grandad. And now this is the end of the taped interview with Mr Adam Ph…"

The tape had come to an end. Freya laughed. "That was well judged, Mark. Or did you know you were getting close to the end of the tape?"

"No, I hadn't noticed. I would have turned it over, but Grandad said he'd had enough."

"So, Dad," said Olivia, "we were right about the body under the grave. Haven't we got enough to go to that police lady with, to get the case opened."

"Well, yes… we probably have enough evidence. But she said 'Chapter and Verse', which means, a timeline for the accident, all the relevant documents, and anything else we can find along the way."

"Dad, this is going to take ages!" Alex exclaimed. "I mean, he's just blown my timeline out of the water."

"Well, just go back through the tape… or your recording of it, and add in whatever facts you can. We'll tidy it up later. I think we should aim to finish this model, and invite a certain lady detective over here. Oh, and see if Grandpa Phipps has found any more useful papers."

"What about the Coopers, Dear?" added Freya. "I reckon we should let Roger hear this tape too."

"Good plan. I'll give Roger a call now, and see what he's up to this week. I mean, are you up for doing a buffet meal or something?"

"Of course, just… see when they can come over."

43

Thursday May 31st 2018 – Milnefield

Roger Cooper grinned as he watched the little model shunting engine slide alongside the down platform at 'Salmsham', on the Phipps' half-completed model.

"This is a really brilliant likeness of the station, Mark. Look, you've even got all the embankment and the brick wall in front of the churchyard."

"Ah, that was Freya. I'm just working on the buildings… those pictures Ted Crozier sent are great but all the buildings are at an angle, or half out of shot. It's taking a bit of time. But it's keeping us occupied."

Roger moved along to the next baseboard, as Mark pointed out where the remaining two boards would fit, once they'd opened up the garage doors and expanded into the garden.

"What I'd really like to do, once I finish this all off, is set it up outside, and then make a short video explaining how the accident happened. We'd need to use half the garden though. But look at this book. This is what you need to look at, Roger, to understand how they sabotaged the signals."

Mark took out an old book which had been recently re-published, dated 1874, written by a signalling expert of the day. In the back were various diagrams of the many different types of signal in use at the time.

"Here is the type of home signal they'd been using on the London & Western for about seven years at the time of the accident. Now, look, there is the signal arm, and there is the rod which connects it to the lens. And there… is the lens itself. That was coloured red."

"Why's there only one lens though?" asked Roger.

"They only needed a red light. White was all clear."

"Ahhhh, so, I get it. When the arm goes to danger, the lens drops in front of the lamp and the light shows red. So… if you removed the lens light, the light shows 'all clear'."

"Precisely."

"Actually, Mark, you wouldn't even need to remove it. Just disconnect the lens arm from the main lever."

"Roger! You've just got it! We were wondering how they were able to put the lens straight back in without being seen. We assumed they'd taken all the screws out, lifted the lens out and then replaced it, all in the space of a minute or so. But undoing that arm would be the work of a few seconds, and same, doing it back up again."

Mark made a note on another sheet of paper he'd been using. "We've been constructing a timeline of every little event… I tell you Roger, this is taking us ages. I'm starting to remember why I gave up doing this research in my teens. Too much like hard work!"

Roger nodded and took a sip from the mug of coffee Olivia had just given him while the two men were pouring over the signal plans.

"Thanks, Livvy. I'm sorry it's just me today. Jacqui's gone to Frome to see an old friend, and

Vicky's still in bed even though she said she wanted to come over today."

Olivia smiled "That's OK, I can sympathise with her. I've been basically dossing most of the week."

Mark turned a page in the old book. "Now, here is the distant signal. This is the exact version they used at Salmsham. You can see it's slightly different from the home, because the lamp is much higher up; that's because of the visibility from Belcote. Now, one thing about these signals... they have a repeater in the signalbox, because the signalman can't see the actual signal, so there's a wire from the signal, back to the box. When the signal arm moves, the wire is pulled and the repeater moves in the box. It's like a little miniature signal right above the lever, so the signalman knows what the distant is doing.

"What, they had all this stuff back then?"

"Oh yeah. It was a pretty sophisticated system they had going then. It was just technologically primitive, by our standards at any rate. Now, see this balance weight here? When the signalman pulls the signal 'off', this wire pulls the balance weight up in the air, which pushes this lever, which connects to the arm and pushes it off. When he wants it to go to danger, he pushes his level forward, which loosens the wire, but the balance weight pulls the wire from the box, and pulls the arm back to danger."

"Got it."

"So... what I reckon this guy Charles Archibald did... I'll tell you about him later... he somehow wedged something, like a metal bar maybe, under the balance weight to stop it pulling the signal arm out to danger, so it was showing 'all clear', and so was the light, of course. But also, he made sure the repeater wire was pulled so the repeater in the signalbox showed the signal was at danger. Now, it wouldn't have taken much to do that, and it would have been easy to remove it all as soon as the train passed, leaving no trace."

"Clever stuff."

"So actually, when you look at the report, and all the evidence they'd collected, the only way all the evidence fitted was if the signals had been tampered with, but I reckon the railway company couldn't bring themselves to believe it, or maybe, thought it was true but wanted to cover it up, so they lobbied to put pressure on the Board of Trade to come down on the signalman and say he messed up."

Roger stared at the model and shook his head. "You know what. I really think we should go public with this. Even though it's my own ancestor who did it all…"

"He wasn't the only one. You should listen to this tape I've got, Roger. We'll have a listen over lunch, while we eat."

"Good idea. Hey, does the line work all the way up here yet?"

"It does indeed, "grinned Mark, "watch this!" and the two men spent a happy few minutes watching the little engine shunting up and down the lines.

Lunch had been a curious affair, as they tiptoed their cutlery around the food so as to eat as silently as possible, while listening to the late Adam Phipps relating his aunt's tale. The tape was stopped twice so Mark or Freya could add comments, but Roger was fascinated to hear the whole story unravelling.

"I reckon we've got a good enough confession there to go to Chloë Smith with. Enough to start her looking at any rate."

Mark agreed. "I think you're right, but I want to present her with a complete story so she has no chance to back out of it. I wonder whether, once we've got it all sorted, to get the local press involved."

"Yes, definitely, but your man for that is Ted Crozier. He knows who to talk to, and who has influence, and so on. I tell you someone else who might be of use, who I am on good terms with – Arabella Templeton-Stubbs."

"Now, why does that name ring a bell?" said Freya.

"Because she's recently become my M.P., and she was the one who stood up in parliament recently and made that comment about giving every male M.P. an attitude test and any who tried to justify any past inappropriate comments about women should be removed. Provoked quite a storm. She's a feisty lady, but also happens to be descended from the old Lords of the Manor of Hallowfield."

"Really? What, Squish Morphy and all of his ilk?"

"I think so. I'll have a chat with Ted, because he knows the history of that family. But I'll talk to Arabella. I used to do a lot of work up at the Manor; in fact, it was me who built five new cottages up there, and renovated the old ones."

"Does she own the Manor then?"

"No, her Great Uncle does. She lives in the Manor Lodge though, and in London, of course. But she's very approachable – I'll give her a call later. If I want to make Salmsham Heritage Centre a reality I'll need friends in high places."

After lunch they went back to the model. Alex was still working on installing the Hill Farm Bridge, which was proving fiddly to say the least. By the time Freya appeared with late-afternoon tea, Roger, Mark and Alex had managed to fit the bridge snugly and securely in place, and were now building up the cutting to the east. Before he left for home, Roger took a few photos of the model, and promised to get Ted Crozier to have a look at them.

"I couldn't resist taking a few along the track towards Salmsham." Roger said, scrolling through the album on his phone so that the others could see the pictures. "Even though it's a model, it gives you a good idea of what the engine crews could see."

After Roger had left, Mark and Freya carried on with the cutting, while Alex started work on the last baseboard, cutting out the tunnel mouth for the fiddle yard.

44

By the end of the half-term week, the Phipps's railway model had been almost completed, and Sunday afternoon saw quite a gathering as the Coopers arrived with Ted Crozier in tow. Olivia's Jake was also there, overseeing the marshalling of the recently purchased model goods trucks into the correct order. All that was missing from the model were the period signals, two period locomotives (both expensive models which Mark had ordered discreetly when Freya was not looking) and the coaches for the passenger train, which were proving hard to source.

Alex had asked to invite Hazel over, and as her father was also a little interested in old railways, the invite had been extended to him too. Geoff Burns was instantly impressed by the model buildings, and got into an animated but polite discussion with Roger about the quality of old buildings compared to modern houses, while Alex showed Hazel the finer details of the model.

John and Fenella Phipps were there too, as John had found a few more family papers which he'd copied for Mark's benefit. John had also brought the first of the two model signals, the distant. He explained it was simpler to make than the home signal as the post was taller and didn't need cutting. It was too late for Mark to formally install it, but he placed it beside the cocktail stick which marked the site of the signal on the model.

Freya's parents were away in Scotland, but Freya had invited some of their new neighbours over.

Once everyone had had a good look at the model, Mark called for everyone's attention and then explained to a large but captive audience the family's theory of how the Salmsham rail disaster was caused, and the immediate outcome.

At the end of Mark's presentation, there were lots of questions asked, many of which were taken up by Ted Crozier. A lively discussion brewed over the merits or otherwise of further investigations, and whether the police should even be concerned with it, when there was so much crime happening right now which had to be prioritised. While this was going on at the 'Salmsham' end of the model, Alex was at the far end, on the fourth baseboard, trying to fit the new distant signal into the base, and explaining to Hazel exactly what a distant signal did. Hazel, who had originally been overwhelmed by the idea of meeting not only Alex's immediate family, but his cousins, and all the extra visitors, was starting to take an interest in the accident. She was also beginning to come out of her shell a little, and she had been put entirely at ease by Alex's parents, who had treated her as if she'd been coming round for years.

As Alex went back over how the signal was sabotaged, Hazel questioned him.

"I get how they did it, but why would anyone want to crash the train, though? That's what I don't get. I mean, even if this Jack Dove guy was a total psycho…"

Olivia, who was standing behind Hazel, reacted to the word 'psycho', nodding and pointing at her brother's girlfriend.

"… it doesn't explain why this other older guy sabotaged the signals. I mean, your Dad didn't explain that at all, did he?"

"You're right. But that's because his granddad knew who was behind it all but wouldn't tell him."

"Well, you know what I think? I reckon it must have been the old farmer – you know, Jack Dove's father, who owned the farm. He would have wanted the squire dead more than Jack Dove."

"Old Farmer Dove? I don't get it. Why him?"

"It's obvious. It was his farm, and we haven't heard much about him, have we. But he had the power. He could have used his son. Then there's that stonemason guy. I bet he worked for the farm sometimes. Also, who let the cows out onto the line, eh? We know that wasn't Jack Dove because he wasn't there, he was out and about. Farmer Dove had so many folk he could pay to do all this stuff for him. I reckon it was him." Like many teenagers, Hazel Burns saw the world in very black and white terms. "He had power over all these people. He did it. I just know he did it."

Alex smiled. "Yeah, well, that's too easy to say, isn't it? But there's absolutely no evidence to link him with the crash."

Olivia joined in. "Alex is right, he'd have left some sort of trail, or someone would have said it was him."

"That's my point, though" said Hazel, who had made up her mind to keep pushing her story just to get Alex's attention, and to rile his sister, "if I was going to do something like this, I'd want to make sure there was no evidence against me as well. That's why he used his son and this other guy. Maybe, to cover his tracks, he even used someone else as an intermediary? Maybe his son didn't even know it was his dad pulling the strings?"

Alex shook his head. "Nah, I don't think so."

"That's crazy, Hazel. You've been reading too many spy books." said Olivia. "Real life's not like that."

"I'm right though. I bet I'm right. And anyway, if we're talking about real life, this whole railway accident was supposed to be real life, and yet you've all decided it wasn't an accident. Where's your so called real life in all of that?"

She went off to find her father, who was once again in earnest conversation with Roger Cooper. Olivia moved in on her brother, who was still fiddling around with the scenery beside the distant signal.

"I told you, that girl's a psycho. Only she could come up with some crazy idea like that. Probably because she'd do it herself."

"Very funny, Livvy. Maybe she's just seeing it as it looks, seeing as she's come in to this fresh without any pre-conceived ideas."

"Huh. She's a killer, Alex, definitely a killer. Watch out, little bro. Still, at least if anything happens to you, I'll know who to blame..." Olivia made knife movements towards her brother's chest.

"Hey, look at this, Mark. Ted's got a few more pictures here." Roger wandered over to Mark, who was busy showing his father the detail on the station buildings, which was based on an old photograph from the 1880s.

"Take a look at this, young man," said Ted, "and see if you can recognise it from the angle."

He waved a photograph under Mark's nose.

"Well, it's the goods yard… from the station, surely. It's a good picture too. Who took it, do you have any idea?"

"John Robert Freeman, in 1877. He was a Somerset historian, very keen on the history of towns and villages affected by the railways. We've got a few of his pictures in our collection. Not enough, mind. I'm sure he must have taken many more which have been lost."

"It's been doctored, though, Ted." said Mark. "Was he a temperance man?"

"What d'ya mean, son?"

"Well, look. There are the old cottages… the ones Roger is renovating. There's High House on the right. But where's the inn? Where's the Dukes Head? It should be next to the cottages."

"Ahhh, well spotted. No, it's not doctored. The Dukes Head we know today wasn't built until after this picture was taken. The old Dukes Head was much further down the road. It's now a set of converted cottages, but when Squish Morpho expanded Hill Farm, he added some extra land south of the railway, and used the old inn as another farm building. Then he had the new Dukes Head built there, where there's just a field… right there." He pointed to the gap in the picture.

"Wait a minute," Mark said, "how far down the road was the old inn then?"

"It's nigh on a third of a mile, son." Ted replied.

"And it's uphill to, isn't it?"

"Aye. You mean, from the inn to the station? Not so steep but, yeah, uphill."

"Well, there's another nail in the coffin of the inquest findings then. Hang on... Alex!!" He called across to his son, who was taking a couple of 'engineman's eye view' pictures from the distant signal. "Where's the Board of Trade report?"

"In that old pilots' case, behind you." Alex came over, rummaged around in his father's old case for a moment and fished out the recently printed PDF. "Use this one, your old one was almost unreadable, Dad."

"I know, I know. Now then, here... here is Jack Dove's statement: *'... I was in the Dukes Head with Connor and Smart, about to have our ale when we heard a long whistle from the train, followed by a terrible sound, like an explosion. We didn't even get our drinks, just went straight out and ran straight up to the station. As we were getting there, there was a big flash and a sort of whoosh and the whole place lit up, I could see carriages piled one on top of the other...'* So, he says he was there in time to see it catching fire, and because he's the hero of the hour, no-one queries the evidence."

"It would have taken him at least two minutes to get there, even if he'd been sprintin'." Ted said.

"Right. And listen to this... this is from Joseph Palmer's evidence: *'...I had to stay in the signalbox to help signal the rescue trains in until Jobbins relieved me. I could not help with the rescue, but I saw some local people rescuing passengers almost straight away. I recognised Jack Dove, he was the first one there and went straight up to rescue people in the top carriage.'* So, he was the first one there, straight up those carriages before any of the railway folk could do anything. He must have been right there when it happened."

"Still, he was still brave to go up there, weren't he?" said Ted. "I mean, the whole lot could've collapsed on him if he'd not been careful."

"Maybe so... but he still lied to the inquest."

"I wonder if he was trying to rescue someone he knew on the train, perhaps?" ventured Alex. "The Squire? Hazel's got a theory that old Farmer Dove was behind it all, but he never even got a mention..." he stopped. It just didn't quite add up.

"Who thinks that?" asked Ted.

"Hazel. My girlfriend. She's the short blonde girl over there, with her Dad." Alex pointed her out, beckoning her over, and then realised it was the first time he'd called her his 'girlfriend' in public. It made him feel quite grown up, especially as everyone just accepted it. "This is Hazel, everyone. Tell them what you were saying back there, about who you think was behind it?"

"What do you mean? About the farmer guy?"

"Yeah, that's it."

Hazel blushed a little, but then recounted the story as she'd seen it. To Alex's surprise, everyone there heard her out, and no-one shouted her down. Ted Crozier was nodding wisely as she spoke.

"The thing is," said Ted, carrying on as Hazel finished, "there were a lot of goings on back then over this railway branch idea. The Squire had become a Director of the line and he was determined to get the branch built at any cost, with the junction right there at Salmsham. But he had no support at all locally. It would have involved cutting back the land belonging to Hill Farm, and wiping out Rosfell Farm completely. Not one other person thought it was a good idea, so once he was killed, of course, his son, the new squire…"

"Squish Morpho?" interjected Mark.

"… yep, Squish Morpho… well, he had it all cancelled, and became the local hero, 'cos then he expanded the farms, everyone had work, and of course we know he helped out the Palmer family a lot too."

"Surely though, he would have known if one of his tenants had conspired to cause a train crash which killed his father?" Roger asked.

"Would he? Well… I don't know. But the lass has a point, because Dove must have had some help, and to be honest, from what I've read and heard about young Jack Dove, he didn't have enough friends to be able to organise such a thing on his own, he was such a nasty piece of work. Maybe he really did have someone else behind him… in which case the Palmer kids got it wrong, didn't they?"

"Well, maybe they did at the time of the crash, Ted," Mark said, "but remember, Auntie Ath… Sarah Palmer, told my grandfather who was ultimately behind it all, but she swore him to secrecy, and he kept his promise to her when I asked him who it was."

As the guests started saying their goodbyes, Mark, Alex and Roger were disconnecting the baseboards ready to store the model in the garage again.

"Well, I suppose, the next step is to sort out the timeline and get ready to present this lot to the Hallowfield CID." said Mark. "assuming she's still interested in hearing us out."

"Oh, she has no choice, Mark. I've seen her a couple of times since she keeps asking how it's going. I say we get her over here in the next couple of weeks and get her started on a proper investigation."

"Well, I'm back at work next week, and the kids are at school so it might take us a bit longer to get everything in order."

"Well, three weeks then. I'll check with my old Dad and see if he's got anything else in his loft as well. You never know, he might find a confession or something."

"These old lofts, eh. My Dad's just brought some more family papers over today. He says he's got yet another load back at home which he hasn't even opened. That's another reason for waiting until we've got all the evidence out before getting Chloë involved. There might be something else in there."

45

Saturday, June 9th 2018 – Salmsham

Arabella Templeton-Stubbs M.P. was not used to meeting her constituents on Saturday evenings in village inns, but she had decided to make an exception for Roger Cooper. She had got to know and like Roger when he had been overseeing the renovation of the old cottages on the manor estate, where she had lived at the Lodge since returning from university thirty-three years ago.

Although she had become nationally famous following her scathing outburst in the House of Commons in the early summer of 2017, Arabella was well-known enough locally, due to her active support for a number of local charitable, social and educational projects, not to attract any unwelcome attention as she marched confidently into the saloon bar of the Dukes Head at precisely 8.00pm.

"Roger, hi!" she called out, giving him a peck on the cheek. "How are you? I'm intrigued by your message."

"Great, thank you, Bella. And thanks for coming over. It's good to see you again, what will you have to drink?"

"Oh, I'm driving, so just orange juice and lemonade, please. And I can't stay too long; Jeremy is fretting about a big business meeting he's got next week, and of course I'll be away in London most of the week."

Collecting their drinks, Roger guided the M.P. to a corner table, where Mark and Freya Phipps sat waiting. After the briefest of introductions, Roger explained their theories about the accident, and how they were interested to know whether there was any family story which had been passed down in the Templeton family.

After listening intently, Arabella told them that she was not a direct descendant of Squish Morpho.

"He was a bit of a dud in that area, you know. He never married, although there were rumours of various dalliances, but we know now that the rumours were just that. In fact, I think he started most of them himself."

"Oh? Why would he do that?"

"Well, of course, we live in enlightened times now, but Squish did not. He was gay, Mark, in a time when it was more than just an imprisonable offence. He would have been excommunicated, and not just by the church. Of course, as the oldest son, he got to inherit his father's titles, the estate; everything, in fact. He was even offered the Directorship of the railway in place of his father, but he declined that. He was only 31 when he inherited, but he was full of energy. He did a lot of good work, really built up the farms, which of course meant the estate prospered. In short, my family owes its present day wealth to Squish Morpho. I mean, he even managed the estate through the First World War, when the government tried to take it over. He staved them off, and did a deal with them to use it as a military rehabilitation centre, and it remained that way until 1921, when he was seventy-eight years old. He died the following year, and then the estate reverted to my grandfather, who, bless him, was not quite as business-minded as his Uncle Squish. But he kept it running – he had some good staff managing it for him. When he died in 1949 it passed to my Uncle Charles, who is still alive; still running the estate at the grand old age of eighty-eight. He has no children either, not that he was gay, but his wife died quite young and he never wanted to remarry. So, when he dies my mother will inherit the estate, and then it'll be passed on to my sisters and me. Although strictly speaking, the estate is held in trust, but obviously we all benefit from it."

"So, are there any papers relating to the accident."

"Oh, there's a huge archive. I mean, every stately home has its own library, but ours takes up three rooms, one on the ground floor, which is on public view, and then two basement rooms. But if there's anything specific we can help you with, I can get our archivist to search for it, or better still one of you could go and search under his supervision. Remember Eddie, who used to look after you whenever we were away, Roger?"

"I do indeed. Lovely chap, always full of smiles if I remember rightly?"

"Oh yes, that's Eddie. Eddie Richmond. Well, he's always worked at the Manor, and he's sort of eased into the role of archivist. Takes it very seriously, in fact he has been studying privately with a view to writing a history of the Templeton-Morphy dynasty, which will be splendidly entertaining, I'm sure." Arabella glanced at her watch. "Listen, I really should go, but get in touch with Eddie and tell him I sent you."

"I will," said Roger. "Can I ask a favour though, Bella? You must know of our local history chappie, Ted Crozier?"

"No. Never heard of him."

"Oh, well he knows you."

"Plenty of people know me, Roger, but I honestly don't recall meeting him."

"Ah well, anyway, Ted knows pretty much all there is to know about Salmsham. Would you mind if we get him involved with this too? Only… well, my idea is ultimately to build a small heritage centre over where the old station is, with a museum devoted to the memory of all those who died in the accident. It'll bring in some tourists but without swamping the place, and might boost the area a bit. Mark here has made a scale model of the station as it was in 1874, with all the surrounding area as well. I plan to put it on permanent display."

"And this Ted Crozier person is reliable? I mean, trustworthy? If we're going to let him near our personal papers, I don't want just anyone poking around in the archive."

"He certainly is. He heads up all the local historical society meetings, and he's used to doing research in the county archives. He'd be a useful help for Eddie. If you name a family in the village from years ago, Ted will give you the full low down on them all."

"Well, then that's fine. I'll let Eddie know that you'll send someone along, and maybe this Ted chap as well. Well, look, sorry to dash but I really must be gone. It's been a great pleasure to meet you all…"

Hands were shaken and cheeks were kissed, and then Arabella Templeton-Stubbs swept out of the Dukes Head without a backwards glance.

"Well," said Freya "I have no idea what to make of that, but I think we're moving forward, Roger?"

"Oh yes, definitely. Bella's a busy woman, but she'll make sure we get access to Eddie and his records. The question is, who's going to have the time to see him if we're all working?" Roger looked at Mark quizzically.

"Good point. I'm going to be snowed under at work, so I can't really take any more time out." Mark looked at Freya. "Do you fancy putting the garden project on hold for a couple more weeks, Darling?"

Freya rolled her eyes. "Well, I suppose so. But I'm not sure I'm the right person to go snooping round in an old archive. I don't really know what I'm supposed to be looking for."

"What if I got..." Roger began, before he was interrupted by a hand on his shoulder.

"What if you got what, Roger Cooper? Taken in for questioning? Done for drinking in an English village inn, without buying one for your favourite detective?"

Chloë Smith plonked herself down beside Roger as Mark and Freya giggled, having watched the DCI approaching stealthily from the bar.

"Hi Mark, hi Freya. I have been hearing interesting things about this mystery of yours. My good friend Mr Crozier tells me I could be arresting someone for murder soon. So, I just need a confession from one of you, or if not, some hard evidence that you didn't do it."

356

"Do all detectives have such a cheerfully sarcastic sense of humour, or is it just the ones I know?" asked Roger.

"Listen, Roger, if you saw the sort of things I see on a regular basis, you'd need one. It helps get me through the long and dreary days. Now, what have you got for me, and where does our male-bashing Member of Parliament fit into all this?"

"Ah you don't miss anything, do you?" grinned Roger. "Well, she's opening up the Templeton-Morphy family archive for us, so we can go and find out if there's anything there which mentions the accident and its aftermath."

"Why is that important?"

"Well, apart from the fact that the Squire was barbecued in the accident, and very well done he was too, by all accounts... we think there was some sort of a conspiracy going on and we're trying to get to the bottom of it. Basically, we're trying to find who had the motive to want to stage the crash. We think we know how it was done, and we think we know who the people were who sabotaged the signals, but we haven't yet found out who was really behind it, and why."

"Are you serious? Do you really know who did the sabotage and caused the accident?"

Mark leant forward. "We think we do, Chloë. We haven't yet got cast iron evidence, but we do have a tape which contains an account of several connected murders. My son is busy putting a detailed timeline together, and we've got a few more documents to find, but we reckon when we put it all together and come to you with most of the solutions to questions you haven't even asked yet, you'll want to be digging even further."

"And," added Roger, "digging up the graveyard. You know we were speculating about someone being dumped in a grave. It turns out, that's exactly what happened. They jumped on this guy, and knifed him several times, and dumped him in the grave."

"Remind me… when was this? 18…?"

"1879." said Mark.

"And you think you know which grave?"

"Yes, we checked all the burials for that month in Salmsham. There was only the one. George Whitmore, the landlord of this place. We've even got a copy of the burial records for the month."

"When will you have all the evidence, do you think?"

"Give us three weeks?" said Mark. "If you could come over to us, as our guest, we'll show you the whole thing. I've… we've built a model of the area, with all the trains, and everything."

"How long will it take you to show me everything, talk me through it all?"

"Well, probably about an hour, plus however long it'll take to look at documents."

"Well, let's say four hours then." Chloë said. "Right, let's put a date in the diary. What's the best day for you folk? Weekends, I presume?"

"Saturday or Sunday."

"Right, let's say Sunday 24th June, at yours?"

"Sounds good. Is that okay with you, Freya?" asked Mark, knowing how she disliked having people invited round without a little bit of consultation.

"Definitely. You must come for lunch or dinner, Chloë. Whichever you prefer. And Roger, of course, bring the family. Let's get Ted over as well."

"Are you sure, Darling? That's a lot of folk to cook for. I mean, it's not another garden party."

"Oh, I'm not doing it all. I'll get my parents over as well, and yours. We might as well go the whole hog and get everyone who's had a hand in this to be there, so if Chloë has any questions, there'll be at least one person who can answer her."

46

It was an unusually cold and wet July day, which compounded the depressing mood that Roger Cooper felt as he stood shivering slightly on the narrow path in Salmsham churchyard, rain from a light but persistent shower dripping from the peak of his cap. DCI Chloë Smith had not yet arrived from Hallowfield, but she had asked Roger to meet the team at 4.00am that morning, and guide them to George Whitmore's grave.

Roger remembered how Chloë had listened intently three weekends ago, as Mark Phipps presented her with not only an eye-catching re-enactment of the Salmsham Railway Disaster, using the hurriedly completed model railway, but a dossier full of every conceivably relevant fact, including Hazel Burns' speculation that old Farmer Dove may have been the unseen person behind the sabotage of the signals. When Chloë had left them, she had promised nothing more than she had when they first told her about the case, so he was a little surprised when she rang him a few days later and asked for his permission, as a relative, to be present at the exhumation of what were probably Jack Dove's remains, which were 'reasonably believed' to be buried underneath another grave at Salmsham church.

Chloë had also asked Mark's permission to exhume George Whitmore, telling him that although she didn't really need it as this was a criminal investigation, out of respect for his family she was asking as many of George's descendants as she could reasonably trace. Mark had agreed straight away, but could not be present at the exhumation. Instead, an elderly lady by the name of Janice Longthorpe, who lived in Hallowfield, and who was another descendant, came in his place. Janice, who was a sprightly eighty-six years old (as she liked to tell everyone) was as fascinated as Roger was about the whole railway saga, and was now busy chatting to Detective Constable Josh Fowler about what the police might do if they could prove that it was indeed sabotage, or mass murder, as she had put it.

Vicky Cooper, who had recently finished college and had no plans to work until she'd found out her final exam results, had crawled out of bed, slung some old clothes on and sauntered up to the churchyard shortly after 5.00am, out of a sort of morbid curiosity. Vicky had spent the first part of her morning chatting up the young detective constable, who was nominally in charge of operations until his DCI arrived later on. The sun was just beginning to peek over the horizon, and the sky was quite clear at first. Vicky had thought the day was going well until Josh had started to talk about his fiancée, at which point she lost interest in him, moved away and stood sulkily on the path. Soon afterwards, the sky clouded over, the wind got up and then it began to rain. She was beginning to wish she hadn't come up after all.

She jumped up and down next to Roger, and rubbed her hands together, blowing on them in a desperate bid to stop her fingers seizing up.

"How long's this going to take, Dad?" she asked, through chattering teeth. "This wind's bitter. We'd have been better off doing this in December!"

"I know. Typical, isn't it? I thought we were in for a long hot summer. I'll go and ask."

He wandered over to the small group of people standing beside a large tent, which had been put up over the grave plot, to enable George Whitmore's remains to be exhumed with some dignity. Janice Longthorpe had started busying herself by noting down the inscriptions on the nearby headstones, much to the relief of the young detective.

"How's it all going, Josh?" asked Roger.

"Ah, you'll have to ask David here. He's monitoring the spade work, as it were." The detective pointed to a figure hunching over the trestle table which had been erected just off the pathway.

David Selby was the Environmental Health representative from the county council. He was dressed in a full-length plastic suit, but had removed his hat, exposing a neatly trimmed head of jet black hair.

"Well," said David, having overheard the question, "they've almost finished uncovering the burial... George Whitmore, that is. What we'll do is lift him in his coffin, and place him into the new coffin, which you can see over there. They'll be taking him to the morgue until they've finished checking the ground beneath him. When they're ready, he'll be reburied in the new coffin."

"Is there anything left of his old coffin then? I thought it would have rotted away."

"Well, it's collapsed of course, but much of the wood is still there. Give them another half an hour and he'll be out of there, coffin and all."

"Thanks, David."

Josh tapped Roger on the shoulder. "Tell you what, Mr Cooper. I've just seen the sexton arriving. He promised us all a cuppa when he got here. Would you mind going to see if he meant it? There's eight of us, plus you two and Mrs Longthorpe."

"Gladly!" said Roger, and he and his daughter turned and walked towards the main church entrance. As they got near to the large double doors, a car pulled up in the layby, and DCI Chloë Smith emerged, pulling her coat on tightly as she walked through the gate.

"Hi Chloë!" called Roger, "we're just sorting a hot drink. Fancy one?"

"Too right, Roger. Tea please, white, two sugars. Is that them over there?"

"Yep. We'll be back in a few minutes."

He pushed open one of the huge oak doors, and made his way down the aisle and past the lectern, to an open door on the right. Mike Morrison, sexton of St. Mary's Church, Salmsham, greeted Roger and Vicky in the vestry. "Kettle's on, Roger. How's it going out there?"

"Oh, quite well, apparently. If you like that sort of thing. They've pretty much got the landlord sorted. He'll be up and about in no time."

"Oh good, good." He nodded, as Roger's dry humour went straight over his head. "We're trying to keep the public away for today, if we can. Actually, the press has been very good. We promised them a few pictures of the chaps working over there if they kept quiet until after the exhumation. The last thing we need is every ghoul coming from miles around to trample around and get in the way. That's why we always do exhumations early in the morning."

"Why, do you do a lot of them?"

"No, but we have done a few in the last few years. Mainly when someone dies locally, and then a relative wants them buried back in their original parish. That's been the reason for all the others. Haven't had any murder suspects dug up before, though. This is a bit of parish history in the making, isn't it? Mind you, I expect there's many more secrets in the ground out there, when you think of all those folk who literally take their secrets to the grave. You could probably write a book with what they all knew but didn't tell about..." He left it there, but Roger picked up on his theme.

"Oh, you mean family secrets, affairs, unsolved crimes, illegitimate children..."

"Dad! You're making the locals sound as if the whole village is one big scandal!" said Vicky, emptying a couple of biscuit packets onto a large plate Mike had passed her.

"You're Dad's right, though, young Victoria. All of these places, they've all got their little scandals through the ages. The thing about the Victorians – pardon the reference - was, they made out they were above all that sort of thing, whereas in some respects they were the worst offenders!"

"Not too many bodies dumped under graves, though, I hope, Mike?"

"True, true… as far as we know." he grinned, filling the large aluminium teapot ready to take to the freezing workers by the tent. "Mind you, you must admit, it's a clever idea if you can get away with it. I wonder how many more there are dotted around the country."

A few minutes later, Roger and Mike carried a large tray of tea and biscuits outside, with twelve mugs, covered by a piece of plastic sheet to keep the rain off. By the time they had got back to the graveside, George Whitmore's remains had been placed in the 'shell', the team's technical term for the new coffin, which was being sealed under David Selby's watchful eye.

"Will you be doing anything with him, Chloë? Or just reburying him?" asked Roger.

"Well, we have had permission from Mark and some of his other descendants, including dear old Janice over there, to take a small sample of him for DNA purposes, just in case he's not who we think he is. We're pretty sure he's bona fide, but seeing as the grave has technically been tampered with all those years ago, I wanted to make sure we'd covered everything. So, they'll take a sample back at the morgue, either bone or tooth, but then he'll be reburied back here again, later on today, or first thing tomorrow."

Two funeral workers slipped past them, bearing the coffin containing George Whitmore's mortal remains out to a waiting van. While they set off on their journey to the Hallowfield Hospital morgue, the exhumation team carried on digging. The team consisted of two people from a specialist company attached to the firm of funeral directors, and two young forensic archaeologists drafted in from Weston University.

Chloë briefed the remaining team personnel, who were in various states of disarray from the soft clay of the churchyard. "Remember folks, if you find anything at all which indicates there's another body down there, stop everything until I can get a SOCO team here, with a photographer."

"How far down are we going?" asked a muffled female voice from the tent.

"Another… I don't know, at least another two feet, maybe more. I think, if we go more than a metre and find nothing we might have to think again."

"Righty-ho!" Came the chirpy reply, and then, almost immediately. "Actually, I don't think you need to worry, Miss. We've got something already!"

"Really? What?" Chloë disappeared into the tent. Roger heard a few muffled voices and then she emerged again, beaming.

"Well, well, well. You guys were right all along. We have ourselves a body. Josh, get onto HQ and have them send SOCO – they'll love this one."

Roger and Vicky exchanged glances. Suddenly, they forgot how cold they were.

"You really think this is him? Jack Dove?"

"Well, we can't be sure, obviously, until we do the DNA tests on him and compare them with you two. But… it follows on from Sarah Palmer's confession."

"So, what now?"

"Well, we wait for Scenes of Crime to do their bit, lift the bones and then do a post mortem."

"Post mortem? Seriously? What can you find out from a pile of bones 139 years old?"

"Evidence of violence. And that's just from a criminal viewpoint. But also evidence as to ID. I mean, we have that picture of him; we can check his facial measurements against the skull shape. But from the criminal point of view, I always try and keep an open mind. SOCO will want to root around a bit more after the body's been removed. You never know, Sarah Palmer might have thrown her knife in the grave to dispose of it, although it's more likely she just cleaned it up and put it back in the kitchen."

"Oh, that's gross!" said Vicky. "Think where it's been... stuck in his ribs!"

Chloë smiled and shrugged. "One piece of meat is much like another, Vicky!"

"Oh, I'm going to be sick in a minute. This is just... oh Dad, why did I come up here?"

"Because if you'd missed it, you'd have always wondered about it."

"Yeah, maybe." Vicky took a deep breath and stared at the tent. By now the team had emerged, and the two archaeological experts were chatting animatedly, comparing notes about their previous excavations.

"How is he looking, ladies?" asked Roger.

"Not very well, Mr Cooper, but to be honest, I don't think he'll get any worse. Would you like to see him?" The older girl, Jennifer, stood up and stretched her back as she spoke.

"Erm... I'm not sure. Vicky? Did you want to have a peek? He is your four times great grandfather, after all."

"Definitely not, Dad. I'm already having nightmares about seeing dead bodies. I don't want any more."

"He won't hurt you, love. He's a bit stuck where he is anyway. You never know, he might be pleased to see you." Jennifer joked, removing her gloves and reaching for a biscuit, as Vicky shook her head resignedly.

Leaving his daughter cradling a warm mug of coffee in her hands, Roger ventured forward to the edge of the tent, and poked his head inside the flap. The younger archaeologist, a post-graduate student who introduced herself as Martina, stood next to him and shone her torch into the deep grave. Roger could just make out the top of a skull, and the outline of an eye socket. A little further down, a long bone was poking through the soft clay.

"That's his left humerus, you know, his arm bone. He's lying slightly hunched up, on his right side, I think, otherwise we'd have seen the other arm. He wasn't laid to rest delicately, that's for certain. We found that rock on his face. Did I hear you say he was your ancestor?"

"Yeah, we think so. If it's Jack Dove. He was my three times great grandfather."

"Gosh. This is a bit weird for you then, isn't it?"

"Yes. Especially as we think he helped to cause the Salmsham Railway Disaster."

"Crikey, yes. We've heard about all that shenanigans. Mixed feelings, eh? I'm not sure how I'd feel about that at all."

"Well, I'm trying not to think about it. And besides, he's not my only ancestor involved with the accident. Another one was the station porter, Arthur Marriott, and he helped to rescue people. Although..." Roger stopped, and realised that Arthur was one of the people who'd had a hand in Jack Dove's murder. "Oh, never mind. It's a bit too complicated to explain now."

They stared into the grave one last time, and then Roger emerged with a "Phew!"

"You alright, Dad?" asked Vicky.

"Well, I'm feeling better than he looks, that's for sure. But I feel a bit numb, actually." He gave his daughter a big hug; she sensed he needed an extra big squeeze and held on a little bit longer.

"Never mind, Roger," said Chloë with a smile, as Vicky finally released him, "we'll soon have him in the warm, all cleaned up, and laid out on a nice shiny bed."

Roger grimaced. He wasn't too sure about the black humour on offer today, what with chirpy archaeologists and cynical detectives.

"In all seriousness, Chloë, what happens now?"

"Well, I'm not yet going to go and dig up Sarah Palmer and charge her with murder, if that's what you mean. Let's just wait and see about the pathology results, DNA tests, and take it from there. I promise I'll keep you fully informed of anything we find out."

By three o'clock in the afternoon, long after the coffin containing the bones of Jack Dove had been removed from the graveyard, and SOCO had finished their investigation, the team finally left. Their tent had been left in place, with a police tape around it. The local press photographer had been allowed to take a few pictures, once the bones had been removed. He was certain he'd be able to syndicate them, especially his shot of the deep, empty double grave.

Sure enough, the pictures appeared in the national press in the next couple of days, and so the people of

Salmsham braced themselves for the inevitable influx of ghoulish sightseers.

By the time the hordes of curious folk (with nothing much better to do, thought Roger) had made their pilgrimage to the churchyard, George Whitmore was already back in his grave, albeit buried slightly deeper than before, and in a new coffin. But all there was to see, for anyone looking, was a headstone and some fresh earth. The team had done a remarkable job of clearing up, and unless people knew where to look, it was quite easy to walk past the grave without knowing that it was a recently disturbed Victorian crime scene.

Meanwhile, down in the village, swarms of upper middle-aged men wearing anoraks wandered around the old railway station with maps and plans and drawings, and the odd photograph. Roger chuckled to himself – how true to life the stereotypical train spotter still looked. He took the opportunity to introduce himself as the person who intended building a heritage railway museum on the station site. One elderly chap, with long wispy grey hair and a Darwinian-style beard, introduced himself as Sidney Pountney, an expert on the history of the London and Western Railway.

"Of course, this wouldn't have happened if the station had been built as originally planned, Roger."

"Oh really? How's that?" said Roger, feigning a deeper interest.

"Well, most of these wayside stations would have had a proper goods siding accessible from both directions, and they were going to run a set of points back there…" Sidney pointed towards the Hill Farm bridge "…and run the extra siding through where the start of the bridge was, and behind the platform. But they couldn't, for a number of reasons."

"Oh, really, well that's interesting Sidney…" Roger started, but was interrupted by Sidney grabbing his arm and looking him directly in the face, uncomfortably close up.

"The first reason is… that large mound of earth there. High House. The landowner refused to let the railway cut back the land towards the house itself."

"Right." said Roger, trying to back away from Sidney's face, which was most definitely too close to his own for comfort.

"The second reason is… they needed the remaining space for the goods yard itself, because they couldn't go any further that way…" he pointed northwards "because the churchyard was in the way. As it is, they were made to build that massive wall to protect the churchyard from collapsing onto the station."

"Right." said Roger again, wondering when this was going to end.

"And the third reason was… they were going to put the signalbox on the outside of the curve so the signalman could see as far round the curve towards Belcote as possible, although in the end they couldn't put it there either, because if they did, the signalman couldn't see up Hallow Hill, so that's why they put it over there." He pointed to the concrete base of the old 'box.

"Quite, so…" Roger tried to stop Sidney, who was on a roll now.

"The final reason was, they were not happy about having facing points in those days, because there'd been some accidents where the points had been wrongly set and trains had been sent down the wrong line. And this bit of line had a large cant so the expresses could go fast around the curve. Putting points in would have caused all sorts of problems with the main line tilting inwards, and the siding having to be level."

"I understand, yes, yes, I see." said Roger, with mock enthusiasm, as if he'd been given next week's lottery numbers.

"So, when you build your museum, you could have all these facts displayed beside your model, which we've been hearing about." Sidney added. "And if you want a consultant, for nothing, I'm your man. I tell you, this would be easily the best thing that's happened to help preserve the memory of this line. I have contacts, you know, and I could get you all sorts of items for this museum, and plenty of volunteers to help you set it up."

Roger smiled and took out his phone, taking Sidney's contact details and assuring him that he would be the first point of contact once they start designing the displays. He waited until Sidney as his friends were looking the other way before sneaking back to his cottage. The last thing he needed was a bunch of railway nutters knocking on his front door.

47

It was some days before the village of Salmsham returned to normal, following the dramatic stories in the national press. The Phipps family visited on the Saturday after the exhumations, stopping to pay their respects at the freshly filled-in grave, and dropping in to see Roger and Jacqui at their double cottage. Jake had come along too, driving Olivia in his own car, so Alex had invited Hazel, who sat holding hands with him in the back of Mark's estate.

"I still reckon it was the farmer dude," said Hazel when they were on their way home again. She actually had no idea whether it was Farmer Dove or not, but she enjoyed the attention she seemed to get from her assertion. "Who else would benefit from the accident?"

"Well," said Freya, "that's a great idea, Hazel, but how would causing the crash ensure the branch line wouldn't be built?"

"'Cos he killed the Squire."

"Yes, but he wasn't to know that the new squire, Squish Morpho, was going to reverse the plans, was he? For all he knew, Squish might have pushed them through even faster."

Hazel shrugged, and looked at Alex, who was staring out of the side window, deep in thought.

Freya thought back to the hundreds of notes and letters she'd read in the last couple of weeks, in the Hallowfield Manor archive. She'd turned up a little nervously on the Tuesday after they'd met Arabella

Templeton-Stubbs, having been contacted directly by Eddie Richmond, the self-styled archivist for the Hallowfield estate. Ted Crozier had declined the offer for the time being, much to Eddie's relief. He could handle one guest rummaging through the archive. Two would have been more of a challenge.

Eddie was waiting for Freya by the public entrance area, and led her around the back of a staircase, to a door marked 'Authorised Staff Only'. As they descended two flights of well-lit and richly carpeted stairs, Eddie told Freya that she would have a staff badge before the day was out, and showed her into the basement library.

"It's actually two rooms, as you can see. This is the main working room here; the other room is just rows and rows of shelving, floor to ceiling."

Freya took a good look around. There were three very large map tables down the centre of the main room, with several chairs and high stools dotted around them. There were a couple of boxes out on the farthest map table, and some papers strewn across in front of them.

"I'm currently working on collating all of the correspondence, accounts, and collected books from each decade. At the moment I'm stuck in the 1780s. The account books are fascinating. All of the squires kept really good records; every purchase, every bit of income and expenditure, and there's actually a library accounts book, separate to the main estate accounts. I mean, this family really had a sense of their history and heritage. They must have known we'd still be archiving stuff in the 2010s, and sure enough, here we are."

"Eddie, this is amazing. Where do I start looking for the accident records?"

"Well, the accident was 1874, so I suggest you start over here, maybe around 1870." Eddie led her to a set of waist high records on a corner shelf set around a pillar, just before the doorway between the two basement rooms. "Here you go. You'd probably be best to start with the correspondence. All I'd ask is you keep everything in order, and in the unlikely event that the Squire pokes his head around the door, just tell him you're my assistant, and you're a volunteer with a keen interest in local history. Whatever you do, don't mention that you're looking into the railway accident; it's a sensitive issue."

"Is it? Why's that?"

"What, you mean, apart from the fact that the Squire was killed in the crash? Well, there was a lot of hoo-ha around that time, arguments about the expansion of the estate, relocation of farms, and so on. Actually, the new Squire was a popular man, and rejuvenated the farms and, of course, preserved them from the possible onslaught of the railway extension. But he was also rumoured to be gay, which brought a certain amount of shame on the family at the time."

"Of course. Well, I'll be sensible then. But what if I find something of significant interest?"

"Well, of course, this is all private, so you can't make copies of any of it. But you CAN copy the information from it, and also, see these document numbers on each sheet. They're unique. If you come in here with one of those, I can find any document in about three minutes. So, if you find anything meaty, note the contents, and the number. Oh, and let me see it, because I need something to excite me from time to time. Annual crop yield figures per acre, and per field, and per farm is not something which turns me on, so to speak."

"Thanks Eddie. I'll get started."

To being with, Freya was not sure exactly what she was looking for, but within a few hours, she was familiar with the very precise filing system, and had been ploughing through various letters and notes. All correspondence had been filed in the date and time order that the item was received, so a thread of correspondence between two people may not be immediately obvious until several letters had come to light. After a few small items had turned up, Eddie allowed Freya to use her phone to copy the documents, on condition she did not show anyone else the contents or the picture.

"If you type a transcript of a letter in the archive, that's fine as long as you clear it with me first. But please don't let any of these photographs go public, otherwise we'll both be in the muck, and of course, you'll be barred from coming back here."

Freya had agreed, and carried on. By the end of the first day, she had found a few notes about the proposed branch line, but nothing major. It was interesting that the Squire's correspondence had been mixed with that of his children, which made it easier to follow the threads when they were writing to each other, which was a frequent occurrence. Matters became more confusing with correspondence from outside of the family, as only the incoming letters were on file. Eddie explained that the Squire kept a separate 'outgoing letters' book, which was kept in a different part of the basement. Once this had been located, Freya was able to start making sense of some of the Squire's more detailed business concerns.

Before she left that day, Eddie Richmond reached into the drawer of a large oak desk which was underneath yet more shelves along the front wall of the basement, and pulled out a staff badge.

"This will not only allow you access into here, but it has a magnetic strip, so you can get into the main part of the manor, but I hope you won't be trying to do that unless I'm with you. The Squire doesn't take kindly to new people who haven't been introduced, and I think it might be better if he doesn't really know you're here, not that we've got anything to hide. But, the less he knows about your presence here, the less he can object, okay?"

"Thanks, Eddie, you've been a great help. I'll be back tomorrow, if that's okay?"

"Of course... now you know the way, just sign in at the entrance like you did today, and then come straight down. If anyone asks, you're my assistant for the next few weeks, all unpaid voluntary work, naturally!"

"Naturally!" she smiled, shaking his hand.

A couple of weeks later, by the time of her fifth visit, she found she had made some good progress on the events leading up to the accident. Ted Crozier had eventually accompanied her on one of the visits, and spent most of his time chatting to Eddie about local events not connected to the railway. In the end, Freya had carried on alone, as before. Every time she found something of possible interest, she jotted it down in a little notebook, taking care to note the document numbers as Eddie had said. Each evening she had spent a couple of hours at home typing her notes up, and sending them to Mark, who added anything relevant into the timeline that their son had painstakingly drawn up.

As Freya had discovered, when the plan to build the branch line had first been mooted by the old Squire, Francis, back in early 1871, Squish, his elder son, had been all for it. It was Squish's younger brother Fraser who'd objected loudly. Fraser saw himself very much as a speaker for the rights of the common man, hence his clerical training and subsequent ordination as a vicar. His father had cheerfully ignored his objections. Freya allowed herself a few smiles at the way the Squire simply refused to rise to the bait, despite frequent outbursts by letter or little handwritten notes.

Only later on, once the Squire had become a Director of the London and Western Railway in June 1873, had Squish Morpho become more wary of his father's plans. But he had never objected to them in the way his younger sibling had. He simply asked his father to temper his enthusiasm until they had done more work in the sand quarries to see what the longer term prospects were. It appeared that Squish had felt there was not enough sand left to be quarried to justify building a new railway line, which would probably only run at peak capacity for a few years before falling into misuse, leaving a scar across their land, empty farms and a displaced labour force. The Squire disagreed, naturally, and so there was a fair amount of correspondence between the two. Most of it was business-like, although there were a couple of letters in which tensions began to appear, with one in particular telling Squish in no uncertain terms that he should stop complaining and support his father's plan in full.

Every night, Freya tidied up the papers she'd been reading, and replaced them in the old-fashioned box file, taking care to re-tie the ribbon inside the box, which had helped to secure them. Her first day in the archive had been tiring mentally and visually, but now she was more used to the work and had paced herself. On this particular day she was feeling pretty pleased with the amount of information she'd gleaned.

"See you tomorrow, Eddie."

"Bye, love. Safe journey." Eddie's voice came from behind one of the many shelving units which protruded into the main archive room.

As she walked back to the car, Freya's phone buzzed. She glanced quickly at the screen, expecting a message from either one of her children, or Mark. But it was her mother, saying "Call me as soon as you can. Exciting information!" She opened the full message, and then pressed the 'phone' button.

"Hello Darling… thank you for calling back. Listen, I've been doing a bit more tracing and you'll never guess what? Well, your Jack Dove…"

"Hang on, Mum! Slow down, let me get into the car… okay, what were you saying?"

"I traced Jack Dove's father. Well, he was a true bastard."

"Who, Jack Dove? I know. Nasty piece of work…"

"No, no, Dear. His father, George Dove. He was baseborn. No father given. But listen, his mother was a chambermaid at the Manor house, and she was only fifteen when she had him…"

"Hang on… at Hallowfield Manor?"

"That's right, Dear. Hallowfield Manor. Now, George Dove was given the tenancy to Rosfell Farm on his marriage in 1840, to Sarah Sutton. Sarah Sutton's grandfather was the previous farmer, and he died in 1840. The thing is, George Dove was only nineteen when he married Sarah, but she was twenty-six; quite a bit older, you see. Something doesn't quite make sense to me. Oh, and George's mother died in 1835, aged twenty-eight. So, someone must have helped her to bring him up. It can't have been his grandparents because they both died before he was three."

"What are you saying, Mum?"

"Well… perhaps George Dove is the illegitimate son of the Squire of the day? Why else would he be given the farm tenancy?"

"I don't know. Right… look, Mum, you've got loads of info there, but could you email it through, because I'm about to drive home. I've actually been working in the archive at Hallowfield Manor, so my head's spinning."

"Right-ho, I'll do that now. Be ready for a lot of data. Bye bye, Dear, and drive carefully!"

Freya ended the call, and then rang Mark. "You going to love this. Jack Dove's father was illegitimate… and his mother worked up at Hallowfield Manor. Are you thinking what I'm thinking?"

"I'm not really thinking much at all at the moment, Darling. I've got my head full of sales targets… I've got another blessed meeting first thing tomorrow morning."

"Well, get this. What if… just what if George Dove was the illegitimate son of the Squire? Seeing as his mother was a fifteen-year-old chambermaid at Hallowfield Manor. Mum thinks it must be him."

"Crikey… if that's the case, Jack Dove would be the Squire's nephew! That's much more of an incentive to kill off the Squire, isn't it? That would make him one step nearer to inheriting the estate. The only thing is, he'd have to murder Squish and his brother, and any other siblings."

"True. It's all speculation anyway. But Mum's sending the data through in an email, so I'll have a good look at it then and see if any of it makes sense."

"I've just thought, Darling," said Mark, suddenly sounding much more attentive. "We've got Jack Dove's DNA being tested as we speak, and that'll be compared to Roger's DNA. I wonder if we could get the DNA from the Squire, or his family, and compare that…. I'll ask Chloë, she can only say no, can't she? But if we don't ask, we may never know."

As she drove home, Freya thought about her research at the manor house. She had something new to get her teeth into tomorrow, and wondered whether any current family members at the manor had known about the son of the chambermaid…

48

Monday 16th July 2018, Hallowfield Hospital

DCI Chloë Smith greeted the four visitors by the reception desk in the hospital morgue. Roger, Vicky, Mark and Alex had chosen to come and see the mortal remains of Jack Dove, having heard from the detective about the forensic evidence taken from the skeleton. Both Jacqui and Freya had declined the offer of a viewing, and Olivia was equally against the idea, saying the thought 'creeped her out'.

Chloë led them into a waiting room and sat them down. She sat opposite them, and took out some papers. Although she knew everyone quite well now, she automatically slipped into her 'voice for bereaved relatives', and spoke more softly to them than she had in the Dukes Head, Salmsham.

"Right. Normally, you would view the body from here, through that big window on the wall behind you. But as there's not much left of him... he's all bones, we've laid him out on the table and you may come into the room and look at him, but you absolutely must not touch anything, OK? He's the victim of a crime..."

"But is he actually, Chloë?" asked Roger.

"Oh yes, definitely. I'll get the pathologist to show you how we know that. But I would say, if you've never seen a dead person before, and you feel uneasy at any time, you can just come out and come back into here, okay? I mean, if you've seen skeletons in

382

museums and the like, he's much like that, to be honest."

Mark nodded as the detective carried on.

"The main difference is, we know who he is, pretty much; we know what he looked like from that photo, and so he's someone we know, and he's related to you two, Roger and Vicky. So, however much he may have been a baddie, he's still a fairly young man who was murdered, so we always try and treat him with the respect we'd give anyone who we knew who's only just died, okay?"

"Right." said Roger, grimacing.

Vicky bit her lip and looked at the back of her hands, while Alex was beginning to wish he was somewhere else. He was fascinated by the thought of seeing the bones of Jack Dove, but suddenly Chloë's words had struck a chord deep within him, and he felt like an intruder in a very private affair. "After all" he thought to himself, "he's not my ancestor, he's Vicky's."

"Right," said the DCI, "I'll just go and get the pathologist, and then we'll go in."

There was a long silence after Chloë left the room, then Mark piped up. "I wonder what the evidence is for the crime that she was on about, Roger."

"Yeah, me too. Maybe they put a bullet in him?"

"My granddad only mentioned Sarah Palmer's knife though, didn't he? Oh well, I suppose we'll know in a moment."

They heard footsteps in the corridor, and then Chloë opened the door gently, and stood back to let her colleague in. "Everybody, this is Jonathan McCann; he's the forensic pathologist who did the post mortem on Jack Dove."

Jonathan McCann was a short but skinny red-haired man in his early forties, with piercing blue eyes and a cheerful visage. He smiled at the assembled group. "Hello, everyone. I gather you are all descendants of our Mr Dove."

"Not all of us," said Mark. "Roger and Vicky here are; I'm their cousin but not via Jack… it's complicated, but we are here because we've been doing the background research behind this investigation, and we think that a couple of our common ancestors had a hand in Jack's… well, death."

"Oh, I see. Sounds like quite a family. Well, someone had a hand in it, that's true. He was definitely murdered." Jonathan sounded quite cheerful about the whole affair. "This will be most interesting for you, I'm sure. Now, we're going to go in and see him. He's laid out on the table for you, and I've got some interesting clues about his death, which I'll explain to you."

They followed Jonathan into the viewing room. Roger went ahead of Mark, then Vicky, who rather unexpectedly grabbed Alex's hand as he moved into the room beside her. He squeezed her hand tightly as if to say "I'm strong, I'm okay" but he felt faintly uneasy.

Chloë brought up the rear and shut the door behind them, clicking the main lights on as she did so. Double checking that the blind over the window to the waiting room was firmly in place, Jonathan lifted back the sheet which had been placed over the remains.

There was a collective gasp from the onlookers, as they looked at the skeleton of Jack Dove, lying on a metal tray which had been placed on the viewing table. The bones were dark brown, with blackened blotches. Jonathan explained that the discolouration of the bones was consistent with them being buried in clay for well over a hundred years.

Alex could not bring himself to look at the skull; instead he marvelled at the feet, the bones of which had been carefully laid out – he hadn't realised quite how many there were. He squeezed Vicky's hand a bit more.

"He's all present and correct. There are no missing bits, every bone was there in its rightful place, so he was complete when he was put in the grave. Actually, he was probably dropped in… he was lying slightly hunched and a little bit onto his right-hand side, but none of his limbs are broken. However, the first thing you may notice is this…" he pointed to the skull. Alex forced himself to look. He noticed Vicky was still looking at the feet.

"The left side cheekbone is shattered." said Jonathan, pointing to the fracture while holding up the missing fragment of cheekbone in his other hand. "Now I believe this happened around the time of his death; it certainly wasn't an old injury. A large piece of rock was found lying beside his head in the grave. It was probably used to smash him in the face while he was still above ground. Either that or it was thrown very hard onto him once he was in the grave. Where it was found indicates that it was most likely the second of those things."

"Is that what killed him then?" asked Roger.

"Oh, I doubt it. It might have contributed to his death, but I think he would have died anyway. Look at these markings on his ribs."

385

Jonathan picked up a rib from the table, and held it up in front of them.

"Can you see this line here? And another, here? There are several of these. I counted seven in all, on different ribs. These are the knife marks, where the blade has scraped the bone. They're pretty deep too. If I had to speculate I'd say it was a pretty savage attack. At least three of the thrusts would have got him right in the heart, but even if it hadn't he would have bled to death pretty quickly from all the other wounds."

"Bloody hell." Roger said slowly. "This is almost unreal, isn't it?"

"Also, if you look at this vertebra here, you'll see a slight nick on one side. That was most likely caused by the tip of the knife going right through his chest to his backbone. So, the ribs show he was stabbed in the back, but he was probably stabbed from the front too. Which came first I couldn't say."

Mark nodded, still staring at the rib which the pathologist was holding up in front of him. "Well, according to our second or third hand evidence, she stabbed him from behind while he was arguing with two other people, but then she just kept going, I suppose, to make sure. It's crazy. I mean, we had a confession, but we weren't really sure what to believe. But here it is."

"Can we go now, Dad. Please?" said Vicky uneasily. "I'm feeling a bit faint."

Chloë opened the door to the waiting room, checking that there was no-one else there. "You go and sit down, Vicky, and wait there. We'll be out in a moment or two."

Vicky pulled her hand away from Alex's. He was busy looking up and down the skeleton.

"How tall was he, Mr McCann?" he asked.

"Well, we measure the femur there, the thigh bone, and from that we reckon he stood around a hundred and seventy-six centimetres. That's just over five foot nine inches. He's a pretty sturdy chap too, and there's evidence he was fairly muscular. We can analyse his diet as well. In fact, there are lots of things we could find out, but as this is a criminal investigation we're not going to spend too much time on that sort of thing; that's more the job for a forensic archaeologist."

"We are doing a facial reconstruction though." Chloë said. "We still have to formally identify him. Because this is an old case, we can't push things through quite so fast, but then again, it gives us more time to be much more thorough."

Once everybody had agreed they had seen enough, Jonathan replaced the sheet over the skeleton, and everyone filed back into the waiting area. Saying his goodbyes, Jonathan went back into the viewing room to arrange for the remains to be put back into storage.

"Oh, Chloë, did we mention what we found out about Jack Dove's father?" Mark asked, as they were gathering up their belongings ready to leave the mortuary.

"No. What about him?"

"He was a bastard. Baseborn, I mean. Illegitimate. We reckon there's a chance he could have been sired by the Squire's father."

"Bloody hell, Mark. You lot could write a book about this case! There were lots of bastards born in those days, you know. What makes you think the Squire was the father, and not someone else?"

"George Dove's mother Jane was a fifteen-year-old chambermaid at Hallowfield Manor. George was baptised in Salmsham, so she must have been sent to live there – in whose care we don't yet know. But then, when he was nineteen, he married the farmer's granddaughter, who was older than him, and got given the tenancy of the Rosfell Farm, over and above the farmer's son. Now, you don't get stuff like that handed to you on a plate, especially if you're illegitimate. Not unless you have people supporting you in high places."

"Gosh, you're right. So, if that's the case, our friend in there is descended from the Squire."

"Correct."

Chloë puffed her cheeks out. "This case gets better and better. I tell you what, I wish all my investigations were this fascinating. Right, I'll get a DNA swab from the Squire. It won't take long to find a match, if there is one. But don't be surprised if there isn't!"

"Ah… well, can I ask a massive favour?" Mark suddenly realised how he may be compromising Freya's work at the archive. "The current Squire knows nothing of this, but Arabella Templeton-Stubbs is in the know. In fact, she was the one who sent my wife to search in the Hallowfield Manor archives. You might be better off asking her for a DNA sample."

"Now who has friends in high places, Mark? Okay, I'll give her a try. I do know her a little, so I'll see if she'll go along with the idea. Please everyone, don't talk to any of the press about this. You can just see the headlines if they catch wind of it. Let's keep it simple and let them bang on about the railway sabotage, and Jack Dove's murder, without them finding a political angle to twist everything with."

49

"I can't believe there's nothing here. Not a single mention of Jane Dove. Nothing." Freya sighed as she stared at a pile of documents spread out in front of her on the map table.

"Maybe there's nothing to find, Freya."

Eddie Richmond had left his own research papers and come across from the far table to look over what Freya had found so far.

"What year is this?"

"Years, Eddie. 1820 to 1823... there's not a word about her, nor about any bastard children. Nothing about supporting her, or anything. Plenty about the Squire's sons, Francis, and poor little Michael, who died aged 4 months. But absolutely nothing. No hints. I give up." Freya sighed, and started stacking the documents back into their rightful order.

"Unless, of course," she continued "all the documents have been removed."

Eddie Richmond bristled at this. "Now look, Freya, remember, this is a private archive. The family weren't keeping stuff just for the likes of you and me to read years later. This material here was essential so the family themselves could refer back to it. They had no motive for removing anything – they would be the ones referring back to it, no-one else."

"Right. Sorry Eddie. Of course, I'm seeing this through twenty-first century eyes. It wasn't a research project for the family."

"Precisely. Besides, you know," started Eddie, "you jumped to a big conclusion about George Dove being the son of the Squire. There was a large population of healthy virile males around Hallowfield Manor and Salmsham in 1821. When was George born?"

"17th May he was baptised, at Salmsham. There's no record here, but it's in my notes."

"Okay," said Eddie, "so assuming he was no more than a month premature, he would have been conceived around July, August or possibly even September 1820."

"Yes, that's right."

"So, let's have another look at the 1820 household journal. I presume you've already got it out?"

Freya sighed deeply, and pointed to the large volume on her right. "Here it is."

"Right. Let's have a quick glance."

Eddie leafed carefully through the pages of the large, lined book, checking dates as he went.

"Right. Now, on June 5th 1820, Squire James, his wife Alice and their baby son Francis – he's the one who became Squire and was killed in the crash – they went to Ireland for the summer, staying at her father's estate in Tyrone, where they resided for... nearly five months. The estate was left in the capable hands of their steward, one Peter Fitzjohn. According to this record, the next few months were spent carrying out essential repairs to the building, and lots of cleaning as well. You need to look at the year records if you want any more information about Jane Dove. What it does seem, though, is the Squire wasn't there to sire a child with her. Someone else must have done the dastardly deed, obviously."

Freya sighed once more. "That's blown our theory out of the water then. Mark will *not* like this. I've checked everything. She's not mentioned once."

"Well, you can't argue with the facts, Freya. George Dove can't possibly be the illegitimate son of James Templeton-Morphy."

Mark was in his office at work when he took the call from Freya, and immediately rang DCI Chloë Smith.

"Hi Mark! What is it this time? Don't tell me, Winston Churchill's father is a suspect too?"

"No, sadly Chloë, not as much fun as that. Although the headlines would be truly sensational! No, Freya's just called and said that Jack Dove's father could not possibly be the illegitimate son of the Squire, as the Squire and his wife were out of the country at the time George Dove would have been conceived."

Mark explained in more detail what Freya had told him, and apologised for throwing a possible red herring into the mix.

"Don't worry about it, Mark. This is how these investigations go; we get an idea, we test it, we get surprises... not everything turns out the way we expect. We've already got Arabella Templeton-Stubbs's DNA, which'll be checked anyway. I'm expecting results in the next couple of days, and I'm sure she'll be very relieved not to be related to him."

"Okay. So, what happens now?"

"We'd like to ID Jack's remains for certain, and then get him reburied in a proper grave. There's no more evidence to get from him now. A couple of the forensic folk from Weston University have had a good look around the bones and taken lots of photos. Someone else at the uni is doing a facial reconstruction, which is up to them, of course. We're interested to see it and compare it to the photos, but it's not part of our investigation."

"You mean, you're not paying for it!"

The DCI laughed. "Damn right, Mark. If someone else wants to offer a free service, why should I disappoint them?"

Mark put the phone down and thought about what they'd discovered so far. It'd been almost too easy to make a few wild suggestions, which then turned out to be correct. Maybe the George Dove scenario was one wild guess too far. He had to admit, they'd just immediately assumed that, if his mother was a chambermaid at the manor, then naturally the squire was the father. It would teach him not to jump to too many conclusions.

There was still one thing niggling him, though. How was it that George Dove got the tenancy for the farm, over and above his father-in-law?

Two days later, Chloë, Roger, Mark and Freya were seated on a huge sofa in the drawing room at Hallowfield Manor, while they waited for the arrival of Arabella Templeton-Stubbs and her renowned uncle, Charles Fraser Webster Templeton-Morphy, otherwise variously known as Squire Morphy of Hallowfield, or Lord Hallowfield.

Chloë had called the meeting, as she wanted to get everyone together to hear the results of the post mortem on Jack Dove, and also her thoughts on where the investigation was headed.

They had been served tea by an elderly lady attendant; not a traditional butler then, noted Mark, more like an ageing waitress in an olde worlde tea room.

"Any chance of giving us a heads up before they get here, Chloë?" asked Roger.

"Nope." She stirred her tea. "I promised the Squire that I wouldn't tell anyone before him. He's been kept in the dark somewhat. For a start, he hadn't realised there was an investigation into his family's affairs, only about the accident and murder of Jack Dove. He certainly didn't know your wife had been in the archives, Mark. I expect Arabella has been trying to talk her way out of that one for the last couple of days…"

As she spoke, the door opened, and the Member of Parliament walked in, followed by her uncle.

"Hello everybody, Nice to see you all again. I'd like to introduce you to my uncle, Lord Hallowfield."

For a man of 88 years, Hallowfield looked exceptionally fit. Tall, upright, and slender but not fragile, he offered his hand to each visitor in turn. He smiled but not warmly; his eyes betrayed a suspicion that events were not to his liking, although he seemed genuinely pleased to welcome Roger to his home again. "Lovely to see you again, Roger." he said with a light upper class drawl, fresh out of the 1930s. "Glad to hear you're still working on those Salmsham re-developments despite all the fuss. *Ne illegitimi te carborundum*, I say."

"Haha thank you, Sir." said Roger, grinning at the irony of the 'bastard' reference. "I'm winning, I think. Just got to plough on and ignore the abuse."

"Quite so, quite so. Right, well, I gather you all know more about this to-do than I do, so I'd appreciate being put in the picture, Detective Chief Inspector." His last words were said slowly but pointedly, as he stared at Chloë Smith, his steepled hands forming a cage with his thumbs beneath his chin and his index fingers resting on his lips, as if he was daring her to speak.

"Of course, Sir." Chloë said. "Well, you must be aware that we opened an investigation into the murder of a man who was known to have disappeared in 1879. Mark here had got some family papers because his ancestor was the signalman at the time of the railway disaster…"

"Oh really. The scapegoat. Yes, I knew all about that." Hallowfield nodded, still staring at Chloë.

"… oh, you did? Okay, well, anyway, one of the signalman's daughters made what was a dying confession to Mark's grandfather, telling him that the person responsible for the disaster was a man called Jack Dove, the son of George Dove, the farmer at Rosfell Farm. She claimed in this confession to have conspired to murder Jack Dove, and drop his body into a freshly dug grave the night before a funeral. We excavated the grave last week and found that this confession was essentially true. There was indeed a second body underneath the coffin."

She paused to let the words sink in. Hallowfield remained immobile. Mark had the distinct feeling that either he was used to playing poker, or he knew more than he was going to let on.

"We have carried out a post mortem on Jack Dove, and found evidence that he was stabbed at least seven times, and thrown into the grave. He was also hit on the face with a rock, although we think that may have happened after he was in the grave and probably already dead. Whether he was dead or not, the rock broke his cheekbone."

Hallowfield took a breath, and intertwined his fingers. "So far, you have mentioned this man Dove, but I assume there's more, otherwise you wouldn't have asked to see me here."

"There is more, Sir. Please bear with me, because it's quite a complex story. We are fairly sure that Dove and an accomplice, probably a stonemason named Charles Archibald, caused the railway crash deliberately, by tampering with the signals so they gave a false 'all clear' to the crew of the express train, so they didn't stop and then they collided with the goods train. And of course, your ancestor was killed in the crash."

Hallowfield nodded once, and raised his eyebrows, as Chloë continued. "We've done several DNA tests on the two bodies we exhumed…"

"Two bodies? I thought you said there was just this man Dove?"

"Well, we exhumed and also tested the man he was buried beneath, who was the grandfather of the signalman's daughter. Her mother's father. He was the landlord of the Dukes Head, Salmsham at the time of his death. So, the family knew there was a funeral the next day, hence the timing of the murder."

"I see. Buy why are you telling me this."

"Well, Sir. We needed to identify Jack Dove, and Roger here is a direct descendant… his three times great grandson. The DNA confirms this, but… I don't know if Arabella has mentioned to you but we also took a DNA sample from her, because we had some reason to believe that Jack Dove's father may have been the natural son of your ancestor's father."

"Rubbish!" said Hallowfield. "Out of the question. We'd have known about this if it was the case."

"Yes, quite. I'm sure you would. And since Freya here has been searching in the family archive she has discovered that this story was a non-starter and had no foundation whatsoever."

"Precisely." Hallowfield said. "And may I ask, how is it that this lady is using our private archive? Was this your idea, Arabella?"

"Yes, Uncle. I told you, Eddie needs some help with his research and Freya is just helping him to speed things up a little. We had a lot of questions which needed answering. Eddie was glad of the extra help."

"Very well, but I still don't understand why you need to tell me all this."

"Because we have the results of the DNA test, and it shows that Jack Dove IS related to you, but not as distantly as we would have expected."

There was a collective gasp from the visitors. Mark and Freya exchanged glances, Roger blew his cheeks out, and Arabella looked quite shocked. Her uncle remained implacable.

"What exactly do you mean, Chloë?" asked the M.P. "Are you saying he's an ancestor of ours?"

"Oh no, that wouldn't be the case. No, but we can establish closeness of the relationship, and when we look at the dates of his birth, we think he was the natural son of your ancestor, Francis. The Squire who was killed in the crash."

"Patently absurd!" said Hallowfield. "We would have known about this if it was the case."

"Well, Sir. The DNA evidence points to the facts. However, if you'll allow us to do some more research in your archive, we may be able to find documentation…"

"Out of the question. I'm not having the police burrowing their way through our family affairs, no matter how old." Hallowfield began to stand up. Arabella sneaked a quick glance at Chloë, and nodded swiftly as she made to help her uncle.

"This is a police investigation, Sir. Not only into the murder of Jack Dove, but the potential murder of the 21 victims of the Salmsham Railway Disaster, and several other people since, including Jack Dove's own daughter, and also the suspicious death of your great uncle, Squish Morpho…" she let her words hang in the air. What the Squire did not know was that she had arranged with Arabella to over-exaggerate the powers of her investigation, to overcome his objections to searching the archives. In fact, not only was she skating on very thin ice, but she had no desire to use police resources when she had plenty of willing volunteers available.

"Squish? Suspicious death? I… didn't know that."

"We have reason to believe that he died suddenly, soon after being given a clean bill of health. We think his death may need reinvestigating."

Chloë was really sticking her neck out now. She'd made that one up on the spot, totally against the rules.

Hallowfield sat down again. "Very well, what do you need from me, then?"

"Just your permission to research the archives, Sir. In fact, although this is a murder enquiry, the murderer is dead, so there's no huge rush. With your permission, we would like to have just one person… maybe Freya here… just working at her own pace without disturbing Eddie Richmond's work in any way."

Freya leaned forward. "I can assure you, Lord Hallowfield, Eddie Richmond is very strict and will not let me touch anything without his supervision, and I also promise you that I will not disclose anything to anyone other than the people in this room."

Hallowfield snorted. "Arabella? Did you put them up to this?"

"No, Uncle, I really didn't. But it really won't harm the reputation of the family. All families have skeletons in their closets, you know. We just happened to dig one of them up for real."

After a brief pause, Lord Hallowfield nodded. "Very well then."

"Thank you, Sir." Chloë continued. "We are only interested in three time periods. Jack Dove's birth… we've obviously got to sort out what went on then. The time of the accident, and then the death of Squish."

"Fine. Well, you carry on. Bella, perhaps you'll show everyone out."

"Yes, Uncle." Arabella led the visitors out into the long corridor, to the top of the main staircase.

"Listen folks, wait in the café for me. I'll see Uncle back to his room and then come and grab a drink."

A few minutes later, they were all sitting in the corner of the café. As far as they could tell, no members of the public recognised the M.P. as she had dressed down for the day. The staff, of course, knew better than to make a fuss and draw attention to her.

"Phew – well done Chloë" said Arabella. "I thought he was going to explode when you mentioned Squish."

"That was a complete lie, Bella, sorry! His death wasn't suspicious at all as far as I know. And even if it was, it's got nothing to do with the railway disaster."

"Okay ladies, brilliantly done, but I'm confused. What happens now?" asked Roger.

"We will file a report for the Coroner – believe it or not, he will hold an inquest, but of course, nowadays there's no jury. We have already had his permission to rebury the body. But we will also be asking the Railway Accident Investigation Bureau to re-open the investigation. It won't be a large-scale thing, and it'll most likely be delegated as a research project for Weston University. They've already supplied those two forensic archaeologists for the exhumation. I think they have an interest in this from a historical perspective."

"They've probably got two or three PhD students lining up to research this." Freya grinned.

"Hmmmm. So once all the facts are out in public, I suppose we may get a formal pardon for Joseph Palmer." Mark said. "That's good. My family has always said he was wronged. Maybe this will help to right things."

Chloë laughed. "Mark! Are you crazy? You may have exonerated your ancestor, but now his daughter and heaven knows who else are implicated in two, three, maybe four murders."

"True! The press will have a field day." he laughed.

"While we're on the subject of family background, may I just say that I have also got two ancestors who were killers. So there. "Roger licked a finger and scored a 'one' in the air. "Which means... I get to build the museum in Salmsham. Just got to get planning permission, buy the land at the old station, convince the locals... oh no. I see more bloodshed!"

Arabella smiled. "Thank you all for keeping this out of the press. My connections, I mean. I'd like to help out, Roger, if I can, so if whatever you need to drive this museum idea forward, let me know."

"Thanks, Bella. And thanks for your time too."

"I was down here anyway today; despite what people think, us M.P.s do work for our living. I was visiting a school in Weston earlier on, and tonight I'm speaking at the local Farmer's Union Annual Meeting, but this was a welcome intrusion into the day, and I'm as good as home so for once I don't feel rushed."

50

August 2018 - Salmsham

Alex and Hazel held hands as they stumbled side by side along the pathway beside the old railway line. While the rest of the Phipps family relaxed in the garden of the Dukes Head, they had elected to go for a long walk, as Alex was keen to show Hazel the real countryside around Salmsham. They had started at the old station, and headed towards Belcote Crossing. The tyre tracks left by the farmer's tractor had hardened in the summer heat, and even the best walking boots could not iron out the unevenness underfoot. Every now and then, one of them would trip and the other would stop them from falling. At least, that's what Alex told himself, while secretly feeling thrilled that he was holding her hand. He didn't care what his sister thought, most of the other boys in his year fancied Hazel, so he was amazed to find himself the object of her attention. He tried not to think about what it was she liked about him, because he assumed it was probably a misconception on her part. He dreaded the day she might say "Ah, sorry Alex, you're actually quite a let-down really… byeeee!"

Olivia and Jake had started out with them, but soon stopped to take a rest by the remains of Hill Farm Bridge. Hazel, however, had demanded to see the site of the distant signal.

"This is weird, Alex," she said, "walking along beside the old track. I hadn't realised how good your Dad's model was. I mean, I can actually tell we're nearly there, even though all these bushes are growing and everything."

"Yep. Well, it was Mum who did all the model scenery. She's pretty good at that sort of thing. Dad's better with the mechanical stuff. Here we go."

They stopped, and Alex pointed out the remains of the signal pulley sticking out of the ground.

"To think, that Charles Archibald guy stood right here, and tampered with the signal. Right here, on this spot. It seems unreal, doesn't it?"

Hazel nodded, and squinted into the sun as she looked back down the line.

"Alex, you know Archibald said he was close to the bridge, you know, back there, when the train went by, then he walked home and left his tools, and then went back to the station to help after the accident?"

"Yes, that's what he said in court. But if you remember, the defence counsel didn't believe him."

"I think they really should have pressed that point. He would have to have been here to put the signal back to red after the train went past. How long would it have taken him to go back to the bridge?"

"At least ten minutes, at a brisk walk." Alex shaded his eyes and looked towards Salmsham Station. "And even if he'd run, probably five minutes."

"Exactly. What a liar! And no-one challenged him."

"No. But he didn't really lie about the signals, did he? They *were* white, but only because he'd tampered with this one, and Jack Dove had tampered with the other one back at the bridge."

"Crazy people." Hazel said. "But, you know what, I think I was right about Farmer Dove. What if he found out that Jack Dove wasn't his son, and that it was the Squire? He's got two reasons to cause the accident and kill him. One, because the squire shagged his wife…"

"Hazel!" Alex was shocked to hear his girlfriend use what he considered to be a coarse term.

"… and two, he was going to lose his farm. I wonder if they can ever find out if it was him?"

"I really don't know. I think that policewoman's got it all sussed."

"The police don't act on hunches though; they only accept evidence."

"That's not true. They have to have a hunch first, then test it. Like we did about George Dove. Then Mum did some research and found out he couldn't have been the older squire's son. He wasn't around when she was… um… made pregnant." He blushed, but Hazel hadn't noticed.

"Ah, all this business is so confusing. Why isn't life straightforward? Why can't we just sort it all out and then do something else?"

Alex laughed. It was true; for the last six months he'd thought of little else than the accident and all the surrounding family intrigue. He kicked around the base of the signal again.

"You know what. I'm going to lift this old bit of metal here, and keep it as a memento." Alex knelt down and started to pull the small metal post out of the ground.

"You are completely mad, Alex Phipps. Where are you going to put it?"

"With our model. I tell you what, I'd like to find something other than that old car part in the station. I bet if we dug down far enough there we'd find some remains of the crash."

"What, after a hundred and forty-four years?" Hazel kicked a stone across the path.

"Why not. Did you know, they just identified a chimney from one of the locomotives that crashed at Hawes Junction in 1910. It was lying in a field nearby. They'd knocked it off to move the engine on a truck so it wouldn't hit any bridges on the way. That was a hundred and eight years old and it was still there."

He pulled the piece of metal away in his hand. It had a small pulley wheel on it. Satisfied, Alex led Hazel back along the path towards the station. In a few minutes, they were back past the old collapsed bridge. There was no sign of Olivia and Jake.

"That's really quite a sharp bend ahead. Imagine steaming round that at seventy!" he commented. "Then... they were about here when they saw the goods train ahead."

Hazel shuddered. "This is freaking me out; it's too real. Let's get back to the pub, Alex. I need a drink."

A few minutes later, they were back in the garden at the Dukes Head, and Alex was surprised to see his grandparents there. John and Fenella Phipps had only just arrived and were still saying their hellos to the rest of the family.

"Nan. Grandpa! This is a nice surprise." said Alex, hugging Fenella. "I didn't realise you were coming over. Dad never said."

"I only found out just after you left." Mark said. "Grandpa texted me to find out if we were in."

"It's closer, and quicker to get to here than yours from Frome." John added. "But look, Marcus. I think you'll be interested in this."

He handed his son a medium sized, fairly bulky buff coloured envelope, with 'To Mark Phipps. Not to open until after my death' written on it.

"Who's it from?" asked Mark

"Your grandfather. Heaven knows how I missed it when I was clearing his stuff originally, but if you remember, there was a large suitcase full of papers. I just tipped them into a smaller case and forgot about them. I've just been through it all again."

"What's in it?" asked Mark

"I don't know, Son. I haven't touched it."

"Before I open it, anyone want another drink?"

Everyone did, and so it was another ten minutes or so before Mark Phipps carefully undid the metal split-pin style fastener on the flap of the envelope, slipped his hand inside, and pulled out a small notebook. Opening it, he saw a heading inside the second blank page. 'Salmsham railway murders'.

"Oh my goodness. This is Grandad's little diary he was telling me about. He said he didn't know where it was, but I bet he did." Mark flicked through the pages. "Crikey, look at the writing. Pages and pages of it! He must have sat down after Auntie Ath had confessed and tried to recall the whole thing."

"Can I have a look please, Dad?" Alex leant over towards his father and made to grab the diary, but Mark held it back.

"I think you should at least give me the chance, Alex. This is addressed to me, after all. For all you know, it might contain a clue to buried treasure."

"I suspect" said his wife "that it's more than that. This could be the final piece of the jigsaw. Go on, let's hear an extract."

Mark flicked open a page and read the neat but very fine writing.

"OK, here goes: 'Jack Dove lied when he said he left the railway to work on the farm. He didn't leave, he was sacked. He was fiddling the railway out of money by sending more of the farm's produce by rail and not declaring it all. Also, he was always mucking about, playing tricks on the staff and some passengers. Isaac Kemp had him dismissed but had to be careful because his father was a big customer of the station.' And so on. Interesting stuff. That's another grudge Dove would have had against the railway then."

Mark skimmed through a couple more pages.

"Ah… listen to this: 'They first suspected Jesse Smith was an accomplice when they got a friend to chat to him and he admitted he'd lied in court. He'd not been walking from the farm to the bridge, he was already on the bridge keeping a look out while D – that must be Dove - fixed the signal and gave him the bolt. As soon as the train went past Smith went up the ladder and put the bolt back in the spectacle arm while D went off around the front of the station to be a hero, and then Smith ran under the bridge to help him.' My God, that's how they did it then! This is absolutely amazing. I wish I'd known this all those years ago, Dad."

John Phipps looked somewhat crestfallen. "I'm so sorry, Marcus, but it's never an easy task clearing out someone else's bits and pieces, while you're grieving. I had so much to deal with. The papers were filed for another day; I just forgot about them."

Mark shrugged. "It's okay – we've got it all now. I need to read this all, get it transcribed and then put the whole thing together with what we already know. Then, and only then, we should go public."

"Mr Phipps, could you do me a favour please?" Hazel asked politely.

"Depends what it is, Hazel. I'm not buying you a glass of wine if that's what you're expecting. Oh, and please call me Mark."

"Okay, erm, Mark, could you look at the end and see who was actually responsible for the whole thing? You know, see whether I was right about old Farmer Dove or not."

"I could, but I think that would spoil the fun, wouldn't it?" Mark grinned.

Everybody else agreed with Hazel. There was such a clamour that Mark was about ready to close the diary and put it back in the envelope, but then they were distracted by the arrival of the Cooper family. As they all greeted each other, Vicky slipped herself down next to Alex and put her hand firmly on his arm, much to Hazel's annoyance.

"Alex, I wanted to thank you… for helping me through that stuff last week" she said. "I'm still having nightmares about that fricking skeleton though."

Alex nodded. "Me too. I couldn't look at his eye sockets. Scary stuff."

"What a pair of wusses!" Hazel said, coldly glaring at Vicky. "He can't do you any harm, can he? He's dead. That means he's not going to leap up and hurt you."

"You didn't see him though, Hazel. You could see the knife wounds and everything, on his ribs." Alex was beginning to feel queasy again.

"Anyway, thanks Alex, you're the best!" said Vicky again, kissing him on the cheek. He felt a rush of blood to his face.

"Fine then." Hazel turned away from him and pointedly joined in a conversation between Mark and Roger about the diary. Roger had just suggested the same as Hazel – that Mark look at the end of the notes and see who was behind it all.

He resigned himself to doing just that. It took him several minutes to find the information they all wanted. It wasn't on the last page, or even the previous few pages, but tucked away halfway down a page where he almost missed it. The name that sprung out from the page made Mark gasp with surprise.

"Oh crikey!" he said slowly. "I didn't expect that. I… I can't tell you here. I think we need to get straight in touch with Chloë about this."

"Oh, come on Mark. You can tell us!" said Roger.

"No… I can't. I really can't. The less people who know this right now, the better." He looked anxiously at Freya, willing her to back him up.

"You can tell us, Mark. Honestly, it's not as if MI5 are snooping around." As she spoke, the whole table went quiet.

Mark looked around nervously. "No, but the press are. This is… this has to come out, but in the right way. I'm going to take it straight to Chloë. You'll just have to bear with me."

Amidst loud groans from the others, Mark snapped the old diary shut, and put it back in the envelope, carefully folding back the metal tags.

"Oh for God's sake, Dad!" snapped Olivia. "Now you're just being overdramatic. Honestly, this happened a hundred and forty-four years ago."

"Yes it did. And it has repercussions today, which we're not going to talk about in public, right now."

There was a brief silence, and then Roger suggested that they might all like to come over to the old station and look at his plans for the museum and heritage centre. "I'd like your opinions please... as many as you like. I've got some ideas, but the more input we all have the easier it is to make plans."

51

Ten minutes later, they stood in a huddle on the concrete base of the old signalbox, as Roger detailed his ideas. He'd already looked into buying the station land back from the manor, and was looking into leasing the old trackway for at least half a mile in each direction.

"Then we could lay down some rails again. But the first stage is to do this signalbox, then the platforms. I probably won't rebuild the complete old station, because apart from anything else, it wouldn't be practical as a museum. No, what I plan to do is build a massive glass roof straddling the whole thing, so the station itself becomes the museum, then me and Mark can spend the rest of our lives adding to it bit by bit." He and Mark grinned at each other.

John Phipps was impressed. "There's just a couple of things though, Roger. First, the planning permission, and second; where on earth will you get the funding from for all this?"

"I'm working on those things, John. But have no fear. I've got some very powerful folk interested in this, and I've already got some potential funding for the initial work, and that's before I apply to the lottery or anyone else."

The younger members of the group had split off, and were sitting silently on the old trackway between the platforms. Olivia and Jake were sitting up, holding hands, their backs to the old churchyard.

Alex sat cross legged opposite them, between his girlfriend and Vicky.

It was Vicky who broke the silence.

"This is all so weird. To think of all those people who died right here, and some of them are buried just up there in that churchyard. I mean, they are literally right there. We sort of bury them and think they've gone away but they haven't."

"Freaky" said Olivia, nodding. "Please have me cremated, folks. I don't want to be dug up in a hundred years' time."

"Oh God, yeah, me too!" said Alex. "I don't want anyone poking around holding my ribs up in front of a bunch of onlookers. I still don't get why Dad won't tell us who is responsible for the crash though. I mean, we've all contributed to this investigation. It's not as if we're kids, really, are we?"

"Most of us aren't." Olivia said pointedly. "No, I think he's just trying to be a big patriarchal figure, only it's not working. Unless it was a German plot or something big like that."

Jake shook his head. "We weren't fighting the Germans in 1874, Liv."

Olivia raised her eyebrows. "I know, Mr Supernerdy, it was just a figure of speech. But it can't be that serious now. I mean, what's the secret?"

"I still reckon it was old Farmer Dove behind it all." Hazel said.

"No it wasn't, Hazel" said Jake. "There's no way that would be a big secret with us, seeing as we've already discussed it. And, there's no evidence for it."

"Fine." Hazel looked away, wondering what she was doing here anyway. She hadn't realised quite how jealous she felt about Alex being close to Vicky.

He seemed quite keen on his cousin, or rather, he let her kiss him and that was just so wrong, and also she was a lot older than him. Apparently she had a boyfriend, but Hazel had never seen him. While the others chatted aimlessly about the museum idea, she worked herself into a deep anger. Annoyed that Alex hadn't noticed how worked up she was, she got up without a word, and walked off towards Hallow Hill. No-one called after her, so she carried on.

At the end of the remains of the station platform, the old trackway became very overgrown and almost impassable, but Hazel had a fairly thick pair of jeans on, and a jacket which prevented all but the worst brambles scratching her arms. She pushed her way through into the foliage, carefully avoiding the nettles leaning across what appeared to be a pathway. Either side of her were thick bushes. She wondered who this piece of land belonged to, and why they hadn't bothered to keep it clear. As she pressed on, she passed through what seemed to be a tunnel of trees, and realised that she was in a much deeper cutting than the one at the other end of the station. The high redbrick wall on the right looked like an extension of the churchyard wall, while to her left the steep cutting was lined with a sloping forest of broad trees, their foliage towering high above her. Surprisingly, at this point the trackway now became more passable, but it looked as if no-one had been this way for a long time. Clearly the dog-walkers of Salmsham and Hallow Hill were no longer using this part of the path.

Hazel pressed on, still fuming about Alex and his cousin. What if they were in love? Where would she fit into this? She had to admit she really liked Alex, and his parents, although his sister was not someone she cared for. Anyway, she didn't want to lose Alex yet, if only because she wanted to see this mystery out. Yes, that was it. She'd see who the culprit was and then dump Alex, or at least, feign indifference and find out if he really cared about her or not.

Her phone vibrated in her back pocket. She carried on stumbling along the path as she looked at the screen. It was a message from Alex. "Where u? We about to go home. We at old bridge cant see u."

She replied "Went towards Hallow Hill. Cmn back now Gimme 10", pressed send and then looked up and almost jumped out of her skin.

She was about to scream, then she realised that the large black bovine face was backing away from her. Recalling what Alex had said when they were walking past a field of cows earlier, she made herself appear very wide by stretching her arms out, and walked forward boldly, maintaining eye contact with the cow, which backed away suddenly, shuffling its hooves, then turned and ran up a steep path to the right. Another cow, already on the path, turned and ran back uphill too. Then Hazel saw the barbed wire right in front of her, and realised she had stopped just in time. Spotting a small wooden section of fence a few yards to the left, she climbed over and dropped to the ground, which seemed a little firmer now.

Hazel glanced towards the retreating cows and wondered they were going. Then she saw that the old brick wall on the right of the cutting had finished, and the cutting slope had fallen away sharply in the space of less than a hundred metres. Walking across the trackway, she followed the cows up the narrow sloping pathway. At the top, she found herself at the edge of a field, where her two bovine friends had joined the rest of the herd. The field was fenced off away to the right, while the remains of a hedgerow marked its boundary on her left; it had obviously been allowed to lapse into disrepair. The opening in the old boundary was as wide as a large gate, so any creature could come and go easily. She remembered Alex saying how the old railway bed was now owned by the farms again, so their animals were free to roam on the old trackway.

Looking across the field, she saw a farmhouse in the distance. Of course – this must be Rosfell Farm! So this might be… no, thought Hazel, this *must* be where the breach in the fence occurred all those years back, letting the cows out onto the line, causing the delay. That was the trigger which started the whole affair; the accident, the accusations, the revenge murders. More than ever, Hazel felt that her hunch about old Farmer Dove was right; who else could have co-ordinated the action but George Dove, a man who had the motive, the means, and the manpower to carry out his evil deed.

Her phone rang. She slipped it out of her back pocket and swiped the screen with her index finger.

"Hi, Haze, where are you? We've been waiting for ages…" Alex sounded worried.

"You'll never guess where I am! I'm at the top of the railway cutting, by the field and I can see Rosfell Farm house from here. This is where those cows were let loose on the line. I tell you, Alex. I really was right about Farmer Dove. I'll take a few pictures, and then come back."

"Okay, Dad says 'no worries, but be careful', and Vicky says 'mind the barbed wire', it's lethal."

Twenty minutes later, Hazel emerged from the brambled pathway and found Alex and Vicky waiting for her. Alex gave her a massive hug, and she was surprised that Vicky seemed genuinely pleased to see her back safely.

"I was a bit worried about you, Hazel. I cut myself on the barbed wire and then fell and twisted my ankle awhile back, so I never go that way anymore." Vicky told her. "But you can follow the track of the old railway line all the way to Hallowfield once you're past the farm."

Hazel thanked her, and grabbed Alex's hand hard. Glad to be back in familiar surroundings, she was relieved to have his attention again.

While his wife drove them home, Mark listened intently to Hazel's story and agreed that they hadn't really given much thought to how the cows had got onto the line originally.

"If you think about it Mark, George Dove had the motive, because his farm was being taken away from him; the manpower with all those farm workers, and the livestock which he could let loose, and the money to pay people off. I would probably have thought of doing something like that if I was worried about my future. It must have been him, surely."

"Mmmmmm. You make some very interesting points there, Hazel. You've got quite an imagination, haven't you! Remind me not to cross you in the future." Mark turned and grinned at her.

"I might kidnap Alex if you do" she laughed.

"Ah, well, there'll be no payout if you do that. You can keep him."

"Thanks, Dad!" Alex smiled as Hazel nestled up to him and put her head on his shoulder.

52

Extracts – Adam Phipps' diary,
transcribed (with full names) by Mark Phipps

'When he came back from the prison, Joseph Palmer was a broken man. Fortunately, Squish Morpho had taken pity on the Palmer family, and told them he knew Joseph had been framed. He gave Joseph the job of groundsman at the manor, with his own cottage.

Soon after he was released, Agnes Palmer died. Ath's parents [Sarah Athey neé Palmer] were very distraught. The inquest said she had died of a fit, and was prone to them, but no-one in her family seemed to know about this. Agnes told Ath that Jack Dove had raped her many times, and threatened to beat her if she told anyone. When she found out she was pregnant he beat her until she miscarried. It was why she couldn't marry Arthur. He'd asked her several times but she had said to wait until he could support her properly then she could leave the manor. She didn't tell him about the rapes or the miscarriage, but Ath told him at the funeral and he vowed revenge on Jack Dove. It was why he joined Hubert Palmer and Ath in their plot.

They planned that Jack should have an accident, but then her grandfather died, the landlord. Her uncle Joe Sands was the gravedigger, so they got him to dig a deeper grave and swore him to secrecy, but he was happy to do it when they told him about Jack Dove's involvement in framing Joseph. They lured

Jack by sending a message from Arthur saying he had some information which Jack might find interesting, and arranged to meet him at the Dukes Head. They knew his regular route went through the churchyard and Arthur confronted him there. Jack told Arthur he didn't know the half of it, and that more people were behind the crash. Jack threatened Arthur so Hubert joined in, but then Ath jumped him from behind. She said "This is for Agnes, and James, and Caleb, and my father, and your wife, and everyone else who you've hurt." She kept stabbing him. She didn't want to stop, and once he was down and on his back, she stabbed him again. The men had to pull her off him. They both then kicked him and hit him with rocks so they were all part of his murder. They threw him in the grave, threw the rocks onto him, and covered him in earth. Later on, Uncle Joe helped cover him and tidy the graveside. After the funeral Arthur couldn't keep his mouth shut. When Farmer Dove asked about Jack's whereabouts, Joe said he was digging the grave and saw Jack Dove walking past and then down the road. He was the last person who saw him alive, and they believed him of course.

Then a couple of years later Ath's mother died and once again the whole family was in mourning. Joseph never really recovered from losing his wife, and died a broken man just 58 years old. Before that, though, Ath's sister Katharine had married Arthur Marriott. She had always had a soft spot for him, and it was him who she had been to see on the night of the crash, but she saw him kissing Agnes and was too scared to tell anyone. He became smitten with her, but the marriage was not a happy one. Arthur was badly affected by everything, and Katharine could not get through to him. They had a son they called James after James Palmer, and two girls, but they quarrelled a lot, and when he confessed the murder to Katharine she was shocked, and soon after this he fell in front of a train and died. Ath thinks Katharine had something to do with it, though she always denied it. His wife and children saw it happen so they were all very upset.

Meantime Jack Dove's daughter Harriet married John Brooks and had two children. Brooks was good friends with Arthur Marriott and he found out about the killing and told Harriet. Arthur had boasted he'd done it with Hubert Palmer, but didn't mention Ath. Later on, Harriet's husband died and she became close to Hubert, who had never married. He'd never had a woman apparently, and was pleased to have the attention of Harriet, but it was a trap, and she arranged to meet him at his work on the railway in Salisbury and then pushed him onto the electric rail, and made out it was an accident. But she was friends with Ath, and Ath realised it wasn't an accident, so she lured Harriet out for a walk by the quarry, confronted her and killed her with a metal pole, and threw her body into a pit in the quarry. By the time they found her a year or so later they couldn't tell how she'd died and assumed she'd fallen.

Meantime Ath had been working on the railway, and was also good friends with Squish Morpho, the squire, because of all the help he'd given them. She did some more digging and realised that there was more behind the accident than Jack Dove and his cohorts. She was talking to Squish Morpho about it not long before he died, and realised he knew a lot of details that had never been made public. She told him she suspected he knew more about the accident, and he confessed he had plotted to cause it, and had intended that the engine crew would be blamed. He had fallen out with his father over some family matters, and then the railway branch plans, and his father threatened to ruin him if he opposed him. Squish was queer and this was not public knowledge. Squish had Jack Dove and a stonemason in his pay, and he wanted Dove to make sure his father really died in the accident, but they had not expected the fireman to survive, so they had to stitch up Joseph and have some witnesses lie in court. Squish also bribed the Board of Trade man, he was also queer. His final report was a complete whitewash, and didn't really bear scrutiny. He was retired after the report was published, and never allowed to go near an investigation again. Squish had not expected Joseph to go to prison.

Ath was angry with Squish and wanted him to suffer too, but she could not bring herself to hurt him because he had always been kind to her, and he was very remorseful, but she told him she had plans for him, but then he died suddenly and the matter was put to rest.

Ath was pleased to get this off her chest. She knew she was guilty of murder, but said that had justice been done from the start she would never have set out to kill anyone.

Adam Phipps, Xmas Eve 1946'

53

Loose Ends – The Future

Lord Hallowfield sat impassively staring straight ahead, a habit he had developed over many years of sitting through endless tedious meetings. Facing him across the massive oak desk in his study was his niece, Arabella Templeton-Stubbs, M.P., and DCI Chloë Smith of Hallowfield CID.

"Uncle, this is not as bad as it sounds. Every family has skeletons in its closet. If we try to cover this up, the press will haul us over the coals. If we condemn it, and then show support for the re-opened enquiry, and a proper memorial…"

"It'll ruin the estate." he interrupted.

"Not if we do it my way. Besides, I think right now I have a lot more to lose than the estate. If the press suspects any sort of cover up, my political career will be over before it starts."

"How much of this affair do you actually know for a fact? You only have this… Sarah Athey woman's third hand confession. I presume you have found no evidence in the archives."

"Not at first" said Chloë "but Freya found plenty of very interesting correspondence between Squire Francis and the Board of Trade in late 1873 and early 1874, relating to the development of the quarries to the north. The Liberal government of the day was not terribly keen to encourage the railway extension, but then there was a surprise general election called, and Gladstone's government was unexpectedly defeated.

The new Tory government was keen to encourage this development and supported Francis's plans for the extension. However, Freya found some more private correspondence between Squish and the old President of the Board of Trade, Chichester Parkinson-Fortescue. It seems Squish had something on him, and this was probably why the plans had been discouraged. But after the election, Squish had no direct influence anymore, so he had to act quickly. The government fell on February 17th, and the accident took place on March 12th. Squish wasn't the only one who wanted his father out of the way; there were a few very powerful local figures who wanted to undermine the whole quarrying development in the area. We suspect that they helped in the planning of the accident, and of course Jack Dove was an ex-railway worker so he knew very well how to create the accident in the first place."

Hallowfield raised his eyebrows, and fixed his stare on the DCI. "Go on."

"We've also found correspondence which shows that Francis Templeton-Morphy pretty much gave the Rosfell Farm tenancy to George Dove, as long as he married Sarah Sutton and brought up their love child, Jack, as his own. As far as we can tell, the marriage was happy and the three daughters of the marriage were actually George's. But we also found evidence that Squish knew that Jack Dove was his half-brother, but Jack did not know. Squish used Jack's reputation as a local bad boy to his advantage; if it happened to destroy his half-brother in the process, so be it. We know Squish also bought off Archibald, the stonemason, who had been working for the manor for years. There were others; Jack Dove took them on and used money and threats to make sure the accident happened."

Hallowfield took a deep breath, and then looked quizzically at his niece. "What do you say to all this, eh, Bella? This... bloody awful mess. What do we do?"

"I know what I'm going to do, Uncle. Write the book on the whole thing. It'll be part of the fascinating history of the Templeton-Morphy family. And I'll support the building of the museum and memorial to the train crash victims – all of them, including those affected by the collateral damage, as it were."

"I suppose there's little point in me saying 'over my dead body', because I'm not going to be around for very many more years, am I." Lord Hallowfield seemed engulfed by a great sadness, and suddenly looked and sounded very frail.

"Uncle... look I know this is a shock to you..."

"No! No... it's not a shock, Bella. Not in the way you imagine. No, I've known about all this... *mess* for a long long time. My father knew most of it. He kept it to himself at the time, but told me when I was a young man. I just prefer the way things were in the old days, when one would hush this sort of thing up. It might not be right by your modern standards, but it was for the best back then. I'm just not as open as you, Bella. I can't bear the thought of all our family's dirty linen being washed in public."

"Uncle, it's no different than our early history, you know. The family didn't gain wealth and land by keeping a stiff upper lip and avoiding controversy. They fought for it, and that was just as bloody as this. In fact, much more so. I'm sure if I was writing about something that happened three hundred years ago, you'd be fascinated. You wouldn't be… ashamed."

Lord Hallowfield nodded.

"Go ahead, Bella. Write your book. I can't stop you. You will have to live with the consequences, good or bad. I would rather not be involved though."

"What I don't understand" said Alex "is why everyone had to keep these little secrets. If they knew who'd actually caused the accident, why not just go public. Why keep sending little coded messages to each other. Why not just speak out?"

The extended Phipps family were sitting in their dining room, along with Freya's parents, Olivia's boyfriend Jake and Alex's girlfriend Hazel. It was the final weekend before the start of the new school year, and the gathering was something of a family tradition since Alex had started secondary school four years ago.

"For the same reason" said Mark "that we didn't talk to the national press about Arabella's relationship to Jack Dove. It would have had serious consequences."

"But that makes no difference, surely?"

"We know it doesn't. But get a sensationalistic press and a sharply divided political system and the first thing that happens is facts get distorted, people believe what they want to believe, and Arabella would be ripped to shreds. It's all about perception, not truth."

"So what you're saying, Dad" Olivia chimed in "is that your grandfather still thought there would be consequences if he had named Squish Morpho as the evil mastermind behind the accident?"

"Correct. Either for himself, or for the current squire… or for the eventual truth. I think Auntie Ath wanted it all to come out, but not until long after she was gone, and I think my grandfather Adam respected that."

"But the trouble is" said Alex "there were so many people dying around Salmsham, or on the railway, that I'm starting to suspect they were all being bumped off."

Sheila Bagley butted in at this point. "I know what you mean, Alex, but I will just say that some of the other deaths which looked suspicious really weren't. Arthur and Katharine Marriott's daughter Mary-Ann was only twelve when she died. I thought might have been another victim of Harriet Brooks, but she died of pneumonia. And then there was Roger's grandmother, Josephine Marriott – Arthur's granddaughter – who died in another train crash in Thirsk in 1967. That was nothing to do with any other event – she was travelling to see a relative."

"Ah, yes. We looked at that too. We downloaded the Thirsk accident report from The Railways Archive" Mark said. "There was no way that could have been sabotage; a freight train going in the opposite direction derailed, and one wagon ended up fouling the main line as the passenger train was going the other way. It was an axle breakage. You couldn't have made that happen if you'd tried."

"Still" said Olivia "I think I'll keep clear of the railway for the time being, with our family's track record – and there was no pun intended there!" she added, as everyone else chuckled.

Three months later found a large gathering at the site of the old Salmsham Station. A marquee had been erected in the car park, and all of the Phipps and Cooper family were there, along with many prominent members of the village community, huddled groups of railway enthusiasts, a smattering of local reporters, and two local TV reporters. Arabella Templeton-Stubbs M.P. addressed the crowd as she proudly announced the formation of the Salmsham Railway Heritage Society.

"Our aim is to put right the wrongs of the past, by publishing the results of the recent re-investigation into the original railway accident, and the subsequent tragic events which have repercussions even today. The physical embodiment of this you will see being constructed over the next twelve months, with the building of the Salmsham Railway Heritage Centre."

There were a few cheers from the crowd, and some applause, which died down as the M.P. continued.

"This centre will house a museum, a model of the original railway station and its surroundings, and a memorial to every person who died in the accident. But just as importantly, we propose to rebuild and restore the station and its various buildings to its former glory. Ultimately we intend to relay about a mile of railway track so we can exhibit some railway stock from the past. So, ladies and gentleman, I would now like to declare this project started by inviting Mr Roger Cooper to lay the first brick in the wall behind me."

She stood back as Roger held up a large breeze block, and then placed it onto the concrete foundation which he'd dug over the previous few days. Once again, there was applause from the crowd, then the TV reporters began to ask questions. Fortunately, Arabella was by far the best known person there, and everyone else was able to circulate freely in the background.

As the press were able to report the following day, the Centre had been set up as a charity, with Arabella as the Chair of Trustees, which included Mark Phipps, Geoff Burns (Hazel's father), Professor Richard Hart of Weston University, and Reverend Peter Lockett of the Parish of Salmsham and Belcote. An unpaid management team reported to the trustees, headed up by Roger and Jacqui Cooper, and including Sidney Pountney, Freya Phipps and Ted Crozier. Despite a few pitfalls and objections, and with the aid of many volunteers, within a year there was enough to see at Salmsham Station to attract a fair number of visitors to the museum and restored platforms, while work continued to progress. It would be two more years before the building project was complete, and another year before the track was once again laid. The Hill Farm Bridge was also rebuilt but could only be accessed on foot from the south of the line. Due to a change in the farm boundary many years previously, visitors would have to stop in a small picnic area just across the bridge.

Sidney Pountney's pride and joy was the replica 1869 home signal, which stood in its original position. In a re-enactment of the disaster for a documentary, Sidney proudly demonstrated for the camera how the signal was sabotaged by Jack Dove and Jesse Smith. He was also able to show just how difficult it would have been for Jack Dove to clearly be able to see anyone up the signal from his position at the crash site.

On Tuesday 12th March 2024, one hundred and fifty years to the day from the Salmsham Railway Disaster, Mark Phipps proudly unveiled a large bronze life-size replica of the express locomotive with statues of the two enginemen in their positions on the footplate. A plaque on the side listed the names of those who had died, and also remembered by name the railway workers who were on duty at Salmsham that day.

As he and Freya stood and watched the small crowd of onlookers, Mark reflected on how much had happened here, not only in the century and a half since the disaster, but also in the six years since his son had found the forgotten folder. Alex Phipps stood in front of his parents and traced Joseph Palmer's name on the plaque with his finger.

"I wonder if Joseph would be pleased or not, with how it's all turned out, Dad?"

"Ah yes. Well, I think that's another one of those facts which we'll never know the answer to." replied Mark, as he and his wife wandered off to mingle with the crowd.

ACKNOWLEDGEMENTS

A number of people have influenced this book and enabled me to develop the initial idea for a historical railway mystery into the finished product.

My late father nurtured my early interest in the railways of yesteryear, and a former neighbour, the late John Anderton, made many trips to the Severn Valley Railway with me and my younger children. Members of my family, both living and dead, have encouraged and assisted me with my genealogical research over the years. Some of our family's stories are more fantastic than any work of fiction!

Huge thank-yous are due to my friends Lorna Edwards, for listening to the developing plot as we plodded our way along Hadrian's Wall last summer; Nia Williams for her guidance and encouragement; Richard Peake for his advice and intimate knowledge of police work; Emily Fisher for her youthful perspective; the real Chloë Smith (who is nothing like her namesake in the book!) for additional inspiration; Alexandra McRobie and Hazel GoldenSmith for help with additional names; my old RGS friends who asked to appear in the book (and do so in various guises.) Finally, a massive thank you to my dear wife Ann who has put up with the various plotlines as they evolved over the past few months.

Thanks are also due to The Railways Archive, the British Newspaper Archive, and Ancestry.com for allowing references to their services in the story.

Printed in Great Britain
by Amazon